ANNALENA McAFEE

Hame

The Fascaray Archives

VINTAGE

1 3 5 7 9 10 8 6 4 2

Vintage
20 Vauxhall Bridge Road,
London SW1V 2SA

Vintage is part of the Penguin Random House group of companies
whose addresses can be found at global.penguinrandomhouse.com

Copyright © Annalena McAfee 2017
Maps copyright © Joe McLaren

Annalena McAfee has asserted her right to be identified as the
author of this Work in accordance with the Copyright,
Designs and Patents Act 1988

First published in Vintage in 2018
First published in hardback by Harvill Secker in 2017

penguin.co.uk/vintage

A CIP catalogue record for this book is
available from the British Library

ISBN 9781784705237

Printed and bound by Clays Ltd, St Ives Plc

Penguin Random House is committed to a sustainable future
for our business, our readers and our planet. This book is made
from Forest Stewardship Council® certified paper.

to Ian

'Here's tae us! Wha's like us?
Gey few, an they're aw deid.'
Scottish toast, traditional

'A language is a dialect with an army.'
Attributed (erroneously) to linguist
Max Weinreich, 1944

CONTENTS

PAIRT ANE

Incomers

Hameseek

Ah lang fur hame,[1] *lang fur the keek*[2] *o hame.*
Gin onie goad has merked me oot agane
Fur shipwrack, ma ruchsome[3] *hert can dree*[4] *it.*
Whit haurdship hae Ah lang syne tholed,[5]
At sea, in fecht! Brang oan the trial.

Grigor McWatt, efter Homer, 1942[6]

1 home
2 sight, glimpse
3 tough
4 suffer
5 endured
6 From *Kenspeckelt*, Virr Press, 1959. Reprinted in *Warld in a Gless: The Collected Varse of Grigor McWatt*, Smeddum Beuks, 1992.

THE FIRST SIGHT OF THE ISLAND FROM THE EAST HAS REMAINED essentially unchanged since the Vikings arrived in the eighth century, crossing the Clinch Straits in their longships with rape and pillage on their minds.

Today's visitor, travelling on the ferry and anticipating a little hiking, sightseeing or a dish of prawns and a sing-song in the pub, sees the same distant wide green platter surmounted by a central conical peak that greeted Sigtrygg Barelegs and his warriors when they hastened across the sea to lay waste to the island and its inhabitants.

The low whitewashed buildings of today's Fascaray were, of course, absent in 795 when the Pictish natives, alerted by lookouts on Beinn Mammor to the curved prow purposefully skimming the waves towards Finnverinnity Bay, cowered in their summer settlement on the western strand of Lusnaharra, while up at the Priory, on the tidal islet of Calasay, sandalled monks scrambled to conceal chalice, paten and reliquary casket before the heathen onslaught.

Much of the land would have been forested with Caledonian pines, 'majestic green cluds, cumulonimbi pierced by heiv'n-aimed spears', as McWatt later described them. Local needs for fuel were then modest and the timber industry, which was to denude the indigenous forests, was more than a thousand years in the future, as were the dark regiments of Sitka spruce sent marching over Fascaray's hills in the twentieth century by modern plunderers – English accountants exploiting tax loopholes for their clients.

But these changes, along with the single-storey croft houses and byres, the fishermen's terraced cottages, the Big House, kirk, manse, rudimentary howff, or inn, the nineteenth-century innovation of Finnverinnity Pier and the narrow granite Temperance Hotel, the twentieth-century arrival of general store and post office, primary school, gift shop, tea room and museum and the architectural extravagances of the Balnasaig Centre in the north-east, have no more shaped and defined Fascaray than has the spindrift blown in on its storm-lashed shores.

The island, part of the Fascaredes archipelago, is a remnant of an extinct Neoproterozoic ring volcano rising from a forty-metre seabed plateau to the 874-metre peak of Beinn Mammor, comprising granite, gneiss, pyrite and gabbro igneous Moine rock – 'a granite ballad', in McWatt's phrase – and has been inhabited for more than eight thousand years.

Fascaray's diverse geological features, its lochs and hills, highlands and lowlands, peat bog and forests, its beaches of blonde machair grass and ivory sand, scattered shells and strewn boulders, its steep cliffs and deep caves, contained within the span of a small island that can be circumnavigated on foot in a single summer's day, have in more recent times earned the island the sobriquet 'Scotland in Miniature'.

Its ancient sites – the Ring of Drumnish, a jagged circle of standing stones west of Balnasaig; the rubble of Mammor hill fort; Killiebrae's broch tower guarding the northern sea passage towards Doonmara cliffs; the Mesolithic shell middens, dating from 6,700 BC, found in the caves of Slochd and Clochd; the remains of the Neolithic village above Lusnaharra, uncovered after a storm in 1902; the ruins of St Maolrubha's Priory on Calasay; the Heuchaw cairn burial chamber and the roofless cleared clachan villages scattered across the island – suggest their own narratives.

Tacitus gave the first account of the archipelago when he described the fleet sent north in AD 80 by Agricola, his father-in-law, who, as recently appointed Roman Governor of Britain, wished to chart the boundaries of his new territory. They must have sailed in the time of Junius, the month we now know as June, for Tacitus describes the never-ending light of high summer in the empire's northernmost insulae.

'The length of their days is beyond the measure of our world: the night is clear, and . . . so short one can scarcely tell the twilight from the dawn. But if the clouds do not hinder, they say that the sun's brightness is seen all night, and nor sets nor rises but passes across the sky.'[7]

If the fleet had sailed in December – a month of deepest mirk, affording a brief chink of grey light, like the 'swift clang o a dungeon

7   Tacitus's *Life of Agricola*, quoted in *Scottish Pageant* by Agnes Mure Mackenzie (Oliver & Boyd, Edinburgh, 1946) and in *Scotland: the Autobiography* by Rosemary Goring (Penguin, 2008).

door', as McWatt wrote, in a seemingly endless night – it would have been a different story. Tacitus noted the fertility of the soil, a sky 'foul with frequent rain' and the wide dominion of the sea – 'not only against the shore does it rise or fall, but it flows in deeply, winding and piercing among hills and mountains, as if in its own habitation'.

The Fascaradian Picts and their Neolithic and Mesolithic predecessors left no written account of their time on the island, and in the eighth century, on Calasay, the peaceful and literate monastic followers of St Maolrubha (pronounced Mail-ruva; sometimes Latinised as Rufus) were more interested in reflecting on the meditations of their order's founder, and his martyrdom at the hands of pagans in 642, than in recording temporal matters. It was left to asset-stripping Norsemen to give the first description of Fascaray (from the Gaelic *foisneach* – friendly, peaceable – and the Norse *ey* – isle).

You can read a near-contemporary account, wrapped in a caul of the bombastic supernaturalism they went in for, of the Viking's 795 expedition to the island in the *Fascaringa Saga*. This was virgin, fertile land – *En groenn ey av fridr og blidr* – and if it harboured an unviolated maiden – *moer* – or two, and a shaven-headed pacifist *munkr* in sackcloth quivering over a hoard of treasure, so much the better. The invaders, men of appetites, might have been briefly diverted by the Finnverinnity Inn if it had been there, but they had no need of a pub; they brought their own carry-out, *mangat* – sewed in leather sacks – a dark ale brewed from heather, which stiffened their purpose and gave a murderous edge to their enterprise.

The *Fascaringa Saga*, compiled by unknown scribes sometime between 800 and 820, is an unremitting inventory of lust, greed, casual brutality, sorcery and power struggles among Viking gods at vengeful play. It incidentally delineates the island's topography, its hills, watercourses and early settlements as precisely as any twenty-first-century hikers' handbook but is reticent on the precise nature of the mortal warriors' activities on Fascaray, under the leadership of the infamous Sigtrygg Barelegs, of whom it was written: 'no edged weapon could harm him, and there was no strength that yielded not, no thickness that became not thin before him'.

A better guide to historical fact was the Benedictine monk Cedric Horven, a lucky survivor of Sigtrygg's massacre at the Dalriadan mainland monastery of Achadh an Uinnseann (Field of the Ash Tree), now Auchwinnie. Cedric emerged from his hiding place to write of the invaders' progress across the western Gaelic kingdom and described subsequent events at Auchwinnie's neighbouring convent of St Dorcas.

Hearing news of the Norsemen's advance, Mother Abbess Ulla had summoned her community at midnight and told them of the pagan desecration of holy sites, the slaughtering of men and boys, and the forcing of women – matrons, maidens and nuns – into wantonness. She appealed to divine mercy to deliver them from 'the wrath of the barbarians and to preserve the sanctity of perpetual virginity' and exacted from her congregation a promise that they would, in all things, obey her command and present an example of chastity 'not only advantageous to them but also eternally to be followed by all virgins'.[8]

Mother Abbess Ulla then 'took a sharp knife and cut off her own nose and upper lip down to the teeth. The sisters witnessed this horrible sight, saw that it was admirable in its purpose and effect, and passed the knife from one to the other, each performing the same act upon herself.'

At dawn the brigands, having plundered another nearby monastery and chapel and slaughtered the monks, descended upon the cloister to press the holy women into debauchery. The shocking sight that greeted them – the mutilated faces of the virgins, their praying hands red with unwashed blood, their robes stained and stiff with gore – banished, for the moment, all lustful thoughts. Sigtrygg and his men fled in disgust but, even in their haste, took time to set fire to the convent and ensure that the hideously disfigured nuns could not escape and offend the eyes of other Norsemen. Mother Abbess Ulla and her community, their honour intact, perished in the blaze and ascended to heaven, according to Cedric, in the full glory of martyrdom.

Leaving behind the scorched and bloody fields of Auchwinnie, Sigtrygg's marauders set sail from the mainland, rounded high eastern cliffs and plunged towards the giant, bird-ringed boulders of Plodda and Grodda – uninhabited islands that formed a guano-streaked corridor of rock at the end of which Fascaray, a bright hummock of green with

---

8   Cedric Horven, *Chronica Minora*, vol. 2, cited in *Flores Historiarum* by Roger of Wendover (1236) and in *Annals of Invasion AD 480–1265* by Matthew Paris (Elgin University Press, 1972).

a pyramidal peak in its centre, rose from the dark sea – 'an emerant blinterin in a starnless nicht sky', as McWatt put it.

If, like their gods, these raiders had possessed the gift of flight, they would have looked down on a small island, eight miles by three: two overlapping ovals broadly shaped like a cloak clasp, a *brosje* – though coarser minds, or those with a poor grasp of Old Norse, might have characterised it as two *brosjts*, or female mammaries – with a coastline marked by steep cliffs in the north-west, white sand coves fringed by long machair grass in the south-west and north-east, and a wide indented harbour rimmed by a pebble beach in the south.

Swooping down to the eastern base of Beinn Mammor mountain, which rears up from the island's green heart, Thor or Freyja would have seen their own reflections gazing up from the wide black looking glass of Loch Och. On the western flank of Mammor's long ridge, little Dubh Lochan would have offered an additional hand mirror for vainer gods. Across the east of the island like a broad silver sash, from Ruh headland in the north to Finnverinnity in the south, runs the fast-flowing River Lingel. The ubiquity of water – glinting through sodden swathes of peat bog, sparkling and flashing in Fascaray's glens, forking like thunderbolts down hills – gives the impression that in this sea-girt place it is the island itself rather than the sky above it that is the source of light.

Half a mile offshore from Ruh, airborne deities would have spotted a smaller mound of green, like the diacritical *sirkel* of the Old Norse alphabet. This is the tidal island of Calasay. If Fascaray is Scotland in Miniature, Calasay – with its little Loch Aye; its unassuming hill, Mambeag, 'a bashful brae, bending the knee to braggadocio Mammor', according to McWatt; its murmuring burns and trickling falls; its compact northern cliffs and its curved micro-strip of machair coastline, a nail clipping to Lusnaharra Strand's new moon – is a Pocket Fascaray, a faint but faithful echo of its bigger neighbour, to which it was, and remains, connected by a strip of sand passable on foot twice a day.

Some twelve centuries after Sigtrygg's raid, Grigor McWatt first sighted Fascaray in 1942. In an inversion of the Viking experience, McWatt wrote, it was the island that conquered him. He was on a char-tered fishing boat bringing elite troops to a commando training school in requisitioned Finnverinnity House. It might have been his first view of the island to which his name, as 'the Bard of Fascaray', was to become as immutably linked as Wordsworth to the Lakes, Clare to the Fens and Crabbe to Suffolk, but as McWatt famously said, it was also a home-coming – or, to be precise, 'a hamecomin' – to his ancestral island, the ancient redoubt (seized after the Vikings had slunk away, sated, with their spoils and their hangovers) of the Fascaray McWatts (Gaelic: MacBhàidh), a sept of the noble clan McCawker, or MacCaulker (Gaelic: MacCuilcheachdh) whose motto is *'Autem videtis me'* – 'Now you see me'.

A Granite Ballad – The Reimagining of Grigor McWatt,
Mhairi McPhail (Thackeray College Press, 2016)

Sea Thirlt

Ah maun gang doon tae the sea agane, tae the lanely sea and the sky,
An aw Ah speir is a heich boat an a starn tae gae her by,
An the whurl's fung and the wind's sang and the white sail's shooglin,
An a grey haar on the sea's face, and a grey dawk brakkin.

Ah maun gang doon tae the sea agane, for the caw o the rinnin tide
Is a gurly caw an a vieve caw that wullna be denied;
An aw Ah speir is a blashie day wi the white cluds fleetin,
An the skoosht spairge an the dirlt spume an the pewlie's greetin.

Ah maun gang doon tae the sea agane, tae the gangrel tinkie's crib,
Tae the pewlie's wey an the whaul's wey, whaur the wind's like a snellit chib;
An aw Ah speir is a scurrivaig wi a lauchin cantie yairn,
An saucht dowre an a douce dwaum whaun the pliskie's neath a cairn.

Grigor McWatt, efter John Masefield, 1944[9]

9   From *Kenspeckelt*, Virr Press, 1959. Reprinted in *Warld in a Gless: The Collected Varse of Grigor McWatt*, Smeddum Beuks, 1992.

My own first view of the island is unpromising. I barely glimpse Fascaray during the rough crossing from the mainland port of Auchwinnie. 'Look!' I say with sham cheerfulness, pointing through the rain-streaked porthole at a distant grey strip of what I take to be terra firma tipping crazily on the churning sea. 'Land ahoy!'

My nine-year-old daughter, Agnes, a valiant traveller who's never been carsick, chooses this moment to reveal she's a poor sailor in a swell. We huddle in the cabin of the ferry and I stroke her hair as she throws up in a paper packet provided by the skipper, our pose a parody of an art-history cliché – Madonna and Child in Wet Anoraks with Sick Bag. For this we've left New York shimmering in the heat under a cloudless sky.

It's still raining heavily when the boat finally pulls into Finnverinnity Harbour and we join the queue of passengers waiting to disembark. A sudden hot panic grips me as I realise I've lost sight of our luggage. It's not in the corner of the deck where I had carefully placed it, half hidden under a tarpaulin sheet with other cases and backpacks, next to a sack of post, bags of grain, boxes of groceries and containers of engine oil. Now it's my turn to feel sick. I knew I should have kept it with us. There was no space to stow it near our wooden bench in the cabin when we boarded. But we could have held on to some of it, instead of following the other passengers' leads and piling our bags at the back of the boat. Our luggage has gone. Vanished.

This is serious. It's not just all our carefully chosen possessions (the pre-packing selection and editing process was especially painful for Agnes) but my laptop, edited printouts of draft chapters of my new book – not all of them emailed or copied to the memory stick in my purse – copies of the precious letters, photos, documents, and 70,000 words of *The Fascaray Compendium* notebooks, typed up by me over two months, printed out and marked up with my own irretrievable pencilled annotations.

I can almost hear Marco's voice from 2,600 miles away rising above the clamour on the boat. 'Why the hell didn't you just use Track Changes? Then at least you'd have all your work on a memory stick?' 'Because,' I mutter to myself, a stereotypical screwball American lady, 'I *like* working with pencil and paper, goddammit!' Agnes, recently prone to embarrassment over her parents' behaviour in public, doesn't seem to have heard me, nor have my fellow passengers who, until now, appeared to be benign young families, wisecracking construction workers, a bunch of teenagers recovering from a heavy night on the mainland and hikers in primary-coloured waterproofs frowning at the view. Suddenly they're all recast as villains.

The disappearance of our luggage feels a greater crime than mere theft; it's an existential assault, a vengeful god's payback for my wilful obliteration of our life in New York. You want to trash your life? Here – try this.

I'm making a mental inventory of what we have left in my carry-on bag – passports, check; credit cards, check; cash, check: phones, check; iPad, check. No! I slipped my iPad into my black case before we got on the ferry – when I see Agnes's purple suitcase: bought for this trip after hours of deliberation in Bloomingdale's with her father. Someone towards the front of the line, one of those ingratiatingly jocular construction workers, is holding it and I'm making my way towards him, incensed.

In New York – yes – we expect this sort of thing and we're on constant alert for opportunistic raids by the needy and the greedy. When so many Haves exist in close proximity to so many Have Nots, it's the Have a Littles – the ones without good security and insurance – who lose out. So we're careful. It's part of the deal in high-density city living. But here? So much for 'the Friendly Isle'. How low can you get? Stealing a child's suitcase!

My way is blocked and I'm about to shout (do they have cops here?) as the bag and the thief's broad back shrink into the distance, when I look up and see a group of islanders in glistening rainwear standing on the dock above us. Teenagers loll against the harbour wall while a grinning old couple look down at the boat and wave an umbrella at a red-headed young woman in front of me. Now, as if choreographed, the teens walk over to join other islanders and together they form a chain with the ferry's skipper, the first mate and the passengers at the front of the line, who are beginning to climb the pier steps onto what is disingenuously called 'dry land'. They're passing the boat's cargo, the sack of post, bags of grain, boxes of groceries, the cans of engine oil, and all the luggage, our luggage, Agnes's bag, mine, the document box, up the stairs and along the dock to the harbour wall where they set it down gently in an orderly pile.

The islanders disperse and Agnes and I are alone. The rain has intensified – it's like standing under the power shower in my Cobble Hill gym. My former gym. Agnes puts up her hood and gamely insists on manoeuvring her own case, which has wheels and a long handle. 'A granny bag' she calls it, approvingly. My own two suitcases, also wheeled, are larger and I balance on them the sealed, waterproof box containing my copies of the rudimentary archive that's more valuable than any of our possessions.

Still smarting with shame at my metropolitan misanthropy, my first response to the vista – the long, low line of whitewashed crofts curving round the bay, the dark hills whose tops are hidden in clouds – is dismay. This is to be our home for two years. For this we've given up our comfortable rent-controlled apartment in Brooklyn, Agnes's place at a friendly public elementary school with excellent math scores, our friends, stores and cafes, concerts and cinemas, proximity to airports, railroads, other cities, other lives? My daughter's father? My relationship?

Agnes, though, has perked up. She's seen the grocery store, distinguished from the other whitewashed buildings by the red pillar box at its entrance and a faded advert for ice cream in its window.

'Ice cream!' she says, instantly won over.

We go inside and I announce myself to a cautious young South Asian man behind the till. He directs me to the post-office counter where a woman, pale, middle-aged and unsmiling, looks up briefly from a stack of parcels and asks: 'Are you Mhairi McPhail?' As if another American with a nine-year-old child would abandon her life, travel all this way and put up with the discomfort and grim weather in an effort to pass herself off as me. At least the postmistress pronounces my name correctly: Mhairi as in Marry, not Myri, or Mary, or Marie. Not even, as some Gaelic purists insist, Varry, or any of the other weird variations that made me, as a chippy teenager, consider changing my name to Jane.

She rummages in a drawer, hands me the key and points left, in the direction of our rented cottage, number 19. I let Agnes choose an ice cream – a strawberry cone scattered with beads of coloured sugar – and as she laps it rapturously in the rain I feel another stab of guilt. Poor kid. What have I let her in for?

Our new home is four doors down from the Finnverinnity Inn which, even now, at 10.30 a.m., is crowded. A group of men – scarlet cheeks, florid noses, sepia teeth – make their way outside with their drinks to smoke and talk and stare at the sea. They gaze at us as we walk past, their heads turning in chorus-line sync to follow our progress and gauge our destination. Inside the pub an accordion wheezes prissily, leading some scattered singing. I hope the noise doesn't travel. My key jams in the lock and when I manage to push the door open a gust of musty air almost fells me. Agnes looks back at the smokers and waves. One of them returns a small, uncertain salute.

The light switch doesn't work and outside the storm has worsened, casting a deep midwinter gloom. Everywhere else in the UK, in Europe, it is summer, the season of warmth and heady languor. At home in New York it's heatwave time – riot weather, Marco used to call it – when the city empties, leaving it to those of us who actually enjoy the *chaleur* or are too poor to head for the Hamptons. It's my favourite time of year in Brooklyn. Anyone who spent at least part of their life in Scotland will never take a spell of cloudless skies and unbroken sunshine for granted. And I have brought my daughter here to this place, dark as a subway tunnel, cold as Alaska (in August!). What kind of mother am I?

I grope my way to a side table, tripping over a large cardboard box – our groceries, ordered in advance, sent over by boat from the mainland supermarket and presumably conveyed here by the altruistic human chain – and switch on a lamp. The room springs into relief. There is a coal-effect electric heater in the fireplace flanked by two threadbare tartan armchairs. Next to the side table is a floral couch with suspicious stains suggesting incontinence or violence. The rug, patterned with a series of concentric purple and grey swirls, looks like a weather map: a deepening band of low pressure in the West Highlands, squally showers, gale-force eight, imminent.

I sigh as I scrutinise the pictures on the wall – Highland cattle peering winsomely under ginger tresses in a variety of native settings: by water-falls, hoof-deep in heather, mooching in machair – when I hear Agnes upstairs. She is squealing with pleasure. I find her in the smaller of the two attic bedrooms, bouncing on her narrow bed.

'Awesome, Mom! Look. I can see the sea.'

You can see the sea, okay. Grey and foam-flecked as dirty suds.

You can see nothing but the sea.

'WHEN A MAN STANDS ON THE SHORE LOOKING OUT TO SEA, HE stands at the littoral of his unconscious,' wrote McWatt. Up in Calasay, he would walk the machair strand daily in all weathers, scooping up handfuls of small bright shells, 'the puir man's traisure', gathering kelp and dulse seaweed in a wicker creel, and searching for useful flotsam tossed ashore by recent storms. He would watch the seabirds engage in their 'genocidal airborne ballet', turn his poet's eye on the 'benign jaundice' of the wild primrose, the 'Parkinsonian tremor' of the harebell, or on the Fascaradian orchid, with its 'cluster of tiny livid mouths silently ululating on pale stems'.

Even in the wildest weather, he never tired of the view from the back window of his croft house, An Tobar, past the low stands of birches, oaks and alders huddling for comfort against wind and storm, across the sweep of cliffs to the ocean in all its moods under its 'turbulent twin' the sky, and out beyond the skerries – the uninhabited rock islands which rose from the sea like so many 'fantastic beasts couchant, inspiration for the winged griffons and twisting hell-hounds of Celtic art'. In the distance the Fascaray Head lighthouse – built in 1844 by Robert Louis Stevenson's uncle Alan and manned, until automation replaced them in 1989, by a succession of bearded recluses with drink problems – swept its nightly 'Cyclopean beam' over the phosphorescent seascape.

The most familiar photograph of McWatt, a black-and-white portrait taken in 1981, is used by Charles Knox-Cardew in *A Vulgar Eloquence*,[10] a scholarly survey of world vernacular literature. The portrait shows the 'Bard of Fascaray' aged sixty, in his late-middle period – he still had more than three decades of writing life to go – squinting sceptically at the view, a fat sleek-haired otter in his arms and a Border collie at his feet. McWatt is a grizzled, kilted figure with fierce blue eyes blazing under a lofty brow. A briar pipe is clenched between his teeth and tendrils of

10   Glenton University Press, New Jersey, 1987, 732 pages.

unruly grey hair escape from a beret, which he wore instead of the traditional tam-o'-shanter 'bunnet', Knox-Cardew suggests, 'in tribute to the
Auld Alliance and the French poets Baudelaire and Rimbaud'.

In addition to the beret, McWatt's idiosyncratic version of Highland
dress substitutes the lace jabot at the throat with a spotted handkerchief
of the sort tied to a stick as improvised hand luggage by fairy-tale vaga-
bonds, and instead of cross-laced ghillie shoes and knee-length socks
he wears mud-crusted rubber boots; we can't, therefore, vouch for the
presence or otherwise of the ornamental *sgian-dubh* dagger, customarily
tucked into the right sock.

A Granite Ballad – The Reimagining of Grigor McWatt,
Mhairi McPhail (Thackeray College Press, 2016)

Agnes is asleep and I sit, jet-lagged and haggard, at the kitchen table in our new home staring at the picture of McWatt in Knox-Cardew's daunting book as if it might vanquish my night terrors and offer a clue – justification would be too much to ask – as to what the hell I'm doing here.

McWatt's kilt – in McWatt tartan, as the captions always say – is unremarkable but the sporran seems comically large, like the pelt of a scalped Pomeranian. Knox-Cardew is an American academic who, to judge by his author photo, wears a bow tie, horn-rimmed glasses and a pocket square in tribute to the Wasp Ascendancy. He derives the title of his book from *de vulgari eloquentia* – 'the people's language' – Dante's approving term for literature written in Italian rather than Latin. Alongside reflections on Boccaccio, Dante, Chaucer, van Maerlant, Ngũgĩ wa Thiong'o, Barbour and the non-Tagalog literature of the Philippines, Knox-Cardew devotes a 110-page chapter to the 'Bard of Fascaray', treating McWatt with patronising deference throughout.

His research didn't apparently extend to a trip to Fascaray, or even Scotland. I guess the Glenton University Press advance didn't cover the fares. Nor has he read a single volume of *The Fascaray Compendium* manuscripts. Nobody has. That's my job – though Knox-Cardew alludes to their existence, describing McWatt as 'a Hebridean Pepys whose masterwork, a magisterial survey of his island through time, remains as yet unpublished'.

A Vulgar Eloquence is described on the jacket as a 'collective critical biography', and it's heavy on criticism, of the reverential literary sort – too much trocheeing and spondeeing for my taste or purpose – and light on the lives. It's also, unsurprisingly, out of print. My research assistant in Glasgow, Ailish Mooney, a diligent Irish postgrad, managed to track down a copy from Innerpeffray Library – borrowed only twice according to the date slip on the inside cover and stamped 'withdrawn' – and sent it to me in Brooklyn. I didn't, in the end, have time to open it until Agnes and I were on the plane here from New York and even then I found myself drawn to the inflight magazine and the safety instructions card – 'in the event of landing on water . . .' Who are they kidding? – before I finally gave in and opened Knox-Cardew's book at the McWatt chapter. My eyes fell on the last paragraph of the third page.

His reimagining of world literature through the multifaceted prism of the Scots language may have been his life's work; his celebrations, in his columns for the *Auchwinnie Pibroch* as well as in his sweeping, as yet unpublished, magnum opus *The Fascaray Compendium*, of the culture and flora and fauna of the island may have provided the connection with community and the natural world that sustained him in bleakest times and awakened many to the beauties of his corner of the Highlands; his rumbustious menagerie may have met the emotional needs of this solitary man, brought some warmth and humour into his life and inspired a generation of naturalists; his spare and elegant memoirs may have redefined the genre; his popular histories, polemical journalism and political activism undoubtedly sharpened his understanding of his own past and enriched modern Scotland's sense of its identity; but it was five verses and a four-line refrain – dismissed later by him as 'thon skitterie wee sang' – scribbled on a pack of Sweet Afton cigarettes during a 'lock-in' in the Finnverinnity Inn, which earned Grigor McWatt his fame, whatever wealth he managed to accrue, and the priceless freedom to pursue his Muse.

I resisted a surge of dismay, closed the book and turned to my child, who was now asleep, her head resting against my arm as we sped, six hundred miles an hour, towards our new home. Looking at the tender curve of her cheek I wondered again – did I really want to spend the next two years alone with my daughter, sequestered in a remote corner of the planet, serving as handmaiden to a dead poet, accidentally famous for a single pop song which he disowned, a reclusive graphomaniac who might have loved the natural world but, from everything I've read, didn't care too much for people?

Thrawnness

Oot o the nicht that haps me,
Mirk as the cleuch frae powl tae powl,
Ah thank whitiver goads micht be
Fur ma unvinkishable saul.

In the fyle claucht o mishanteredness
Ah havnae jouked nor greeted.
Ablo the lounderins o chance
Ma bluidy heid is nae defaited.

Ayont this place o fash an tears
Lours but the grue o hinmaist scug,
An yet the assizes o the years
Wull airt me wicht. Ah wullnae pug.

Ah dinnae care if bampots prate,
Aw haurdships Ah can thole.
Ah'm the high heid yin o ma fate,
The skipper o ma saul.

Grigor McWatt, efter William Ernest Henley, 1946[11]

---

11   From *Kenspeckelt*, Virr Press, 1959. Reprinted in *Warld in a Gless: The Collected Varse of Grigor McWatt*, Smeddum Beuks, 1992.

McWATT BEGAN HIS LIFE'S WORK TOWARDS THE END OF WORLD War II, in an army tent pitched in the grounds of Finnverinnity House, the northern seat of Fascaray's absentee laird, Montfitchett. The house, known locally as the Big House, had been taken over by the British government for use as a secret training school for commandos and Special Operations Executive agents. It was a gruelling course but somehow, on a narrow camp bed under canvas in the shrubbery, between Herculean manoeuvres, remorseless tests of strength and endurance and late-night instruction in the dark arts of sabotage and murder, McWatt began to write the first of the notebooks that would become *The Fascaray Compendium*.

In this first volume, his focus was on island history. 'A dwelling has stood on the site of Finnverinnity House, commanding the curve of the bay to the west of the harbour, since the early sixteenth century . . .' were the opening words. Knox-Cardew, who didn't have access to the *Compendium* but was aware of its broad themes, speculated that 'during those dark days, it may have been a comfort to him, as it has been to others, to retreat to the past in an attempt to make sense of the challenging present'.

Over the years, McWatt rewrote and enlarged his chronicle of Fascaray's ancient and medieval past, drawing on published histories and archive material. The peripatetic minister Donald Monro, known as the Dean of the Isles, visited the island in 1563, McWatt wrote, 'during what seems to have been a rare interval of peace and prosperity'. Monro noted in his *Description of the Western Isles of Scotland*[12]: 'ane castle of Fasquarhaye, pertaining to Malcolm McQuhatt by the sword but to the bishop of the isles by heritage, with ane fair orchard . . . roughe country, with pairt of birkin woodeis, maney deires and excellent for fishing'. Monro also gave the first account of the annual 'guga hunt' – the catching, killing and

12 William Auld, Edinburgh, 1774.

smoking of young solan geese or gannets – 'a tradition that continues to this day', wrote McWatt.

Two years after Monro's visit, three months after her marriage to Darnley, Mary, Queen of Scots, is said to have attended the wedding of Malcolm's daughter, Mariota, on the Isle of Fascaray. 'Sources suggest that the doomed queen stayed in what was then a modest castle or fortified house with a walled courtyard, called simply Finnverinnitie,' wrote McWatt. Mary is said to have visited the house again, 'seeking refuge after her escape from imprisonment at Loch Leven Castle in 1568, and left a touching thank-you note, written in French, to her hosts'.

In the mid seventeenth century, Oliver Cromwell sent a fleet to sack the castle and subdue the troublesome clan McWatt, whose members had remained stubbornly loyal to the House of Stuart. 'It was then,' wrote Grigor McWatt three centuries later, 'that God showed his true colours as a clansman.' A two-day storm sank the parliamentarian ships in sight of Finnverinnity Bay and forty-two English sailors were drowned.

Subsequently, 'God's sympathies were diverted elsewhere'; within seventy years the clan chieftain, Aeneas McWatt of the McWatts, fell on hard times, his impoverished kinsmen were scattered and in 1698, the year of the ill-fated Darien venture that cost Scotland its independence, Finnverinnitie and its land had been taken over by the rival McGlaisters (Gaelic: McGlabhcadair; motto: '*Quid vobis quia non praeteribit*' – 'Whit's fer ye'll nae gae by ye') who later set about building a new house from the ruins of the old in the baronial style, with eight octagonal turrets topped by corbelled conical roofs clustering round the central stem of the ancient castle.

The writer Martainn MacGilleMhartainn, or Martin Martin, visiting the island in 1700 in the footsteps of Dean Monro, found Fascaray 'in good heart, despite the recent reversal of clan fortunes', and observed: 'The Natives are generally a very sagacious people and quick of Apprehension; several of both Sexes have a Gift of *Poesy*, and are able to form a *Satyr* or *Panegyrick ex tempore*, without the assistance of any stronger Liquor than Water to raise their Fancy.'[13]

But strong liquor, Martin noted, was as much a part of Fascaradian life as Poesy and Panegyrick. He enjoyed the hospitality of Domnhall

13 *A Description of the Western Islands of Scotland* by Martainn MacGilleMhartainn, published by Andrew Bell, Cross-Keys and Bible, Cornhill, 1703.

McGlaister at Finnverinnitie Castle and wrote: 'Their plenty of Corn was such, as dispos'd the Natives to brew several sorts of Liquors, as common *Usquebaugh*, another call'd *Trestarig, id est Aquavitae*, three times distill'd, which is strong and hot; a third sort is four times distill'd, and this by the Natives is call'd *Usquebaugh-baul, id est Usquebaugh*, which at first taste affects all the Members of the Body: two spoonfuls of this last Liquor is a sufficient Dose; and if any Man exceed this, it would presently stop his Breath, and endanger his Life.'

Famously, hospitality of a more frugal sort was offered to Bonnie Prince Charlie by the McWatts, then living in reduced circumstances in Calasay, when the Young Pretender fled the Scottish mainland after the crushing of the '45 rebellion. Grigor McWatt cites Neil MacEachan's *Narrative of the Wanderings of Prince Charles in the Hebrides*,[14] a first-hand account of the royal fugitive's flight. The prince, disguised as an Irish servant woman, had distant sight of Finnverinnity House when he arrived at the island by night on a French frigate. He ruefully declared it 'ane douce and gentill place' but was advised to steer clear of the house on account of the incumbent McGlaister's English sympathies. The prince spent the night in 'a hummel wee shielin with the puir but leal McWhatts of Calasie', according to MacEachan, before resuming his journey.

By the time the travel writer Thomas Pennant arrived in 1769, the McGlaisters were absentee lairds, Scots in name only, enjoying the rewards of their loyalty to the Hanoverian Crown in a 300-acre estate in Leicestershire, while 'the houses of the Scotch peasants are the most wretched imaginable and shocking to humanity'. Many Fascaradians had been 'cleared' – violently driven off the land – by the island's factor (estate manager or bailiff), set on making 'agricultural improvements' for his masters. Pennant noted the 'melancholy aspect of Finnverinnitie House, commanding the wide eastern bay, with very fine oaks and horse chestnuts in the garden. Its noble family have left North Britain and swallows are making their nests in the bold stucco of the upper apartments.'[15]

Four years later Dr Samuel Johnson, visiting the island with his Scottish amanuensis James Boswell, found the house 'romantically

14 Edward Black & Sons, Glasgow, 1750.
15 *A Tour in Scotland, and Voyage to the Hebrides 1772* by Thomas Pennant, John Monk, 1774.

derelict',[16] and by the time Dorothy Wordsworth visited Fascaray in 1803 she could exult in the 'most pleasing romantic effect of the scene – like a barren Ullswater, interveined with water, empty of people, and with a few ruined cottages, built simply like savages' huts, scattered among fir trees that made a delicious murmuring in the wind'.[17]

McWatt continued: 'After the second wave of brutal evictions failed to make the land sufficiently profitable for the profligate McGlaisters, Finnverinnity House, along with the island, was sold towards the end of the nineteenth century to a Bristol tobacco merchant who restored the central crenelated fortress, added two wings, a Gothic tower and an open turret above a castellated porte cochère entrance.' The silhouette of the extended house was, and remains, 'dominated by 23 ornate chimney stacks of varying heights and design which squat on the building's dark mass like giant chessmen'.

For more recent history, McWatt drew on Fascaray's 'living reference library' – the Finnverinnity Inn – and it was there he learned that 'the celebrated Glasgow architect and designer Charles Rennie Mackintosh is said to have visited the house at the turn of the twentieth century'. Design historians have attributed to Mackintosh the handsome master bathroom in the Big House, with its pea-green sanitary suite and chequered black-and-green tiles with Japonaiserie-style thistle motif.

In 1929, Percy Mere-Stratton, Lord Montfitchett of Godalming and Mayfair, bought the island and its main estates, Finnverinnity and Balnasaig, 'as a playground for his pals', wrote McWatt. Three times a year the new laird would travel up with his shooting and fishing parties wearing brogues, houndstooth plus-fours and matching cap, for what McWatt called 'a spot of recreational colonialism', while Montfitchett's wife, Lady Muriel, 'the buck-toothed, etiolated heiress to a pomade fortune', played cards with her smart friends, 'chain-smoking theatrical types imported from London who had a horror of mud, cold and midges and rarely ventured outside the house'.

For Montfitchett's triannual sprees he maintained a staff of twenty-two

16 *The Journal of a Tour to the Hebrides with Samuel Johnson, LL.D* by James Boswell, Malone, 1785.
17 *Recollections of a Tour Made in Scotland, A. D. 1803* by Dorothy Wordsworth, John Campbell Shairp, 1885.

at the house all year round, men and women – mainlanders, some English – stringently divided by rank and responsibilities. As well as a cook and a housemaid, a butler, groom and stable boy, there were kitchen maids, parlourmaids, laundry maids, ladies' maids and a footman.

The factor oversaw the land and tenants, three ghillies and four stalkers assisted with the fishing, stag hunting, capercaillie and pheasant shooting, and a young man known as 'an occasional boy' cleaned and set the fires in the reception hall, drawing room, dining room and each of the eighteen bedrooms when a full house party was in residence. He also maintained order among the guns and rods of the tack room and – the only task he enjoyed – set off a rocket across Finnverinnity Bay to welcome the arrival and signal the departure of the laird. Shonnie MacDonald of Lusnaharra, a fourteen-year-old piper and fiddler much in demand at the island's *taighean ceilidh* (ceilidh houses), was employed to stand in the open turret in all weathers to skirl the Montfitchetts and their guests into dinner.

Provisions were conveyed by boat from Auchwinnie to Finnverinnity Pier, where they were loaded onto carts pulled by Clydesdale horses and taken directly to the house.

The hierarchy within the house was reinforced by rules governing communications between servants (few, and only of a business nature – unauthorised liaisons would result in immediate dismissal) and between servants and islanders (none – servants were confined to the house and its grounds and, again, instant dismissal would be the price of fraternisation with locals).

During the ten months of the year when the laird was not in residence, the servants busied themselves cleaning, dusting and airing the empty rooms each week, laundering unused bedclothes to keep them fresh, cleaning windows each month and polishing and repolishing furniture, guns, shoes and rods.

The factor and ghillies controlled vermin, raised the pheasant chicks and did their best to keep down poaching. 'If the factor had extended his field of operation to the maintenance of the island's small and fragile infrastructure, to its crofts and cottages, to the needs of its tenants, he would have had little time for other duties but Lord Montfitchett instructed him to ignore crofters' complaints about their crumbling, windowless homes –

the *taighean dubh* blackhouses, smoke-charred, heather-thatched drystone hovels which many islanders still shared with their cattle,' wrote McWatt.

Like many of its insular neighbours, Fascaray was too remote from the mainland to be connected to the national grid and the only regularly functioning generator, located in the main village of Finnverinnity, mostly served the Big House. Islanders drew their water from wells, and self-dug pits screened by ramshackle wooden sheds served as toilets. Domestic rubbish was piled outside crofts and when the piles got too unwieldy they were shovelled onto the open decks of fishing boats and buried at sea.

Most Fascaradians accepted this squalor and hardship as the status quo. If the injustices of the Highland Clearances, when Montfitchett's predecessors had forcibly evicted many Fascaradians to make way for the more profitable *caora mhor* (big sheep), were alive in local memory, so too was the sense of defeat against overwhelmingly superior forces. Resignation and stoicism were regarded as Fascaradian virtues.

But even the most passive islanders were provoked to anger when news reached them in 1932 that Lord Montfitchett had issued an order banning children from playing on Finnverinnity beach. The laird – 'beneficiary of, but not necessarily an advertisement for, an Eton and Oxford education', wrote McWatt – also did his best to thwart plans for the expansion of Finnverinnity School.

'Send them to the damned mainland, if education's what they want, though I can't think what good it's going to do them in the bally bog', he was reported to have said.

The schoolteacher, Miss Elspeth Millar, daughter of a minister from Resolis, was said to have been as scandalised by the laird's language as by his attitude. But the islanders were powerless. There was no higher authority to appeal to. Montfitchett was their laird and they were his serfs, and Sammy Nelson, his factor, with 'a face like a nippy sweetie', as Effie MacLeod, would later say, was his enforcer. 'This was the arrangement, the social contract, and they were all bound by it; always had been and always would be,' wrote McWatt in 1945.

A Granite Ballad – The Reimagining of Grigor McWatt,
Mhairi McPhail (Thackeray College Press, 2016)

The Pushion Tree

Ah wiz ragin at ma pal:
Ah telt ma wraith an it gied ower.
Ah wiz ragin at ma fae:
Ah telt it nae, ma wraith eikt power.

An Ah wattered it wi tears,
Greetin sair ootthroo the years;
Wi whids an sleekit chairm,
An smirks Ah kep it wairm.

An it eikt baith day an nicht,
Till it buir an aipple bricht.
An ma fae behaud it shine.
An he kennt that it wis mine,

An tae ma croft he stole,
His greed he couldnae thole;
In the morn Ah seen wi glee
Ma fae ootstreekt aneath the tree.

Grigor McWatt, efter William Blake, 1948[18]

18 From *Kenspeckelt*, Virr Press, 1959. Reprinted in *Warld in a Gless: The Collected Varse of Grigor McWatt*, Smeddum Beuks, 1992.

I'm woken by a blinding flash. Sunshine. I come round to full conscious-
ness blinking at the white walls of my new room which, in the purifying
blaze of light, summons a memory of our suite in a Sedona spa resort – a
birthday break, during which Marco had proposed again, I'd refused
again and Agnes had been conceived in a reconciliation tryst. Ten years
ago. Breakfast here, though, will not be a leisurely berry granola with
cold-pressed wheatgrass served by wait staff filling in between acting
jobs. We must fend for ourselves, with whatever frugal supplies the
Auchwinnie store has provided.

Outside, apart from the cry of seagulls and the faintest tidal sigh,
there is no sound. Curled next to me in the bed is Agnes, who crept in to
join me at midnight. She is still asleep, warm and fragrant as oven-fresh
brioche, clutching her quilt. Trying not to disturb her, I lift my head to
look through the window. Under a cloudless blue sky the sea is opales-
cent turquoise; it could be the Gulf of Mexico, or the Aegean.

Agnes stirs, raises herself from the pillow and gazes out of the
window.

'Wow, Mom. The sea! It's awesome!'

Her accent is as pure, deep-dyed American as her guileless high spirits.
Unlike her mother, whose neutralised mid-Atlantic diction testifies to a
rootless past – Scotland, Canada, England, New York – and whose recent
absence of any discernible enthusiasm might, in 1950s Hollywood, have
seen her hauled up before McCarthy's House Un-American Activities
Committee.

After breakfast, we prop open our front door and get to work. I put
my laptop, the box of letters and the manuscript out of harm's way, on
top of the kitchen cupboard. Agnes is an eager assistant and we roll
up the hideous carpet and put it in the shed in the small yard behind
the house. We move the fake-coal heater – I'd rather freeze than warm
my hands in its feeble glow and I'm willing to sacrifice my daughter's
comfort as well as my own on the grounds of taste. But no sacrifice is

necessary. Behind the electric heater is a hearth with a functioning, perfectly acceptable fire basket in which a real fire has been carefully laid, with paper (the *Auchwinnie Pibroch*, eighteen months old, headline 'DOG RESCUED AFTER NIGHT ON MOUNTAIN'), firelighters, kindling and logs. Hypothermia will not be necessary. We stow the heater in a cupboard under the stairs. Back in the sitting room, we sweep and mop the stone floor and lay a plain rush mat which Agnes has found in a corner of the shed.

Animal lover though she is, she agrees that the cattle portraits are excessive – 'tacky', she says, though she looks a little longingly at a photograph of a calf and its mother in the grounds of a ruined castle and asks if we can keep it. I tell myself that it will read as irony to my New York friends, as if any of them will ever cross the Atlantic to see it. We stash the rest of the portraits in the shed. I replace the light bulb and switch the nylon lace shade for a rusting utilitarian tin cone – a relic from a ship, probably, the sort of artefact metropolitan loft dwellers would ransom their children for – also retrieved from the shed. From the airing cupboard we take out extra blankets, soft lambswool in the colours of heather and moss, and drape them over the chairs and couch.

The kitchen is easier. We fold away the plastic tablecloth with its oppressively chirpy print of teddy bears tucking into gargantuan breakfasts. I check Agnes for signs of regret but she is firm.

'No way,' she says.

Beneath it, after a good scrub, is a pleasingly plain and serviceable pine table.

The bathroom is fine, apart from the china lady whose frilled nylon skirts conceal a spare toilet roll. I pick her up. Kitsch, of the unironic sort, corrodes the spirit. But a little moue from Agnes makes me change my mind. Okay, I can live with it. Taste is another tyranny. She smiles, a sweet victor's smile, pats the china lady gently on the head and asks if she can go outside.

'Please! I'll only be ten minutes,' she says. 'I just want to go to the beach.'

I look along the road. In our two hours of work, a handful of pedestrians have walked by, heading to or from the pub or store, or both, and two quad bikes and the occasional rusty Land Rover have cruised by at strolling pace. Speeding wouldn't be possible on these rutted roads. The sea is busier, with several small fishing boats bobbing in the wake of a big workhorse ship carrying its cargo of hothoused salmon and mussels to the mainland from the industrial fish farm beyond Plodda and Grodda. The sturdy ferry, its red trim giving it a children's-book jauntiness, is on its way back from Auchwinnie, and the white triangles of the pleasure yachts, out from the mainland for a brief fairweather voyage on this beautiful day, carve lazy arcs in the sea. Concealing my anxiety about non-existent road traffic, I watch my daughter cross safely to the shore then I go into the kitchen to unpack our groceries.

This is plain fare, dismayingly so to a North American with vegan inclinations and borderline gluten intolerance. It's the food of my parents' generation, who were raised in Scotland in a post-war world of scarcity when, if it ever came up, the notion of actually taking pleasure in what you ate, or failing to eat every last morsel on your plate, would have been considered decadent. I know we can survive in a world without quinoa, arugula and cilantro, but will it be any fun?

Agnes, though, has never been much of a gourmet and fancy farmers' market goods are of no interest to her. A boiled egg, a piece of toast, would do just as well. Simple, undemanding appetites seem to have skipped a generation. But she tolerates my needs and impulses and was always endearingly receptive to her parents' more adventurous culinary experiments. She is supremely adaptable and will be content with whatever Auchwinnie's supermarket has to offer.

Upstairs, there is little to do except open our suitcases and put away clothes and shoes. From my bedroom window I watch the clouds massing, obscuring the sun and leeching colour from the sea. My dark-haired daughter walks, absorbed, along the pebble strand, occasionally stopping, eyes drawn to a particular stone or shell, which she bends to pick up and turn in her hand. She has the gift of concentration – unlike her mother, who is shamefully distractable when it comes to homemaking.

Apart from my document box, our heaviest case contains our books. Instead of the fashionable stories for nine-year-olds – didactic tales of bullying, body dysmorphia, family dysfunction and the joys of diversity – Agnes has brought old favourites, mementoes of her earlier childhood, before the fall, when she was part of an old-fashioned, two-parent family and the future was fixed. I set out the books on the dresser – *The Little Prince, Treasure Island* – classic novels in early editions given to her by her father when she was way too young, and a recent vintage addition, *The Treasure Seekers*. I suspect they're more cherished for the pretty illustrations than the stories. She's also brought a Nancy Drew, *The Clue of the Whistling Bagpipes* – another Goodwill find from her father – an anthology of Grimms' fairy tales, *Eloise at Christmastime* and, in a classic regressive move, her baby books – Sendak, Browne and Ahlberg.

She couldn't be talked into an e-reader though I've brought mine, containing a library of classics I'll never live long enough to read. I've also brought a back-wrecking selection of books that weren't available in digital form, among them Knox-Cardew's clinically obese critical study.

There is a souvenir of my own past – my grandfather's 1936 Blackwood edition of the *Fascaringa Saga*, as revered and little read in our household as the family Bible. As well as my past, there is also my present – the 1964 *Selected Verse of Hugh MacDiarmid*, poet and figurehead of Scottish nationalism, in the Raucle Press edition with an introduction by his erstwhile friend Grigor McWatt; *Warld in a Gless*, the complete collection of McWatt's 'reimagined' poems, from 1945 to the early nineties; distressed paperback copies of his two slender volumes of memoir, *Forby* and *Ootwith*; and *Frae Mambeag Brae* and *Wittins*, the Stravaigin Press selections of his essays and newspaper columns for the *Auchwinnie Pibroch*.

Ailish Mooney also unearthed a Festschrift pamphlet of reminiscences of McWatt – *Poet in a Landscape*, published by Auchwinnie Press in 2000 with interviews with fellow Fascaradians to celebrate the poet's eightieth birthday. My grandfather refused to be interviewed – he had left the island behind more than half a century ago, he said – and his lack of grace was matched by its subject; McWatt tried to suppress the booklet by buying up as many copies as he could and burning them. Here in my hand, in its softback plaid cover (the McWatt tartan again – overlapping grids of purple and mustard on a field of blue), is one that got away. I riffle through its unexceptional pages – '"He's a private man," says Marsaili MacDonald, proprietor of the Bothy guest house. "He wouldn't like the fuss of this book, wouldn't like people talking about him."'

There are three other Fascaray-related curios – Jim Struan's *Silent Killing for Cubs and Scouts*, a self-published memoir of the Finnverinnity

House war years, and two accounts of more recent and arcane local history: *Reflections from the Pilgrim Path*, a book of pious New Age flummery by Neville Booth, one of the founders of the Balnasaig Centre, which has been drawing the credulous comfortably-off for 'spirit-channelling' retreats for forty years, and *The Wisdom of the Wilderness Within* by Evelyn Fletcher, Booth's former partner and current high priestess at Balnasaig. All three fail to mention the island's most famous son.

And then there is my own book, *The But'n'Ben Baroness*, my brief and justly unregarded life of Isobel Grant, the doughty amateur collector who founded the Am Fasgadh Highland Folk Museum on the island of Iona in 1935. She deserved better than this thinly worked-up dissertation, published by Aikenhead Press, a Scots-interest American imprint so small, with a print run so negligible that it might as well have been a vanity outfit. I carry the book as a talisman, I guess; my own regressive keepsake, a reminder, in case I ever begin to founder on our chilly desert island, of the busy, work-obsessed student I once was, with a promising career ahead of her.

It's also part of the reason I'm here; it certainly wasn't my interview performance (thirty apologetic seconds on my strengths, an impassioned thirty minutes on my weaknesses) with the Auchwinnie Regional Development and Enterprise Board that finally landed me the job. My family connections can't have done any harm. My grandfather, Hector McPhail, like all the Fascaray Five, has the status of a minor deity round here. The commission for a book on McWatt that I'd wangled from Alma, my old editor at Aikenhead, now editor-in-chief at Thackeray College Press, must have helped too. But Isobel Grant swung it.

I stare at the cover photograph of the formidable spinster. She stands in tweed skirt and oversized glasses at the peeling door of a croft which, thatched roof apart, could be number 19. I'm not sure whether to curse her or thank her.

I feel a sudden need to step outside, to inhale the salty air and gaze at the sea. For a moment I'm vindicated as the sun breaks through the gloom, casting a sparkling net across the sea – this crazy move, all the unnecessary upheaval, was necessary after all.

One minute of exultation, then the clouds sweep back and the midges move in. Tiny, numerous and relentless, they swarm at my lips and my eyes. On the shore, they've descended on Agnes too and she runs towards me, laughing and swatting her face. I look down the street where, outside the pub, the smokers flail their arms against their own insect hordes. I run inside with my daughter and slam the door. I must look out those midge hoods.

In July and August, on rare days of startling and sustained heat, dragon-flies as blue as the cloudless skies shimmer over cushions of moss by the burn while the midges, who abhor direct sunlight, are nowhere to be seen. Out to sea, somnolent groups of whales pass like cortèges of cruise ships and around them dolphins and porpoises joyously arc and dip as if stitching the ocean's silken canopy of turquoise, gentian and cobalt.

By the shore, wild roses are viscera pink against the vaulted blue of sky and sea, and the machair is scattered with orchids like fuschia pine cones. At the rocky margins around Loch Aye, flag irises – *seggie flooers* – bristle like the golden spears of a pygmy army and swallows swoop and dive over the water, pecking at it and sending out concentric circles of waves, making long-playing records of the loch's black skin.

Guillemots, razorbills and screaming seagulls plummet from the sky, swooping to scoop up shellfish from the shore. They carry mussels and clams up as high as the tallest Caledonian pines then open their beaks and drop the shells, smashing them on the rocks to yield up the viscous pelagic hearts. Clamorous chicks, balls of pure down, emerge from eggs hidden beneath the samphire and sea wrack and the glinting cargo of seashells. There is treasure at every step.

As sunset trails its scarlet pennants in the west at the end of our long summer days, glittering fountains of mackerel fry spray up from the enamelled sea like silver confetti as the tiny fish flee unseen predators.

Here, poised between sea and sky in this limitless azure sphere, it is possible to imagine that man can live at peace again, set aside the deadly squabbles of tribe and territory, reconnect with nature and re-enter Arcadia.

Then the day darkens, storms descend and relentless rain turns this Eden into a bleak and chilly hell, reminding us that the world is not always benificent. And out beyond the Mhor Sgheir reef, north of Lusnaharra, the Carracorry whirlpool, which has been known to swallow rigged ships whole, is at its most dangerous during the half-ebb spring tides of high summer, when the weather is at its most benign.

Grigor McWatt, 1945, *The Fascaray Compendium*

INVENTORY OF SCOTS WORDS DESCRIBING
CLOUDS, CLOODS OR CLUDS

berk – a covering of clouds, overcast

ceul – motion of clouds in wind

goog – a heavy, dirty cloud

grum – a dark patch in the sky indicating a storm

hert-sair – a cloud resembling a broken heart

hum – an overcast sky

kerfin – drift of small clouds

kyrie – passage of clouds before wind

mirlie-backs – cirrocumulus cloud formations

muirbreak – deluge of rain on moorland

owerga – a rising bank of black cloud

pouthered lawyr – a fleecy white cloud resembling a lawyer's wig

prattick – an unusually heavy cloudburst

roarie bummler – a bank of storm clouds

rouk – thick, misty cloud

scull-gab – a cloud formation resembling a human skull

skub – high, hazy, drifting cloud

thwankin – clouds mingling in thick and gloomy succession

tumald – an intense downpour

voaler's-crammacks – cirrus clouds, like goat hairs

watter-mooth – a burst rain cloud

windy-rogs – lines of clouds indicating bad weather

yackle – small white clouds shaped like teeth

yagach – heavy mass of cloud portending loss or disaster

Grigor McWatt, 1946, *The Fascaray Compendium*

IN A DOCUMENTARY MADE FOR BBC SCOTLAND IN 2007, SEVEN years before McWatt's death, Allan Logan, the literary critic and outspoken nationalist, compared the Bard of Fascaray to Walter Scott 'in the impact their respective work has had on the national sense of self'. McWatt had little time for Scott, dismissing the romantic novelist as a 'fawning Uncle Tam, with a taste for pageantry, who courted English autocracy', but he graciously accepted Logan's view that the work of 'the foremost poet of the Fascaradian archipelago' had brought 'the glories of Scotland, the sublimity of our hills, our seas and rivers, our cascading falls and limpid lochs – defying colonisation, neglect, and the self-cauterising spirit of the dispossessed – to the attention of the wider world, and ultimately returned our land to us'.

Old film footage – a jerky home movie in faded colours made by an amateur fan in 1962 – shows the poet in his early forties wearing the familiar kilt and beret, beating the bounds of Calasay with a skittish Border collie and a shy teenaged boy, identified as McWatt's assistant Donald MacInnes. In fisherman's sweater and army fatigues, young MacInnes, supervised by McWatt, chops wood, carries a bucket of water from a well and rolls playfully in the grass with a creature that looks like an overweight ferret. (Those familiar with the life and work will know that this is Marty, McWatt's pet pine marten, part of the ungovernable menagerie that featured in some of the poet's lighter and best-loved columns for the *Auchwinnie Pibroch*.)

The old footage is interspersed with Logan's interview with the poet, nearly half a century later, filmed at the fireside of An Tobar. At one point, Logan asks McWatt, then aged eighty-six, if he is ever lonely, if in his 'splendid isolation' he misses 'the society of others'. The poet takes the pipe from his mouth and spits in the hearth before answering.

'Lonely?' he repeats, incredulous. 'Open your eyes, man. Step outside and look around. Apart from my extended family – the dogs, the otters, pine martens, wild cats, the coos and hens and goat, the visiting seabirds and seals – I know every lichen-covered rock, every hill, every granite pinnacle and glacial corrie, every burn and rivulet, every gorse bush, rowan tree and hawthorn, every primrose and harebell, as I would know a much-loved face down the years. I've seen this place in every season, all weather, watched the islands on the horizon shimmering in heat haze, buffeted by blizzards and dissolving in haar, seen the sea as blue as Eden's own ocean and as black and gurling as hell's cauldron. I know the call of the greylags, the silver fanfare of the whooper swans and the chatter of chaffinches busy at their nests in the alders as if they were the cries of my own weans. Tell me, how the devil could I possibly be lonely?'

A Granite Ballad – The Reimagining of Grigor McWatt,
Mhairi McPhail (Thackeray College Press, 2016)

My small cache of correspondence between McWatt and Lilias Hogg, the Flooer o Rose Street and Muse o Menzies', is a start. But only a start. I exaggerated its extensiveness and significance to the Auchwinnie Development Board, and to Alma at Thackeray College Press, because I wanted the job and the book deal. I've got to do better than this. There's some extra-literary curiosity about the Hogg–McWatt affair; it's the stuff of vintage, high-end gossip even among those who've barely read a word of his work, a staple of the culture sections of the posher papers in a narrative he would have loathed – a story of the doomed love of a beguiling girl for an unattainable and much older poet genius; a kind of Bloomsbury-of-the-North subplot, with added whisky and incidental bagpipes.

The fact that the only surviving picture of Lilias Hogg was taken in her early twenties has been good for the myth. Their story has been bracketed with other 'poetic grand passions and star-crossed lovers': Dante and Beatrice, Petrarch and Laura, Lowell and Blackwood, Dylan and Caitlin, Hughes and Plath. One Saturday supplement, struggling to come up with editorial to justify its Valentine's Day advertising spread, used pictures of Virginia and Leonard Woolf alongside photographs of Lilias Hogg and Grigor McWatt to illustrate a feature on 'lofty literary passions that took no prisoners'.

Then there is the tantalising 'other woman' angle. The enigmatic 'Jean', later derided by a bitter Hogg as 'the murky quine [dark lady] of your sonnets'. For fourteen years, Lilias had believed that she herself was the sole inspiration for McWatt's love poems and that their marriage was inevitable. She never recovered from the blow dealt by news of his secret affair.

Hogg and McWatt even made it into the tabloid press – *Me* magazine – though here their story was served up as a cautionary tale of a woman who ruined her looks and her life (word order reflecting the hierarchy of loss) by spending too much time hanging round creative sorts in bars.

Janis Joplin, Billie Holiday and Amy Winehouse were also cited in the piece, which described McWatt as a 'songwriter' rather than a poet.

There is no record of his views on the press version of his relationship with Lilias but the fact that he refused to give interviews on the subject indicates his position. The references to Lilias Hogg that I've seen so far in *The Fascaray Compendium* are few and oblique. But the Auchwinnie Development Board and Alma at Thackeray Press are keen on this angle. My two bundles of letters, one skimpy, the other chunky, their value in inverse proportion to their dimensions, give us only fragments of the real story. McWatt's letters to Hogg (the small bundle, plus three postcards, ranging in dates from 1958 to 1988) are a fraction of their total correspondence. Written in black ink on unlined blue notepaper, these letters were preserved by Hogg and passed on to me by Edinburgh University Library. We know that she returned a number of his letters to him in despair or pique and that, strapped for cash, she also sold some of his letters to an Edinburgh book dealer. My researcher, Ailish, is trying to track these down from Glasgow.

My haul of letters from Hogg to McWatt, covering the same period, is more extensive but less useful; they're carbon copies which she retained – Lilias had an eye to posterity even then – and the blue ink is smeared and faded. She probably tried to hawk them to the book dealer too but they would have been worthless. With luck, I might find some of the originals in Calasay. With more luck, I might locate the McWatt letters that Hogg returned to him. I am, I know, counting on a lot of luck here.

The keys to the enterprise hang from an iron ring, sinister as Dark Age manacles. I feel like a jailer as I rattle them. They'll open the doors to his house in Calasay and, I hope, unlock a hoard of truth-telling treasures, illuminate the life and work of the Bard of Fascaray, for my book as well as the museum, secure my job and consolidate my new life here. My new life, and my daughter's.

Johanna McAllister, the young part-time administrator of the Fascaray Trust, who has been taking care of the Calasay site, assures me that the house and McWatt's remarkable library, housed in a converted byre, have been kept intact since the poet's death in January. She goes in every week, making the journey on quad bike, negotiating the tricky tides across the strand from Ruh, to dust and air the rooms, check that the rain hasn't got in, the burn hasn't risen under the floorboards or the wind hasn't blown the roof over the cliff.

Apart from the rest of the *Compendium* notebooks, there are stacks of paper there for me to go through, she tells me. 'Letters, pamphlets, bills, receipts, goodness knows what. All safe and dry so far. I've put a box of stuff under the desk in the house for you to make a start.'

Also awaiting my attention is a collection of agricultural implements and other artefacts of island life, amassed by McWatt over six decades and stored in a cart shed on his croft. I must go through it, catalogue it and bring the best of it to the new museum in Finnverinnity.

'There's an unbelievable amount of stuff, just sitting there,' says Johanna. 'I've struggled to sort through it all. That lot, and the library . . .'

My taped interview with Effie MacLeod (done in June on a brief trip to Scotland — a four-day festival of jet lag, bad food and bad faith) has been digitised, copied and transcribed by the assiduous Ailish Mooney. Ailish is also pursuing other McWatt biographical leads, collating a comprehensive list of recordings of his song, 'Hame tae Fascaray', while in her spare time completing her MLitt in Archives and Record Keeping at Glasgow University. She sounds better equipped for my job than I am.

I need more — anything — on McWatt's childhood, which is a black hole in terms of documentation, and I have to trace surviving SOE veterans to piece together his war years. McWatt's memoirs are almost parodically unforthcoming and include only a handful of cagey sentences about these key periods of his life. The Scots have never been good at kissing and telling. Preliminary enquiries, made by phone and email before I left New York, got nowhere and I was too preoccupied with packing up my life, and my relationship, to pursue them further. Ailish, of course, is on the case.

There is the new Grigor McWatt Heritage Centre and Fascaray Museum, funded by his estate and the Fascaray Trust, to set up for official opening at the end of December — less than four months away! I need to choose and collate archive material and exhibits, get some narrative coherence on McWatt's biography and the history of the island, and somehow find time to write my 40,000-word book on McWatt's life and work, provisionally titled *A Granite Ballad*. There are the poems to deal with: his last three collections — *Teuchter's Chapbook*, *Thoog a Poog* and

That's Me Awa – will be added to a new complete edition of his verse, along with any unpublished poems I find.

But my most monumental task is *The Fascaray Compendium*, McWatt's vast seventy-year journal and survey of the island's folklore, history, flora, fauna, and community life, which comprises 22,000 pages – more than eight million words, inscribed by fountain pen in his minuscule handwriting, prim as an embroidery stitch, in 276 softback quarto notebooks. A bundle of them, 1945 to 1970 – one hundred notebooks weighing a total of 57lb (almost as heavy, I note, as my daughter) – was expensively couriered to me in four boxes to Brooklyn so I could start work on the manuscript to prepare it for publication. I did what I could before I got here. So much typing; I felt like a fifties stenographer. Johanna will help and there is provision in the budget for another typist, but I must edit it, compile an index, with Ailish's help, and usher it finally into print in seven hardback volumes in two years' time, 2016 – two and a half years after the poet's death. I ask myself how I signed up for all this and the answer comes back: Marco.

He'd initiated the whole thing as a joke. The notion that I might actually apply for the job never occurred to him. It wasn't so funny when I was offered it, and accepted. But as I unpacked the boxes from Auchwinnie in our tiny apartment in Degraw Street and saw the scale of the task, I began to have serious doubts. All the lexicons and inventories (of moss, seashells, birds . . .); all that history (surely told better and more impartially elsewhere?); the perpetual drafts and redrafts of poems and essays; the journal entries with their minutiae of local gossip, decade after decade; recipes. Recipes, for chrissakes – I nearly chucked the job on the spot. Then Marco walked in and saw me on my knees, hair scraped out of my eyes in a bun, peering over my reading glasses (a recent and aesthetically unhelpful addition), sorting through the slew of pastel-coloured notebooks on the floor. He laughed and made some slighting comment about a schoolmarm grading papers, and that did it; our fates were fixed. I was Fascaray-bound within a month.

The remaining 176 notebooks currently in Calasay are soon to join their companions, packed up and returned by me via courier from New York, in two fireproof safes in the Fascaray Trust office. A selection of them will eventually be shown in the museum, where they'll rest in climate-controlled, UV-screened display cases on electronic cradles which will allow their pages to be turned every few months. A colleague at the National Library of Scotland has offered to talk me through some of the conservation issues. I can combine a meeting with her in Edinburgh with my planned interview with Donald MacInnes, McWatt's former assistant, in October. Lilias Hogg's sister Dolina McPartland, a retired math teacher, has finally agreed to talk to me, too. I should set up the interview with her soon before she changes her mind, or dies. It'll be tricky – both interviews will be tricky – but even so, the thought of leaving Fascaray is accompanied by a treacherous heart-leap of pleasure. Three days after we get here, I'm already plotting my escape.

I can leave Agnes with Johanna, a busy, functioning single mother whose daughter Ailsa is Agnes's age. Agnes will be fine, I tell myself. By some miracle of genetic recombination, despite the neuroses of her embattled parents, despite the upheaval of their break-up and relocation to this strange place, Agnes will always be fine.

On cue, reinforcing my guilt, the door opens and my daughter stands there, eyes wide, a look of delight brimming on the perfect oval of her face.

'Mom! Look!'

She holds out her hand and something glints in the curve of her small palm.

'Treasure!' she says.

'It's pyrite,' I tell her. 'Fool's gold.'

She bites her lower lip, downcast.

'That's mean,' she says. 'I am so *not* a fool.'

'Oh, Agnes. That's its name. Fool's Gold. A common mineral,' I explain. 'You can find it all over the Scottish Highlands.'

'It's pretty, anyhow,' she insists, still injured by the imagined insult.

She places the rock in her bowl of shells and pebbles on the window-sill as I look out at the shifting sea, grey as the Finnverinnity roof slates and sealed beneath a lid of grubby cloud.

Top Floor
33 St James's Square
Edinburgh
11 July 1959

Griogal Cridhe [Beloved Grigor],

Why so cold and silent? What have I done? I know you need to work. I know you need your island and your sea and your space and solitude. But I thought you needed me too. When I saw you walk into Menzies' unannounced, my heart leapt. You'd come for me, I thought. But all night, as you talked to the boys, and glanced over at me only fleetingly, I was in agony. And then I did the stupid thing and flirted with Sydney. What an idiot I was. If I couldn't ignite your desire I wanted to inflame your jealousy. I'm covered with shame and I despair that instead of drawing you to me, I've driven you away forever. Please forgive your Flooer. Life would be intolerable without you.

Yours (always, whether you like it or not), Lilias

———————————

*An Tobar
Calasay
Fascaray
14 July 1959*

Leal-hertit Lilias,

I'm sorry that I caused you such pain. I give what I can give. You understand my work more than anyone and know that, like the thistle, I evade the grasp and thrive in wild places.

43

Dinnae greet
Oor twa sauls, whilk are ane,
Tho Ah maun gang, arenae
Breuken but expandit
Like gowd tae spirlie thinness clourt.

Gin they be twa, they are twa sae
As stieve twin diacles are twa,
Thy saul the siccar fit, maks nae shaw
Tae flit, but doth, if th'ither dae.

An tho it in the middlins sits,
Yet when th'ither hyne stravaigs,
It heelds an glaggers efter it,
An staunds upricht, as that comes hame.

Sic wull thou be tae me, who maun
Like th'ither fit asclentit pairt,
Thy stieveness maks my circle suith
An maks me feenish whaur Ah stairt.

Aefauldlie, Grigor

———————————

Lilias Hogg pinned the handwritten verse to her wall and it survived her chaotic life and many house moves to hang above her bed in her final, pitifully threadbare flat in Shrub Place Lane. The poem[19] was eventually published in 1992 and the original is in the Fascaray archive, yellowed by time and cigarette smoke, with the rusty ghosts of thumbtacks in each corner.

A Granite Ballad – The Reimagining of Grigor McWatt,
Mhairi McPhail (Thackeray College Press, 2016)

———————————

19 'Valediction', efter John Donne, 1959. *Warld in a Gless: The Collected Varse of Grigor McWatt*, Smeddum Beuks, 1992.

22 August 2014

Inventory of possessions I have hauled 2,600 miles east from New York to this remote boulder in the North Atlantic Ocean.

Correspondence between Grigor McWatt and Lilias Hogg: Digital scans and printouts of postcards and letters from McWatt to Hogg – 25. The letters were preserved in their envelopes, on which the postage stamps were, as on all McWatt's correspondence, carefully attached upside down. Digital scans and printouts of carbon copied letters from Hogg to McWatt – 134.

Photographs: 12 prints – spanning 1945 to 2011, showing McWatt from 25 to 90 years old – taken from scans of the originals, held in the National Library of Scotland archive in Edinburgh.

One laptop: containing aforementioned scans of letters and a compressed file of 2,000 pages scanned from *The Fascaray Compendium*; draft chapters of *A Granite Ballad* (I also have an edited printout of the first two chapters); audio recordings and a transcription (maddeningly inaccurate) of my interview with Effie MacLeod, as well as every recorded version of 'Hame tae Fascaray' that Ailish has managed to unearth. (She's located 53 so far and I've only managed to get through half of them. Agnes calls it 'that hee-ra-haw song' and puts her hands over her ears whenever she hears it.)

One memory stick: containing copies of some of the above.

My journal: Pilar suggested I write a blog from my new island home. I'd rather perform open-heart surgery on myself with a *sgian-dubh*. Suppose it doesn't work out here? A public, online, real-time account of my mental and physical disintegration, from self-loving boasts to self-harming sorrow, might please Marco but it would mortify me. I'm holding back for now with a carbon-based, A4-format, lined, green spiral-bound hardback; plenty of scope for second thoughts, private regrets and emendations. The first entries are 19, 20 and 21 August. Apart from them, nine pages of notes and this inventory, the rest of the journal is vertiginously empty.

Books: Miscellaneous. Cited in 20 August entry.

Clothing: various, mostly water and windproof.

Midge hoods: two khaki net shrouds, said to be the only defence against Scotland's pitiless no-see-ums.

Toiletries: various, including noxious sprays which claim (falsely, I now know) to provide a chemical defence against the midge.

My daughter: who comes with her own inventory.

And, taking up more time and mental space than all of these –

My cerebral swagbag: an airport carousel's worth of guilt, hopes, anxieties, regrets.

BY THE MID 1930S, EVEN THE ENGLISH HAD BEGUN TO BAULK as the Laird of Fascaray's High Toryism veered towards home-grown fascism and then Nazism. Montfitchett was not alone, of course; his friends and fellow peers, the Lords Rothermere, Redesdale and Brocket, members of the notorious Anglo-German Fellowship, were also taken by the new German Chancellor's bracing style and visionary outlook. Redesdale's daughters, Unity and Diana, pin-ups of the movement, had visited Finnverinnity for a week of grouse shooting; photographs taken on Mammor ridge show them windswept and comely in tweeds and lisle stockings, jaunty pheasant feathers in their felt halts.

In April 1939, when pictures appeared of Montfitchett in Nuremberg, grinning at Hitler's side during the Führer's fiftieth-birthday celebrations, revulsion was expressed in every newspaper except the *Daily Mail*, whose proprietor, Lord Rothermere, warmly congratulated their mutual Austrian friend on his annexation of Czechoslovakia.

But with the outbreak of war, Montfitchett had the grace to pipe down. He went to America to join his ne'er-do-well son Torquil, who evaded military service by making a startlingly young but advantageous Yankee marriage and was dabbling in real estate in Connecticut. 'Lord Montfitchett sat out the conflict, bickering with Muriel over martini pitchers, in a rented Italianate mansion with a nine-hole golf course on the north shore of Long Island,' McWatt wrote in *The Fascaray Compendium*. The laird's unappetising alliances were, however, not forgotten. Back in the UK, the War Office's decision to requisition Finnverinnity House as a training school for commandos and Special Operations Executive agents seemed to islanders like natural justice.

'This dreich land o bog, hill and bracken, riven with secret glens and girt by a mercurial sea, is an invigorating paradise for those of us of a Spartan disposition,' wrote McWatt. The north-western region of Scotland encompassing Auchwinnie on the mainland, Fascaray and the scattered clusters of uninhabited islands that encircle it, is known in Gaelic as *na criochan cruaidhe* – the harsh frontier or, in the idiomatic Lallans Scots of McWatt, 'the marounjous ootlaund'.

Its enfolded glens guarded by crags and peaks, its treacherous bogland and dense woods, fast-flowing rivers and plunging waterfalls, serrated coastline and inaccessible coves walled by tumbled rock, its capricious seas and wild weather, made it a perfect training ground for Winston Churchill's elite troops of commandos and special agents.

In the wake of the catastrophe at Dunkirk in 1940, the British government developed a new military strategy. Men and women, some from enemy-occupied countries overseas, were to be trained in guerrilla methods of sabotage, silent killing and survival then sent abroad to aid the resistance movements.

Whitehall dispatched military officers to Scotland, looking for likely headquarters where officers and other ranks of both sexes could be billeted while undergoing the arduous selection process which would qualify them for admission to the SOE, the Special Operations Executive, a crack corps schooled in the art of ungentlemanly warfare. The large houses of the region – castles, Victorian shooting lodges, Greek-revival mansions and Edwardian baronial follies – were earmarked; usefully they were already empty, since even in peacetime their owners, based in England, visited infrequently and, with the outbreak of war, had decamped entirely. The blandly named Ministry of Works conducted the requisitioning on behalf of the 'Inter Services Research Bureau', a cover name for the SOE.

The new military strategy became known in the north as 'Ssh . . .' – not a reference to the secret nature of its work but an acronym of 'Scotland's Stately Hames'. *Na criochan cruaidhe* was identified as a Restricted Area and road and rail routes were patrolled by the army and in some places sealed off entirely with barbed wire and armed security posts. The two railway stations at Auchwinnie – Auchwinnie East and Auchwinnie West – gave access to trainees, munitions and supplies, and in addition provided useful targets for demolition practice. Population in the region was minimal and those who lived there had the habit of discretion – 'they had managed to keep secret the presence of Bonnie Prince Charlie some years before,' as McWatt later pointed out.

There was little protest from most of the usurped aristocrats, who consented to do their patriotic duty when they received assurances that, after the war and British victory, their property (in most cases their third or even fourth 'home') would be returned intact. No such guarantee could be offered to them in the event of a Nazi victory. Given his politics, Montfitchett was more ambivalent and wrote a letter of complaint, nobbling an old school friend in the War Office to register his protest at what he called 'this Bolshevik appropriation and wholesale destruction of private property'.

The Labour politician Hugh Dalton, Minister of Economic Warfare in Churchill's coalition government, had been given the task of setting up the SOE and he replied to Montfitchett expressing polite sympathy. 'But given the current circumstances, we regretfully have to proceed with this arrangement. We will, however, use our best endeavours to ensure that the property is returned to you in the condition in which we found it.'

In a memo[20] for his departmental files, attached to a copy of his correspondence, Dalton was more forthright. 'Lord Montfitchett appears to own a number of alternative residences throughout the British Isles, in Europe – occupied and free – and in Africa. I cannot believe the requisitioning of Finnverinnity House will cause him undue hardship.'

Under the laird's orders, telegrammed from London, Mrs McIvor, the widowed housekeeper of the Big House, arranged for much of the furniture to be sent into storage at Fort William before she was mothballed herself to wait out the war with her invalid sister in Peebles, and Finnverinnity House began to receive its first intake of would-be commandos and SOE agents.

Although Mrs McIvor had done her best to clear the house in the time available, senior officers and high-status instructors – civilian and military – were able to make use of several guest bedrooms which were still comfortably appointed, while women trainees (seven in all, over five years) were given Mrs McIvor's quarters: two windowless rooms and a bathroom off the scullery. Other officers slept on camp beds laid out in a dormitory arrangement in the main bedroom and in the attic nursery and servants' quarters where, because of their distance from the first-floor bathrooms, the men used a large blue-and-white porcelain bowl

20 Released to public scrutiny by the UK National Archives in 1971 under the thirty-year freedom of information rule.

decorated with dragons — later identified as a priceless Chinese Quianlong jardinière — as a communal 'chantie' or chamber pot.

The ballroom was turned into an officers' mess with an improvised bar built from the hull of an abandoned fishing boat, wedged under a presiding portrait of one of Montfitchett's ancestors who had made his fortune selling opium in China (the jardinière was a spoil of his trade). His permanent expression of displeasure seemed appropriate. Outside, for lower ranks, tents and Nissen hut bunk rooms were erected on the lawns and bathroom facilities set up in the shrubbery.

The recruits were a disparate bunch: professional soldiers and gung-ho amateurs, volunteers from British battalions, among them McWatt, who joined the SOE at twenty-one, after a brief period of schoolmastering in the Borders. Fate or fortune brought him home to the Highlands, 'to which', as he wrote in *Forby*,[21] his first volume of memoirs, 'as with Rabbie Burns, my heart has always belonged'. There were also exiles from Continental Europe, men and women determined to tough out the final gruelling selection process and earn the right to stay on in this unforgiving place, acquiring the lethal skills required to return home and aid the resistance.

In addition, 'Warfare Weekend' courses were set up for volunteer members of the British Home Guard, described by Jim Struan in *Silent Killing for Cubs and Scouts*[22] as 'a rag-tag bunch of part-timers most of whom had failed to get into the regular army'. They served as 'demonstration troops', showing real recruits what was required, playing the part of the enemy, guarding targets or pursuing the trainees across the hills.

The Home Guard's lack of soldiering skills made them the butt of jokes for the trainee commandos from the regular army, who were themselves mostly regarded as low-status 'drones' by senior officers who had more in common with the absent Lord Montfitchett, leaving aside his unpalatable political views, than with many of the trainees. McWatt later noted that 'even here, in extremis in the marounjous ootlaund, the social stratification of the British class system was as ancient and inexorable as

21 Virr Press, 1962.
22 Buirlie Books, 2003.

the Ring of Drumnish', though foreigners were exempted and stamina and courage, or their opposites, were not, as events proved, the prerogative of a single class or nationality.

A Granite Ballad – The Reimagining of Grigor McWatt,
Mhairi McPhail (Thackeray College Press, 2016)

The Isle of Fascaray

Ah'll awa aff an gang the nou, an gang tae Fascaray
An a wee bothy build there, o cley an simmen straw;
Nine bean-raws wull Ah hae there, an hinnie bees an aw,
An bide alane in the bee-lood shaw.

An Ah shall hae a wheen o saucht, for saucht comes dachlin slaw,
Dachlin frae the mornin's haar tae whaur the chirker sings;
There midnicht's in a glimmer an nuin's a heather glawe,
An forenicht's fu o the lintie's weengs.

Ah'll awa aff an gang the nou, for aye thru nicht an day,
I hear loch watter laippin wi laich soonds 'gin the shore;
While Ah staund in the city wynd an oan the tarmac grey,
I hear it in ma sair hert's core.

Grigor McWatt, efter W. B. Yeats, 1944[23]

23 From *Kenspeckelt*, Virr Press, 1959. Reprinted in *Warld in a Gless: The Collected Varse of Grigor McWatt*, Smeddum Beuks, 1992.

24 August 2014

When I first told friends and colleagues in New York about my move, they were appalled.

'Taking time out to think things over, we understand,' said Hobi. 'Getting away for a while, maybe. But two years? Where the hell is it anyway?'

I pointed out the island on a map.

'Wow!' she said. 'The He-brides!', pronouncing it as if it were a community of transgendered newly-weds. 'Isn't that where they made *The Wicker Man*? I love that movie. All those crazy islanders! Hey, are you sure about this?'

There was some curiosity about my publishing deal, which made me uncomfortable until I hit on the perfect way to shut down the subject. Asked what the book was about, I would reply 'poetry and identity'; it cleared a room in seconds.

When I phoned my parents in Toronto to tell them about my new job they responded with the same wary approval they'd expressed ever since ninth grade when, after a series of cyclonic rows, I'd made it clear that all future decisions about my life would be taken by me, and only me. I should have known better than to expect them to be pleased that their daughter was returning, garlanded with academic and professional success, to their homeland from which they had high-tailed, without a backward glance, many decades ago.

'Well, if you're happy about it? And Agnes is happy about it . . . ?' said my mother.

'What about Marco?' was my father's tentative question.

'Marco doesn't come into it,' I said.

They didn't press me further.

'A major sulk . . .' was Marco's response when it was clear I was serious.

This was rich. He'd seen the job advertised online – the Auchwinnie Regional Development and Enterprise Board in north-west Scotland was looking for a curator, archivist and editor to set up the new Grigor

McWatt Heritage Centre and Fascaray Museum. He printed out the ad and left it on my keyboard – we weren't speaking at the time – as a provocation. He never expected me to act on it.

'Don't do this to us,' he pleaded. 'To Agnes . . .'

'Who is this "us" of which you speak?' I replied. 'Is this the "us" you were thinking of while you assayed the Downward Dog with Karmic Kate?'

'I don't remember you giving much thought to our family while you were scaling the peaks of ecstasy with De Quincey.'

De Quincey was Pascal, my revenge romance. Typical Marco – now you needed a thorough grasp of English Romanticism to navigate his insults.

'Oh, lay off. You started it . . .' I began.

He changed the subject.

'Fascaray!' He shook his head. 'I can't believe it. It's thousands of miles away. It's cold and damp – and *random*.'

'Random it is not. Maybe you've forgotten – you've forgotten so much else over the last year – my name, my family, my birthplace . . .'

'Give us a break, Braveheart. You're no more Scottish than you're a New Yorker. Get over it. You're an uptight, risk-averse Canadian. Deal with it.'

'Okay. I can take that from an Italian-American whose closest connection to his homeland is the occasional plate of red-sauce pasta in a Bed-Stuy luncheonette.'

That seemed to hit home. He paused, picked up his backpack and turned to leave the apartment. At the door, he swung round with an afterthought.

'Are you seriously going to bring up our daughter in a country where the three major food groups are cookies, fries and liquor?'

That did it. His single sentence expressed years of unspoken contempt for my family, for me.

'You snob!' I shouted. 'So what's this? Pizza Pride? How dare you!'

'Oh, come *on*,' he said. 'I'm actually quoting *you*, for chrissakes.'

He was but, at the time, that seemed beside the point.

Pilar, my closest friend at the Museum of the Printed Word, at least bothered to research my move before venturing an opinion.

'Don't go all New Age on us,' she said.

Her confusion, it turned out, was general. Those few people in New York who had ever heard of the island, or bothered to google it, assumed I was going to work for the Balnasaig Centre, not the Fascaray Trust. It's a branding issue. In some circles – international, bohemian baby boomers and Generation Xers – Fascaray is known not for its native bard or its Land Raid heroes but for the batty cultists, the Balnasaig Seekers, a group of English eccentrics who came to the island in the 1960s to commune with spirits from other realms and went on to create a small empire offering bed, board and cosmic enlightenment to like-minded etherealists.

While to some outsiders the Seekers have become the main event, they're antithetical to Fascaray's history of pragmatism and, above all – as the most cursory reading of McWatt indicates – its hostility to the English. If the Seekers could survive there for so long, I was surely in with a chance.

There's little crossover between the solemn pilgrims who visit the Balnasaig Centre and the folk-music fans who stay in the Bothy bunkhouse, drink single malts at the inn, sing The Song with a warrior passion and follow the McWatt Walk around the island in the footsteps of the late poet. But both are good for business. The bulk of the money for the Grigor McWatt Heritage Centre and Fascaray Museum has come from McWatt himself, who bequeathed his estate – and the substantial royalties from his popular song – to the people of Fascaray. Though the poet had no time for the Seekers, I was told by Gordon Nesbitt of the Auchwinnie Board that 'developments at Balnasaig are part of the modern story of the island and must be represented somewhere in the new museum'. I wasn't going to argue. Pilar needn't have worried, however; I've never had any time for the New Age, a misleading term for a bunch of lazy narcissists who jettison reason and hard-won science in favour of Old Age 'intuitions' and cod medievalism. My views, long held, have nothing, almost nothing, to do with the fact that Marco's squeeze was a teacher of what she called 'Mystic Yoga'.

The cover photograph of Neville Booth's book, *Reflections from the Pilgrim Path: the Balnasaig Story*, taken in the 1960s, shows the author newly arrived on the island in his early thirties, spindly, prematurely bald and dressed with odd formality in a suit, frowning meaningfully at the ancient standing stones of the Ring of Drumnish. He looks the sort of meek, conventional type that the Seekers' hippie followers might, in another context, have described as 'a straight'.

Other photographs show the co-founders of the community in its early years – Booth's then wife Althea, tall and gaunt in a black cloak that gives her the appearance of a resting pipistrelle, and their secretary Evelyn Fletcher, a chubby matron in a floral flock.

The book, with chapters headed 'The Quest for Selfhood', 'The Journey Begins', 'In Search of Soul', doesn't inspire close reading. But McWatt's name isn't in the index – that's my get-out; I don't *need* to read it.

Of course Marco eventually did his research too. He mocked the whole project – 'McWatt was an obsessive; the guy had hypergraphia. He needed psychiatric help, not a museum devoted to his so-called legacy.' I stood my ground. 'You do realise,' he went on, 'that climate change has meant a 67 per cent increase in rainfall on the island since 1961,' to which I pointed out coldly that we're not completely unfamiliar with heavy precipitation in New York. Then he seized on the Balnasaig Seekers as another reason why I shouldn't take the job.

'So you're throwing up everything, travelling all that way, removing our daughter from the life she knows and the people she loves, to hang out in the Brigadoon boondocks with a bunch of obscurantist kooks.'

I could have answered that I would have nothing to do with the Seekers, reminding him that my main task was to organise an archive, set up a museum, write a book, edit and publish another, and that, in pursuit of this end, I would be 'hanging out' with perfectly rational researchers, curators, academic publishers and funding bodies. Instead, I said: 'At least I have no plans to *sleep* with any obscurantist kooks. Incidentally, how is Karmic Kate?'

cuckoo (*Cuculidae*): locally called the gowk, or fool, though we know it is the sleekit cuckoo who is the clever one, since she cannot be fashed to raise her own weans and so lays her eggs in the nests of other birds – meadow pipits (moss cheepers) and dunnocks (whin sparraes) – who make more committed parents and are too gowkit to notice the striking dissimilarity between their own brood and the interloper.

jackdaw (*Coloeus monedula spermologus, Viell*): known as the cae. Resident. Frequently seen in the vicinity of Finnverinnity House. Also sighted in woods above Tilliecuddy by Rab McNab in May 1948. Author and ornithologist Murdoch McMurdo, in his *History of the Fascaradian Archipelago* (1886), mentions it in connection with the Lusnaharra district.

lesser redpoll (*Carduelis linaria, Caberet*): rose-lintie. Seen by Father Col Maclennan near Loch Och, October/November 1946.

magpie (*Pica pica pica*): pyot, pickie-turd. Rarely seen scavenger, though observed by McMurdo in the Doonmara locality. He also surmises from the place name Sguid Pioghaid (Shelter of the Magpies) in the south-east of Calasay that the species was once prolific here.

Scottish crossbill (*Loxia curvirostra scotica*): bowsie spink. Britain's only endemic bird species. It has the good sense never to be seen in England. Resident, breeding grounds in the vicinity of Loch Och. Recently sighted on a Sabbath in the Finnverinnity kirk graveyard by Ranald Paterson, minister of the Free Presbyterian Church of Scotland. Sighting not recorded until the Monday.

shorelark (*Eremophila alpestris flava, Gm.*): according to the Official Handbook of the Birds of Scotland these are unknown in the West but the author saw one in 1944, at dawn, feeding on a heap of decayed seaweed on the shore in front of the Finnverinnity Inn.

siskin (*Carduelis sinus, L.*): totie spink. A small and agile finch with a narrow bill, yellow streaks on its wings and distinctive forked tail. Seen by Tam Macpherson on his farm woodpile at Balnasaig Farm in winter 1947.

skylark (*Alauda arvensis arvensis, L.*): known as laverock. Resident. Most frequently seen by the author on Beinn Mammor. Also sighted by Rab McNab above Lusnaharra Strand.

Grigor McWatt, 1948, *The Fascaray Compendium*

GRIGOR McWATT WAS TO MAINTAIN HIS SILENCE ON DETAILS of his SOE work all his life, but sixty years after the war, Jim Struan, a former commando, published his vivid memoir of the Big House war years, *Silent Killing for Cubs and Scouts*.

'The whole establishment was capable of providing training and accommodation for 150 officers and more than 2,000 other ranks. There were catering staff, administrative staff, domestic staff. It was a world unto itself, an enormous extended country-house party with mud and munitions,' wrote Struan.

'In fieldcraft classes, hard men of the hills taught trainees how to survive in the most brutal weather: making rudimentary shelters; wild fishing for brown trout, sea trout and salmon; trapping, skinning, gutting and cooking rabbits on small fires built with a couple of sticks and foraging for edible fruits and berries. There was bigger game, too, and it was on the hills of Fascaray that the men and women of the SOE learned to stalk, kill and *gralloch* – disembowel – deer, and by extension to dispose of human quarry.' On these expeditions, Grigor McWatt would have learned the skills of self-sufficiency that later served him well in Calasay.

'It was Fairbairn and Sykes, known as the Heavenly Twins, two ex-policemen with distinguished service records from the Shanghai Municipal Police, who, in the wrecked splendour of Finnverinnity House, taught us the art of silent killing and reflex shooting,' Struan wrote.

'We learned how to use knives creatively, how to administer a cosh, wield a deadly catapult, make lethal weapons from tin hats and shovels (excellent for decapitations), how to break free from opponents' holds, get a prisoner in an intractable grip, hog-tie him, dislocate limbs, split mouths, burst eardrums, gouge out eyes and break necks. We called the course "Murder Made Easy".'

On their first day on Fascaray new recruits were sent out on a 'walk', which gave them some idea of what they were in for.

'Carrying our tommy guns and fifty-pound haversacks we slogged a dozen miles in three hours non-stop in driving rain, had a twenty-minute halt for lunch, assailed by infernal midges, then hauled ourselves up to do another four miles in an hour. Our feet were like burning bricks. That night when we finally stopped, famished and exhausted, we ignored our rations. We had other priorities and limped to the riverbank, unlaced our boots and plunged our feet in the pure cold waters of the Lingel. I can still hear the sound, a sweet Gregorian chant of gratitude, as fifty men, trousers rolled to the knees, sighed in unison. We bedded down under the stars while the frost turned our kip mats and blankets into sheets of solid ice, but we were so glad to be no longer walking that we slept like bairns.'

The recruits abseiled down cliffs and waterfalls, and from the roof of Finnverinnity House, practised 'scree running' on the north face of Beinn Mammor and learned, in the calm waters of Loch Och and the rough seas by Plodda and Grodda, to handle kayaks and 'folbot' folding canoes, which would enable them to approach enemy vessels undetected and place magnetic limpet mines on their hulls. Manhunts, known as 'Spider and Fly', were set up – punishing versions of hide-and-seek in which 'quarry' would be given a head start and sent off into the hills with no provisions for days at a time, left to fend for themselves as best they could, regardless of midges, gales, rain and snow, while their colleagues, equally sparsely equipped, would be charged with tracking them down.

'There's nothing like real bullets to sharpen the reflexes. As far as I know the only fatality was a chap who slipped in the snow and fell to his death on Mammor. They brought him down from the hills tied on a pony like a stag. But there were a few near misses, I can tell you, and these games could get pretty rough.'

Occasionally, the commanding officers had to remind the ranks, when they manhandled the 'prisoners' back to HQ, that they were all, in fact, on the same side.

Sick and numb with exhaustion after long slogs in remorseless rain across bogs perfidious as quicksand, tormented by a fizzing nimbus of midges, dodging friendly fire in some of the most inhospitable terrain in Europe, they would file into the Nissen huts to hear lectures on night navigation and sabotage before grabbing a barely edible plate of bully beef and boiled potatoes and collapsing on their camp beds to get some shut-eye before the next day's onslaught.

'There was no let-up,' Struan wrote.

All this physical work in extreme conditions took its toll. 'That was the plan. Eliminate the laggards. It was a test of character as well as of physical fitness. Not everyone received the coveted green beret at the end of the course.' Many – more than 20 per cent of the intake – had the humiliation, after the five-week ordeal, of eventually being 'returned to unit'. The faint-hearts, according to Struan, 'were identified and weeded out pretty sharply. This was no place for weakling boys and girls.'

After such an apprenticeship, the rigours of post-war self-sufficiency on a derelict croft must have seemed a cakewalk to Grigor McWatt.

Fascaray, he wrote in *Forby*, 'had a good war'. The bombing of cities to the south and naval battles to the north in the 1940s were distant rumours, fuelled by occasional news bulletins delivered over Tam Macpherson's crackling wireless at Balnasaig Farm, passed on and embellished in pub and store.

The island was, though, 'buffeted by regular explosions and bursts of gunfire loud enough to rattle crockery and break windows', wrote McWatt, and by night 'the sky was a *son et lumière* of flares and tracer fire.'

'It was like Guy Fawkes Night every night,' recalled Effie MacLeod. 'The farm collies were driven wild by it. The weans too. I don't think embdy slept through the night the whole time the boys were up there at the Big House. Not that the lassies were complaining.'

This was what the Fascaradians called 'the wee pretendy war': the dress rehearsal, with live ammunition, being conducted by trainee commandos and SOE agents at Finnverinnity House. Whatever secret business they got up to in the baronial pile at the head of the bay, on their rare nights off duty in the Finnverinnity Inn the commandos were thirsty, loud, disputatious and free with their money.

Rab McNab, the landlord, worked all hours, serving beer and whisky – of which there was a mysterious abundance – by candlelight long after the electricity generator had shut down for the day. The commandos liked a song, too, and Murdo 'the Fiddle' McIntyre from Doonmara was paid in drink for melancholy airs that would, according to Effie MacLeod, 'bring a tear to a glass eye', or for wild reels that accompanied energetic interpretations of the Highland fling by Paris diplomats, Norwegian academics, Canadian engineers, Czech schoolteachers, Danish farmers, a Jewish mathematician from London's East End, a concert pianist from Krakow and a tulip-growing publisher from Amsterdam, as well as British recruits and officers of every class and background.

Like all Britons in that time of official rationing, Fascaradians faced shortages of sugar, tea and flour, but they were used to a degree of self-sufficiency and continued to produce a surplus of milk, butter, eggs and potatoes. No one went hungry and the recruits up at the Big House were happy to barter chocolate, cigarettes and nylon stockings in exchange for the islanders' bounty of dairy produce and vegetables. The modern invaders brought their plunder to Fascaray and left it there, and if any local maidens were pressed into wantonness, it was with their full consent.

There was a vigorous black market in game – salmon, trout, venison, red grouse and capercaillie – poached unchecked, by islanders and commandos, from the River Lingel and the Finnverinnity Estate since Sammy Nelson, the factor, and his two ghillies had left to fight the enemy in Italy and North Africa. There was money to be made from the Receiver of Wrecks for flotsam washed up on the beach – bales of raw rubber were spotted on Lusnaharra Strand by young Francie and Jamie MacDonald, playing truant from school, and salvaged by their father, bringing in the equivalent of a month's rent and a year's feudal dues for the family. An enormous steel drum containing forty gallons of pure spirit, found at low tide half sunk in the sand below Doonmara cliffs, failed to make its way to the Receiver and was instead shared between the islanders. Some of it was used neat in the Tilley lamps; some, coloured and sweetened with treacle, made a passable dram in social emergencies.

Business on the island had never been better and, reflected McWatt in *Forby*, there was, despite the privations, and anxieties about the island menfolk fighting battles far from home, a 'hectic gaiety – a gather-your-harebells-while-you-may quality – to island life during the war years'. Only Miss Hughina Geddes, proprietor of the Finnverinnity Temperance Hotel, which had fallen on hard times, and Ranald and Wilma Paterson, the island's minister and his wife, longed for the return of the more law-abiding and deferential *ancien régime*. Three miles west up the coast, in the papist enclave of Lusnaharra, Father Col Maclennan, parish priest at the Church of the Sacred Heart and Immaculate Mary – built on the site of the pre-Christian shrine of Teampull Beag – was ambivalent; the SOE boys were lively company in the pub but he was suspicious of their intentions towards the island's young women.

Once the war ended, however, the old order was swiftly restored as Fascaradians returned home from overseas military and naval service and the commandos and SOE officers ('all but one', wrote McWatt in *Forby*, with a reticence approaching coyness) left the Big House and waved goodbye to the island from the deck of a trawler.

On America's East Coast, Percy Mere-Stratton, Lord Montfitchett of Godalming and Mayfair, was packing up after this wartime sojourn, preparing to reclaim his British assets, while across the Atlantic in the laird's Scottish island fiefdom, in a Nissen hut in the grounds of the now-deserted Finnverinnity House, Grigor McWatt shouldered his kitbag and tramped eight miles north to stake a more modest claim on an abandoned clachan on the tidal islet of Calasay.

A Granite Ballad – The Reimagining of Grigor McWatt,
Mhairi McPhail (Thackeray College Press, 2016)

This wee patch of earth we call Fascaray is a bonsai Scotland, a diminutive Dalriada, an atomic Alba, a bright flake of Caledonian confetti in which all our country's marvels, her landscape of unrivalled variety and intensity, her majestic vistas, are shrunk as if by faery command to a manageable human scale, to a perfect snow globe of emerald, amethyst, sapphire and topaz held in the hand of a wonder-struck child. To be in Fascaray is to know and truly understand Scotland in a way that is denied us on the mainland where we are dwarfed by her fabulous immensity.

Just as all of Scotland's natural wonders are contained, condensed, in Fascaray, so is its history. To live here is to inhabit a granite ballad. Brave warriors and barbarous incomers, tribal conflicts and stirring romance, benevolent chiefs and cruel overlords, happy chance and great misfortune are all here in the Fascaradian narrative. Read the story of our island people and you read the story of Scotland.

The year 843 saw the accession of Cinaed mac Ailpin, Kenneth MacAlpin, first King of the Scots. He was the son of a Pictish mother, Máel Muire, a Fascaradian 'dark-eyed daughter of Mammor', and a father from Dal Riata, Kingdom of the Gaels, encompassing much of the west coast of modern Scotland and part of what is now known as Ulster. MacAlpin fused the traditions of both great tribes, subdued and united the warring kingdoms of Alba as well as the seven Pictish kingdoms of Cait, Ce, Circinn, Fib, Ficach, Fotia and Fortriu. His reign saw the weakening of political connections with Ireland, the severance of links with England and several decisive clashes with native rivals in Melrose and Dunbar. Thus, thanks to a daughter of Fascaray, our nation's story could begin.

If history is wealth, we Scots should be millionaires. It might have been envy of our characterful, plot-rich story, or anxiety that the regicidal tendency might be infectious, that provoked Sir Christopher Pigott, the irascible seventeenth-century English parliamentarian, to observe that 'the Scots have not suffered above two kings to die in their beds these two hundred years'. Another outsider, albeit from the more sympathetic nation of Spain, wrote: 'Scots go to war, and when they run out of wars, they fight each other.' While our native hostility and suspicion of each other may be ingrained, it is as nothing – a mere shadow dance – to the contempt we hold for our arrogant southern neighbours.

The English essayist Charles Lamb wrote in 1822: 'I have been trying all my life to like Scotchmen, and am obliged to desist from the experiment in despair.' The feeling is mutual, though in my case the experiment was abandoned early, at my mother's knee, before I ever had the misfortune to meet an Englishman face-to-face. By their works you shall know them, and the works of our English masters were visible all around my childhood home in the benighted city of Glasgow. And here in Fascaray, ancestral home of the Clan McWatt, the Sassenach continues to plunder our resources and traduce our people.

Grigor McWatt, 1946, *The Fascaray Compendium*

25 August 2014

'It'll be fine. You'll see.'

My reassurances, uttered to my daughter, are, I realise, aimed at myself. It's Agnes's first day at Finnverinnity Primary. Her new classmates have already been back at school for a week. Term starts early here. In New York, her friends are still on vacation for another two weeks. She's taking it well. If she's nervous, she's doing her best to spare me.

The school is in a converted two-storey Georgian house, broad and austere, whitewashed stone with black trim, set in woodland above the village. It was once occupied by the factor of the Finnverinnity Estate, a figure inspiring fear and hatred, responsible for evictions and rent collection, the scourge of poachers and, in the first Lord Montfitchett's time, of children. It's a sweet revenge that the island's under-twelves have now claimed his house. Today, the long sash windows which once sternly surveyed the laird's dominion are papered with the pupils' colourful and heart-warmingly inept paintings of red and white boats on a curly blue sea.

The ground-floor rooms – sitting room, drawing room, parlour, kitchen and scullery – have been knocked through and turned into one large classroom with four tables around which children sit, ranked by age, ostensibly absorbed in their work. Upstairs is the headmaster's flat. Despite the reproductive efforts of the island's younger incomers, the steady flow of emigrants leaving Fascaray to seek work on the mainland has meant the school is now almost too large for the meagre population of thirteen children aged between five and twelve.

The head teacher, Mr Kennedy, comes to greet us. He is, in fact, the only teacher, helped out by part-time teaching assistant Johanna McAllister, when she isn't helping me out with the museum and working as part-time administrator of the Fascaray Trust. Niall Kennedy is spare and harried, in his early forties, with professorial glasses and an Irish accent. Agnes takes his hand and walks with him to a table where three girls and three boys of about her age look up briefly then get back to their work. My daughter sits down, gives me a small, fluttering wave – farewell or dismissal – and turns away to open a schoolbook.

I leave the school, walk three hundred yards back past the store and the pub, call in at number 19, where I retrieve my box of documents and head down the road towards my own first day. The Fascaray Trust and the Fascaradian Museum of Island Life (as it is presently called) inhabit two adjoining cottages similar to my own, opened up and extended into the adjacent herring shed, outside which fisherwomen once worked, singing, up to their elbows in blood, wielding the little *cutag* dagger to gut, cure and pack in salt their menfolk's catch before it was transported for sale to the mainland.

Half the street-facing wall of the Trust office has been given over to a large plate-glass window, which lets in little light since it is covered with photographic charts of local birds, fish, wildlife, trees and flowers as well as handwritten cards advertising local services – cleaning, babysitting, pony trekking, rubbish clearance, bed and breakfast, reiki massage – and private sales of gardening tools, a fax machine 'barely used', and frozen venison steaks.

My new office contains an unsteady melamine desk, two plastic garden chairs, a computer of some antiquity with an insanitary keyboard and a printer of similar vintage and unwholesomeness. On top of a metal filing cabinet an electric kettle stands next to an unopened carton of long-life milk, past its sell-by date, a box of tea bags and four 'Fascaray Trust' mugs, chipped and so grimy they must be a biohazard. Over my desk is a bookcase containing a less well-preserved version of my own Fascaray library, as well as 'Fascaray – the Island in Time', a badly foxed photographic booklet compiled by the Fascaray Preservation Society in 1986, and two box files marked 'Boat trips' and 'Local Walks' containing pamphlets, some illustrated with clumsy line drawings of a small figure I take to be McWatt, with kilt and pipe, others with crayoned seagulls, dolphins and an idealised croft cottage, puffs of smoke issuing from its chimney like comic-strip thought bubbles.

I open the filing cabinet and find no files but an unsorted miscellany of papers, some of them bills and invoices, under a half-empty bottle of Johnnie Walker whisky and an open packet of shortbread cookies. I notice a sickening, sweet odour – dead mice? – that seems to be emanating from the museum, separated from the Trust office by a linking door. I push it open tentatively. The smell is overpowering.

Once my eyes adjust to the gloom I make out what must be rows of display cabinets covered with dust sheets, stacks of chairs, three old suitcases, tottering piles of cardboard boxes and, leaning against the back wall, what looks like a giant sarcophagus draped with canvas. Next to it looms a wide kitchen cupboard, its open shelves cluttered with crockery and rusting cooking utensils and, leaning against it, several bulky objects, also shrouded. I peek under the dusty drapery and see a wooden barrel, a garden rake minus most of its tines, a yard brush, an industrial-style fan, big as a jet engine, and a stuffed sheep whose single glass eye peers at me balefully under a hank of crusty ringlets.

The place is festooned with cobwebs and looks like an abandoned junk store. If I had a shred of susceptibility to the supernatural, I'd find it sinister. Instead I find it depressing. More housework. But the abandoned Museum of Island Life, which it is my responsibility to somehow transform into the Grigor McWatt Heritage Centre and Fascaray Museum, can wait. Having spent three days getting our new home in decent shape, I now need to sort out my office.

I fill the kettle and wash a mug. The water, which gushes straight down from the Kilgurnock Falls, fed by incessant rain, makes a fine cup of tea. Well, that was one thing you couldn't get in New York – good fresh water, decent tea. I feel a pang as I remember my keen little helper, who is getting her bearings in her new environment up the road. I hope she is finding her own consolations.

Hame and Loue

Jist Hame an Loue! The wirds are wee,
A bickety peerie puckle o letters.
And yet in aw oor leid's braw glossary,
Ye'll nae find twa wirds better.
Hame an Loue sae cannily proclaim
The muckle pleasures ben the hoose.
There arenae wirds mair douce
Than Loue an Hame.

Jist Hame an Loue! It's hard to spae
Which o the twa wirds bears the gree.
Hame wioot Loue is nae a prumros path.
But Loue wioot hame is fire wioot a hearth.
If ye can, chuise baith. But since I couldnae,
Whit tae dae? My Loueless nature wis nae shame
And here at last in Fascaray,
I find, Loue is Hame.

Grigor McWatt, efter Robert Service, 1946[24]

---

24 From *Kenspeckelt*, Virr Press, 1959. Reprinted in *Warld in a Gless: The Collected Varse of Grigor McWatt*, Smeddum Beuks, 1992.

27 August 2014

By November last year, our relationship – bowed under the strains of his affair with the unhinged yoga teacher and buckled further by my payback fling with Pascal, a young musician with movie-star looks and mayfly mind – had seemed to spring back and resolve itself into solid, sustaining companionship. Love even. We had been tested by a moment of mutual madness and we had survived. We thought we could make it work, Marco and me. Marco, Agnes and me.

He accepted a teaching post in the drama department at Austin, Texas, starting the following May, but as we went through the motions of telling friends, giving notice on our apartment and my job, and packing up our lives, I began to have doubts. Maybe I didn't want to travel with Marco after all, not at the expense of my career. Not to Texas. Not anywhere. Ever.

Our daughter took on the role of UN peace negotiator, attempting to bring these two warring nations together to discuss their demands. We woke up one morning from our respective wings of the Super Kingsize after another frosty night – no talking, no touching – to find Agnes at the foot of the bed with a breakfast tray.

'Happy anniversary!' she said.

Naturally, neither of us had remembered. Even when our relationship was a going concern, we never marked the day of our first meeting. But Agnes loved to hear us retell the story of the awkward exchanges at the off-Broadway after-party, my faux pas, his mock proposal, how we very nearly *didn't* get together – 'which would mean I wouldn't even exist!' she would marvel.

It was ostensibly the prospect of relocation that finally broke us. I had no job to go to in Austin and though the Harry Ransom Center was, and remains, an archivist's mecca, they weren't recruiting. I didn't see myself leading a happy housewife's life in the broiling heat of Texas, with only the drop-off and pick-up times at Agnes's school to measure out my days. What would I do with myself? Take up yoga? The arguments, inevitably, began to focus on the question of trust. The old wounds became inflamed and we fought the old war all over again.

'Why don't you apply for that Fascaray job?' Marco finally said in March – his first words after our latest, week-long, silence. 'Seems perfect for you. Bracingly cold – full of Calvinist miserabilists. You've always said you wanted to go there.'

After I got over my indignation and read the job advert again, I was mildly intrigued.

My bluff had been called and I counter-bluffed. Within two months, after a further post hoc marital squall – *he* accused *me* of selfishness – two interviews in Glasgow and a trip to Pennsylvania to secure my book deal with Thackeray, the job was mine. Perhaps the inherited Scots trait, or vice, of thrawnness – a perverse, sometimes self-destructive stubbornness – played a part in my decision to take up the job. I have to watch this inclination to slice off my nose, Mother Abbess Ulla-style, to spite my face. The injury to the Vikings, and Marco, is only psychic. It's plain who's really suffering here. It only struck me later, when we first boarded the ferry for Fascaray, that I was also holding a blade to our daughter's *mignon* features.

I had thought that Marco might have been stauncher in his defence of our relationship. His affair with Karmic Kate was in the past, as was mine with Pascal, but though Marco was undeniably attached to Agnes, and she to him, he finally seemed to give us up without a fight. It was as if my own affair – simple retaliation, I could see now – had been the greater transgression and my reluctance to jettison my career had been the ultimate betrayal.

In the end, my family history, the need for an anchor, a fixed point in a spinning world, must have had some role in my decision. I was drawn, too, by McWatt himself, as well as by Lilias Hogg, the project, the island, the whole story. But in my dismal new office in Fascaray, with the unseasonal rain slanting down outside, as I contemplate the work that lies ahead, it's comforting to blame Marco.

The Seicont Comin

Birlin an birlin in the braidenin gyre
The seabhag cannae hear the seabhager;
Things brak awa; the middlin cannae haud,
Tapsalteerie is lowsed ootower the warld,
The bluid-dreiched tide is lowsed, an orraboots
The ceremony o aefauldness is drount;
The Scots are wabbit, whiles the skellum English
Swee wi virr.

Grigor McWatt, efter W. B. Yeats, 1946[25]

---

25 From *Kenspeckelt*, Virr Press, 1959. Reprinted in *Warld in a Gless: The Collected Varse of Grigor McWatt*, Smeddum Beuks, 1992.

IT WAS AS IF A SPELL HAD BEEN BROKEN AND THE SERFS WERE finally waking from a 200-year sleep: by September 1946, a year after the war had ended, the social contract which had held for so long in Fascaray was unravelling.

Seven of the crofters had served with the Seaforth Highlanders in France and Italy, where they met many men for whom feudalism was, at best, a quaint historical quirk. Two of the islanders – Ali Mackenzie and Shonnie MacDonald, the laird's young piper – had lost their lives on the battlefields of Europe and their five surviving comrades returned in a rage to the island, to the damp and primitive homes they did not own, to their needy families, to the ancient rules and social hierarchy that constrained them. They could take no more.

'We've won the war for them. And what have we come back to? Nothing!' said Ewan McNeil of Killiebrae, that night of 9 September 1946, in the Finnverinnity Inn, recalled by McWatt in *Forby*. 'Damn all!' He thumped the table and the whisky shuddered in every glass in the pub.

McNeil's mood had not been helped by news that while he'd been dodging bullets and bombs in Monte Cassino, Maggie Macpherson, the green-eyed, auburn-haired eldest daughter of Tam Macpherson of Balnasaig Farm, had become engaged to a Polish officer, an SOE demolitions instructor at Finnverinnity House.

'Shonnie MacDonald and Ali Mackenzie died fighting for the laird's king and country while the laird quaffed Eiswein with Adolf,' said Hector McPhail,[26] another Killiebrae man, who had fought fascism in the Rhine as well as Italy.

Then, stirring from the shadows and rising from his usual seat in the darkest corner of the howff, the taciturn incomer – an SOE blow-in from the Big House who'd stayed on – spoke. '*Dùthchas!*' he declared. In addition to McWatt's own record of the evening in *Forby*, we have a first-hand

26 Grandfather of the author.

account of that speech from Ruddy McIntosh, then a rookie fisherman of twenty, who was interviewed more than half a century later for *Poet in a Landscape*, the Auchwinnie Press Festschrift pamphlet marking McWatt's eightieth birthday.

McIntosh recalled that the Gaelic speakers in the inn were shocked to hear this stranger, 'a *gall*, a fella frae away', use the islanders' word for the ancient way of apportioning tenure according to clan birthright, in which the principle of kindness, to the land as well as the people, was sacred. 'Wha loues the laun, awns the laun, an the laun awns him,' McWatt went on, in Scots rather than Gaelic, his voice trembling with conviction. 'Montfitchett disnae loue the laun. He laithes it – an aw the fowk who bide here.'

It was late, much drink had been taken, and there were roars of agreement. Father Maclennan, acquainted with the inflammatory effects of the *uisge beatha*, held up his hand to silence the crowd. But if anyone thought he was trying to act as conciliator – for blessed is the peacemaker – they would have been mistaken. He had, in his former parish of Barrhead, Glasgow, once attended a meeting addressed by James Maxton and had been much taken by the socialist politician's oratorical style.

'Brothers and sisters,' said the priest, though there is no record of any female presence in the pub at that time. 'Men and women of Fascaray, we have on this fair island of ours, appeased the English lairds for too long. The time has come. Justice demands it . . .'

And so it was, that as dawn broke over Fascaray on 10 September 1946, five determined men, aided by a score of friends and family, women as well as men roused from their beds, grabbed shovels and picks and walked the length of Finnverinnity Bay, past the Big House where Mrs McIvor, who had only returned the previous month from her Peebles exile, was already up clearing, as best she could, the debris left by the departed commandos and airing rooms in anticipation of the laird's imminent return. Using hemp rope from the fishing boats and stakes hewn from Montfitchett's trees, the islanders fenced off ten acres of fertile land, two acres each for the returning soldiers, and began to dig.

The Fascaray Land Raid became a cause célèbre – immortalised in McWatt's song, of course, and later on stage (an agitprop hit at the Glasgow Citizens') and screen (a cult seventies Canadian caper movie)

– and though the five men's test case was finally thrown out of the Edinburgh Court of Session in November and their subsequent appeal, financed by collections in pubs, shipyards and miners' clubs throughout Scotland's industrial heartland, was lost, it was, modern historians have argued, the spark that lit the flame that was to become, decades later, the conflagration of modern Scottish nationalism.

The Fascaray Five – Murdo MacDonald (brother of the late Shonnie), Hector McPhail, Angus McPhee, Neil MacEwan and Ewan McNeil – finally had no choice but to leave the island in search of work and shelter. Most of them headed south, to the shipyards and factories of Glasgow. But though Montfitchett, now widely ridiculed as Herr Montfitchett, had won, and the purloined land was restored to his estate, it was a pyrrhic victory for the laird. Even the minister, Ranald Paterson, turned his face from the laird's entourage when it next disembarked at the pier – Montfitchett, Paterson was heard to say, had a 'regrettably casual attitude to the Sabbath'. Sammy Nelson was refused service in store and howff and abruptly left his master's employment to return home to Fife. Montfitchett imported a stalker from Gloucestershire and a factor from Hampshire, but neither stayed the course. The game shooting was never the same and the poachers always seemed to get the best bag.

Lady Montfitchett's programme of purge and redecoration at the Big House, embarked on the week after the Court of Session ruled against the Fascaray Land Raiders, seemed to the defeated islanders shivering in their damp, insanitary blackhouses, a sinfully extravagant act of spite from a doomed tyrant.

The Gothic candelabrum, which in the glory days of Finnverinnity House illuminated the ballroom with forty candles and had during wartime service been used by a high-spirited Norwegian officer for late-night shooting practice, was dismantled and replaced by a vast bouquet of glass lilies, illuminated by 120 electric light bulbs, which arrived by boat from New York in a crate 'as big as the village school', said Effie MacLeod. A 'society artist' was brought up from London to paint a fresco – lightly clothed muses cavorting in a Cretan grove – in the ballroom. The cellar, depleted by officers with a taste for expensive champagne, was restocked, and crockery, glassware and cutlery – irreparably soiled in Lady Muriel's view – were dumped at sea while new French china,

Waterford crystal glass and Portuguese silver were bought and shipped from Harrods in London.

Bedding and furniture, also 'contaminated' by vulgar use, were burned in a pyre that lit up the skyline and smouldered for ten days. Again, Harrods was called in to provide replacements.

Outside, the lawn – battle-weary from the passage of a thousand army boots and scarred by a patchwork of pale rectangles on which the now dismantled tents and Nissen huts had stood – was dug up and resown. The antlers and bones of dead stags, illegally poached from the hills and barbecued to supplement mediocre canteen food, were retrieved from the rhododendron shrubbery and a new planting scheme, based on an Elizabethan knot garden with box hedges and topiary, was devised by a fashionable French garden designer.

In the stables, a grimmer modernisation programme took place when the Clydesdales and Shires that had been used by troops for exercises were dispatched, under laird's orders, with the returning groom's service pistol and sold for horsemeat. (The groom, an Irishman who had served in the Cavalry Division during the war, left his job at the Big House, and the island, the following day.) But despite all the cleaning up, clearing out and re-equipping, the scarifying fires, purifying submersions and ruthless eliminations, the shipments of furniture, hectares of cream paint and bales of pink toile, this was not a restoration of the *ancien régime* but its last hurrah – 'Marie Antoinette rearranging her lingerie drawer at Versailles in 1792,' wrote McWatt.

This was, of course, poetic hyperbole – no 'National Razor' ever grazed the neck of the Montfitchetts, though late-night talk at the Finnverinnity Inn suggested that the popular will might have been there, if not the means. Nor were the Montfitchetts instantly stripped of their status or wealth. But the old order had suffered a blow and would never be the same again.

Grigor McWatt's song, 'Hame tae Fascaray', written in a half-hour fever of inspired indignation, was first performed in the Finnverinnity Inn during those darkest days, and for the next few years it was played and sung, like the English national anthem on the Home Service, to round off the evening's programme at the pub. Set to the traditional tune of 'The Hills of Tranalla', 'Hame tae Fascaray' was played feelingly at its first airing by Murdo 'the Fiddle' McIntyre, vibrato throbs richly ornamented by grace notes. Solo vocal parts were taken by the formidable amateur baritone and professional poacher Dougal Mackenzie, whose brother had died in the Burma campaign, and by young Hamish McIntosh, whose tremulous voice had a chorister's plaintive purity, giving the combative lyrics a paradoxical edge.

> *Montfitchett rages*
> *In his lair.*
> *Sassenachs beware!*
> *An end tae clearance*
> *An interference!*
> *We'll soon be there.*

The chorus, a bellowed anthem more heartfelt and menacing than the most pugnacious football stadium chant, set the crowd swaying. They were spoiling for a fight.

A Granite Ballad – The Reimagining of Grigor McWatt,
Mhairi McPhail (Thackeray College Press, 2016)

Hame tae Fascaray

Blaw winds,
An dae your warst!
Stormy seas rise up!
Spite lashin rain
An England's shame,
We're comin hame.

Chorus:
Hee-ra-haw, boys,
We're awa, boys,
Gangin hame
Tae Fascaray.

Howl gales,
An screech gulls,
Let the haar descend.
Let thunder crack,
But dinnae fash
We're headin back.

Chorus

Lassies waitin
On the pier,
While the gloamin falls
On knowe and brae.
We're on oor way
Tae Fascaray.

Chorus

Montfitchett rages
In his lair.
Sassenachs beware!
An end tae clearance
An interference!
We'll soon be there.

Chorus

Heather's bloomin
On the braes,
This is oor ain land.
The bonnie hame
Where we belang.
Let's stake oor claim.

Chorus

Grigor McWatt, 1946[27]

IT WAS ANOTHER SCOTTISH POET WHO EVOKED THE DOUBLE-edged 'gift' of seeing ourselves as others see us. This gift, or curse, would, suggested Robert Burns, 'frae monie a blunder free us / An' foolish notion'. If McWatt had guessed at the scepticism with which he was viewed by his fellow Fascaradians in those early days, he might have turned his back on the isle and sailed away with his SOE comrades in 1945. And if he had done so, the cultural loss to the island, and to Scotland, would have been incalculable.

McWatt's minute observations of the natural history of the archipelago, its fauna and flora – he gave his name to a rare blue winter-flowering form of the wild flower lady's bedstraw (*Galium verum*), known as *Galium McWatti*, or McWatt's mattress – as well as its folklore, have enriched our understanding of Scottish island life over the last half-century. His promotion of the Gaelic notion of *dùthchas* – the sense of belonging to the land, a relationship of mutual trust that entails responsibilities as well as rights – foreshadowed the modern ecology movement.

And then there were his translations, 'reimaginings' or 'owersettins', as he called them, which he hoped would 'stell [place] the Scots leid [language] at the hert of the warld's literarie tradeetion'. Scholars and critics continue to argue over the degree of his success in this respect but at the end of the Second World War, to the islanders eking a harsh living from an unforgiving land, he was simply 'a glaikit [foolish] wee man who wrote wan guid sang'.

If McWatt had sought a warmer reception at the end of the war than the suspicion and often frank hostility that greeted him, and all incomers, on Fascaray at that time, if he'd instead hankered after an Edinburgh flat handy for the pubs, if he'd married Lilias and set up home in the city and raised a couple of kids, or if he'd returned home to a bunk, unemployment and drink in a Glasgow model lodging house, our store of poetry and song would be immeasurably poorer and Fascaray would have been consigned to permanent obscurity.

A Granite Ballad – The Reimagining of Grigor McWatt,
Mhairi McPhail (Thackeray College Press, 2016)

Everything is eternal, everything changes. The sandy sickle of coast west of the Calasay cliffs is gilded by strips of fool's gold, copper and silver pebbles that from a distance look like scattered loose change – the leavings of a showy 'scoor-oot', in which coins are thrown to bairns after a wedding. Within a week, the glittering bounty is gone and the bleached crescent is pristine powder once more.

In summer, new islands rise up in the narrow straits between the skerries displaying, on their jeweller's velvet of mossy rock, a shimmering hoard of seashells. Next day, the treasure is nowhere to be seen – buried again. Some mornings offer up a quivering cargo of jellyfish, blue filaments glowing through their translucent mass like a heap of gelatinous light bulbs. By evening, the jellyfish are gone and the beach is ankle-deep in purple seaweed streamers, like the residue of a forgotten Christmas party. Another dawn yields a splendid harvest for the impecunious crofter as the strand turns green as a meadow with edible seaweed – bright skeins of samphire woven with darker threads of dulce. The crofter knows he must busy himself and gather this bounty, for the next day it will have vanished.

On those occasions when my eyes become too dazzled by the infinite beauties of sky and sea, I turn my gaze downwards. Scoop up a handful of shells and you hold in your hand a glowing galaxy of stars, each tiny calciferous flake and whorled chamber, gaudy bivalve and mother-of-pearl fan with its own secret, tumultuous history far older than our own.

Some shells, like the stones at Ruh beach, are stitched with the curious calcareous hieroglyphs of the serpulid tube-worm. Look closely and they seem to spell out an urgent message in the alphabet of an ancient, obsolete language. Warning or imprecation?

Grigor McWatt, 1946, *The Fascaray Compendium*

29 August 2014

In many ways, the MacRaes' abandoned Museum of Island Life is my greatest problem here. It was set up in Finnverinnity's derelict herring shed in 1985 by Padruig and Mikey, entrepreneurially inclined cousins from Lusnaharra whose track record for moneymaking schemes was patchy. Their projects, recorded by McWatt in *The Fascaray Compendium*, had included an ill-fated fish and chip takeaway van ('a salmonella outbreak was never pinned on a batch of their battered cod but suspicions were strong enough to kill the business'), and Paddie's Peds, launched one summer to hire out plastic pedalos off Lusnaharra Strand ('the absence of tourists, the weather, high tides and the local coastguard – called out to rescue Padruig and Mikey when they were carried away by rip tides towards the Carracorry whirpool on one of their own vessels – saw off that enterprise').

No lives were jeopardised by the cousins' venture into local heritage, though McWatt argued in the *Auchwinnie Pibroch* that it compromised the island's credibility. The Fascaradian Museum of Island Life appears to have been an ahistorical emporium of tat offering tea, scones and tablet fudge to bewildered day trippers seeking shelter from the rain, with some loose change to spend and an hour to kill before the ferry back to the mainland.

Agricultural implements, rusted and mud-caked, salt-eroded maritime sundries and oxidised bric-a-brac are carefully, if unconvincingly, labelled by hand. The 'Pictish hoe, about 5th century BC', appears to be, beneath the dried mud, standard-issue garden centre hardware, circa 1980; 'Viking fibula, 8th century' looks less like a penannular brooch or garment pin than a twentieth-century plumber's pipe clamp; and a '*Sgian-dubh* dagger, once concealed in the sock of a kilted Jacobite', dated 1745, is uncannily similar to the Jenners' cheese knife Marco and I were sent from Blairgowrie with a plaid-wrapped log of Crowdie cheese as a Christmas present from my Aunt Bridie.

In one section of the museum, under a paper banner bearing the felt-tipped words 'Peeps into the Past', the walls are lined with acrylic-framed copies of old photographs – glum men, bearded and waistcoated, leaning against crumbling hovels; glummer women in shawls, arms deep in barrels of fish. They are identified in captions as Fascaradians but there are no recognisable landmarks and the images look suspiciously generic.

The MacRaes had applied to the then newly appointed Auchwinnie Regional Development and Enterprise Board for funding. (It was the projected grant, local cynics said, rather than a passion for local history that induced the cousins to set up the museum in the first place.) Their proposal included plans for something called 'The Clearance Experience', in which tourists would be invited to wrap tartan shawls around their macs and plastic ponchos, swap their fleece beanies for woollen bunnets, and stand head-on to a wind machine (the fan) next to the stuffed sheep, enduring five minutes of audiotaped hectoring from an Englishman who exhorted them to get off his land.

But their most ambitious wheeze was the Clan Cubicle, fashioned from an old Woolworths photo booth, which invited visitors, for £2, to select their affiliated clan from a comprehensive list pasted next to the coin slot, to step inside, close the plaid curtains, take a seat on a height-adjustable stool, enjoy a soulful recorded skirl of bagpipes (performed by Donnie and Sorley MacDonald, son and grandson of the late piper Shonnie) followed by a five-minute audio-visual exposition of the key role played by the customers' ancestors in the history of Scotland – 'land of mists and monsters'.

In the MacRaes' account of the national narrative, all roles were key and all popular surnames, no matter how ostensibly un-Scots – Evans, Garcia, Jones, Khan, Patel, Smith, Wang, Stein – had an affiliated clan. Insurmountable 'technical problems' had finally scuppered the project and the prototype booth – my sarcophagus – looms at the back of the museum rusting under its canvas winding sheet.

The grant from the Auchwinnie Board failed to materialise, as did any day trippers, and the MacRae cousins abandoned the herring shed – on which they owed a substantial sum in rent to Auchwinnie Council. McWatt reported the museum's demise with satisfaction in his 21 June 1988 'Frae Mambeag Brae' column in the *Auchwinnie Pibroch*. 'Here on Calasay, the only visitors who are welcome are the winged variety who fill the air with song, drop no litter and go about their own business, leaving us in peace to go about ours.'

Abandoning all the museum's contents 'as collateral', the MacRaes fled Fascaray, Scotland and the continent to open a ceilidh pub in Nova Scotia. A quarter of a century later, it's my job to get rid of all this junk, sort through McWatt's junk, and start over.

Athin the Gyrie o this Yowtherin Leif

Athin the gyrie o this yowtherin leif
There incums glisks o asure hewit,
Untashit braw as is the cuckoo-brogue
Or bonnie jessamine, when strawn aboot
Stravaigin burns by voar, which maks
A gamawow o thon philosophers whase
Anely ettle is tae ease oor molligrants.
Ah hae minded when the winter cam,
Heich in ma chaumer in the rimey nichts
In skiggan licht o the kinchie muin
Oan ilka rissle, speeach an racket
The shaikle spears eiken oot their lenth
Gin the flanes o the ochenin dag,
When aw the laun aroon ligged law
Aneath a dufftie skilderin o snaw.
Sae Naitur's bawbees gie me wealth
Tae gang aboot ma winter's darg wi stealth.

Grigor McWatt, efter Henry David Thoreau, 1949[28]

28 From *Kenspeckelt*, Virr Press, 1959. Reprinted in *Warld in a Gless: The Collected Varse of Grigor McWatt*, Smeddum Beuks, 1992.

WHEN THE ISLAND'S FIRST TRACTOR WAS DELIVERED TO TAM Macpherson at Balnasaig Farm in the late 1940s, McWatt wrote, 'the mixed curse of the twentieth century finally arrived on Fascaray'. Until then, the only motorised vehicles on the island had been Montfitchett's shooting brakes, the military trucks of the SOE training school (transported to the island with great difficulty on a steam drifter from Auchwinnie), and Donald John 'the Shop' Mackenzie's Ford jalopy, used to drive supplies from the pier to the store and to the few areas of the island blessed with a semblance of surfaced road. When the road ran out Donald John would, in the case of old and ailing customers, make the rest of the journey on foot carrying the goods in a creel basket. Younger and fitter householders would have to hoist the goods themselves from the side of the track, where Donald would leave them in boxes under a sheet of tarpaulin secured with stones.

Bicycles, often shared between families and neighbours, were prized but the potholed roads meant they could only be used by the hardy. Shuggie 'the Post' MacLeod used a bike for his daily circuit of the island but had to push it, with his sack tied to the crossbar, much of the way. In fact most islanders simply walked, including the children of Lusnaharra, who hiked the six-mile round journey to school in Finnverinnity each day without complaint, carrying their lunchtime 'pieces' – a can of milk and a scone or bread roll – and the regulation peat for the school fire.

In winter, when nightfall began mid-afternoon, children would be sent home after lunch before the dark descended. On moonless winter nights, Fascaradians would spear burning peats with a sickle and use them as torches, *fàd air corran*, trailing sparks as they travelled to and from their homes. Fields were ploughed using yoked horses – Clydesdales on Balnasaig Farm, smaller breeds on the smaller farms – to pull the harrows.

The arrival of Macpherson's tractor, a Ferguson TE20 costing a scandalous £200, was greeted with scepticism. Many old hands shook their heads and prophesied that the thing was a fad, couldn't do the work of a good team of horses and wouldn't last. Calum Donald 'the Plough' MacEwan, now reduced to helping out Seumas 'the Byre' McKinnon, remained confident to the end of his days that the 'tin beast' was a temporary interloper and told McWatt that for months after the arrival of the newfangled machine, before remembering to apply the brake, Tam would still shout 'whoa'.

Mail and supplies – food, sundries, coal, building materials, cattle feed and, on sombre occasions, coffins – as well as the occasional passenger, were delivered twice a month to the island by the *Gudgie*, a steam puffer boat whose crew – skipper Ali Hume, first mate Malkie McTavish and deckhand Pat Boy Cairns – always received a welcome in the inn. A small open scaffie fishing boat, the *Silver Darling*, a two-masted lugger, built at the turn of the century and owned by father and son fishermen Tormud and Alec Campbell of Finnverinnity, served as a passenger ferry for unscheduled crossings. Such was the difficulty and discomfort of the ten-mile passage – in bad weather no amount of oilskin or waterproofs could prevent passengers and crew getting a soaking on the shelterless deck – that few undertook the journey voluntarily. The trip was mostly made by the sick, who had to be stretchered down to the ferry with great care from the rickety wooden pier lest – as happened to the bad-tempered old mother of Donald John the Shop – they slid head first into the bow of the boat.

'It's a hard life, this island life,' wrote McWatt in *The Fascaray Compendium* in 1949, 'and it breeds a hardy people.'

A Granite Ballad – The Reimagining of Grigor McWatt,
Mhairi McPhail (Thackeray College Press, 2016)

31 August 2014

Even Agnes feels she has to duck against the low beam of the porch, a brick sentry box which puts a small but useful distance between the Calasay rain and the front door of An Tobar, Grigor McWatt's home for almost seventy years.

'What does it mean? An Tobar?' Agnes asks.

'It's Gaelic for "the source".'

'Like ketchup?'

The house would originally, in the time of McWatt's ancestors, have been a single-storey, windowless *taigh dubh*, built with its back to the steep grass-edged cliffs, the ocean beyond and the scouring north-easterly winds. The drystone walls would have been topped with a heather thatch secured with ropes and weighted with stones gathered from the shore. The peat fire was built on the floor in the centre of the single-roomed dwelling and above it there would have been a hole in the roof through which the smoke escaped, inefficiently – hence the name 'blackhouse'.

When Grigor McWatt first saw it in the 1940s, it was derelict, a roofless shelter for foxes and wildcats. He sublet it for a nominal rent from Tam Macpherson, a 'tacksman' farmer with the unique privilege on the island of a long leasehold and security of tenure. For a decade McWatt lived there with sheets of corrugated iron laid over the beams in an attempt to keep out the rain and cold while he set about reclaiming what he maintained was his ancestral home, hacking away at the vicious briars that clung to its walls, using stone from the clachan's other derelict houses to patch it up, and making furniture from stacks of fish boxes washed up on the shore in the violent equinoctial gales.

Now the blackhouse is white, a *taigh geal*, a limewashed country cottage with faded red trim that would make a charming, if rudimentary, vacation let.

'These days I have a slate roof, a fireplace with a flue, windows, a functioning bedroom in my loft and a compost toilet,' McWatt wrote in the *Auchwinnie Pibroch* in July 1962. '*Embourgcoisement* is finally upon me.'

I put the rusty key in the lock and find that the door is already open.

As Agnes steps into the front room, she looks around and says wonderingly: 'Just like a dollhouse! A dirty little dollhouse!'

Dirty is overstating it. Where does she get her exacting standards of domesticity? Not from her father, anyway. The flagstone floors could do with a sweep, I suppose, and the broad hearth which fills almost the whole north wall, with its swinging cast-iron arm and cooking pot suspended by a rusty chain, is blackened with years of accumulated soot and carbonised grease.

'A witch's cauldron!' says Agnes.

I don't imagine the bachelor poet went at the pot too often with a wire brush. But otherwise the cottage is – to my eyes – surprisingly neat and well preserved, without any of the unpleasant smells associated with neglect.

Johanna has done a good job, but not good enough to satisfy my daughter, who surveys the room with awed disgust. Her expression softens and is replaced by a familiar, wide-eyed look of curiosity.

'What does that mean?'

She is pointing at the inscription 'Ou Phrontis', carved on a stone slab above the fireplace.

'Who cares? I don't give a damn,' I say.

She lowers her head and frowns.

'I only asked,' she says.

'No. No,' I say. 'That's what it means. "Ou Phrontis". Who cares? I don't give a damn. It's Greek. A quote from a historian. Herodotus.'

It was also carved in the house of the English adventurer T. E. Lawrence – an improbable inspiration for McWatt.

'Look!' Agnes, fully recovered, wrinkles her nose as she points above the hearth. 'A bedpan.'

All my fortunate child knows of hospitals, she has seen on television.

'No. You put hot coals in it,' I explain. 'Then you wrap it in cloth and slip it into your bed to warm it before you get in. Like an electric blanket.'

She nods, distracted; she's lost interest – a bedpan would have been more entertainingly gross.

Under the narrow north-facing window there is a ladder-backed chair, cane-seated, and a small writing table – an old clerk's desk with brass hinges securing the sloping lid. I lift it, and there, in neat rows, are four pencils – HB – a putty eraser, a fountain pen, bottle of black ink, a silver sharpener, an assortment of felt-tip pens (long dried up) and a pale green notebook, the same faded quarto softback as *The Fascaray Compendium* manuscripts. I open it, restraining the archivist's thrill – like the promise of casual sex, too often followed by disappointment. I turn the pages carefully. I was right to be cautious. They're mostly blank.

What is there in the first few pages is a record of his accounts for December 2013–January 2014. Two columns on each lined page: Expenditure and Income. The column for Income is blank. Four lines from a poem are scored through but still legible – *Awa, saul, the boadie's guest, / Stravaigin's ower, tak yer rest. / Trith's killt sae stap yer greetin, / Though yer whids deserve a beatin.* It's dated 13 January. I don't recognise it as one of his published poems, nor can I guess at the original, if indeed it's a translation. There's not enough here to include in a new collection of his verse. The next entry, on 14 January, the day before his death, is more prosaic: 'Seed potatoes. Ink. Paper.'

So, after a lifetime of hypergraphia, the Hebridean Pepys finally fell silent. The notebook is of little use to me and no interest at all to Agnes. Instead she's entranced by a dish of shells on a small milking stool by the fireplace.

'Wow! His collection is way bigger than mine,' she says, covetously running her fingers through it.

'Don't touch,' I say, sounding sharper than I mean to. 'It's for the museum.'

She slumps, frowning, in the armchair – wing-backed, Victorian, with a plaid loose cover. The poet's chair. How baffled and irritated he would be to see this skinny nine-year-old in her neon-striped socks, rosebud skirt and hiking boots, sulking in his chair.

I haven't the heart to reprimand her again. How many nine-year-olds would willingly accompany their parent on a professional trawl through an unknown dead man's stuff? An *old* unknown dead man, too. It's the only comfortable chair in the room. She's welcome to it. On the other side of the fire is a wooden captain's chair with a grey woollen cushion.

This, I imagine, would be for visitors. No concessions to ease. No invitation to linger. I imagine him saying, as Grandad McPhail used to say – more imperative than interrogative – 'You're not for stopping?'

I tape the ledger in bubble wrap, put it in a padded bag and slip it in my waterproof backpack.

In the window above the desk, between bookends fashioned from two rocks of pyrite, are four volumes of *Jamieson's Dictionary of the Scottish Language*. This is the 1887 edition, published by Alexander Gardner. The red spines are intact and their board covers relatively undamaged, though the fore edge is stained black. I open the first volume – the paper is heavily foxed – and towards the back on pages 552 to 555 ('cumlin – an animal that attaches itself to a person or place of its own accord' to 'curbawdy – active courtship'), there are the tidemarks of damp. But overall the books are in pretty good shape, considering they've been wedged in by this draughty window for so long.

'Wow!' Agnes says, pointing at the bookends. 'Fool's gold!'

The dictionaries will be useful exhibits but I don't want to risk damaging them on the rough ride home. I put them back where I found them; they're as safe here as anywhere. I'm beginning to worry that I haven't judged the tides correctly. It might be a damp journey back across the strand to Ruh.

Agnes, always one step ahead, our earlier snippiness forgotten, is in the kitchen, a small, spartan room dominated by a wide stone sink with a single dripping faucet and an ancient Calor gas stove. She is standing on a stool going through the jerry-built cupboards. Apart from cartons of salt and pepper and a tin of Brodie's tea, there are three boxes, two unopened, of oats, the old Scott's brand whose logo is a Highland he-man in kilt and wife-beater 'simmet', about to hurl a rock into a loch.

'Porridge. Yuck. Your poet ate porridge,' says Agnes.

In his first decade on Calasay, McWatt drew water from the top of the burn before he excavated the old well, whose topaz water was, he said, 'as sublime on the palate as the rarest single malt, without the deleterious consequences of the *uisge beatha* the following morning'.

From the kitchen window, I can see the old cast-iron tub he used to bathe in outside, an inconceivable prospect to someone like me who, until three weeks ago, regarded underfloor heating and a steaming shower head as standard-issue bathware. Pneumonia could be a risk here, even in August. McWatt would set a fire of sticks beneath the tub to heat the water drawn from the well and, as far as I know, never suffered any illness until his death in January. His toilet was a midden pit behind the drystone walls of an old sheep pen. He washed his clothes in the lower reaches of the burn, using stones to rub in carbolic soap, and hung them to dry on rope strung across the fire which, in those early years, blazed on the floor in the centre of his cottage, just as it had done in the black-houses of his ancestors. Fuel was provided by peat, which he cut from the bog, or by driftwood gathered from the strand, and fallen branches from the copse of alder, oak, rowan and pine, bent by the wind gusting in over the Calasay cliffs. The thought of all that manual labour, just to get through the day, makes me suddenly weary.

He cooked in a pot suspended over the fire or on a small Primus stove balanced on a table made from fish boxes, dining, he wrote in his second volume of memoirs, *Ootwith*,[29] 'as well as any laird', which wasn't surprising since the contents of his larder were often poached from the laird's estate. He fished salmon and grayling from the Lingel and trout from Loch Aye, gathered mussels from the strand and, with Dougal Mackenzie, the 'orraman' and ceilidh singer from Killiebrae, took part in Fascaray's illicit deer culls. From the kitchen window you can still see the vegetable garden he dug, with *feannagan* lazybed rows for potatoes. He would kill and eat the rabbits that nibbled at his carrots. With no one to tend it any more, the garden has run to seed and an extended family of rabbits has moved in to reclaim it, in their own herbivorous Land Raid.

Agnes has wrenched open another cupboard and found three cans of mutton stew, a can of haggis, one of evaporated milk, a box of Cremola Foam drink powder (raspberry flavour), a pack of Bird's Custard and a half-empty bottle of Highland Park whisky. Like my daughter, McWatt was not a gourmet, though *The Fascaray Compendium* includes several local recipes passed on to him by some of the older women of the island. He justified the inclusion of these 'receipts', as he called them, by saying they were 'women's varse, part of a long oral tradition that proves once

29 Smeddum Beuks, 1994.

more the distinctiveness and pre-eminence of Scottish culture, despite the suppressions and depredations following the Act of Union'.

His view hasn't boosted his reputation among feminist scholars.

Agnes has seen enough. She's now investigating the bathroom – a conventional 1970s lilac vinyl suite, part of the process of '*embourgeoisement*', more practical but less aesthetically pleasing than the al fresco tub – then races up the twisting wooden stairs into the bedroom, where, before I catch up with her, she stops short.

'Mom! Come look! He's got a cuddly! Your poet's got a cuddly.'

'It's a quilt, Agnes. A cuddly to you. A blanket, or a comforter, to the poet. Poets don't have cuddlies. Or this one doesn't. Didn't.'

I look out of the window and see I was right to distrust myself. I've miscalculated. The tide is already lapping over the southern end of the islet. We have to hurry. No time to visit the byre library and cart shed across the yard. We'll have to save them for another day. I usher Agnes towards the door and then remember Johanna's box of documents. It's tucked under the desk, exactly as she said. Outside, I seal it in more bubble wrap, put the whole thing in an oilskin sack and secure it to the back of the quad bike. Then the midges descend, a thousand shimmering pixels with mean intent, and I fumble for the net hoods. Agnes puts hers on and laughs.

'We're like those burka ladies!' she says, delighted.

'Come on. No time for this. Got to get going,' I say.

She climbs onto the pillion seat and surprises me by leaning across and turning the key to start the engine. No time to protest or ask her where she learned this trick. What else does she know? I blame her father for this osmotic absorption of random information. We ride back towards the shore, outrunning the midges, at a speed that makes us gasp, exhilarated. The last hundred yards of our journey across the Calasay Strand is through six inches of swirling seawater.

Once we reach the dunes I stop to check the documents are dry. I've got away with it.

'Can we do that again, Mom?' Agnes says. 'Please!'

*Inventory of goods brought by Agnes Bartoli from
New York to Fascaray, August 2014.*

Neptune: her stuffed dolphin. A souvenir of babyhood.

Her comforter: which she calls her 'cuddly', a small and disintegrating patchwork quilt, another souvenir of babyhood.

Blue trinket box: a present from her Italian grandmother, Nonna Lucia. When the box is wound with a silver key and opened, a tiny mermaid with a golden fishtail pirouettes to the tinkly sound of Debussy's 'Clair de Lune'. In the box, Agnes keeps her small collection of postage stamps – Italian, British and American – and low-denomination banknotes and coins from the respective currencies. Scottish five-pound notes showing Burns's mouse are especially treasured. Total value, at current exchange rates: $37.25.

Books: miscellaneous, cited in my journal entry of 20 August. These were the stories her father and I teasingly fought to read to her – she was always such an appreciative listener – before the teasing stopped and we just fought.

Planisphere: a star wheel, plus *telescope with tripod* – both presents from her father who encouraged her new interest in night sky-watching, despite my opposition on the grounds that it was a diversionary tactic devised to delay bedtime.

Clothing: various, mostly wind and waterproof.

Shoes: various, including – despite my insistence on their unsuitability for the journey – a pair of pink tooled calfskin cowboy boots.

Another present from Marco, bought at the rodeo during his stint at Tucson.

iPhone (with pink rubber case): a present from her father, also. I am obviously too busy actually raising my child to buy her presents.

WHEN McWATT'S DAILY CHORES WERE DONE IN CALASAY, BY the light of a paraffin lamp he began his apprenticeship as a writer, penning essays and polemic, 'reimagining' classic verse and prose into Scots, making it entirely his own, and – through the 'lang and lanesame nichts' – compiling his masterwork, *The Fascaray Compendium*, his definitive anthology, or 'vade mecum', as he called it, of the island's history, culture, folklore, flora, fauna and community life.

He was, he wrote, 'a true son of Fascaray'; the island's long dark winters, with brief flashes of daylight, and its summers of never-ending brightness had given its name to a particular psychiatric condition – *Morbus Fascariensis*: spells of deep and burrowing gloom alternating with frenzies of elation, often exacerbated by alcohol. In his depression, even the coming of spring – 'thon fause freend' to McWatt – could not cheer him, as the opening of his 1945 poem *The Ort Laun*,[30] a reimagining of T. S. Eliot's *The Waste Land*, indicates.

Sheuchin o the Deid

April is the fellest month, breedin
Laylocks oot o the deid laun, kirnin
Mindin an wissin, eikin
Dreich roots wi voar rain.
Winter glaised us, happin
The yird in ill-mynded snaw, feedin
A wee bittie life wi dried tubers.

For McWatt, as he wrote in *Forby*, the hardships endured in the late 1940s echoed those of the mid nineteenth century when his great-grandfather Aonghas, then a shawl-wrapped toddler, had been driven out with his parents – McWatt's great-great-grandparents – from their small clachan on the islet of Calasay in the terrible times of the *fuadach nan*

---

30 From *Kenspeckelt*, Virr Press, 1959. Reprinted in *Warld in a Gless: The Collected Varse of Grigor McWatt*, Smeddum Beuks, 1992.

Gàidheal, the clearance of the Gaels, by Montfitchett's grasping predecessors, who regarded the islanders as 'primitives', standing in the way of progressive, lucrative sheep farming, deer forests and sporting tourism.

Eviction notices were served but the Fascaradians, already suffering the consequences of the potato blight – like their Irish cousins – had nowhere to go, and one October night, the factor arrived with his henchmen and torched the heather-thatched roofs.

McWatt quoted one eyewitness account[31]: 'Little or no time was given for the removal of persons or property; the people striving to remove the sick and the helpless before the fire should reach them; next, struggling to save the most valuable of their effects. The cries of the women and children, the roaring of the affrighted cattle, hunted at the same time by the yelling dogs of the shepherds amid the smoke and fire . . . A dense cloud of smoke enveloped the whole island by day, and even extended far out to sea. I ascended Beinn Mammor about eleven o'clock in the evening, and counted 250 blazing houses, many of the owners of which I personally knew, but whose present condition – whether in or out of the flames – I could not tell. The conflagration lasted six days, till the whole of the dwellings were reduced to ashes or smoking ruins . . .'

The islanders were urged to emigrate and Sir Charles Edward Trevelyan, who had, in McWatt's words, 'honed his genocidal inclinations as a colonial administrator in Calcutta', was charged with setting up the Highland and Island Emigration Society and expressed the view that a 'national effort' would now be needed to rid the land of 'the surviving Irish and Scotch Celts', to make way for racially superior settlers. He welcomed 'the prospects of flights of Germans settling here in increasing numbers – an orderly, moral, industrious and frugal people, less foreign to us than the Irish or Scotch Celt, a congenial element which will readily assimilate with our body politic'.[32]

A century after his ancestors' eviction from the island, McWatt wrote at his desk in Calasay: 'We're dispossessed and deracinated, but we're nae done yet!'

31 *Gloomy Memories in the Highland of Scotland* by Donald McLeod, Archibald Sinclair, Glasgow, 1892.
32 *Letterbook of Highland and Island Emigration Society*, 30 June 1852, National Archives of Scotland.

The nineteenth-century McWatts failed to board the boat to Nova Scotia with most of their compatriots and instead took the road south where factory work was found and distant family provided temporary lodgings in a Glasgow tenement. Their story was succinctly told in *Forby*, the first of his two autobiographical volumes, later made into a two-part drama series by BBC Scotland, starring Bill Paterson and Phyllis Logan, with Alan Cumming as the young McWatt.

Wee Aonghas's first language, Gaelic, was forbidden at school and like most children of his social class his education ended at fourteen, when he took a job in a textile factory. 'My great-grandfather's exile was complete,' wrote McWatt. 'Internally, he was denied his mither tongue, externally, the wide skies, wild seas and soft green braes of his native land were lost to him and in their place loomed the charred factory chimneys and sandstone tenements, dark as chambered burial cairns, of Glasgow whose Gaelic name, *Glaschu*, in cruel irony, means "Dear Green Place".'

At twenty-three, Aonghas met and married Jeannie McDougall, a seamstress, and when they had their first and only child, Forbes – Grigor's grandfather – the family moved to a tenement in Bridgeton.

Forbes, a sickly child, left school at fourteen like his own father and after a series of manual jobs on the shipyards of the Clyde, married Ina Mackay, who worked in the wafer room of the Gray Dunn biscuit factory. Their son Ossian – Grigor's father – was born in 1900. A childhood bout of TB spared Forbes the greater peril of conscription in the First World War and he went on to find work as a warehouseman in the Templeton Carpet Factory.

Ossian, naturally clever but obliged by economic pressures to continue the family tradition of an abbreviated education, became a fitter on John Brown's shipyard in his teens. By the time he was twenty, he had joined the Communist Party and his political activism cost him his job. He was later taken on as a driver on the Corporation trams, where he met, and subsequently married, Morag McCluskey, 'a pretty young clippie', as McWatt described his mother in *Forby*.

The young couple, who lived in a 'single end' in Maryhill, saw education as a means of self-betterment, having been denied it themselves, and ensured that their son, Grigor, should be better equipped than they were to 'make something of himself'.

In *Forby*, the picture the poet paints of his parents is compassionate – simple but good folk who did their best, within their own limitations, for their precociously clever only child. When he won a scholarship to the local academy, Ossian and Morag 'were that proud, you'd think I'd single-handedly retaken Flodden', he wrote, though he was 'subjected to ribbing from local youths' once his school set about flattening his broad Glaswegian accent into an acceptable version of English (a 'pan loaf voice', was the dismissive term) with only a light inflection and a comprehensive mastery of the old Braid Scots vocabularies – from the Lallans of the Central Belt and Lowlands to the Doric of the North-East – to hint at his origins.

In his scant prose descriptions of his childhood there are few shadows – apart from those cast by the dark cloud of 'poverty and dispossession'. But a fragment of verse, a 'reimagining' of Larkin, enclosed in a 1970 letter to Lilias Hogg, suggests another story.

> *They fuck yer heid, yer maw an paw.*
> *They dinnae mean tae, but they dae.*
> *They stech ye wi the fauts they haid*
> *Chuck in some extra, jist fur ye.*
>
> *Man hauns oan meeserie tae man.*
> *It deepens like the loch o hell.*
> *Get oot as early as you can,*
> *An doan't hae onie weans yersel.*[33]

To lovelorn Lilias, who would have been nearly thirty when she received this poem and – as at least one subsequent letter showed – dreamed of having children with McWatt, this letter must have felt like a dagger in the heart.

A Granite Ballad – The Reimagining of Grigor McWatt,
Mhairi McPhail (Thackeray College Press, 2016)

---

33 From *Kowk in the Kaleyard*, Virr Press, 1975. Reprinted in *Warld in a Gless: The Collected Varse of Grigor McWatt*, Smeddum Beuks, 1992.

Delicht in Rauchle

A douce raivelment o the duds,
Kittles a list tae see the scud
A slippit shawl, an oxter flashed
Maks aw desire fair unabashed.
A keek o simmet gets ma vote,
As does the trailach petticoat.
Straigly cuffs an loorach snuid
Speak mair to me o womanhuid,
Than donsie quines in kythe perjink
Whase airtful weys mak manhuid shrink.

Grigor McWatt, efter Robert Herrick, 1959[34]

---

34 From *Kenspeckelt*, Virr Press, 1959. Reprinted in *Warld in a Gless: The Collected Varse of Grigor McWatt*, Smeddum Beuks, 1992.

LILIAS HOGG, THE SECOND CHILD OF KEITH AND SANDRA HOGG, was, she liked to say, 'born on Hell's Hogmanay': 1 January 1941. On that morning, as the infant Lilias screwed up her eyes against the alien light, opened her mouth and emitted her first protesting yell, four hundred miles to the south, Londoners woke to a changed world and surveyed the damage inflicted by German bombers – the Old Bailey, the Guildhall and a handful of Wren churches had all been hit.

'I was a war baby,' she told Archie Aitken, 'and life's been a battlefield ever since.'

She always described the family home – sandstone, three-bedroomed, single-storey, built in 1935 in Liberton, a southern suburb of Edinburgh – as a bungalow. To her parents and her sister Dolina, it was 'a villa'.

Sandra Hogg was a trained midwife and in later life she would remind her husband and their daughters of that fact and, in particular, that she had given up her career to look after them. Keith Hogg, who endured a quiet war supervising stores at Redford Barracks on account of his flat feet, later became a senior bookkeeper with Jenners department store.

Lilias couldn't wait to flee the suburbs for the city two and a half miles down the road and saw school – a genteel girls' academy – and secretarial college as irritating interruptions in her progress towards the centre of the capital, to the hub of an intellectual and creative world full of colour and free of restraint.

In her early, glory days as an avid teenager skipping college in Edinburgh's bohemian pubs, Lilias struggled to keep up with the talk and the drink. She had more success with the latter than the former. Episodes of melancholy in one so young and winsome were permitted by the middle-aged poets to stand in for a poetic disposition, in the absence of any worthwhile poetry.

Willie McCracken, stung by rejection, cruelly quoted Wordsworth at the capricious seventeen-year-old: *Oh! many are the poets that are sown /*

By Nature; men endowed with highest gifts, / The vision and the faculty divine; / Yet wanting the accomplishment of verse.

Ironic, then, that McCracken's blustery doggerel is forgotten while Lilias Hogg's reputation survives today, if only as the Flooer o Rose Street and the Muse o Menzies', who inspired the twentieth century renaissance of Scottish poetry.

Recent scholars of feminist studies have suggested that Hogg's letters, and the scraps of her verse that survive, reveal a slender, tentative gift that if properly nurtured might have made her the equal, if not the better, of any of the Rose Street poets. But, the Women's Studies' argument goes, even if Lilias had possessed the talent of a Sylvia Plath or an Emily Dickinson, the exclusively male Menzies' Bar set would have celebrated her beauty, delighted in her winning nature, admired and encouraged her capacity for alcohol in those early years and completely overlooked her verse.

Her career path was clear – she wanted to be part of the literary and artistic narrative. In order to finance her progress and pay for the occasional round in Menzies', she found a job as a secretary and receptionist with a printing firm, McDuff's, whose manager took a shine to her and continued to overlook her unpunctuality and regular Monday-morning absences.

'Calendars, menus, cattle market catalogues, orders of service, the odd programme for the Edinburgh Festival gentry, a pamphlet or two for the cracked Fringe set,' as she told McWatt. 'See me! I'm in the publishing business too!'

It was, reflected McWatt in *The Fascaray Compendium*, the French writer Alphonse Daudet who observed in his *Memoir*[35] that 'in southern climes the sun warmed the human core, but "we, the transplanted ones, are seized upon by this homicidal North with its mists and rheumatism, its mournful rains and sleet", and, without any external heat source, we "must resort to hard liquor" to guarantee an interior summer. While winter winds howl through the lanes and wynds of Edinburgh, temperatures are tropical during the long late-night lock-ins in the pubs of Rose Street.'

35 Éditions du Soie, 1872.

McWatt, a celebrator of the Auld Alliance (though, to him, any alliance against England would have done) liked to quote another French writer, Baudelaire: *Il est l'heure de s'enivrer! / Pour n'être pas les esclaves martyr-isés du Temps, / enivrez-vous; / enivrez-vous sans cesse! / De vin, de poésie ou de vertu, à votre guise.*[36] McWatt translated the exhortation for the benefit of the company, into robust Scots: *'Tis the oor tae be bluitert! / Tae jouk oor thirlage tae the knock! / On uisge, poetry, virtue, as ye wish, / G'aun yersels, get rairie, mairchless pished.*

['It is the hour to be drunken! / To escape our fates as martyred slaves of time, be ceaselessly drunk. / On wine, on poetry, on virtue if you wish.']

Virtue rarely came into it.

Drunken excesses that would have been grotesque in a woman older and less favoured than Lilias were indulged and sometimes encouraged. She was picturesque even when intoxicated to the point of unconsciousness, her curls tumbling over her eyes, her rosy lips parted, pale limbs wantonly arrayed.

A Granite Ballad – The Reimagining of Grigor McWatt,
Mhairi McPhail (Thackeray College Press, 2016)

---

36 *Le Spleen de Paris*, 1869.

32 Melville Street Lane
Edinburgh
15 August 1958

Dearest G,

A joy to see you. That white night, you in full flight in Charlotte Square, singing, dancing and declaiming your own divine Book of Revelations like a secular, sexier Billy Graham. And moved by your message, I come forward every time to Testify! Yes, Lord, a joy. But a joy burned through with pain, like a red shot silk in which the slightest movement and glancing light reveal the black depths beneath.

We are, my heart's twin, two minds with one vision. Griogal Cridhe, our separation feels like an amputation, or a cardioectomy, if there is such a thing. All is tired and grey here, since you left. Sydney's high-tailed it back to Stella. Hugh's burrowed into Biggar with Valda for the season, George's away back with his mammy in Orkney and Norman's up in Sutherland en famille, murdering fish and punishing his knees on the hills. That leaves the hardcore. Willie and Archie tore into each other again in Rose Street. Over me! Daft to think my true gallant knight is 300 miles away over the water, while these two bletherskites tulzie to claim me. I seek you nightly in the golden warmth of Menzies' . . . When will you be back to ignite this drab pile of tinder and make a merry bonfire of us all?

Your Ayebidin Lilias

———————

Leal-hertit Lilias,

    The willow warblers are back. I feel it is my duty to count them in, to encourage their return. I fancy that if I were not here to welcome them they wouldn't return from their African pit-stop.

    Edinburgh was a rare pleasure, as it always is. I come to drink at 'the gowden mile' of Rose Street as a Bedouin lost in the Sahara might stumble into an oasis. After months of solitary toil in this intellectual desert, the talk and companionship of my peers in that sheikh's palace of brass and mahogany is like a cooling draught of purest water to my parched mind. And this oasis also has the advantage of dancing girls – chief among them your fair self.

    I will be back, as soon as my duties are done here. Until then, keep my seat warm at Menzies'.

> *E'en wi a simmer's day*
> *Ye're mair louesome an mair lown,*
> *Gurl winds dae shoogle dautie bluims o May,*
> *An simmer's tack hae aw tae cutty speal.*

        Aye, Grigor

———————

The McWatt–Hogg correspondence will be exhibited in the new Heritage Centre and Museum, displayed in glass cabinets as the letters of Fanny Brawne and John Keats were once displayed in the Hampstead museum down south. To avoid offending local sensibilities here, I won't mention Hampstead. It would be like bragging about the Hamptons in the Bronx. Down south, 'enemy country' as McWatt called it, the correspondence between the nineteenth-century lovers was shielded from sunlight by chenille drapes which were rolled back for viewing. Here, in the gloomy north, we won't need the drapes.

Until I came along, there was little enthusiasm from the locals for the MacRaes' abortive Fascaradian Museum of Island Life. Now, it seems, there is a strong community will to preserve it. The Auchwinnie Board warned me that I might face some obstructiveness so, in the interests of local cohesion, I have invited islanders to submit their own suggestions for 'enhancing' the new museum at a public meeting in Finnverinnity Hall in October.

My focus, as outlined by Gordon Nesbitt, chairman of the Auchwinnie Regional Development and Enterprise Board, which oversees the Fascaray Trust, is 'Fascaray's heritage and McWatt's unique perspective on our cultural identity and the island's place in Scottish history', and my role will be to listen attentively to islanders' proposals, express interest, ask them to elaborate and then press on regardless with our own plans, which have already been approved by the funding bodies.

An illuminated timeline of Scots history – a twenty first-century electronic Caledonian Bayeux Tapestry – has already been commissioned from Minka Redpath, an Edinburgh artist, and will run in a strip around the walls, enabling visitors to press buttons beneath key dates, setting off audio recordings of McWatt's prose and poetry, some read by McWatt himself and others by Scottish actors.

But, though my main interest is the letters and documents, the centre-piece of the museum (and here I imagine the sulphuric scorn of the poet) will be a gaudy jukebox – a digital player tricked up to look like a relic from a fifties coffee bar – with access to every recorded version of 'Hame tae Fascaray' from Robin Hall and Jimmie Macgregor in 1959 to Paolo Nutini two months ago. McWatt's shade may fume but the Auchwinnie Regional Development and Enterprise Board leapt at the idea: accessibility and interactivity in one neat, flashing neon-lit package.

Robin Hall and Jimmie Macgregor – 1959
Ewan MacColl – 1960
Jimmy Shand (instrumental version) – 1960
Kenneth McKellar – 1962
The Corries – 1964
Hamish Imlach – 1965
Nigel Denver – 1966
Andy Stewart – 1967
The Incredible String Band – 1968
Moira Anderson – 1968
Donovan – 1969
The Humblebums – 1970
Eric Bogle – 1971
The Wolfe Tones – 1971
Lulu – 1972
The Sensational Alex Harvey Band – 1973
John Martyn – 1974
High Speed Grass – 1974
Average White Band (instrumental version) – 1975
Bob Dylan – 1976
Gil Scott-Heron – 1977
Silly Wizard – 1977
Gerry Rafferty – 1978
Val Doonican – 1979
Jack Bruce – 1980
Simple Minds – 1981
Boys of the Lough – 1982
Big Country – 1983
St Andrew and the Woollen Mill – 1984
Rod Stewart – 1986
The Proclaimers –1989

Runrig – 1990
The Waterboys – 1991
Bert Jansch – 1992
Rab Noakes – 1993
The Chieftains –1994
The Three Tenors – 1995
Dougie MacLean – 1997
Emmylou Harris – 1998
Michael Marra – 1999
Dick Gaughan – 2000
Eddi Reader – 2002
Shooglenifty – 2003
Dolly Parton – 2005
Karine Polwart – 2006
Peatbog Faeries – 2007
Franz Ferdinand – 2008
King Creosote – 2009
Ewan MacLennan – 2010
The Mighty Sparrahawk – 2010
Donald MacDonald and the Islands – 2011
Susan Boyle and the Caledonian Orchestra – 2012
KT Tunstall with Nicola Benedetti – 2012
Callum Rae and The Corellas – 2013
Paolo Nutini – 2014

4 September 2014

In my office, I shove the mangy desktop computer aside and open my laptop. The transcription. A sore point. Ailish had, without consulting me, over-edited Effie MacLeod's interview, removing all pauses, hesitations and interruptions and, more controversially, ironing out Effie's idiomatic grammar and converting her 'Braid Scots' Lallans into Standard English. I was furious at the blunder and complained to Gordon Nesbitt. Irritatingly, he sided with Ailish.

It wasn't a question of cost, he said – the Auchwinnie Board was prepared to pay for a further transcription if necessary – but of demographics and, inevitably, accessibility. The board's business projections show most visitors to our new museum will be heritage hunters from America, Canada and New Zealand who'll need a little help with the language.

'There might even be the odd visitor from England and they'd certainly be stumped by Effie's Scots,' said Nesbitt.

'This is cultural cringe,' I argued. 'Completely against the spirit of McWatt. It's a cowering acceptance that Scots is an uncouth bastard variant of English.'

'Maybe,' said Nesbitt quietly. 'But it's also sound business. Your purist approach will appeal to nats and language nerds. We want to draw more visitors to the museum. Let's not exclude them. More visitors will mean more money for Fascaray. And that's a good thing. Surely.'

This seems perverse, especially considering one of the biggest public supporters of the Grigor McWatt Heritage Centre has been the influential SFSL, the Societie fur the Forderin o the Scots Leid, which, part-funded by the European Union, promotes the Scots language and successfully lobbied for an additional Scottish government grant for the project. For a second, I wonder whether this is a resignation issue. But to walk out only weeks into a new job will look like a failure of nerve rather than a principled stand. I'll put this grievance on hold for a later date when I might be looking for a respectable excuse to get out of here.

Meanwhile, the recording of my original, unexpurgated interview with Effie is safely in storage at Auchwinnie Library, ready to be shipped over and installed in our audio-visual display in the new museum; visitors will be able to hear Effie's authentic voice, even if the transcription has been horribly neutered. And I'll use the real thing – make my own transcription if I have to – in *A Granite Ballad*, and provide a glossary if my editor at Thackeray Press insists.

In fact I enjoyed the interview process – I haven't done fieldwork since my sophomore research in Nova Scotia – though in the end I was more interested in Effie's accounts of island life than in her sketchy recollections of the dead poet.

Listening to her I took an almost indecent pleasure in her language and accent. My own mongrel enunciation was ironed flat in a Canadian convent and further tortured by three scholarship terms in an English boarding school, which elocuted me away from my childhood Scots. Once I arrived in Manhattan in my twenties I felt I'd finally found my place and I did my best to go native, acquiring the trappings of a New York identity – smart-mouthed attitude and bohemian style – in the course of which any trace of my mother tongue was eradicated in favour of a bland, keep-'em-guessing, rootless, if not completely classless, inflection.

Effie's voice, earthy and true, resonated at a visceral level – my cradle soundtrack, not always comforting but ingrained – and it made me nod towards sleep. If Effie had been younger and more alert she might have been offended. But she was away, happy to talk on unprompted until long after the light dimmed.

Transcription of interview with Effie MacLeod,
Margaret Lodge, Stamperland Road, Clarkston, Glasgow,
3 June 2014. Conducted by Mhairi McPhail.

'So, Mhairi – that's a good Scots name, isn't it? I'd a friend once named the same. We worked together one summer at the cigarette factory in Dennistoun. It's all artists' studios now. You wouldn't believe it. You could have knocked me down with a feather when I saw it two years ago. Yes. Mhairi-Ann Galvin, from Bridgeton. We called her Wee Annie. Do you ever answer to Annie? No one ever calls you that?'

What Effie actually said was that she and Mhairi-Ann Galvin had worked '*thegether*' at the factory, which was '*aw they artists' studios nou. Ye widnae credit it. Ye cuid a bund me wi a strae . . . Aye. Mhairi-Ann . . . frae Brigtoun,*' was '*cried*' rather than 'called' Wee Annie. '*Naebdy aye cries you that?*'

'What? Oh yes – Grigor. There's another old Scots name, fit for an old Scots man. Oh, he couldn't have been so old when I first set eyes on him, I suppose. But he was the kind of fellow who always looked old.'

For 'what' read '*whit*', for 'yes', read '*aye*' (which also means always and ever) and for 'oh' read '*och*'. The last two sentences, if faithfully transcribed, would have read '*Och, he couldnae hae been sae auld when I first clapped eyes on him, I suppose. But he wis the kindae fella who aye looked auld.*'

'Yes – it was after the war. I was not much more than a child myself at the time.'

'*Aye . . . it wis efter the war. I wisnae much more than a wean masel at the time.*'

'And your grandfather was a Fascaradian? Hector McPhail was it? One of the Five? Well, my memory's not so good these days but the Five Men, I remember the story well.'

'*. . . No sae guid these days . . . but I mind the story well.*'

'I'd been evacuated to the island from Clydebank – we had the Blitz too, you know. It wasn't just the English. Anyways, my mother sent me away to stay with my Macpherson cousins at Balnasaig Farm. My father, who was a Morrison from Lewis, wanted me to go there, to Stornoway. But the women were always the strong ones in our family and my mother won. She said Lewis was overrun with the RAF and the navy and I wouldn't stand a chance there. If she'd known about the commandos at Finnverinnity Big House she might have had second thoughts. Would you not take a wee biscuit with your tea, Mhairi-Ann? No? Go on – Oh, there's nothing of you. You need feeding up. You're a splinter of a girl . . .'

'*Ye ken . . . Wisnae jes the English . . . I wouldnae stand a chance . . . Och, you're a skelf of a lassie.*'

'It was hard at first. Even though I had family on the island, I was still what they called a "From Away". Like Grigor McWatt too, I suppose.'

'*A wis still what they cried a "Frae Away".*'

'I didn't have much of the Gaelic back then when I arrived on the

113

island. My mother had stopped speaking it in Glasgow when she moved there as a girl. It was thought to be low-class, if you know what I mean. For tinkers and the like. And once I got to Fascaray, though it was banned at the school – they got a hiding with the Lochgelly tawse if they so much as whispered in Gaelic – it was what everyone spoke at home. I soon picked it up though. And then after a couple of years at the farm, Uncle Tam's brother-in-law Donald John the Shop offered me a job in Finnverinnity, with a bed in the back stockroom. Well, to a young girl you can imagine, I would rather have been in Finnverinnity than Balnasaig. More of the action there, if you know what I mean.

'Most of the local lads were away fighting but some of the commando boys up at the Big House were very dashing. They had a nice line in patter. Anyways, I've always been quick – my mental arithmetic was so good we didn't need an adding machine in the shop – and I must have got enough of the Gaelic at my mother's breast to give me a basic foundation, if you know what I mean. Before long I was thinking in Gaelic, though Shuggie and me, once we were married, mostly talked Scots at home. We didn't want to confuse the bairns and hold them back. But I still dream in Gaelic sometimes.'

For 'very dashing' read '*awfie dashin*', for 'if you know what I mean', read the more economical '*ken*'.

'Oh? Grigor McWatt. I remember him well. Wore the kilt. They all wear it now, especially the Americans, but in those days on the island it was only the laird who wore it, at Hogmanay. And he was English. The laird and Grigor McWatt. Yes. McWatt. He struggled with the Gaelic – he could never master it. He used to get hopping mad when we started to speak it in the shop or wherever. He was a funny wee man. Not the laughing sort of funny, no. More the odd sort. He'd come over from Calasay to the inn or for his shopping now and again – stamps, tobacco, maybe a bit of mince, a bag of broken biscuits – or call in to the farm at Balnasaig for a dram with Uncle Tam on his way back from Finnverinnity. Mostly, though, he kept to himself, up there in Calasay, up to his eyes in books.

'Shuggie had more to do with him, taking all those parcels of books up there to him. Grigor liked his books, Shuggie used to say, more than he liked folk. Books came first, then his collies. And then there were all the other animals, hens, wildcats, otters, that stupid creature Marty – the pine marten. McWatt was daft about them, though it ended not so well. Whoever heard of anybody keeping pine martens or otters as pets? As for folk, no, your poet didn't have much time for folk.'

'*Aye, I mind him well . . . He couldnae maister it . . . He'd come over from Calasay for his messages . . . Thon gowkit cratur, Marty . . . Embdy keepin pine martens . . .*'

'Do you have any pets yourself, Mhairi-Ann? No? I was always a great one for cats. They can be very good company when you're all alone. I had to give my last one, Missy, a Persian blue, away to my daughter Moira, who stays in Springburn, when I moved in here. No pets, see. That's the rule. But the matron, Mrs Drumlie, has a wee Jack Russell terrier and she brings him in once a week for the residents to pet. We all have a go. Those of us who aren't away with the fairies.'

For '*very*' read '*gey*', for '*aren't*' read '*arenae*'. It's not so hard, is it?

'I always had a soft spot for horses too. We had them at Balnasaig until the tractors came in – three pair of them, Clydesdales I think they were, two for ploughing and two for carting and two for – I can't remember.'

'*Ah cannae mind . . .*'

'Can't remember their names either, though I had my favourite, a big soft-eyed creature with a star on her forehead and furry hooves. She'd a way of nuzzling me when I went to feed her. And she had two foals, the bonniest wee things. I went about by pony and trap, down to the harbour to get the provisions from the puffer, loaded them onto the trap myself. You wouldn't think that now, to look at me. I can barely get out of my chair here without the help of that nice wee Filipina girl over there, Lin . . .

'There was a byreman, Seumas McKinnon, Seumas the Byre, who looked after the horses and all the cattle and sheep and pigs – he'd muck out ten barrowloads of manure in the morning before he began his day's work in the fields. He was daft on wee Effie Maclean who did the milking, but poor Seumas was much older, not much to look at and a Catholic besides, and Effie'd set her cap at Calum Donald MacEwan, the ploughman, anyway. We called him Calum Donald the Plough. There was a man who did everything else, the carting and heavy work and helping out; he was called the orraman. I can't remember his name.

Dougal, was it? Yes, he was one of the Mackenzies. Oh it was a hard life but we all pulled together.'

'A big soft-eyed cratur ... We cried him Calum Donald the Plough ... Aye, he wis one o the Mackenzies ... Och ... we aw pu'ed thegether ...'

'Uncle Tam kept cows, Ayrshires, as well as the sheep and pigs and he grew oats and hay, turnips and potatoes, a bit of kale. He did the road mending round our corner of Fascaray. But it was like painting the Forth Bridge – you were never done. Once you'd got the road straight up towards Calasay, it was time to go back and deal with the Balnasaig to Finnverinnity stretch. He used the horses for that too, until the tractor came in. A good horse was worth more than gold ...'

'Mair than gowd ...'

'They could be very stubborn, come harvest time after being out for the spring champing at the grass. Could you blame them? They'd gone soft, didn't like the weight of the collar going on them and the noise of the carts, the reapers and the hayrakes, and all that would send them daft so Calum Donald the Plough would stuff their ears with cotton wool. Over at Lusnaharra, Joe McPhee always put butter in the horses' ears to calm them before yoking them up. During harvest they'd work till eight or nine at night, men and beasts. It was hard work on the sunny days, with the heat and the horseflies. But everyone would help. There'd be a drink of oatmeal in a pail of water to keep you going, maybe a jam sandwich.'

'They could be gey thrawn, come hairst ... The heat an the clegs ... There'd be sowans in a cuman ... mebbe a piece an jam.'

'Before I moved to the shop, I'd help with the milking in Balnasaig. That was always the girls' work. Me and Effie Maclean. The two Effies. And I'd make the butter. You'd put the milk in these shallow dishes and after a couple of days you'd skim off the cream and put it in an earthen-ware crock. You'd leave it for three days then you'd churn it with the plunger. That was hard work. I'd muscles like that Charles Atlas. And it was always going wrong. It wouldn't set ...'

'Aye, lassies' work ... you'd ream aff the cream ... then you'd kirn it ... Aye gangin wrang ... thon Charles Atlas ... It widnae set ...'

'What? Oh yes ... McWatt ... [LAUGHS] You're a great conversa-tionalist, hen. I'm getting carried away here. So. Grigor McWatt. Well, he was known to help out at harvest time too. And with the peat cutting. But he could be a sour old devil, skulking round the island, snapping at the children. And he was a mad keen nationalist. Not that I'm against the independents. Not now that is. In the old days, they were a bunch of hotheads. I nearly lost my hand that night they blew up the postbox. Still got the scar. See? Just by my thumb. No? Just there. No?

'Yes, most of the time he'd be walking around with a face that could have tripped you up it was that long. It was the poetry, I suppose. Thinking all those big fancy thoughts can't make you too cheerful. He'd no time for incomers, either. That was me. Up from the south. I was lucky I wasn't English or I would have got dog's abuse from him. But he was surly and I won't take rudeness. I told him "I suppose you think I came up the Clyde on a water biscuit?" That shut him up.'

'*Aye . . . Thinking those big fantoosh thoughts . . .*'

'But he could be awful kind too. I mind him giving away a catch of herring to Marsaili and Jessie MacDonald, who'd been widowed by the Big Storm. That was some night. Sea nearly as high as Mammor, the *Morag May* lost, with Marsaili's father and Jessie's brother too. Wee Margaret in the shop lost her daddy too, poor soul. McWatt wrote a poem about that, if I remember correctly.

'*If I mind right . . .*'

'He wrote a good song, too, I'll give him that. "Hame tae Fascaray". A fine tune as well, but the fellow who played it, Murdo McIntyre from Doonmara, Murdo the Fiddle, never got any credit for it. A good-looking fellow Murdo in his youth, but a devil when drink was taken. Like all the men, except my Shuggie. That was the only way to get McWatt out of the pub – if any visitor to the island, knowing no better, saw him in the inn and asked him for a verse of his song, he would rush out the door, deeply offended. Some of the local children, little devils they were, used to shout to him in the street – "Gangin hame!" You should have seen the look on McWatt's face!'

'*Breenge oot the door, black-affronted . . . The local weans, wee devils . . .*'

'So is it the poetry you like, Mhari-Ann? I'm keen on a good poem myself, though I always prefer the cheery sort. They always had a nice wee verse or two in the *Sunday Post*. Francis Gay. Do you remember him, Mhairi-Ann?

'Count your blessings instead of your crosses; Count your gains instead of your losses; Count your joys instead of your woes; Count your friends instead of your foes.

'There's a lot of comfort in a poem, Mhairi-Ann. Do you not think?'

I overlooked Larkin/McWatt's advice about reproduction (*doan't hae onie weans yersel*), and I wouldn't dematerialise Agnes now if I could, but I made it my project to '*get oot*' early and fled my family at the first opportunity. Books were my exit permit, my get-out. So I got out, though I've spent a lifetime waiting for an entry visa to get in. Somewhere. Anywhere. As I address the difficulties of my new job in this isolated place, a place with which I can at best boast a theoretical connection, I feel a sudden billowing bleakness. This, I remind myself, was my partner's idea. Or rather my ex-partner's. Marco has set me up. A trap. And I've walked right into it.

I have to watch for this misery, make sure it doesn't erode Agnes's lovely blitheness.

After a morning spent with Oonagh McKinnon at her family's small sheep farm in Lusnaharra, Agnes announces that, no, she won't have lamb cutlets for lunch today.

'Have you ever actually held a lamb?' she asks with passion. 'Like, in your actual arms? They smell a bit funny but they are *so* cute. Papa always says my name means lamb in Latin. Why would I want to eat myself?'

Thus, my daughter informs me she is now a vegetarian.

'Though I suppose since I eat fish that makes me a fishetarian.'

'Pescatarian,' I tell her.

'Pest?' she bridles. 'How am I a pest?'

'You're never a pest. Put your boots on again. We're going to Finnverinnity House.'

'To Aaron's house?'

'To his garden. We're going to do some more research.'

'I *love* research.'

She scrambles to lace her boots, zips up her jacket and is at the door. She can't wait to get going. Looks like *Morbus Fascariensis* has skipped this generation after all.

*

Lady Montfitchett's post-war efforts to rid Finnverinnity House of any association with its proletarian occupiers were not entirely successful; a remnant of the obstacle courses and shooting ranges set up by the army to test the skills of would-be commandos can still be seen in the grounds of the Big House today. An abandoned bothy on the east side of the walled garden was deployed by the SOE as a 'mystery house' with pop-up tin targets to sharpen the reflexes of apprentice snipers. These days it is used as an overspill junk room by the twenty-first-century owners of Finnverinnity House, described by Johanna as 'a couple of harmless old German hippies and their kids'.

The Schneiders, through Johanna, have given me permission to root around in the outbuilding to look for anything that might be of use to the new Fascaray Museum. The Schneiders are in Auchwinnie for the day and there's no sign of life at Finnverinnity House as we walk up the drive, an unkempt swathe of gravel, ground elder and thistle. Rain-sodden Tibetan prayer flags flap limply from the peeling porte cochère and a Saltire and a skull-and-crossbones Jolly Roger fly at half-mast from the turret.

In the bothy, Agnes is entranced, stepping past the old bicycles, the upturned Silver Cross pram, outgrown toys – 'Hey! Elmo from *Sesame Street*! – rusting tools, seatless cane chairs, empty preserve jars and the paraphernalia of innumerable abandoned hobbies: a fretsaw, a candle-making kit, a knitting machine.

Leaning against the far wall is a six-foot coffin-shaped strip of sheet metal – one of the original targets for the trainee agents' shooting practice. It's rusty and pitted with bullet holes but you can still make out the crudely painted facial features and the faded lettering which identifies this target as 'The Laird'. Cleaned up, it will make a quirky addition to the museum.

'That is *so* creepy,' says Agnes, delighted.

I have my doubts about Mr Yeats's Lake Isle of Innisfree. It cannot always be said of my own island that 'peace comes dropping slow'. Fascaray – and my sub-insular corner of it, Calasay – is not invariably a serene place in which to work. My house rattles in the ninety-mile-an-hour winds like the tin cup of an unregarded mendicant. In gales and hailstorms I think of my time as a commando – it is as if I have come under sustained machine-gun fire from all sides. Of the unremitting rainfall we have endured, at best it can be said that drought is never a problem here.

We do, however, suffer a drought of another kind – the intellectual variety. The only reading material one is likely to see on Fascaray, apart from the Bible, is the *Sunday Post* newspaper, or *Film Weekly* magazine, or the occasional detective novel by Agatha Christie. The island minister has, of course, a thorough knowledge of the Scriptures and Psalms, in both Gaelic and English; our island schoolteacher might, I imagine, stretch to a novelette or two, and while the parish priest of Lusnaharra has a sound knowledge of the classics, in the original Latin and Greek, as well as the poetry of W. B. Yeats and Banjo Paterson, he remains indifferent to my passion for the rich tradition that originates here beneath our very noses.

I have to travel south-east, to the Sassenach-haunted streets of Edinburgh, to find compatriots who share my ambition to revive the great Scots literary tradition, championed in that city in the eighteenth century by Robert Fergusson, whose gutsy varse in our native language inspired the insipid imitator Burns. We hope to do Bold Rabbie Fergusson better service. Such is the caprice of posterity that few have heard of him in Fascaray, though even the most drouthie toper in the Finnverinnity Inn can recite a line or two of Burns.

Yet among unlettered men on this wind-buffeted island, there is real poetry to be found – a living poem, in the elemental moments of daily existence. There are few more exhilarating, manly pleasures, and few

121

greater challenges to character and human resourcefulness, than those called upon the sailor by the demands of the sea.

To join the crews of the small herring boats, skirting the Carracorry whirlpool and sailing thirty miles out beyond the Mhor Sgheir reef, is to jettison the superfluities of the modern world and inhabit one of the great Norse sagas, or to journey with Odysseus himself across the Aegean's wide back. The ocean is bestial behemoth and beckoning odalisque many times over in a single voyage.

And a journey on a Clyde steam puffer – the stumpy cargo boat that brings essential supplies to grateful islanders in all weathers – is more than a Neil Gunn short story; a simple-minded Para Handy cannot do justice to this narrative. It would take a capacious novel, by Margaret Oliphant or John Galt, or even that big blusterer Scott, to begin to delineate the full range of characters, settings and experiences the average puffer deckhand encounters in a single week.

'*Tuig thus' an t-eathar, 's tuigidh an t-eathar thu*,' they say. Ken the boat and the boat will ken you. Here on Fascaray we are all men of the sea, subjects not of some foreign monarch or remote parliament, but of the weather and the tides. The Finnverinnitian, they say, is a crofter with a boat, and the Lusnaharran a fisherman with a croft. Up at Calasay I also try my hand at both disciplines, with modest success. I get by. My daily darg [work], however, is retributive larceny. I pick the pockets of the English tyrants who have robbed us of our birthright, take the best of their verse, with all its unjust advantages, and, by a process that is part linguistic, part alchemical, I reimagine it, offer it to my people and make it Scotland's own.

My chief aim is to reclaim a poetry worthy of the Fascaradian fisherman, the peacetime commando of the waves, who can know both the profound terror and the euphoria that come from mastery of nature at its wildest. My varse – this is my hope – will be like the ocean: timeless, capricious, elemental and indomitable.

Grigor McWatt, 1948, *The Fascaray Compendium*

10 September 2014

Despite close scrutiny of the official records and Ailish's long hours at the SOE archives in London (after which we had a small wrangle over her expenses), we still haven't come up with anything on McWatt's war service.

Jim Struan arrived as a trainee to the Big House in 1941 and stayed on as an instructor until late 1943, when he was sent to Italy and the Balkans. I tracked him down to Aberdeenshire, where he has been living for the past 25 years with his partner Eric. Jim, as historian of the Fascaray SOE alumni, keeps in touch with the dwindling and ancient band of survivors dispersed throughout Europe and America, and arranges annual reunions in London. He has tried to be helpful to our project here in Fascaray and we've had several friendly but fruitless exchanges of letters and phone calls.

'McWatt . . . McWatt? I've heard of the poet, of course. And the song. He wrote that, didn't he? The Hogmanay standard. Gives me the boak [makes me sick] to be honest. Bit of a character, by all accounts, wasn't he? But I can't recall him at Finnverinnity for the life of me.'

Jim has asked around, he says, but so far no one has any recollection of Grigor McWatt at Finnverinnity House. He promises to ring me if he hears anything useful. In my office I pick up Jim's memoir. The only photograph, a black-and-white picture taken in the grounds of the Big House in 1943, shows a group of young men and women in attractively distressed fatigues, grinning, arms draped around each others' shoulders as if on some hearty summer camp excursion, or a Ralph Lauren photo shoot, rather than enduring a dry run for hell. It occurs to me that most of them were younger than I am now.

I check the index again. Magical thinking. Do I honestly believe that McWatt's name, which wasn't in the index when I last looked, which Jim can't recall in this context, will suddenly appear there? No mention. Of course not. It's as if Grigor McWatt, before 'Hame tae Fascaray' brought him his unwelcome fame, had not existed, though several islanders have testified, then and since, to his presence at the Big House, and particularly at the inn, during the war years, and his poem 'The Sodger' is eloquent testimony to his active service. It's another missing link, which McWatt's biographer conveniently passes over in a few glib sentences.

'His return to the island was as a hero,' writes Knox-Cardew, 'one of that exceptional, courageous band of men and women, an elite corps of spies and saboteurs, destined for dangerous work assisting local resistance movements in occupied Europe. Based in Finnverinnity House, appropriated for the purpose from the absentee landlord Montfitchett, McWatt plotted and played his part in the defeat of Nazi Germany.'

The Sodger

Gin Ah shud dee, ween anely this o me,
That there's some neuk o furrin lea
That is aye Scotland. There shall be
In thon fouth yird a fouther smurach derned;
A smurach Scotland buir, collit, mak't awaur,
Gied her flooers tae loue, her paiths stravaiged,
A bouk o Scotland's souchin Scotland's air,
Dicht by the burns, blest by suns o hame.
An think, this hert, all evil chucked awa,
A pulse in the ayebidin mind, nae less
Gies somewey back the thochts by Scotland gien;
Her sichts an soonds; dreams cantie as her day
An lauchter, lairned o pals; an douceness
In herts at saucht, ablo a Scottish heiv'n.

Grigor McWatt, efter Rupert Brooke, 1944[37]

37 From *Kenspeckelt*, Virr Press, 1959. Reprinted in *Warld in a Gless: The Collected Varse of Grigor McWatt*, Smeddum Beuks, 1992.

'So your grandpa was a hero too, like the poet?' asks Agnes, looking up from her school books.

'Kind of . . .'

My grandfather, Hector McPhail, was two years younger than Grigor McWatt. They probably shared a dram and exchanged a few gruff words in the Finnverinnity Inn after Hector returned to Fascaray in 1945 from war service in Italy. They might have fought together in mainland Europe, but back on the island they certainly would have worked side by side, sleeves rolled, sweat breaking on brows furrowed with purpose, each spadeful of soil avenging centuries of injustice as they defied the law by staking out the 'reclaimed' acres during the Fascaray Land Raid. Hector might even have sung 'Hame tae Fascaray', McWatt's ballad of pride and belonging, at its first airing in the Finnverinnity Inn in 1946.

But I'll never know what Hector thought of McWatt, whether my grandfather found him a kindred spirit or an oddball, whether the poet inspired respect, scepticism or grudging affection. I never knew my grandfather well but, from what I remember, he was always better at the grudging than the affection, and his hostility – to his neighbours, his children, to the English (he could have made common cause with McWatt on that one), to Catholics, to 'the quisling Labour Party', to intellectual pretension, to unlettered imbecility, to people – was one of the reasons my parents emigrated to Canada in 1979.

'Was my grandpa Dougal a hero?' asks Agnes, pen poised over an empty page.

'In a way, I suppose.'

If heroism consists of building some kind of life with few advantages, turning your back on a family that made you miserable, starting again among strangers and never, ever complaining, I suppose my father qualifies.

We'd heard that Grandad McPhail 'drank', especially so after Grandma's death, and though we intuited our parents' disapproval and, on our rare visits back to Scotland, we heard him speak in a funny, indistinct way and once saw him stagger and fall like a cartoon character – a strangely menacing cartoon character – as children we had no understanding of what this 'drinking' actually meant. Didn't everyone 'drink'? That's what you did when you were thirsty.

As we hit our teens and began our own experiments with chemical mood-changers we understood at last and Hector's unwholesome thirst gave him an outlaw glamour. It didn't last. Hector foreswore drink, adding alcoholics to his list of hate figures. This was probably fortunate for him in health terms, and for his relationship with our parents, which defrosted to a state of dutiful chilliness, but for my brother and me it was a loss. In sobriety, our grandad became an uninteresting old man.

When I won the scholarship to Turville Chantry, the expectation was that during vacations I would travel north of the border to stay with family in Scotland – Aunt Bridie in Blairgowrie or older cousins in Cumbernauld – and visit Grandad, who had become a punctilious sender of birthday postal orders. But the competing offers of holidays in the swanky London town houses, country estates or French villas of my wealthy classmates – who had taken me on as you might an exotic pet – were irresistible.

Towards the end of my grandfather's life, I remember enduring a starchy visit to his tenement flat in Govan where he lived alone with a small dog – a live yapping version of the staring porcelain 'wally dug' twins on the mantelpiece. The flat smelled of furniture polish and disinfectant and I remember feeling only boredom, embarrassment and a fierce yearning to get away.

'And is Papa a hero?' asks Agnes.

'Maybe, honey . . . Maybe to you, anyway.'

In my twenties, when I visited the UK my life was too busy and interesting to find time to call on an old relative whose connection with me felt purely notional. He became, like many lonely people, a monologuist. Now, of course, I wish I'd had more patience, and curiosity. If he did give me his first-hand account of the Fascaray Land Raid, or his impressions of the Bard of Fascaray, I wasn't listening. My sweet-natured daughter would have listened. But I was always too arrogant and engrossed in the small dramas of my own life. Now I'm paying for my carelessness. I must unearth this story the hard way.

The Hidlins Fowk

Smue at us, pey us, bygae us: but dinnae aye forget;
Fur we are the fowk o Scotland, that niver hae spaiken yet.
There's mauny a bowsie fermer that wauchts less cantily,
There's mauny a free French paisant mair walthie an waesome than we.
There's nae fowk in the hail warld sae mauchtless an sae cannie
There's hunger in oor pechans, there is lauchter in our een;
You lauch at us an loue us, baith quaich an een are wet:
Ainlie, ye dinnae ken us. Fur we havnae spaiken yet.

We hear men speakin for us o new laws strang an douce
Yet nane o them can speak the leid that we speak ben the hoose.
An mebbe we'll rise hinmaist as Frenchmen rose afore
Oor radge comes efter Russia's radge an Ireland's michty roar.
Mebbe we are meant tae merk wi oor rammies an oor rest.
God's geck for aw high heid yins. An mebbe whisky's best.
But we are the fowk o Scotland; an we havnae spaiken yet.
Smue at us, pey us, bygae us. But dinnae aye forget.

Grigor McWatt, efter G. K. Chesterton, 1950[38]

38 From *Kenspeckelt*, Virr Press, 1959. Reprinted in *Warld in a Gless: The Collected Varse of Grigor McWatt*, Smeddum Beuks, 1992.

'Is this really it?' Agnes asks, as we pick our way across the moss-furred rubble in Killiebrae Glen. 'People actually lived here?'

'Yes. People lived here. Including your great-grandfather.'

'But where are the houses?'

'At your feet. These stones were once walls that supported roofs thatched with heather. Whole families – parents, sometimes four or five kids, sometimes more – lived in these houses, with their dogs and their cattle. And look, those smaller stones – the line of them across there by the burn – must have been an enclosure or a wall round a small garden. Maybe a pigpen.'

I hadn't briefed her properly. Clearly she'd thought we'd be visiting a cute cottage and peeping in at the room where ninety-one years ago Hector McPhail, her ancestor, lay gurgling in his cradle. I've brought her here under false pretences.

'But there's nothing here!' she says indignantly. 'If anyone ever did live here, if it ever really was a village, a giant must have stomped his way across it, flattening houses, and all those families and cattle.'

'Well, in a way, that's what happened.'

'Not a *real* giant?'

'No. Your giant is a kind of metaphor, a figure of speech, meaning he, she or it represents something else – it could be progress, economics, politics – trampling heedless across small lives in these communities.'

I lose her at metaphor. She is weaving between the stones trying to make sense of this place in her own way. As am I; a global citizen, choosing to renounce the pleasures of the world, getting down on my knees, metaphorically, and burrowing back to the dank omphalos, to someone else's past, to the dead poet's retreat and my grandfather's unhappy home. Not a bad response to heartbreak. Original, even; swapping one desolation for another. But watching my daughter running through the ruins, I chide myself for putting her through it too.

She stops at a large boulder stained with yellow lichen.

'This is it!' she says. 'My great-grandfather's house.'

'How do you know it's his house?'

'I don't. It's a metaphor.' She pats the stone tenderly. 'Poor Hector.'

Tomorrow I'll revisit another dead man's house, though there will be plenty of material evidence – too much, maybe – of the life lived. Oppressed by the prospect of all that sifting and cataloguing, I wonder if Hector's home, and the entire clachan of Killiebrae, sets a better example than An Tobar. Let it all decay. Ashes to ashes. The future's the thing.

Agnes, though, is enthusiastic.

'Can I come with you to the poet's house tomorrow? Please!' she begs.

'Come on, Agnes. You know it's a school day tomorrow.'

'But it'll be like a treasure hunt!' she says, then pauses, struck by a fresh thought. 'Is that another metaphor?'

The Dishantit Clachan

Douce Killiebrae, bonniest clachan o the glen,
A place o unco sonsieness tae all wha ken,
Where smuin spring arrayed her kilt o flooers
An simmer hung her chairms frae ilka bouer,
Where bairnies ran aboot in blithesome play
An birdies sang their joy ootthrou the day.
Hoo aften hae Ah daundered oer yer green,
Where couthie cantieness wis ayeweys tae be seen.
But sonsieness has fled, aw chairms awa,
Yer bouers are broukit, bairnies gone an aw.
Whit cruel hert can tak sic braw delicht
An turn it intae derk an hooshit nicht?
In this dishantitness we see a tyrant's haun,
As mirkest meeserie stegs the sculdered laun.

Grigor McWatt, efter Oliver Goldsmith, 1960[39]

39   From *Kowk in the Kaleyard*, Virr Press, 1975. Reprinted in *Warld in a Gless: The Collected Varse of Grigor McWatt*, Smeddum Beuks, 1992.

PAIRT TWA

Cauld Handsel

AS HE SETTLED INTO CALASAY AFTER THE WAR, MOST OF McWATT'S forays down to Fascaray were made to the Finnverinnity Inn, where an increasingly infirm Rab McNab still presided in the rosy glow of candlelight. McNab thought McWatt a 'queerie fish', but he was used to irascible customers – some of the fishermen could get carnaptious after a few nights at sea – and the publican handled the poet efficiently when drinking got out of hand, calming McWatt's outbursts while avoiding condescension. More than once McNab, not entirely sober himself, transported his cantankerous customer home on a cart hitched to Tam Macpherson's cuddie [horse], mindful of the tides on the Calasay Strand.

McWatt visited the village store rarely, calling in only to buy tobacco, or paraffin for his lamps, a few slices of bacon or a pound of mince, or stamps from the post-office counter. The young sales clerk was Effie Morrison, known as Effie the Shop, to distinguish her from Effie 'the Milk' Maclean at Balnasaig Farm. (After her wedding to Shuggie the Post, Effie the Shop became Effie MacLeod.) Once she took on the job of running the island's telephone exchange, she could claim a comprehensive knowledge of every islander's joys and travails. McWatt, however, remained an enigma.

'He just came in for his messages [shopping] and left. He wasnae one for the local gossip,' said Effie MacLeod, although his observations in *The Fascaray Compendium* show he had a keen eye for local news. In his early years on the island, his lack of Gaelic would have been an impediment to social intercourse in the store, where locals who had been happily conversing in Scots would switch to Gaelic as soon as an outsider walked in.

'He could be gey thrawn [very stubborn]. But he was aye mannerly,' Effie Macleod told me.

McWatt occasionally helped out at the Balnasaig harvests and communal peat cutting – exercises in reciprocal altruism for all the islanders, who were rewarded in kind with labour on their own smallholdings and peat banks, with seed potatoes, a pat of crowdie and, in McWatt's case, a guaranteed welcome and occasional dram at the farm with Tam Macpherson on his way to Finnverinnity. McWatt also joined in several of the traditional 'guga hunts', in which the men of Fascaray sailed to the rocky islets of Plodda and Grodda, scaled the cliffs and caught, skinned and smoked young gannets, though he was said to have had no head for heights and remained in the boat during these annual excursions.

He ventured out with the fishermen only 'when skies were unclouded and seas were calm', according to Tormud Campbell, owner of the *Silver Darling*. The poet was 'neither use nor ornament when it came to hauling in the herring', Tormud reported in a humorous aside in *Poet in a Landscape*. McWatt, unusually for a commando though not for a fisher, could not swim and some felt he didn't pull his weight when out on the boat; challenged by Roddy McIntosh for failing to help the crew with the lobster pots in a force nine, McWatt was said to have replied that he was 'here to observe, rather than to participate'. Tormud and his son Alec had to intervene before a fight broke out on the bucking boat.

At Calasay, McWatt's labours on his croft gradually began to pay off. He rebuilt the crumbling north wall of the house, glazed windows, made his home as watertight and windproof as it could ever be and, using an old boat mast interleaved with struts made from salvaged barrels, built a staircase to a loft bedroom. He fertilised the land with seaweed and cattle dung and grew kale and turnips as well as potatoes and carrots.

He had few visitors. According to Effie MacLeod, McWatt 'mostly kept himself to himself in those days. He was the loner type of fellow. Not much of a conversationalist — except in drink. Then you couldnae stop him. Sober, though, he liked to listen, and he went round collecting the island yairns and receipts and the like. He always had time for the old ones, listening to their crack, stories about ghosts and fairies. They maybe thought he was a bitty touched, but they were aye glad of the chance tae blether. Most of the time, though, he cooried doon in Calasay.'

He took regular deliveries of large parcels of books, most of them second-hand, in quantities that made Shuggie groan as he slung the sacks over the crossbar of his bike. At Ruh, Shuggie had to dismount and push the Raleigh across the strand to Calasay. If he didn't get the tides right he ran the risk of getting his feet wet, wrecking his bike or even being stranded with McWatt for the night.

'That happened once or twice after we were married,' Effie MacLeod told me in our interview at her Glasgow nursing home. 'Shuggie would aye come back with a sore head the next day. What else was there to do up in that place, if you werenae writing or walking, but drink? Though Shuggie was moderate in his habits, compared to some.'

McWatt eventually housed his books in the library he built from an abandoned *bathach*, or byre, sheltered by a copse of birches to the west of his croft. He plastered and rendered its interior walls, built shelves from driftwood gathered from the shore, covered the roof in neat overlapping slates and tightly sealed the windows against rain.

'He takes mair care o thon library than he does o his ain hoose. I'd rather be a book than a man up at Calasay,' Shuggie told his wife, and in later life the retired postman would put his disabling lumbago down to those years spent shouldering sacks of books to McWatt's remote library.

When the poet wasn't cultivating his croft, building his library, or milking Flora, his shaggy, extravagantly horned 'Hielan coo', he sat at his desk by the back window, or in rare days of fine weather on a folding camp chair by his front stoop, writing, reading and struggling to learn, or relearn as he said, Gaelic.

The more personal entries in *The Fascaray Compendium* reveal that when the *Morbus* took hold he would sit for hours morosely observing nature through the fogged glass of the window until he would be forced out of the house by his importuning collie, Luath, who would race round the bounds of Calasay while McWatt strode the hills and shores, stooped to examine wild flowers or seashells, turned over stones and examined moss and lichen 'as if they contained the secrets of the universe', gazed upwards to note the passage of birds from Iceland, Siberia and Africa and observe the unfurling drama of the clouds and the shifting moods of the sea.

In happier intervals, his personal summers, heedless of sleep he wrote his verse and laboured to improve his home further, installing a wood-burning stove, diverting a supplementary water supply from the nearby burn, and 'reimagining' world literature into the Scots language.

During these most productive periods he would break from his writing only to call in on the older inhabitants of the island, who welcomed a visit – even from an incomer (a distant clan connection has never impressed the hard-line amateur genealogists of Fascaray) – in their lonely blackhouses. McWatt would take notes for *The Fascaray Compendium* as they reminisced, mostly in their second language, Scots, about their childhoods, the old ways, the spirit world and hauntings, and about miraculous cures at the former pagan shrine of Teampull Beag in Lusnaharra. Over cups of scarlet tea and a *strupag* (home-made bun), these *bodachs* and *cailleachs* (old men and women), nominally Christian – Catholic or Free Church Presbyterian – would tell stories of the island's ghosts as if they were gossiping about neighbours. 'This mix of the earthy and the numinous is the essence of Gaelic realism,' wrote McWatt.

There were tales of widows with second sight who foretold storms and predicted death, witches who blighted crops and thwarted romance, water kelpies who spirited away children, teasing *sidhe* fairies, selkie seal women who ensnared fishermen, and Seonaidh the volatile sea god who had to be appeased with a cup of ale.

Then, off duty, McWatt would return to the inn, wild with argument and song. He shared Father Col's fondness for whisky – 'a wee goldie' – and a stushie [bantering row] about politics and poetry in the low-beamed intimacy of the Finnverinnity Inn. Though the poet was not a man of God he was ecumenical in his acquaintances; he also liked to play chess at the manse with the teetotal Presbyterian minister, Ranald Paterson who, on account of his sabbatarian beliefs, was available for 'The King's Game' only six days a week. McWatt was even seen once in the company of the minister at the Temperance Hotel, where the elderly proprietor Miss Geddes, famous for her home-baking, laid on a special Friday high tea. It was said, though, that after ten minutes in the hotel's chilly lounge, the poet disdained the sandwiches, thanked his hostess politely, filled his pockets with scones and made his way swiftly over to the Finnverinnity Inn.

A Granite Ballad – The Reimagining of Grigor McWatt,
Mhairi McPhail (Thackeray College Press, 2016)

The Solitude O Nicht

It wis at a ceilidh —
Ah lay in a dwaum, kennin nocht.
The fadin flooers fell aboot ma heid.
When Ah got tae ma feet still bluitert,
The birdies hud flit tae their nests.
Anely a few pals hung aboot.
Ah ganged alang the burn — follaein the muinwaik.

Grigor McWatt, efter Li Po, 1949[1]

1   From *Kenspeckelt*, Virr Press, 1959. Reprinted in *Warld in a Gless: The Collected Varse of Grigor McWatt*, Smeddum Beuks, 1992.

15 September 2014

It's raining steadily as I cross the strand to Calasay on the quad bike. My waterproofs are so wet I might as well have swum across in high tide. Inside the house I kick off my sodden boots and struggle out of my jacket, leaving them in the porch in the vain hope that they might dry there. This time I move around the house more methodically, opening drawers and putting documents of interest into folders. Trouble is, there seems little of much interest.

Johanna did a good job with her preliminary selection of material, now in two boxes in my office. What's left are drawers of old pens, business cards – the Raj Curry House in Auchwinnie; 'The Vital Spark', a local electrician; a taxi firm in Edinburgh – impenetrable bank statements, old chequebooks (three fat rolls of them), leaking AA batteries, a broken flashlight and a stack of bills from an Auchwinnie vet for treatment of Gyp, McWatt's last collie and the final survivor of his menagerie.

By the desk are two old pottery preserve jars – mass-produced, mid twentieth century – painted with kilted warriors. The glaze is cracked and there are chips on the rims. They'd probably fetch a couple of dollars apiece in a vintage sale. One is empty; the other holds a clutch of tobacco pipes, an unsavoury wooden bouquet of sticky black bowls and chewed stems. I pick one up gingerly. To real McWatt aficionados they'd be serious relics, containing the DNA of the great man. I can't escape the feeling that my good degrees in anthropology, heritage and museum studies were meant to equip me for more rewarding and hygenic tasks than this.

I think again of the Could Have Beens. I could have stuck with the Museum of the Printed Word in New York. It might, with time, have developed into a viable concern and, once the investment and politics had been sorted out, it could even have been interesting. It had the added virtue of being located in New York, which would have avoided upheaval, allowing us to stay on in Brooklyn, though once Marco was out of the picture we would have needed to find a smaller apartment.

There was a highly paid post at the new Museum of Pet Apparel, set up in Trenton by the ex-model ex-wife of a Russian energy magnate, but the cost to my dignity would have been too great. If woman could live by prestige alone, I might have gone for the job at the Frick, but woman, and in particular single woman with daughter to support, can't. It was only part-time and temporary and the salary would barely have covered our rent.

On McWatt's dresser, next to a chess set – a copy of the medieval pieces found on the Isle of Lewis in the nineteenth century – I find a cork box and, dutifully, but with a singular lack of curiosity, prise it open with a screwdriver. Agnes would be beside herself with excitement. My scepticism is justified – again; it contains a neat ball of rubber bands. Next to the box is a peppermint tin filled with postage stamps, second class. Like my exiled nationalist parents, reluctant subjects of the Queen even in faraway Canada, McWatt always stuck the stamps upside down on envelopes as a protest against the English monarchy.

Outside, a wind has got up, hurling raindrops against the window like handfuls of gravel. I struggle into my wet boots and jacket and cross the courtyard to the byre, flinching at the biting cold and dismissing thoughts of Austin and that relentless sunshine. I was never going to live there, whatever Marco said. I push open the door fearing the worst, but all is clean and orderly, like the stacks in a small provincial library. I look more closely. A large provincial library. From floor to rafters the shelves cover all four walls, leaving just enough space for the wide barn doors in the east wall and two sash windows in the west. Ten feet up, accessed by two ladders, a wooden platform runs around the higher shelves. The remaining *Compendium* notebooks are on the middle shelves of the north wall, 176 of them, almost five feet of faded spines; 14,000 pages, maybe five million more words, demanding my attention.

I pick out an armful, put them in my bag and turn to a low shelf, double height for reference books, on the west wall: *Collins Encyclopaedia of Scotland*; Elspeth MacLeod's *Illustrated Encyclopaedia of Scotland*; *The Covenanter Encyclopaedia*; the Royal Scottish Geographical Society's *Encylopaedia of Scottish Places and Landscape*. A small white label is fixed to each spine and on it, handwritten in black ink, is a number – 032, 032.1, 032.2. The Dewey Decimal Library Classification System. McWatt was nothing if not thorough. And a man of his time. I did a semester at the Center for Dewey Studies in Carbondale, Illinois – where I met Alma, a fellow Scot, who went on to become my editor at Aikenhead Press and is now editor-in-chief at Thackeray – and, though a detailed understanding of the system is as useful now to the modern archivist as is a facility with horses to the average city cab driver, I've always taken a nerdish pleasure in matching category to number.

Inevitably, poetry is the largest section in McWatt's library, taking up the remainder of the wall, all the way up to the rafters. I choose a shelf at random. There is a copy of Quiller-Couch's *Oxford Book of English Verse*, one of *Palgrave's Golden Treasury*, a *Penguin Book of Contemporary Verse*, a *Norton Anthology of English Literature* and a *Faber Book of Modern Verse*. The first, a former public library book, stamped 'withdrawn' on the date slip, has a split spine and signs of insect infestation; the *Palgrave's*, also second-hand, some English kid's discarded school prize, has detached boards and evidence of mould growth; the pages of the paperback Penguin are brown and frilled, as are the pages of the Norton; while the Faber, apparently acquired new around 1965, the date of publication, is in comparatively good condition with only a slight UV discoloration of the jacket. All are identified by a sticker numbered 821 (English Poetry). These are thrift-store and *bouquiniste* finds, bought for cents, and some are in such poor condition they'll defeat the most skilled conservationist. There's nothing here of antiquarian value; the library's true worth is as a guide to McWatt's creative life. There's plenty to investigate, but not now. I have the tides to think of.

I lock up again and run back to the house, shivering. Austin was never an option, though I did seriously toy with the idea of Oklahoma, specifically the Gilcrease Museum in Tulsa. As in Austin, the temperature there right now would be in the high eighties. Agnes would have loved all the Old West and Native American collections, and Tulsa's comparative proximity to Austin might have worked too, in terms of Marco's access to Agnes. But in the end I lost my nerve. Tulsa, home of the evangelical Christian Oral Roberts University, was never going to be our kind of town, though the accommodation would have been less primitive and the climate, and probably the welcome, would have been more congenial than in Fascaray.

Here, even the dead are against me. McWatt seems to have taken up residence in my brain and is constantly denouncing me as a fraud. Okay, I silently tell him – closing up his drawers, bundling the notebooks into a box and his papers into my backpack – my accent may be transatlantic and my tastes and experiences may be bourgeois-cosmopolitan. But I'm as Scottish as you are. Or were.

I close up the house, clamber onto the quad bike and make my way back to Finnverinnity through the implacable rain. Yes. What could have been. And then there was my relationship with Marco. The biggest Could Have Been of all. I might have hacked it after all as a 'trailing spouse', an academic's contented partner in Austin, swimming in Barton Springs, jogging round Lady Bird Lake, enjoying the music scene, though not necessarily the musicians – my dalliance with Pascal inoculated me against that special brand of folly. As for Marco, I could have been a little more French about it all, overlooked his indiscretion and moved on. And would our little girl, gamely coping with her new life as the child of a single parent marooned on a patch of damp peat floating in the North Sea, be more deeply secure if I'd capitulated? Instead, I tried to get even, with near-fatal results.

I've bored my friends beyond endurance on the subject of my failed relationship. Now I'm beginning to bore myself. This ancient mariner needs to find another subject. It might as well be Grigor McWatt.

The Rhame o the Aunceant Taury

The Sun nou rase onwith the richt
Oot o the sea cam he,
Still dernt in haar, an on the caur
Ganged doon intae the sea.

An the guid sooth wind still huffed ahint
But nae douce bird did follae,
Nor onie day for scran or play
Cam tae the taury's hollae!

An Ah hae done a hellish thing,
An it would dunt them raw:
For aw averred, Ah killt the bird
That made the souch tae blaw.
Ah gowk! said they, the bird tae slay
That made the souch tae blaw!

Grigor McWatt, efter Samuel Taylor Coleridge, 1947[2]

---

2   From *Kenspeckelt*, Virr Press, 1959. Reprinted in *Warld in a Gless: The Collected Varse of Grigor McWatt*, Smeddum Beuks, 1992.

16 September 2014

Agnes was never a complainer, though she occasionally asked, after she'd spent time with certain of her friends in Brooklyn, 'Mom, why are you being so posh?' She knows the story. It's not my fault. I'm under no illusion that a tendency to pronounce words as if impersonating a minor member of English royalty will impress my daughter's friends. Still, Agnes is mortified. Posh does not go down well in some Brooklyn circles. 'Courtney says you talk like you're Mary Poppins or something,' she told me. Posh does not go down well in Fascaradian circles either.

English, or my own buffed-up version of Canadian English, was not my first language, though if you heard me speak you might find this hard to believe. My mid-Atlantic accent is essentially a North American version of old-guard BBC, upper received pronunciation, that outmoded signifier of a top-tier private school, Ivy League education and a trust fund, none of which I possess.

Honed in compulsory elocution classes in St Maria Goretti's and polished out of all recognition by my scholarship year in Oxfordshire, my voice suggests 'the love child of Katharine Hepburn and Alastair Cooke', Marco would say in the days when he liked me; 'the bastard offspring of Princess Anne and Gore Vidal', he would say more recently, when he didn't.

My 'a's – if I don't watch it – are long, I take a baaarth rather than a bath, every consonant is pronounced, and the endings of my words are, despite my best efforts, ringingly enunciated. But, though I can almost pass as posh among North Americans susceptible to a notion of Old World *noblesse* (useful in job interviews and when meeting museum donors and corporate sponsors), I've never been able to shake off the feeling that I'm an impostor and that any minute I'll be unmasked – pronounced, that is, with careful deliberation, as *unmaaarsked.*

I swear Margaret Mackenzie smirked at me in the shop this morning when I bought some groceries.

145

'I can *do* Scots, if you'd prefer, ya cheeky besom,' I felt like hissing in my broadest Glaswegian, which can come out when I've had too much to drink. Or when I'm angry. But I've only been here a month; too early to be making scenes or enemies. All in good time.

The Herkeners

'Is there aebdy there?' speired the Traiveler,
Chappin on the muinlit door;
An his cuddie ramshed the gress
O the forest's ferny floor;
An a birdie flew oot the turret,
Abuin the Traiveler's heid:
An he knyped oan the door agane a seicont time;
'Is there aebdy there?' he said.
But naebdy cam doon tae the Traiveler;
Nae heid frae the leaf-fringed sill
Hinged owr an keeked intae his grey een,
Where he stuid kittelt an still . . .

Grigor McWatt, efter Walter de la Mare, 1947[3]

3   From *Kenspeckelt*, Virr Press, 1959. Reprinted in *Warld in a Gless: The Collected Varse of Grigor McWatt*, Smeddum Beuks, 1992.

THE FORWARD-THINKING EDITOR OF THE *AUCHWINNIE PIBROCH*, Roy Fraser, visiting Fascaray in the late 1940s for a fishing weekend, overheard McWatt perorating in the Finnverinnity Inn on the historical and cultural case for Scottish independence. Fraser spotted the poet's potential as a lively contrarian and signed him to write a weekly column for the paper. The fee the *Pibroch* paid for 'Frae Mambeag Brae', as the column was called, was small, even by the standards of the day, but to the impoverished poet, subsistence crofter, beachcomber and occasional fisherman, two decades before his song royalties began to roll in, the column provided a significant and regular boost to his income.

Remarkably, he continued to write for the *Pibroch* for the next sixty-six years, seeing off nine editors and three proprietors, until a month before his death in 2014. The columns reflected the preoccupations of *The Fascaray Compendium*, with subjects ranging from politics and history (local and national), poetry and the natural world, to island life, customs and lore, as well as accounts of the latest mishaps in his menagerie and the antics of his sheepdogs (he went through them, like his editors, at a rate) and, above all, even in his lightest columns, making the case for the singularity and supremacy of Scottish culture.

In June 1947, McWatt achieved a degree of national attention in Scotland when he used his column in the *Auchwinnie Pibroch* to lambast the film adaptation of A. J. Cronin's bestselling novel *The Green Years*[4], and, by extension, to condemn the entire *oeuvre* of the much-loved, internationally successful Scottish novelist.

'It takes a good deal to get me out to the pictures,' wrote McWatt, 'particularly when, as last month, the seasonal gales make any crossing to the mainland cinema from my island home unpleasant, if not hazardous.'

The big screen offered no solace.

'The most mawkish, preposterous and unrecognisable picture of

4   Published by Gollancz, 1944. Film adaptation, directed by Victor Saville and
    starring Charles Coburn and Gladys Cooper, 1946.

our native land and its inhabitants was presented in 127 excruciating minutes,' he wrote.

It wasn't just the simplicity of the plot he objected to but the phoney accents of the Anglo-American cast – 'loch pronounced as "lok"; dance, which as every Scot knows rhymes with ants, is rendered "dawnce"; bonny is given an unintended echo of the charnel house when it is delivered as "boney"; banks become "benks"; and so we are given that iconic Scottish setting and song – The Boney Benks of Lok Loamin,' he continued.

The only pronunciation they got right, he maintained, was of 'aye', which, 'once they crack it and realise it rhymes with the Isle of Skye rather than Mandalay, or Fascaray, is hard to get wrong. But fired by their success, they cram it into every sentence, at the expense of sense, and give the impression rather of excitable Mexican rancheros than natives of proud Scotia.'

If you were seeking something to say in favour of the film, McWatt argued, 'you could acknowledge that it is faithful to the book – the one as bad as the other – and there is consistency in that the dour and foolish characters on both page and screen bear as much resemblance to a true Scot as does that preening Englishman Laurence Olivier to your correspondent.

'It is bad enough that the Hollywood panjandrums get us so wrong, and care so little about us that they make no attempt to get us right, but the real criminal in this enterprise is Cronin, one of the highest paid authors in the English-speaking world, who has presented this abominably lightweight and false image of his own country. By the time the travesty drew to a merciful close, I left the cinema in a rage. If I had happened to meet any Hollywood film magnates or highly paid authors that night, I could not have accounted for my actions.'

News of McWatt's sustained insult travelled as far south as Glasgow, where the *Sunday Post* newspaper reprinted half of it word for word – without paying him a penny, he noted bitterly – and mounted a feeble defence of Cronin.

'Heart-warming stories for hard times,' wrote the *Post*'s columnist Francis Gay. 'Only a nipscart would be unmoved by Cronin's inspiring prose.'

The controversy earned McWatt a reputation as a professional curmudgeon on matters Caledonian – a reputation he gleefully accepted – and soon he was receiving invitations to Glasgow (travel expenses included) to take part in BBC Scotland arts programmes.

He was born, he said, to be 'a proud Berserker in the manner of the ancient Viking heroes, visiting wrath, or *riastral*, upon the enemy – in my case Anglocentric philistinism – with no quarter given'.

It was at the BBC studio in Queen Margaret Drive that he first met Christopher Grieve, better known as the poet Hugh MacDiarmid, and over a stiffener in the hospitality room, a friendship was ignited that would place Grigor McWatt at the heart of what later became known as the New Wave of the Scottish Cultural Renaissance.

A Granite Ballad – The Reimagining of Grigor McWatt,
Mhairi McPhail (Thackeray College Press, 2016)

150

Oan First Keekin intae MacDiarmid's Thistle

Muckle stravaiged Ah i the realms o gowd,
An mauny guidly states an kinricks keeked,
Roon mauny westlin islands hae Ah bin,
Which makars leal tae Apollo haud.
Aft o wan braid expaunse whaur Ah'd bin tellt,
That deep-brou'd Homer ringed as his ane glebe,
Yet did Ah niver braithe its purest saucht,
Tae Ah read MacDiarmid scrievin in fu flaucht;
Syne Ah felt some leuker o the skies
Whan a new starnie gleeks intae his ken;
Or like creesh Cortez whan wi aigle een,
He gowped at the Pacific — an aw his men
Leuked at each ither wi a camsteirie ween —
Lownin, upby a tap in Darien.

Grigor McWatt, efter John Keats, 1948[5]

5   From *Kenspeckelt*, Virr Press, 1959. Reprinted in *Warld in a Gless: The Collected Varse of Grigor McWatt*, Smeddum Beuks, 1992.

IN ADDITION TO A STEADY INCOME, McWATT'S COLUMN IN THE *Auchwinnie Pibroch* provided him with a larger and more engaged audience than was ever available at the Finnverinnity Inn. Throughout the late 1940s he wrote passionately in support of the ill-fated Covenant petition for a devolved Scottish Parliament and in 1949 he reached an even wider audience when he used his column to condemn a speech given at the Auchwinnie Academy prize-giving by the regional director of education, Harry Elliott, who had called for the elimination of Scots 'dialect' in schools arguing that it 'handicaps its speakers, is not pretty and its literature is small'.

'They have robbed us of the Gaelic, these Uncle Tams,' wrote McWatt in 'Frae Mambeag Brae' (the *Pibroch* column was reprinted later in the *Scotsman*), 'and now they wish to rob us of our other ancient, robust and poetic tongue and to deny us our great tradition of Dunbar, Barbour and Fergusson. Well, I have a good Scots saying for Mr Elliott – "Shut yer geggie, ye wee nyaff, an awa an bile yer heid."'

McWatt also expressed support for the Reverend Paterson, whose recent scathing pulpit attack in Finnverinnity kirk on the Duke of Edinburgh, young husband of the English Princess Elizabeth, for playing polo on a Sunday made it to the front page of one London paper. 'I am not, myself, strictly a sabbatarian,' wrote McWatt, 'but I am a republican, and any attack on these idle foreigners who claim our land as their fiefdom is welcome for whatever reason, from whichever quarter.' Less controversially, he wrote about the excavation of the Neolithic chambered tomb at Heuchaw, the pleasures and perils of mushroom foraging, and the seasonal invasion of compass jellyfish on Calasay's beaches. The income from his column allowed him the luxury of more frequent journeys to the mainland. He would catch a morning boat for day trips to Auchwinnie to meet the *Pibroch*'s editor, Roy Fraser, at the Fisher's Airms pub, and his friend Andrew McMillan, who ran the Auchwinnie Press printworks, which in 1959, under the imprint Virr Press (later Smeddum Beuks), would begin its long professional association with McWatt by printing *Kenspeckelt*, the first of the poet's five volumes of self-published verse.

McWatt would also watch the occasional matinee at the Auchwinnie Astoria and visit the local Carnegie Library, a two-storey building of pink Corsehill sandstone, built in 1905 in the beaux arts style. These days the library is closed, apart from the small reference section at the back where the local archives are stored. The rest of the semi-derelict building houses a thrift store and a food bank for the region's poor. But even in its well-funded mid-century years – backed by a civic-minded local authority that believed books were a route to self-improvement, supported by church elders who, though their own reading needs were entirely met by the Scriptures, endorsed a secular 'house of books' as an alternative to inn and sin – Auchwinnie Carnegie Library could never rival McWatt's own collection of Scottish literature, history and verse.

Four or five times a year in the late forties and early fifties, Murdo 'The Fiddle' McIntyre, who lived in heroic squalor in Doonmara, would move into An Tobar for a week to take care of the animals, allowing McWatt to travel further afield, to Glasgow for occasional TV or radio appearances but more usually to Edinburgh. The poet would not be drawn on the details of his visits to the capital.

'Twa things you couldnae ask Grigor,' said Effie MacLeod. '"Gie us a sang." And "How wis Embra? Nice wee break?" . . . That's three things, ken.'

He refused all invitations to England. The Poetry Society in London made several overtures and only once did he appear to waver, when in October 1948 he received an invitation from Muriel Spark, then the society's general secretary and editor of its *Poetry Review*.

'I might be persuaded to meet you, Miss Spark, in your native Edinburgh and give a reading there. But London? Never!'

According to Knox-Cardew, McWatt 'always maintained that his inspiration, the well-spring of his art, was his love of Scotland, and of Fascaray in particular, but some have argued that it was his hatred of England – like his friend MacDiarmid, he cited 'Anglophobia' as his hobby – that was the greater passion'.

A Granite Ballad – The Reimagining of Grigor McWatt,
Mhairi McPhail (Thackeray College Press, 2016)

The Stone of Scone, also known as the Stone of Destiny or, to give it its correct Gaelic name, the Clach Sgian, is the ancient coronation stone of the kings of Scotland. It was given to our people by Fergus Mòr Mac Earca of Dalriada in the fifth century. Seven centuries later, in 1296, it was stolen from us by the thuggish English warlord Edward I, who had anointed John Balliol, a Frenchman with estates in England, Scotland and France, as a puppet King of Scotland.

It was this same Edward, who rejoiced in the designation *Scottorum malleus* (hammer of the Scots), who had recently demonstrated his strength and moral courage by expelling England's Jews and confiscating their property to finance his acquisitive ambitions. Having equipped a large and barbarous army, Edward swept into Wales. This brutal invasion was a mild warm-up for his adventures in Scotland, where the marionette King John surrendered without a fight and Edward's progress was merciless; he sacked towns, massacred inhabitants, razed castles to the ground and slaughtered the Scottish army with his superior forces until two thousand Scots nobles and landowners, including my own shamefully pusillanimous forebear Dougal McWatt of Fascaray, were compelled to gather in Berwick and sign the 'Ragman Rolls', a document acknowledging Edward as their king. The tyrant appointed an English viceroy to rule us, English officials to run our administration and left English soldiers garrisoned in our towns. The theft of the Clach Sgian was the final indignity.

The measure of the man, Edward, of his sneering coarseness, can be seen in his parting remark as his henchmen conveyed the sacred slab of red sandstone southwards. '*Bon bosoigne fait qy de merde se deliver.*' That he spoke in Norman French does not lessen the insult. The most polite English translation would be 'to divest oneself of faeces is a good thing'. And what did he do with this self-described manure? Why, he took it to Westminster, put it under his throne and sat on it.

Centuries later, there it remains, warming the posteriors of English monarchs who still lay egregious claim to Scotland's land and Scotland's people.

Grigor McWatt, May 1950, Auchwinnie Pibroch[6]

6   Reprinted in *Frae Mambeag Brae: Selected Columns and Essays of Grigor McWatt*, Stravaigin Press, 1985.

18 September 2014

Outside, Glasgow is *en fête*. Flag-waving crowds mingle in the sunshine as a bagpiper, red-bearded, wearing T-shirt, kilt and hiking boots, tunes up – long, ominous drone followed by penetrating squeal – then blasts into 'Scotland the Brave'. Inside, this cool glade of improbably tall, skinny chairs is hushed and decorous, a shrine to Charles Rennie Mackintosh, Scotland's foremost architect and designer, if your taste runs to art nouveau, *japonisme* and improbably tall, skinny chairs.

Dolina McPartland's insistence that the only day she is available for an interview is Referendum Day, when all of Scotland has been granted a holiday, suggests that she is a 'No' supporter; while the affirmative tendency make merry outside, for her it's business as usual. She pours her tea and glances out of the window at the good-humoured throng below. Excited children, faces painted blue and white, hold blue balloons and wave small Saltire flags while their parents carry banners declaring 'Yes!'. Agnes, staying with Johanna and Ailsa while I'm away, would have loved this. Dolina McPartland, née Hogg, shakes her head, tuts – confirming my hunch about her sympathies – and turns her sceptical eye across the narrow table to me.

She is a neat elderly woman in unseasonal lilac tweeds pinned at the lapel with a brooch of silver, amethyst and white fur – a rabbit's foot. Agnes would be scandalised. I strain to see a trace of the Flooer o Rose Street in Dolina's small, crimped face but the Lilias I'm hoping to glimpse in her sister is the sensuous laughing girl caught in a single photograph in one moment of happiness fifty years ago, before her heart was broken and chaos took its toll. Of course Dolina doesn't look like Lilias. Even Lilias didn't look like Lilias for long.

*

'I've strong views on the man, as you can imagine. He was a fraud. All bluster and bombast. His poetry? I wouldn't give you a penny for it. Doggerel as far as I can see. But that's not the point. He could have been Robert Burns for all I care. He destroyed my sister's life. That's all that concerns me. I've been badgered by the press and by that puffed-up American biographer to speak about McWatt countless times. I wanted nothing to do with it. They printed lies, painting my sister as a nymphomaniac, an alcoholic, a hopeless hanger-on, an autograph-hunter with a father fixation and a daft passion for anyone calling himself a poet. But Lilias, for all her shortcomings, was far more than that, before and after she knew McWatt.'

'. . . Don't push me. I've agreed to this conversation under duress. I don't have long left myself now and it seems this is the only way of restoring my sister's name. But if for a moment you try my patience, it's over. You understand? . . .'

'. . . The feminist perspective? The feminists have been every bit as bad as the other sort. Sometimes worse. Instead of presenting Lilias as a victim of her inadequacies, a dipsomaniac fall-girl whose life was a cautionary tale against the evils of drink and unseemly ambition, they make her out to be some sort of martyr-for-the-cause. But she wasn't "oppressed by the male sex". It was one man who did for her and one man alone. Your precious poet, McWatt . . .'

'. . . No. We weren't what you'd call firm friends throughout our childhood, Lilias and me. Sisters – siblings – rarely are. She was too wild for my taste. I was always the cautious one, obeyed my parents, applied myself to schoolwork. She was cleverer than me but hated any kind of confinement. She was keen to provoke and explore. She led me into trouble more than once. And usually ensured that I got the blame. But when you get older you see things more clearly. She was an innocent too, hungry for life, for experience, and for love.'

'. . . She could have done anything. She wrote beautifully – you've seen her letters. She was gifted. She tried her hand at poetry and, though I'm no expert I can tell you her poems were every bit as good, if not better, than anything McWatt ever wrote. She'd a beautiful singing voice and a sharp wit. She also had the makings of a successful painter, according to people who know about these things. If only she'd applied herself. But she never applied herself to anything, except her doomed love for an unworthy man who was incapable of returning any affection. She was a romantic soul and he saw that and preyed on her. He led her on.'

'What drew him to her? I'm more interested in the other question: what on earth did she see in him? She was seventeen, for goodness' sake! Half his age. They'd call it child abuse now. I know he wasn't the only "poet" in her life – that whole shower in Rose Street took advantage of her, saw her as an adornment, a bauble, and delighted in her for a moment then cast her aside when her lustre faded. But McWatt, from the safe distance of his precious island, played her, and his other women too, I'm sure, like a fisherman reeling in a salmon. And how he reeled her in. Then he left her floundering on the bank and walked away.

'He would flatter her and make promises, then there would be months of unexplained silence. Maybe his distance played a part in her yearning. The others – all the self-important poets – fell for her, one by one, in their different ways. But McWatt was always just beyond her reach. She could never have him, and the more she realised this, the more she wanted him. She became convinced he was The One, that the pain she felt was a kind of transcendent love. She thought his meanness and elusiveness were the signs of great genius and the torments of a soul too sensitive for this world, a soul that could only be healed with the balm of her love.

'And then there was the final blow. The other woman, Jean. Lilias's rival. The discovery of this other woman's existence, of his parallel affair, was really a death blow to Lilias. She chastised herself as a fool and felt she'd been the dupe in a long, bigamous marriage. This Jean assumed a mythical power in Lilias's mind. From the skewed perspective of her misery, my sister exalted the other woman and debased herself further.

'You say your Heritage Centre will preserve McWatt's legacy? Well, here's his legacy – lies, treachery, a promising young life destroyed, and all the grief and guilt I feel for failing to save my sister. Grief and guilt I will take to the grave. Put that in a display case in your museum.'

attery – stormy, bitterly cold wind

bensill – violent storm

blaud – buffeted by wind

blenter – wild, gusty wind

blowdir – sudden blast of wind

bluister – squally, violent wind

dreeffle – a sudden, brief gale

dyster – a stormy wind blowing in from the sea

flaff – a puff or gust of wind

gandiegow – a squally wind, usually accompanied by rain

gousterous – dark and blustery

gowl – howling wind

grashloch – wild, blustery storm

grumlie – unsettled, blustery

gyndagooster – a sudden, sweeping storm

hash – a strong wind usually accompanied by rain

jauchelt – tossed about in high winds

katrisper – extremely strong gale

kav – stormy winds throwing up sea spray or spindrift

nizzer – wild, blustery blizzard

peuch – a light puff of wind

reeshle – whistling wind

snirl – bitter wind

souch – soft sound of wind

spindrift – sea spray swept by violent winds (Scots word now in general use)

teuch – rough and windy

ventulacioun – air current

winwersht – low spirits brought about by constant buffeting of wind

Grigor McWatt, 1951, *The Fascaray Compendium*

19 September 2014

Yesterday Glasgow was a carnival. Today it's a funeral. I cross George Square from my hotel, weaving through groups of stricken kids wrapped in flags. They hug each other or squat on the tarmac, silent as the statues around them: of the Scots – Robert Burns, James Watt and Walter Scott – and of the non-Scots – Gladstone, Prince Albert, and an equestrian Queen Victoria, whose raised sceptre and haughty stone features seem to carry an extra charge of triumphalism.

Two pretty student girls, Saltires painted on their cheeks, carry a home-made placard – 'We Will Not Bow Down' – and pose for photographers hunting images for press post-mortems on the referendum and tourists snapping the zeitgeist for Facebook posts. There are a few morning drunks on a Braveheart binge, topping up from the night before, political defeat lending a heroic quality to their drinking. Outbreaks of defiant singing rally the crowd; 'Flower of Scotland', that woozy lament, 'Freedom's Road' and 'Caledonia'. Yesterday's bagpiper is here, still shrilly asserting Scotland's bravery.

I'm meeting Ailish nearby in the merchant quarter of the city, where imposing eighteenth-century sandstone warehouses that once sheltered bales of slave-grown tobacco, sugar and tea have been turned into imposing sandstone malls selling bespoke toiletries, designer clothing, and cups of coffee costing the annual income of an eighteenth-century merchant's footman.

Ailish is a sharp, chillingly earnest brunette who exudes brisk disdain – for McWatt, 'he's not exactly Yeats'; for Lilias, 'she was her own worst enemy'; for the Scots, 'they don't have the gumption to have a decent Rising. They're way too fastidious', and, I sense, for me.

But she is doing the work the Auchwinnie Board is paying her for: tracking down documents, digging out recordings of McWatt's songs and attempting to trace anyone still living who might have something illuminating to say about the Bard of Fascaray. So long as she is doing her job, that's fine. I don't have to like her, or she me.

Tentatively, for I know I've already lost the battle, I raise the subject of her transcription of my interview with Effie MacLeod. I don't want her neutering any more Scots-language material. I cite the support for our project from the Scots Leid society. She is unrepentant.

'It's all daft,' she says. 'There's no Scots Leid, or language, or whatever they want to call it, except maybe Gaelic, which is derived from Irish anyway and is spoken by one per cent of the population.'

I'm taken aback by her hostility.

'Well, that wasn't Grigor McWatt's view,' I say.

She doesn't ease off.

'All this language pretence is pure politics. There are about four Scots dialects and ten subdialects, and they're all variants of English with a bit of Norse thown in.'

'That's not the view of the Scottish government either,' I offer weakly, thrown by her aggression.

'Of course not. It's not in their interest, is it? We've got the same thing in Northern Ireland with Ulster Scots. All that "hamely tongue" Ullans bull. If you can say you're a minority language, there's European Union money in it.'

'Well, maybe there is,' I say, counting out coins to tip the waiter. 'And maybe some of that money's paying our wages. So let's try for a more positive attitude?'

Making my way to catch the train north I recross George Square. There's a sudden jostling as a group of skinheads – ruder elements of the 'No' campaign, one holding a Union Jack aloft – run jeering through the dispirited band of 'Yes' supporters. Skirmishes break out and I dodge through the traffic to watch from the safe distance of North Hanover Street as the police arrive. Good thing I didn't bring Agnes, I tell myself.

The crowd thins and peace is restored swiftly. The only real damage inflicted seems to be on the dignity of City Chambers, whose grand Italianate facade has been sprayed with graffiti reading: 'Obey Your Queen'. Mourning resumes. The bagpiper starts up again and, under the monument of Walter Scott, a young guitarist strums and begins to sing in a high, nasal whine. The two girls with painted cheeks stand next to him, their arms around each other, their placard at their feet, swaying gently as they sing the chorus.

> *Hee-ra-haw, boys,*
> *We're awa, boys,*
> *Gangin hame*
> *Tae Fascaray.*

TOWARDS THE END OF HIS FIRST DECADE ON THE ISLAND, ONE of McWatt's mysterious jaunts to the mainland coincided with the disappearance of the Stone of Scone – the traditional coronation stone of the ancient kings of Scotland – which was removed on Christmas Day 1950, from beneath the English throne in Westminster Abbey, London.

After news broke of the theft (or 'restitution of the monumental soul of Scotland', as McWatt brazenly described it in the *Auchwinnie Pibroch*) five beefy men from London in dun overcoats and trilby hats arrived on the ferry. They spent a good deal of money in the inn, where an attentive Rab McNab also furnished several rounds of drinks 'oan the hoose' in an unprecedented display of generosity. This gave young Jamie MacDonald, earning pocket money working as a 'pot boy', enough time to borrow Shuggie the Post's bike and get over to Calasay to warn the poet that the polis were on their way.

The men in trilbies didn't suspect a thing, and after dispatching three bottles of malt and a number of Scotch eggs, they persuaded Tam Macpherson to drive them up to McWatt's croft on a trailer hitched to his tractor. It was no one's fault that the tides were against them and that, once the trailer got stuck in the mud on the Calasay Strand, the five Special Branch officers had to dismount and walk in their city shoes through sea, sand and bog all the way back to Balnasaig Farm, where they spent the night in the silage byre on a bale of straw.

In the morning, once the tide was in their favour and they finally reached An Tobar, the officers' interrogation techniques were said to have been compromised by the previous night's ordeal. They left the island in a hurry – Rab McNab waved them off from the pier with a cheery 'Haste ye back!' – and no charges were ever brought.

When questioned on the subject in the inn, McWatt would give an enigmatic smile, shake his head and draw deeply from his glass. In his column for the *Pibroch* the following week, he cited Lord Byron's condemnation of Lord Elgin's theft of the Parthenon marbles: 'In *Childe*

Harold's Pilgrimage, the Aberdonian poet Byron laments that the antiquities of Greece had been "defac'd by British hands"', wrote McWatt. 'For Greece, read Scotland, for British, read English.'[7]

The Stone of Scone was found at Arbroath Abbey the following April and four Glasgow university students were identified as the culprits. McWatt was finally in the clear as far as the authorities were concerned. For some Fascaradians, however, the island's eccentric poet had as good as lifted the Stone himself. He never contradicted them.

A Granite Ballad – The Reimagining of Grigor McWatt,
Mhairi McPhail (Thackeray College Press, 2016)

7   *Auchwinnie Pibroch*, 17 March 1951. Reprinted in *Frae Mambeag Brae: Selected Columns and Essays of Grigor McWatt*, Stravaigin Press, 1985.

ask – sky covered with grey clouds or haze; slight rain

domra – veil of clouds; obscuring fog or mist

fowg – variant of fog

gloor – faint sunshine through haze or rift in clouds

gum – haze; mist; fine film of moisture or condensation

haar – cold mist

halgh – spume; mist; sea spray

ime – condensation; rising vapour

Neptune's uouue – fog

ramfeezle – obfuscation

reik – column of cloud

rouk – sea fog; mist with the appearance of smoke emanating from the earth

scowman – gloomy appearance or haze

shokk – mist; drizzle

stim – haze; mist; film on glass

Grigor McWatt, 1952, *The Fascaray Compendium*

Agnes has asked to stay up late. Tormented by guilt over my absences, mental as well as physical, I agree. She's set up her telescope at her bedroom window and insists on talking me through the constellations.

'The really brilliant thing, see, is that in Scotland, in this part of Scotland anyway, they've got the darkest skies in the whole of Europe. Super clear. No light pollution. No cities. No traffic. No malls. No nothing.'

'Mmm. Brilliant!' I say, without conviction.

I put my eye to the lens and feign excitement at the wobbling flashes of light skidding across the boundless dark. Agnes studies her star chart and points.

'So that one, the one with the long handle, is the Plough. It's spelled like "plowg-huh" but you say "plow". And that one, two stars up from the handle . . .'

She is her father's daughter in so many ways. When I first met Marco, I was taken by his random enthusiasms and weird passions – for 1930s comic books, bread-making, open-source software, tabletop ball games, English Romanticism, Czech pre-war advertising art, the Nordic harmonium repertoire, British radio comedy of the 1950s and astrophysics. He plays the spoons – that I ever found his hobo drum solos appealing now amazes me – and he knows everything there is to know about the ecology of plant epiphytes, the common and Latin names of wild flowers, English music-hall theatre and Bauhaus textile design. I suppose, for a while, I was just another of his random enthusiasms and weird passions. He made me laugh and lifted me up through my spells of what I guess was *Morbus Fascariensis*. It worked for a while.

One long night at a dinner with some of his sillier summer stock friends, after two hours of his stoned exposition on the subject of *The Goon Show*, I had my Titania moment; I stirred from sleep to find my handsome, clever, creative beau was a dim, braying ass.

His effusiveness, his fads and his odd, unnecessary expertise began to drive me crazy.

'Doesn't anything depress you?' I shouted at him one morning, after hearing him whistle – 'My Old Man Said Follow the Van' – in the bathroom. The fact that I recognised the tune made me even angrier. His useless knowledge was, after years of proximity, taking up valuable houseroom in my brain. It was like secondary smoking; exposure to this stuff, his stuff, was diminishing me.

We had argued through the previous night and now he was gazing in the mirror, his jaw a Santa's beard of shaving foam, pursing his lips and whistling. Whistling! – the mating call of the optimistic numbskull.

He looked hurt.

'Our relationship depresses me,' he volunteered finally.

Now we were getting somewhere.

He wiped his face and left the apartment. Possibly to pursue his latest enthusiasm – yoga.

I watched him go, his broad back in the faded green T-shirt with its contour map of sweat patches, the sandals, the low-slung cargo shorts. Shorts, for chrissakes. Where were we living? The beach? How old did he think he was? Now I even found his shorts offensive.

'And then in the south, which is that way – Mom? Are you listening? – in the south, when it's really dark, if you're really lucky, you can see the Milky Way.'

'Mmm . . .'

Odd to think that I foresook my *puer aeternus* for his younger brother. His figurative younger brother, that is. Marco doesn't have a younger brother. But if he ever required one and held auditions, Pascal would have been called back for a second interview. Younger brother, not twin. Pascal was a slender faun to Marco's chunky satyr, taciturn rather than effusive but with soulful eyes and the same dark hair, more plentiful in Pascal's case. The boy was talented, played slide guitar with an art-school band with a cult reputation in Williamsburg, and sang like an angel: an angel with a repeat prescription for antidepressants and what seemed to be a daily marijuana habit.

What did I care, or even notice at the start of our affair, if he'd barely read a book in his life, possessed no discernible sense of humour, spoke in banal epithets derived from some self-help huckster – about life forces, energies and spiritual connections – and his body of knowledge amounted to a few interesting chord shapes on the guitar and a degree of digital dexterity, plus a sketchy appreciation of indie fashion and an instinct for cool?

As I began to grasp the extent of Pascal's shallowness, I persuaded myself that it was a good thing, that he was an *enfant sauvage*, and that his unencumbered intellect was a restful sanctuary, a white-walled Zen temple offering welcome refuge from the clamorous cosmopolis of Marco's mind. The key to this self-persuasion was the sex, which was terrific – at the beginning. Added to the thrill of novelty, after years of fidelity, was the fieriest spice, the habanero chilli of revenge. The yoga teacher may have been usefully flexible but she was my age, if not older. I knew Marco, too, and three months into his affair with his yoga teacher, he began to show signs of disenchantment. I doubted whether he and Karmic Kate, a martyr to her food allergies, would be having as much fun in the sack as I was with my beautiful, smooth-skinned, limber, rock princeling. Pascal's surprisingly luxurious sublet – a white-glove luxury condo in a converted printworks in Tribeca with triple-aspect windows, ambient lighting, chef's kitchen (unused) and an assemblage of low, pale furniture – seemed a perfect stage set for an affair. What did I know? What does anyone know?

'And if you're real lucky you can see this thing where the sky kind of dances with coloured lights. It's called the aura boralis.'

'Aurora borealis. Northern Lights,' I say. That much I know. From Marco, of course.

Bonniest of lassies,

Despair I cannot thole. We will certainly meet soon for a quaich or two in the old haunt. I am caught up here with my duties – Roy has asked me to write an extra column this week for the Pibroch. Donald is sick – this younger generation, yourself included, seems to lack the robustness of my own – and I cannot leave the laddie to take care of the menagerie. Caesar, Luath's successor, is arthritic himself now and has to be coaxed into a walk, Bluebell the coo has mastitis, and Darnley and Mary the otters are, I fear, reverting to a feral state. But dinnae fash yersel. I'll be back in Rose Street soon enough.

Aye, Grigor

––––––––––––––

27c Jamaica Street
Edinburgh
18 July 1964

Oh, Grigor. 'Soon enough' is never soon enough for me.

Your Lilias

––––––––––––––

The weekend. Specifically, Agnes's weekend. I owe her. The wind is brisk and we're walking straight into it as we set off for our hike from the trail head by Dubh Lochan. I can barely hear Agnes's chatter – about school, about who said what and did which to whom – and my McWatt Walk pamphlet is almost wrenched from my hand by a sudden gust.

The weather is too wild for the picnic – English muffins with smoked salmon – I've optimistically brought in a backpack and, when the rain breaks, we seek shelter in one of the Slochd caves, marked on the Ordnance Survey map as Uamh a' Chlàrsair Chaillte, which the pamphlet tells us is the site of 'a famous supernatural occurrence'. I curb my sneer. Folklore sells. This is Agnes's day, I remind myself: I am leaving my work behind and doing something with my daughter. Whatever she wants. Does it make me a bad mother that I secretly rejoiced when, rather than asking to go see some Disney movie at the cinema on the mainland or spend the day in Auchwinnie's noisy, over-chlorinated pool, she asked to go for a walk? Here?

Ailsa McAllister had told her about the cave and this bad mother rejoiced again when she saw it was part of the McWatt Walk itinerary. I've been meaning to check it out. Either the Heritage Centre and Museum does something with this strand of the story – produces a 'Spirit Sightings' wall map, or some such nonsense aimed at the gullible Balnasaig tendency, as well as a better brochure, maps and nature trails for Sunday strollers and serious hikers – or we scrap it.

Our picnic is finished and packed away but, sitting on my waterproof, spread over a boulder in the gloom of the cave as the rain batters down outside, we're not ready to leave. I sense Agnes is disappointed. But she soon rallies.

'Tell me the story again,' she asks.

I take out the damp pamphlet and, using my flashlight, read it out once more.

'"Uamh a' Chlàrsair Chaillte, the Cave of the Disappearing Harpist, is said to be the site of an incident that took place there three hundred years ago. The harpist, playing a lament and finding the weather suddenly inclement,"' (when, I wonder, is it ever clement?) '"took shelter with his dog in this deep cleft in the rock. Still plucking away at his harp he wandered further into the labryinth of caves and was never seen again."' His dog, though, was said to have emerged a week later from a hollow at the mouth of the Cannioch all the way round the coast to the west. '"The animal's eyes were wide with fear, he was whimpering, and every hair had been singed from his body. It is said that if you stand by the blow-hole near Doonmara cliffs, you can hear the lament of the lost harpist drifting up from the chambered caves below."'

My daughter's teeth chatter in the moist chill of the cave; perfect conditions for incubating a chest infection.

'Suppose it was true,' she says. 'That the harper got lost. Who saw him go into the cave? He was alone with his dog. Did he go into the store or something and say "I'm just going to shelter in that cave"? And suppose he really did disappear. Couldn't he have just, like, drowned or something? And the dog could have got lost too and maybe missed his master and . . .'

She would love to be terrified by the story, just as she'd like to believe in fairies but, like her parents, she's a hard-boiled rationalist. (The 'Mystic Yoga' was an aberration in more ways than one, Marco assured me when he ditched Kate and came running back to me. Too bad I was otherwise occupied at the time.)

'I bet the dog wasn't really burned. Just frightened and hungry,' she adds. 'His fur might have fallen out because he hadn't eaten anything for days.'

She's a born sceptic, scorns tooth fairies and despises Easter Bunnies but, in a mutual conspiracy, we're both holding out for Santa Claus. I'm not sure who's indulging whom here. Our last Christmas – our last Christmas as a family – was, on the surface, an ur-Noel, as faithful a version of the twinkling midwinter ritual as any merry family feast orchestrated by Charles Dickens. Agnes was our sweet, heartbreakingly appreciative Tiny Tim, wishing 'God bless us every one'. Marco did his best, and so did I. Agnes, opening her stocking with exorbitant glee, declared: 'It wouldn't be Christmas without Santa.'

As we wait for the squall of rain outside to pass, she walks deeper into the cave's gloom. I switch on my flashlight again and follow her through a narrow passageway. She crouches in what looks like a grotto, sifting cautiously through the charred remains of a bonfire. She's also a born collector, whose indiscriminate urge to acquire worthless artefacts might, I sometimes worry, be an early sign of compulsive hoarding. Here, again, she is her father's daughter. Marco pays $200 a month for a storage unit in Long Island City to house his pinball machines (the Star Trek and Addams Family models), boxes of VHS cassettes, 78 rpm records by Paul Robeson, Sophie Tucker and Whispering Jack Smith, his father's collection of German beer steins and an array of chrome mid-century kitchen equipment. As a professional archivist and curator, I should be receptive to the impulse. Instead, I'm impatient with personal clutter, equating it with chronic sentimentality; forgivable in a child, perhaps, but in an adult an obvious case for cognitive behavioural therapy.

'Mom?'

In her cupped hands, Agnes holds a small piece of blackened driftwood.

'Can I take it home? Please?'

Her little face is radiant with delight and, though custom and practice should tell her otherwise, she expects me to share her pleasure in this filthy object.

'It's like a kind of fish,' she says. 'There are its eyes and those lumpy bits are its fins.'

I overcompensate – her collection, unlike Marco's, has not yet reached critical mass – and I lean in, shining the flashlight on her cupped hands. The shard of wood is about two inches long, notched, with a single hole at one end.

'Wow! Interesting!' I dissemble. 'Well, okay. As long as you wash your hands properly when you get in – Look! They're black! – and keep this thing well away from the kitchen.'

'Promise!' she says. 'I'll put it with my shells in the window.'

Her teeth are chattering again. It's time to go.

I ask her suddenly: 'Do you miss Brooklyn?'

She pauses, weighing up her reply. Agnes doesn't give glib answers.

'No,' she says finally. 'I don't miss Brooklyn . . . But I wish we still lived there.'

The rain has stopped and in our dark corridor of rock the sun unfurls a path of light at our feet. We walk back along it to the cave's mouth and, shielding our eyes from the glare, step into the sparkling landscape.

I ask Agnes what she wants to do now.

'I know, Mom! Let's go to the blowhole at Doonmara and listen out for the harper!'

Brek, Brek, Brek

Brek, brek, brek
On yer cauld grey stanes, och Sea!
An Ah wud that ma gab cuid mooth
The thochts that ris up in me.

Och, braw for the fisher's laddie
That he heuchs wi his sister at spiel!
Och, braw for the sailor loon,
That he sings in his scowe as weel.

An the byous ships gang on
Tae their hyne aneath the brae;
But och for the pap o a vainisht haun,
An the soond o a vyce that's awa.

Brek, brek, brek
At the fit o thy cleuch, O Sea:
But the neshie mense o a day that is deid,
Will niver come back tae me.

Grigor McWatt, efter Alfred, Lord Tennyson, 1948[8]

---

8   From *Kenspeckelt*, Virr Press, 1959. Reprinted in *Warld in a Gless: The Collected Varse of Grigor McWatt*, Smeddum Beuks, 1992.

Fascaray's vernacular domestic architecture is disappearing. Modern plumbing has yet to arrive – although it was the Scots who invented the flush toilet, it is taking an unconscionably long time for the people of Scotland to benefit from the contrivance. The *taigh beag*, little house – a dry toilet, or cludgie, in a lean-to shed – is an innovation considered by some islanders to be showy to the point of pretentiousness. But the windowless *taigh dubh* – with a corner pen for cattle, built on a slope so their *keech*, manure, slides out through a drainage channel – is now an endangered species.

The natives of Fascaray generally no longer share their blackhouses with their animals (though one *bodach* in Killiebrae, Wullie Maclean, brings in his heifer and keeps her behind a partition in his front room when she's about to calve, and a *cailleach* in Doonmara, Peigi MacEwan, once the island howdie, or midwife, still allows her hens to roost inside above her head on the rafters. 'They're company,' she explains.

Most lairds are too tight-fisted to shell out the cash to lift their tenants from picturesque medieval poverty (picturesque, as long as you are standing some distance, and upwind, from the hovels) to tidier 1950s penury. So the islanders do it themselves, with varying degrees of success and, understandably, little consideration for aesthetics or tradition. Aesthetics and tradition come at a price few here can afford. In the 'improved' blackhouses there are now glazed windows, though some crofters use cheaper polythene sheeting rather than glass; earthen floors have been concreted over; 'box bed' mattresses on frames have mostly replaced pallets of straw on the floor; and the turf roofs are gradually disappearing under sheets of rusting corrugated iron.

But some things will never change. There is still the peat fire – though now in a hearth at one end of the house discharging its smoke up a brick lum – there is the dresser, where the humble household crockery is displayed with pride, its patterns and glazes flickering in the light of the fire, and the *seise* bench against the wall where the visitor sits, tea and scone – a *strupag* – or whisky in hand, and listens, enthralled, to the stories of the house.

'*Fàilte. Tighinn ann.* Come you in . . .' is the invitation, unvarying and irresistible, from the island's oldest residents. Their stories told *aig cois an teine*, round the peat fire, are often of the supernatural – of kelpie waterhorses, of presentiments of storms and shipwrecks and terrifying apparitions of the inconsolable dead, of the omnipresent *sidhe* fairies, mostly benign, though with an inclination to mischief. No older Fascaradian goes for a walk in the woods without spotting the fairy rings – circles of stones, wild flowers, or mushrooms, or indentations in the soil – that prove the wee folk are busy and numerous in these parts.

Superstitions are commonplace, particularly in relation to fishing. A red-headed child encountered by a fisherman on his way to his boat spells disaster and the story goes that in Lusnaharra, the ginger-haired McKinnon children, all seven of them, are asked to stay indoors – 'ben the hoose' – when the men go out to fish. The devil, Auld Nick, also known as Black Donald of the Whids, or lies, is a regular visitor to the island and his maidservants, the witches, are ill-favoured spinsters or widows.

One old fisherman, Tearlach MacDonald of Killiebrae, told me that his father Lachlan had seen the local witch's black cat sneaking out of his chicken coop and had hurled a rock at it. Lachie was a good shot and hit the miscreant smack on the head. It crumpled to the ground with a piercing yowl then gathered itself up and slunk back across the field to his mistress's mean croft. The next day the witch, an unmarried woman of sour disposition, was seen around the clachan with a bandage on her head and a black eye.

It is not through the stories of kings and queens, battles and covenants, warriors and statesmen that we understand ourselves best but from folklore, the people's history, passed down by our ancestors, preserved and embellished by local storytellers, *seannachie* bards, enshrining in story and song the beliefs and customs that continue to shape us, define our sense of right and wrong, good and evil, sustain us through inevitable sorrows, lighten dark days with seditious humour and celebrate the numinous glory of the natural world around us. You can tell a country by its folklore. We have a living tradition of stories, music and song, *orain luaidh* waulking songs, weaving songs, fishing songs, ballads of love and lament, *puirt-à-beul* mouth music and the ceilidh. And the English? They have the Home Service, *The Archers*, cricket and morris dancing.

Grigor McWatt, 1952, *The Fascaray Compendium*

No childhood pictures of McWatt survive. In Knox-Cardew's book, the earliest photograph of the poet, the original of which is in the National Library in Edinburgh, is a studio portrait of an intense young man in his mid twenties whose inordinately high forehead, under an asymmetric pelt of black hair, seems to have been stretched by the burden of thought, and the features – the fierce eyes underscored even then by shadows, the surprisingly feminine nose, the pursed mouth – crowd towards his resolute chin. He is wearing a stiff suit (this is his pre-kilt era) with a silk tie and some kind of floral buttonhole – heather and harebell, at a guess – and his formal pose, one elbow uncomfortably crooked on a shelf or mantelpiece, is a photographer's cliché of the day intended to evoke manly self-possession. Instead he looks like an under-slept schoolboy playing dress-up in his father's clothes. Ninety-two pages later the poet is transformed into the familiar bad-tempered, pipe-smoking wraith in his sixties wearing beret and kilt.

Between these two poles of age, we have a photograph of McWatt in his early thirties, fully kilted by then but hatless, puffing at a pipe and glaring across the sea from the Calasay cliffs behind his croft. Ten years later, in 1962, he is in the same outfit, with the addition of the beret, addressing a political rally at Auchwinnie, where he stood, unsuccessfully, as Scottish National Party candidate for Westminster. By his side is a bashful young man in long shorts, holding a sheaf of papers. The caption identifies him as Donald MacInnes, then aged seventeen, McWatt's 'assistant' and leader of the party's local youth wing.

Young McInnes features again – photographed from above as he lies laughing on grass starred with daisies, wearing a kilt himself and a fisherman's jersey, playing with what looks like a strangely attenuated smooth-haired cat – Marty the pet pine marten, whose antics were the subject of some of McWatt's more homespun columns in the *Auchwinnie Pibroch*.

The teenager is also photographed standing solemnly with McWatt at the head of Loch Shiel on the Scottish mainland, framed by the hills of Sunart and Moidart, beneath the Glenfinnan Monument which marks the spot where Bonnie Prince Charlie raised his standard to claim his rightful kingship of Scotland and where, as McWatt wrote in *Forby*, one of the poet's ancestors, Alexander McWatt, served as piper to the prince.

The only photograph of Lilias Hogg in the chapter – the only photo of her unearthed so far – is faintly blurred, giving the impression of movement, of someone always on the run, evanescent and impossible to pin down. She has the minted prettiness of youth: bright eyes – the photographer's flash gives her a look of bedazzlement; pale unblemished skin; wide full lips; abundant curls and generous breasts. Attractive enough, though I wouldn't have had her down as the Muse that inspired a generation of poets. Her head is thrown back as she laughs at something or someone to the left of the photographer; I find it hard to believe that the joker is McWatt. There isn't much evidence so far that comedy was one of his strengths.

I may be wrong, as in so much else. There's the poet in another photograph with a wide vulpine smile, full pint in hand, with MacDiarmid and MacCaig, leaning against a bar – Menzies', the caption tells us. Above them on a wooden shelf, a long brass rail supports a row of bottles which glint festively. On the same page, McWatt, in his mid thirties, is photographed alone with MacDiarmid. Both are smoking pipes and grimacing at a tea trolley in the hospitality room of BBC Scotland's studios in Glasgow.

I mustn't be distracted. I should be looking for new material, not retreading the old. I put the book back on the shelves in the alcove.

'Mom?'

I turn to see Agnes holding out a small posy of yellow flowers, bright as a fistful of morning sun. Marco would have given us their Latin names, species and genus. So, it now occurs to me, would McWatt; he'd throw in the Scots and Gaelic names for them too. We find a vase and put them on the mantelpiece.

'There!' she says, head cocked, stepping back to appraise the vase, the room and me. 'That's better.'

bog cotton, cotton grass (*Eriophorum angustifolium*): known as mappie's fud. Food for butterflies. Used to dress wounds, stuff pillows and make wicks for candles. Ubiquitous by Beinn Mammor.

buttercup (*Ranunculus*): known as yellae gowan. Ubiquitous. Favours, like all Fascaradians, proximity to water.

butterwort (*Pinguicula vulgaris, Lentibulariaceae*): known as modalan, badan measgan and steep-gress. Used as a charm against witchcraft. Cattle that eat it are said to be immune from malevolent elvish arrows. It is also said to protect the bonniest bairns from kidnap by covetous fairies, who like to replace healthy infants with wan and sickly substitutes. Maggie MacGregor of Kilgurnock tells of a woman watching over a newborn baby in a croft in the clachan of Tilliecuddy who overheard the conversation of two passing *sidhe* at the window. One said: 'We will take it.' The other insisted that they could not because 'its mother partook of butter made from the milk of a cow that had eaten the badan measgan'.

common ling or heather (*Calluna vulgaris*): known as fraoch, or ling. Ubiquitous. Used for making brooms, creels, ropes and thatched roofs, etc. The staple diet of grouse. Cattle prefer the mion-fraoch – the young growth that emerges once the old growth has been burned. The green tops were once used to make heather ale, *mangan*, favoured by the Vikings (see the *Fascaringa Saga*).

gorse (*Ulex*): also known as broom and whin. Lemon-hued, coconut-scented, ubiquitous in the spring and, with the million-starred constellations of celandine, the tender primroses and the yellow crotal lichen – the poor man's saffron, used to dye woollen cloth – turns Fascaray into a shield of shimmering gold.

lady's bedstraw (*Galium verum*): a froth of yellow, honey-scented flowers in high summer. Grows in the machair of Lusnaharra and Calasay and on the grassy shore west of Finnverinnity harbour. Used as a dye for wool, to heal skin disorders, ease childbirth, stop bleeding and calm the troubled soul. A rare blue variety flowers in winter and is found on a ledge below Calasay cliffs.

lesser meadow rue (*Thalictrum minus*): known as ruebeag. Found in rocky outcrops in Killiebrae Glen. Tea made from its dried flowers is said to cure rheumatism.

marsh chickweed (*Stellaria palustris*): known as *fliodh-uisge mór*. Grows in puddles and pools and can be mistaken for watercress. Heated on stone it is used to cure festering wounds on hands or feet.

syme, meadow rue (*Thalictrum maritimum*): grows on the rocky shore east of Finnverinnity and beneath Doonmara cliffs. Flowers in August.

tansy (*Tanecetum vulgaris*): yellow flat-topped button-like flowers. Flowers late summer through to autumn. Ubiquitous. Aromatic, used as a strewing herb with southernwood (*Artemisia*: laddie's loue) on *taigh dubh* floors to make the house smell sweeter.

trefoil (*Lotus corniculatus*): known as triffle, cocks an hens, bairnie's baffs, birdie's fit. Cluster of yellow pea flowers, often with red streaks, pollinated by the 'common blue' butterfly and seen all over the island from April to September.

violet: not for us Wordsworth's solitary 'violet by a mossy stone / Half hidden from the eye!' In Fascaray, the sweet violet (*Viola odorata*), wild pansy (*Viola tricolor*), common dog violet (*Viola riviniana*) and bog violet (*Viola palustris*) – known locally as cuckoo-brogue (Gaelic *bròg na cuthaige*) – come mob-handed, turning our banks, braes and woodland into vivid, scented cerulean plains that dizzy the senses and reproach the grey spring skies.

wood anemone (*Anemone nemorosa*): known locally as jessamine.

yellow-flag iris (*Iris pseudacorus*): known as the seggie flooer. Flowers in June. Abundant in wet habitats and on shore-lines. Fringes Calasay Strand and Loch Aye.

Grigor McWatt, 1953, The Fascaray Compendium

IT'S CLEAR FROM THE CORRESPONDENCE WE HAVE, FROM HIS journal entries in the *Compendium* and his *Pibroch* columns, 'Frae Mambeag Brae', that McWatt was conscious of his place in history and of the political, as well as the literary, significance of his work.

In the early 1950s he joined the Scottish National Party, whose founders – in its earlier incarnation as the Nationalist Party of Scotland – had included his friend MacDiarmid. Whether or not McWatt had been directly involved in the 'reclamation' of the Stone of Scone, he openly and habitually engaged in nationalist-related acts of civil disobedience. All the stamps on the envelopes containing his twenty-two letters to Lilias Hogg are carefully fixed upside down – 'staunding the English Queen Lizzie heelster-heid' – an act of treason according to the English statute books. Between 1952 and 1954 he wrote three columns for the *Auchwinnie Pibroch*, as well as numerous letters to the *Scotsman*, the *Glasgow Herald* and the Aberdeen *Press and Journal*, protesting against the description of the new monarch as 'Queen Elizabeth II'.

'The English may have assented to the rule of two Lizzies, but we Scots have only suffered under the yoke of one. Call this yin by her rightful name, Queen Elizabeth I, until we dispose of English monarchs altogether,' he wrote in the *Pibroch* in June 1953, a week after the young Queen's coronation in Westminster.

In October that year, the old King George the Sixth, 'G VI R', red pillar box outside Finnverinnity post office was finally replaced with a modern version, bearing the Queen Elizabeth the Second, 'E II R', gold insignia. The following month, just before dawn on 30 November, the feast day of St Andrew, patron saint of Scotland, an explosion was heard across Fascaray. Men and women scrambled from their beds, dressed hastily and emerged dishevelled into the cold night air. Some thought buried munitions left behind by the SOE commandos were to blame. A few ex-servicemen, naval as well as army, fancied, as they struggled into wakefulness, that they were back fighting the Hun, the Japs or

Mussolini's Fascists in the darkest days of the war. Others assumed Mrs Wilma Paterson's newfangled cylinder gas cooker was the culprit.

In an entry in *The Fascaray Compendium*, McWatt described the scene.

It was Effie Morrison, running in curlers, dressing gown and slippers from her bedroom at the back of the shop, who first found the fragments of shrapnel flung by the force of the blast as far as the pier bench. She picked up a large triangular shard – red and black, vaguely familiar – and screamed as her fingers were burned by the heat. As she ran to the shore and knelt to immerse her hand in seawater, another figure emerged from the open door of the shop. It was Shuggie the Post, barefoot and bare-chested in long cotton drawers and, in the panic, heedless of the shocked stares of some villagers, who assumed he would be chastely in his single bed at his mother's house in Finnverinnity. Shuggie pointed at the charred and twisted stump that now stood in place of the old post box and sprinted to Effie's aid.

'Now who would do a daft and dangerous thing like that?' he asked, as he wrapped her hand in a bandage torn from his good work shirt.

They all had their suspicions, as did the police, and the talk on the island was of little else. Effie Morrison's brazen 'suppin o the kale afore the Grace' with Shuggie, which would, under normal circumstances, have animated island gossip for months, if not years, was forgotten as Fascaradians told and retold the story of the Finnverinnity Bomb.

There were rumours that the Scottish Republican Army were involved and McWatt, in what his critics denounced as an ill-judged, crowing column for the *Auchwinnie Pibroch*, seemed in no hurry to dissociate himself from the shadowy movement with alarming connections across the Irish Sea. For the second time in four years, Special Branch officers descended on the island and McWatt was questioned once more. Again, police could find no evidence for his involvement in the explosion. In his writing and in person, he always referred to it with unconcealed glee as 'an act of sedition', though he expressed regret about Effie's hand.

The replacement pillar box arrived three months later — until then residents had to bring their mail in person to Effie, who had recovered fully but, some felt, wore her bandages rather longer than was necessary. After the incident, Effie the Shop became known as Effie the Hand.

In his column in the *Auchwinnie Pibroch* in April 1954, McWatt reported that the new postbox bore the image of the Scottish Crown rather than the insignia of an English monarch.

'It is a small victory, but a victory nonetheless,' he wrote.

A Granite Ballad – The Reimagining of Grigor McWatt,
Mhairi McPhail (Thackeray College Press, 2016)

The 1707 Act of Union was a union in the sense that the slave's connection with his master is a partnership of equals. It was Darien that did for us. This pestilential strip of jungle and swamp on the isthmus of Central America now known as Panama, along with the perfidy of the English, the mischief of the Spanish and – let us finally acknowledge it – the justifiable resentment of the native Kuna Indians, was our undoing as a nation. It had started so promisingly – a wildfire of optimism had burned through Scotland, from the blackhouses and crofts of the Highlands and Islands to the satanic mills of the central belt. And once more our wee, o'erlooked island of Fascaray played a disproportionately large role in this story.

We should have known better; optimism was a phenomenon rarely observed north of Hadrian's Wall since the Battle of Bannockburn. Our seers and *seannachies* could have told us: it would not end well. And neither did it. The premise was reasonable enough: England had her Empire – much of it administered and policed by Scots exiles – why should not Scotland, with her ingenuity and propensity for graft, have her own?

In 1698, after years of famine and hardship, the proposal, to fund a naval fleet and set up a trading base and colony in the New World, ignited the imagination of Scots of all castes from all corners of the land. Our own wee Empire! 'He won't be looked upon as a true Scotchman that is against it,' wrote Lord Basil Hamilton. Subscriptions – amounting to half of Scotland's capital – were raised in grand estates and Highland clachans, merchants' town houses and Glasgow slums.

As one historian later observed, the Darien venture was 'an amazing yet natural product of that curious blend of cold, thrifty common-sense and poetic idealism found in Scotsmen'. Thrawnness, our word for the peculiarly Scots quality of perverse intractability, also had a hand in it. There could have been no greater spur to the venture than the news that the English, who did not take kindly to other nations' imperial aspirations, were fiercely against it.

Six ships set sail from the port of Leith in July – taking a circuitous route to avoid the hostile English navy – with 1,200 Scots sailors and would-be colonists on board and a cargo of periwigs, clay pipes, Bibles, serge frock coats and finest tweed. The first mate of the *Capercaillie*, the last ship to sail, was a Fascaray man, Farquhar McWatt.

The voyage was trying enough – one merchant was so troubled by seasickness that he sought drastic relief by tossing himself overboard to his death – but the destination was intolerable: a climate so hot and humid it was habitable only by the hardiest Kuna Indians, and infested by disease-bearing insects so large, vicious and deadly they made the colonisers nostalgic for the innocent wee midges of home. We had, it emerged, been badly misinformed. There was not a great demand for wool garments and powdered hairpieces in the relentless heat of Darien. In what must surely have been an ironic reference to the landscape and climate they had left behind, the Scottish colonists called this malarial inferno New Caledonia.

Our Fascaradian first mate perished, probably of yellow fever, two weeks after landing in Darien. Inevitably, most of his compatriots were not long in following him. The English threatened their own trading partners in the region with war if they did any business with the Scots interlopers; the Spanish, based in neighbouring Colombia, besieged the New Caledonian port; and the Kuna, who had no time for any of the Europeans, did their best to undermine the venture using guerrilla tactics. Disease and starvation did the rest.

Three hundred survivors finally made it home to a country now so broke it became a supplicant of England. The English bribed those wealthy Scots who had lost money in the Darien scheme with a full repayment of their investment. Within a decade, the Act of Union had been signed and the long, quarrelsome, woefully unequal marriage of inconvenience between England and Scotland was officially solemnised. The Scots people, apart from the coward few bought for 'hireling traitors' wages', became the Kuna Indians of Old Caledonia, without the necessary expertise in effective guerrilla tactics, exploding pillar boxes notwithstanding.

Grigor McWatt, 1954, *The Fascaray Compendium*

BY THE CLOSE OF 1955, MONTFITCHETT WAS DEAD — DECAPITATED in a crash in his convertible Riley, in which he was touring the lanes of Surrey, England, with Alicia Rivers, a vivacious Rank starlet, who also lost her head in the accident.

Not much German was spoken in Fascaray, but when the grisly story was confirmed, via a week-old copy of the Aberdeen *Press and Journal* which arrived on the mailboat, *Schadenfreude* was the only word to describe local reaction to the news. 'The motor car has usefully served the purpose of the guillotine,' wrote McWatt.

Rab McNab had largely relinquished the running of the pub to young Jamie MacDonald – now a strapping 21-year-old with the valuable characteristic in a barman of a personal distaste for drink – but on the night the news broke, McNab was helped down the stairs from his attic room, to which gout and liver trouble now confined him, and he raised a trembling glass in the bar to the Fascaray Five as the the pub rang to the sound of McWatt's song. Hamish McIntosh, the original boy tenor on the night of the ballad's debut a decade ago, was now a wiry fisherman and construction worker in his twenties and he belted out the words with tuneful passion. On this evening of tears, rage and laughter, 'Hame tae Fascaray' seemed even more of a battle cry than a love song or lament.

> *Heather's bloomin*
> *On the braes,*
> *This is oor ain land.*
> *The bonnie hame*
> *Where we belang.*
> *Let's stake oor claim.*

The celebrations may have been in questionable taste. They were also premature. Montfitchett's son Torquil, a weedy fellow who had been glimpsed more than two decades earlier as a teenager in the garden of the Big House sullenly swatting midges during one of his father's visits north, had inherited the title and the estate. The laird was dead. Long live the laird.

A Granite Ballad – The Reimagining of Grigor McWatt,
Mhairi McPhail (Thackeray College Press, 2016)

In my early twenties, having acquired an education and the beginnings of an interesting career in New York, I became the sort of wild child against whom, when the time comes, I will warn my daughter.

To my Stakhanovite curriculum vitae – anthropology at UC Toronto; an MA in museum studies from NYU; a semester in library studies in Illinois and a course in curatorship in Grenoble; placements at the British Museum and the Pergamon; my monograph on Isobel Grant – I added drugs, drink and reckless sex. I had spent my teens being a good girl, striving for and mostly achieving A grades which, I suppose, in my doggedly unaspirational family home amounted to a kind of rebellion. Now I was an A-grade bad girl. But though I partied all night in Manhattan and Brooklyn with the smart club kids – art students and actors, always between jobs and mad for pleasure – I had a shameful secret. Though I tried, I could never entirely extinguish my work ethic. While my amusing friends languished in bed moaning theatrically, only rising at 4 p.m. to attend to costume and make-up for the evening's revels, I'd been doing drudge work since early morning at an ill-paid post uptown in the stacks of the Marquand Archive.

By night we were flappers at the brink of the twenty-first century, hitting the contraband hooch and Charlestoning our young lives away. But with dance music still pulsating in my skull, the taste of the last cocktail and who knows what else in my mouth, my mind straining for clarity through a cataclysmic comedown, I always managed to haul myself out of whatever bed I happened to find myself in, shower off the excesses of the night, swap my gaudy party clothes and Doc Martens for unexceptional corporate threads and mid-heeled pumps and report for duty. And here's the thing – I enjoyed duty.

Apart from the fact that the job helped pay the rent on my crummy room in Hell's Kitchen, I liked my colleagues, who were superficially staid but had arcane expertise and complicated needs and rivalries. I liked their private dramas. I even 'liked' the colleagues I disliked. The workplace was one big dysfunctional family and I liked big dysfunctional families – as long as they weren't my own, didn't get in the way of the work itself and I could leave them at the end of each day. There was structure. I yearned for structure. I enjoyed teamwork, or the process of attempting to herd a disparate group of people with competing interests towards a single purpose, and above all I took pleasure in the quiet discipline of reading, sorting and categorisation. My party friends, many of them the beneficiaries of trust funds, would never have understood.

Hal, an on–off boyfriend with vague ambitions to work in film and a father in oil, lay in bed one morning at 7.30 watching me dress for work. His expression was quizzical and, raising his index finger with exaggerated effort to point at his own handsome face, he said, 'Consider the lilies of the field, they neither toil nor spin, yet even Solomon in all his glory was not arrayed like one of these.'

Yes, standing in my cut-price approximation of a business suit, last night's thrift store indiewear stuffed in a holdall, bracing myself for the morning subway ride, I felt shame; a drab worker bee trying to pass in a hive of magnificent queens.

In Fascaray, getting my daughter ready for school, feeding her, keeping chores and laundry under control and sifting through the detritus of Grigor McWatt's life, partying is no longer an option – raucous late-night revels at the Finnverinnity Inn have little appeal – and I have all the work I need.

As for Handsome Hal, he's no longer handsome. He's dead. After his third time in rehab, each stint the price of a good college education, he picked up where he left off, acquired some oxycodone pills, crushed them, diluted them and injected the solution – a respectable party dose by his usual standards but fatal after his recent clean-up.

That's when I climbed off the carousel. Just in time. That's also when I met Marco Bartoli, then an aspiring playwright working as a summer stock stage manager. As it turned out, Marco liked working too.

The devil, they say, has all the best tunes and here in Fascaray, where the extended wake for the late laird continues unabated, it seems the papists of Lusnaharra are even closer to Black Donald of the Whids than the rest of us and have access to his beguiling songbook.

I did not have the dubious privilege of meeting William Buchanan, a true Holy Willie, late minister of the Finnverinnity Free Church of Scotland in the parish of this island until 1941. He arrived here in the late 1920s, one of the missionaries sent by the Free Church to scare the daylights out of sinful islanders and turn them towards the stern mercies of his god. Buchanan's influence lingers, even under the comparatively benign regime of his successor at the manse, the Reverend Ranald Paterson.

Above Finnverinnity Harbour, the Temperance Hotel still stands, where the ageless Mistress Geddes still presides over unimpeachably clean rooms and substantial though joyless repasts. But there is more custom, as well as life, down the road in Rab McNab's boisterous howff, ably managed by young Jamie MacDonald – nephew of Fascaray Land Raider Murdo and of Shonnie, the piper soldier who perished in the war – and the Finnverinnity Inn has been permanently *en fête*, as our Auld Alliance partners might say, since news of the departure to the Great Ayebidin Grouse Shoot of our late and unlamented laird.

Music and dancing may still be frowned on, officially, by the most God-fearing Presbyterians, but attitudes have relaxed since the 1930s when the Reverend William Buchanan refused to solemnise the marriage of Morag McIntosh and Donald MacEwan, two devout young members of his own congregation, until Morag's family destroyed the handsome violin – 'the devil's recruiting machine' – that once belonged to her grandfather and hung over the fireplace in the family home. In the event, Iain McIntosh, Morag's younger brother, burned an old fiddle – donated for the purpose by Murdo McIntyre of Doonmara – and hid the treasured instrument in the byre. It has since been brought out and dusted down to perform good service at many a local hoolie, though never on a Sabbath.

Times change, but in this matter not sufficiently quickly to my mind. The inn, of course, has long existed outside the pale and accordingly serves the devil's drink to the sound of the devil's music. And some Wee Free affiliates can be seen there on weekday evenings, tapping their feet to a cantie reel and imbibing 'a richt guid willie-waught'. But Saturday evening – Sabbath Eve – and the Sabbath itself are dreary and silent as the tuim throughout the east of the island. Around Finnverinnity on the Lord's Day, harvests are suspended, peat gathering stops, no boats set sail, no washing is hung, no cows are milked, no eggs are gathered, no children play, no flowers are picked, no cheerful youth purses his lips to whistle a merry tune. Instead, in Presbyterian households, the long days and longer nights are spent in close Bible study and it is still to Lusnaharra and its Romish denizens – whose priest, who enjoys a tune himself, permits his parishioners to milk their cows after Sunday Mass and turns a blind eye to the occasional Sabbath ceilidh – that one must look for any sort of weekend divertissement.

Grigor McWatt, 1956, *The Fascaray Compendium*

TORQUIL MERE-STRATTON, THE NEW LORD MONTFITCHETT, HAD grown up to become what was called in the English and American newspapers 'a socialite'. *Who's Who*, a copy of which was found in Auchwinnie Carnegie Library by Miss Elspeth Millar, listed his hobbies as poker, backgammon, blackjack and baccarat. Unlike Burns, or McWatt, Torquil Mere-Stratton's heart clearly belonged in Monte Carlo, rather than the Highlands.

But in the immediate aftermath of Percy Montfitchett's death and without his bullying presence, his son made several exploratory journeys up to Fascaray, bringing with him his American wife Minty, a buxom woman whose family had made their fortune selling gunpowder during the civil war, and their sons Clarence, eleven, and nine-year-old Peregrine, who in photographs at the time wore identical high-collared suits, and expressions pitched between bewilderment and resentment.

On their initial visits, the new laird, his wife and sons were accompanied by an entourage of English servants whose manner so offended Mrs McIvor that, the morning after they first arrived, she left permanently on the mailboat for Peebles.

There were, however, signs of more positive change under the new dispensation. The minister and his wife received an invitation to 'cocktails' at the Big House, and although Ranald and Wilma Paterson were of the temperance persuasion and their strict sabbatarianism usually extended to Saturday evenings, they made an exception for the new laird and were able to report back that 'improvements and plenishments' had been made to the house.

A 'loggia' – 'a fantoosh name for a big porch', said Effie MacLeod – had been constructed, a mahogany cabinet containing a television set had been installed in the drawing room, the billiard room had been redesignated as a 'den' for Torquil, and the old game pantry and flower room had been stripped out to make a 'rumpus room' for the boys. Torquil and Minty, said the Patersons – despite the laird's insistence, the minister and his wife still found it a painful impertinence to call them by their first names – had been most hospitable.

Over at Lusnaharra, Father Col Maclennan would have had no difficulty accepting the offer of a cocktail. He was now in his seventies and increasingly unsteady on his feet, but he could still say Mass, perform baptisms and marriages, mete out penances and see off the dead. Francie MacDonald and his cousin Donnie gave the priest regular lifts to the Finnverinnity Inn in their old Fordson tractor with its shattered windscreen whenever they were heading over to see Jamie, shipping fish from the pier or getting the family's 'messages' from the store. But no invitation from the Big House came for Father Maclennan. Sectarian barriers were firmly in place.

At the school, then based in Finnverinnity's village hall, Miss Millar was struggling with the new intake of pupils. There was something of a population boom at Lusnaharra, McWatt reported in the *Compendium*. 'Amateur "sociologists" at the inn believe there is a connection with the post-war success of Glasgow Celtic football team, which has taken the Coronation Cup, to the consternation of Finnverinnity, which has always been a Rangers village and is undergoing something of a population decline.'

The island's older children who were fortunate enough to receive secondary education were sent over to the two mainland schools – Catholics to St Maolrubha's and Protestants to Auchwinnie Academy – to board each week. The non-denominational Fascaray School in Finnverinnity, which took all-comers, now had thirty children, more than double the number Elspeth Millar had taught when she'd first arrived on the island from Resolis sixteen years earlier as a naive and idealistic young schoolmistress.

Another teacher was recruited – the minister and his wife, in conjunction with the dominie (schoolmaster) at Auchwinnie Academy, had the final say on the appointment – and Grigor McWatt noted in the *Compendium* that 'when Miss Janet Thomson of Buckie was first handed off the mailboat at the pier by skipper Ali Hume and first mate Malkie McTavish, Jamie MacDonald and his brother fought like Cain and Abel for the right to carry her suitcase to the schoolhouse'.

Torquil Mere-Stratton's new bailiff, Lionel Spicer (he dispensed with the term 'factor' but, wrote McWatt, 'that was the only concession to modernisation in the arrangement'), created a stir when he arrived on the island. Tam Macpherson's youngest daughter, Sheena, over at Balnasaig Farm was, according to Effie MacLeod, 'daft on the fellow' and compared him to the Hollywood actor Stewart Granger.

To the pub regulars, recorded McWatt, 'Spicer lacks humour or charm and has never bought a round of drinks. Any symmetry in facial features or signs of heroic musculature are a matter of indifference, if not suspicion.' He was also English – 'another patronising southern imperialist' – and, if he was an improvement on Sammy Nelson, in that he gave the impression of listening politely to crofters' complaints and requests, 'he listens, apparently attentively, and then ignores them just the same'.

A Granite Ballad – The Reimagining of Grigor McWatt,
Mhairi McPhail (Thackeray College Press, 2016)

10 October 2014

Agnes is on her mid-term break. She wanted to see her father in Texas but we agreed that the journey was too long for her to make on her own and, with double jet lag to contend with, it would be too disruptive. She took it well, but while the other kids her age are meeting at Oonagh's house in Lusnaharra today and at Kirsty Campbell's in Finnverinnity tomorrow, Agnes says if she can't go to Texas she'd rather spend her holiday with me in my office.

'I won't make a noise, honest,' she says. 'Please. You won't even know I'm there.'

She brings her school bag with a stack of books, some writing paper, a drawing pad and some paints and brushes – she has a project to get on with – and we set her up with a jar of water at a table in the window. I've taken down the wildlife posters so we have an unobstructed view: a shaft of sun plays across the grey sea like a searchlight, then it's gone, the sky darkens and the rain starts. She's silent, as promised, while I get on with my work, clearing out the old museum next door – Johanna has hired a dumpster, delivered by cargo boat from Auchwinnie, and we're slowly filling it with the MacRaes' trash.

I return to my desk and log on to my computer. Nothing happens. I try again. The screen is dead and I curse loudly. Agnes puts her finger to her lips and tiptoes up to my desk. Her fingers play, prestissimo, over the keyboard then she presses the return key with a decisive jab and the computer whirrs into life.

I start to thank her and she puts a finger to her lips again and goes back to her work. Chastened, I return to mine.

INVENTORY OF SCOTS WORDS DESCRIBING
AN UPROAR, FIGHT OR CONTROVERSY

bulyor
clamihewit
collieshangie
dindy
fecht
gilravage
guddle
gurryshang
habber-galyo
hubbleshew
killiemahou
klamoz
kurdy-murdy
peloo
pudder
rammie
rickibeekis
rippet
roukle
rumballiach
shangan
shicavy
speeho
steuchie
strabash
stracummage
stramash
strebogle
stushie
threap

towrow
tuilyie
tulzie

Grigor McWatt, 1957, *The Fascaray Compendium*

The feudal system of landownership seemed intact and even strengthened after the judicial failure of the 1946 Fascaray Land Raid, but a decade later, even with a new laird in place, the first signs of fundamental social change began to appear on our island. 1956 was the year of the hard winter and the Big Snow. It has also become known as the year of the Big Thaw, when the demands of nature at her harshest brought islanders of all religious persuasions together in an unprecedented way.

It did not start well. The courtship between Jessie Mackenzie (Presbyterian) of Finnverinnity, daughter of church elder Donald John the Shop, and Francie MacDonald (Catholic) of Lusnaharra had scandalised both communities. Stern words had been issued from the kirk pulpit denouncing 'this godless union' and Father Maclennan had taken Francie's mother aside after Mass to express his concern. 'There are plenty of decent young Catholic girls around. Francis has no need to consort with a Protestant,' he told Kitty MacDonald.

But the young couple, defiant in their ardour, slipped away from their homes in November, caught the mailboat to Auchwinnie then the coach to London, where they found factory work and separate accommodation in a youth hostel. They were married three weeks later in Hendon register office with two passing strangers – a student nurse and a train driver – serving as witnesses. The Fascaradian fugitives spent their wedding night in a room above the Welsh Harp pub on the North Circular Road and returned home to present their outraged families with a fait accompli.

Accommodation for young married couples is limited on Fascaray so the newly-weds had to live apart for several months with their respective families, whose continuing fury they hoped to appease by seeking blessings for their marriage in kirk and church.

Minister and priest reluctantly agreed, only after the Reverend Paterson received private assurances from Jessie that their children would be brought up according to the tenets of the kirk, while Francie told

Father Col in confidence that any offspring would be baptised and raised as Catholic.

A day was set for a morning blessing at Finnverinnity kirk, to which Francie would be driven from Lusnaharra on a trailer hitched to his cousin Donnie's old Fordson tractor. The austere ceremony would be witnessed by Jessie's family, who would then wave her off as the couple were driven the three miles back to Lusnaharra for a blessing at the Church of the Sacred Heart and Immaculate Mary in the presence of the MacDonalds.

But on the eve of the ceremonies, the weather turned wild and the island, usually protected from the cruellest winters by the benign influence of the Gulf Stream, was buffeted by the fiercest blizzards in living memory. Several steamers seeking shelter from the gales dropped anchor out beyond the bay and islanders woke the following morning to white silence. The Big Snow had spread its dazzling canopy over glen and hill, smothering the landscape and muffling all sound.

The road between Finnverinnity and Lusnaharra, an extended cart track, was obliterated by three-foot drifts. Older members of both congregations muttered that it was God's way of showing his disapproval for a headstrong young couple's shocking disregard for tradition. The younger generation was more forgiving – and resourceful.

At Lusnaharra, Donnie MacDonald, handed out shovels and spades, while over at Finnverinnity, Alec Campbell's son Wee Eck organised a work party with the bride's brother, John Donald 'the Fish' Mackenzie, and the groom's brother, Jamie, 'borrowing' tools from the Big House gardener's shed.

Two hours later, the two work parties, Presbyterian and Catholic, broke through the tunnel of snow and met a mile and a half from their respective villages, shook hands, shared a dram from a hip flask and waved through the Fordson, its trailer, now decorated by the McKinnon sisters with garlands of holly and ivy, bearing a relieved Francie on his way to join Jessie at the kirk. There Ranald Paterson, swept up by the wave of goodwill, overlooked the fact that the blessing was finally taking place two and a half hours later than scheduled while over in Lusnaharra Father Col was similarly accommodating when the party finally arrived there after nightfall. He made a point of warmly welcoming John Donald and Sarah Mackenzie, who had, despite the earlier veto of their parents, chosen to accompany their sister, the new Mrs MacDonald, to the blessing at the Church of the Sacred Heart and Immaculate Mary.

The memorable dance that followed in Lusnaharra was enlivened by the music of Murdo 'The Fiddle' McIntyre and the bride's cousin Iain McIntosh, who played on the family violin which had, two decades earlier, almost been consigned to flames by a minister who would have taken a far sterner view of the celebration of the MacDonald-Mackenzie union.

Grigor McWatt, 1957, *The Fascaray Compendium*

By 1 p.m. the rain has cleared and the sun is stirring behind a thick wedge of cloud. Agnes and I leave the office and take our sandwiches and flask of tea outside and sit on a wooden bench by the pier.

'It's okay to talk now?' she asks.

I laugh. 'Of course, honey. It's lunchtime!'

'Just checking . . .'

She swings her legs as she stares out to sea where a faded column of rainbow shimmers on the horizon.

'Watergaw!' she says.

'What?'

'Watergaw. That's what they call a broken rainbow here. That's the name of Dot and Lori's hotel, too.' She turns and points at the former Temperance Hotel, refurbished and reopened last year, above the harbour.

'Nice word. And clever of you to pick it up. You're really getting the hang of this place.'

'Mmm . . .' she says. 'It's not hard if you just listen. You know Oonagh? She's Catholic, which means her favourite colour is green, and she supports Celtic soccer club? That's Glasgow Celtic. Like kind of Irish Scottish? Not the Boston Celtics that Papa likes. That's basketball. Kirsty Campbell is Presbyterian, which is kind of Protestant, and her favourite colour is blue because she supports Rangers soccer club? That's Glasgow Rangers. Not the Texas Rangers. That's baseball.'

'What about you? Who do you support?'

'I guess I'm like you and Papa? I don't really have a religion so I don't have a soccer club . . . And my favourite colour is a rainbow. A watergaw.'

'That's my girl. You don't have to choose.' I put my arm round her. 'Keep your options open.'

Even now, though I grew up in North America, where we have bigger fish to fry in terms of community conflict, I'm conscious of the tribal traditions here. Sunday in Finnverinnity is still the 'dreichest' day, whatever the weather, a legacy of centuries of dour churchgoing, despite the absence now of any place of traditional worship on the island. Perhaps it's race memory, or too long spent in the company of my parents, despite my best efforts, but I have an ear for the distinctions, the subtle gradations of names and preferences that can give away faith affiliations; the Irish whiff of incense and the panoply of saints – Kieran, Brigid, Anne-Marie – the resinous tang of Scots Presbyterianism – Malcolm, Jean, Duncan, Effie. But the old boundaries are dissolving and these days, in former zones of Catholic holdout and Wee Free redoubt, names can cut both ways and all the recent Hebridean Kylies and Darrens and Chantals are usefully mixing up the old certainties.

'But Oonagh and Kirsty are really good friends. I mean *really* good friends,' Agnes says.

'Well, that's an advance.'

'What's an advance?'

'Going forward.' I watch her frown. 'Never mind. It's good, is all.'

Marco was, like most Italians, a happy and unconflicted ex-Catholic but I'm the anxious product of what used to be known as a 'mixed marriage': in my case, Protestant father, Catholic mother. The Gallaghers, my mother's family, were Irish immigrants who came to work in the Scottish coal mines just after the First World War, and my father, Dougal, was, like his own Fascaradian father, nominally, a Presbyterian. Dolores Gallagher, a typist in a law firm, first met Dougal McPhail, a steelworker, in the early seventies at a dance in Green's Playhouse, Glasgow. The improbably named Sensational Alex Harvey Band were playing. Dolores had told her parents she was going to a special novena at St Andrew's Cathedral and was staying over in town with a friend.

It was rare in those days for couples from either side of the religious divide – and there were only two sides – to get together. They were Capulets and Montagues, transplanted from the plains of medieval northern Italy to the west of Scotland's late-twentieth-century industrial sprawl. In Glasgow in the 1970s, star-crossed romances rarely ended in double suicide but young people caught dating 'one of them' were in serious breach of community protocol. Your religion was instantly identifiable by your name, the school you went to, the songs you sang and, as is apparently still the case, the football team you supported. Wearing the wrong colour or bawling the wrong ballad in the wrong part of town could get you in serious trouble. Though the signs and signifiers have become blurred – there are laws against sectarianism now and the old songs have been cleaned up – there are apparently still those who regard religious hatred as a cherished part of Scottish heritage and feel it's their personal mission to keep the flame alive.

'And Aaron Schneider, he says he's a Druid, which is like the really old, old religion here? But he's from Germany and he supports Munster, which is like monster only different?'

'Does he have a favourite colour?'

'If he does, he won't tell me.'

The first dance my mother attended was in the parish hall of her local Catholic church in a mining village in Lanarkshire. Teenagers came from miles around – the youth club passed for nightlife in those days – to queue outside for admission to the church hall, where they were met at the door by the parish priest who asked them each in turn to recite the Hail Mary. Those who stumbled over the words were sent on their way. Only the faithful, those who could recite the entire prayer as fluently and rapidly as a tobacco auctioneer, right down to 'Now and at the hour of our death . . .', were admitted – boys to the left, girls to the right – for an evening of chaste jigging to the sounds of Amen Corner and the Yardbirds on the parish Dansette.

'Black!' Agnes declares.

'What?'

'Black. I think that's my favourite colour. And I support the Boston Celtics. I don't care if it's not soccer.'

'That's right. Stand your ground.'

My parents stood their ground, courted in secret to avoid scandal and after two years announced their engagement to their horrified parents. The young couple tried to appease both sides by avoiding kirk and church and opting for a civil marriage ceremony at the City Chambers. Instead, they found they'd compounded the original offence and only close friends, and Dolores's sister, my aunt Bridie, attended the wedding. Relations had not improved by the time my mother fell pregnant with me and soured further when I was born – my Land Raid hero grandfather Hector wanted a kirk baptism, Dolores's father insisted on a Catholic christening. My parents held out against both. When I was four years old my father accepted defeat and a job at the steelworks in Hamilton, Ontario. Canada was neutral territory, with a long history of harbouring Scottish refugees from conflict and hardship.

'Mom?' Agnes tugs at my sleeve. 'Maybe turquoise? Maybe that's my colour? That's like blue and green, mixed together?'

'Great idea!' I say.

The watergaw has vanished and the sun with it. It's raining again. We put up our hoods and, as we run back to the office, the rain turns to sleet.

blawthir – wet weather turning to sleet

blirtin – squally snow shower

feefle – swirling snowfall

feuchter – light fall of snow, individual flakes

flaggie – soft snow in which footprints can be seen

flindrikin – lacy covering of snow on ground

fyole – light covering of snow

fyoonach – dusting of snow on ground

glaister – thin covering of snow or ice

glutherie – slushy

grimet – thin patches of grimy snow through which the earth is visible

pewlin – blanket of snow

scruif – a thin crust of ice or snow

skelfs – large snowflakes

sleekie – shower of rain and snow

snaw-ghaist – mirage or apparition seen in snow

snaw-pouther – fine driving snow

sneesl – begin to rain or snow lightly

spitters – light gusts of small flakes

stark – dense snowfall

wridy – covered in snowdrifts

Grigor McWatt, 1956, *The Fascaray Compendium*

18 October 2014

A month on and the blue-and-white 'Yes' posters remain in some Lusnaharra windows – hard to tell whether defiance or inertia is the guiding principle – and in Finnverinnity post office, where we go to pick up supplies for our picnic, the newspapers are still full of reflection and argument about the referendum. They won't let it go. There's little sign of jubilation from the victors; those who voted 'No' to independence are keeping their heads down.

Margaret Mackenzie serves us with a politeness that could read as disdain. Whatever her position on the question of independence, I can't imagine her hopes for Scotland's future involve extending much of a welcome to outsiders.

The trail head is just west of the Big House, where the Saltire still flutters next to the Jolly Roger. At first our path is easy, wide and well defined with a gentle ascent beside a small burn flashing copper in the sunlight. As Agnes skips along the grassy track, her talk is of school, her soap opera of friendships and fallings-out, plans for Halloween, Christmas and Hogmanay.

After a while I stop listening and her chirruping voice blends with the exultant songs of wintering skylarks and snow buntings. Someone – probably Marco, who taught me to recognise birds in the first place – once told me that birdsong is not the liquid distillation of joy it appears to human ears but a shrill announcement of territorial imperatives. 'Vamoose! Mine! Get outta here!' Over and over. One of several facts I wish I could unlearn.

We pause by a rocky outcrop to swig from our water bottle and Agnes clambers to the top of a boulder and takes out her phone to photograph Finnverinnity's harbour below us, its broad indentation and long concrete pier lapped by indigo water under a blameless blue sky.

'I'm taking pictures of our walk to send to Papa.'

I step aside like a guilty starlet evading the paparazzi. Another bird, a lapwing, starts up its song, its tiny whoop-whoop like the distant call of the NYPD.

We press on and soon the path becomes narrower and steeper. The weather is changing. Low clouds race in and begin to crowd out the blue. The small burn has become a waterfall which spills over the path. We have to watch where we put our feet and Agnes's conversation slows as she picks her way more carefully up the hill.

'Tell me again how you and Papa met?'

Suppressing a sigh I tell her the old story – the friends, the bad musical about a superhero who loses his powers and finds love, which I hated and, as it turned out, he'd written and directed, the fact that we couldn't stand each other. Loathing at first sight.

'At first,' she reminds me. 'But then you really liked each other?'

'Yes.'

'And he proposed to you within, like, five seconds?'

'Kind of. You know the story.'

'So your friend Olivia introduces you – "Mhairi . . . Marco". "Marco . . . Mhairi" – and he says . . .'

'"Marry? We've only just met."'

She laughs as if she's hearing the story for the first time. I won't spoil it by reminding her of what she knows already and must make her sad – that eventually we came to loathe each other again. Who said first impressions were always false?

We've reached the col and before the path picks up again we have to cross a wide tract of soggy peat starred with strange white flowers – small plumes of fluff on spindly stems.

She changes the subject.

'Can you make T-shirts and stuff out of bog cotton?'

So that's what it is.

'Probably not.'

Although the land is flat it requires more care in crossing. We're properly dressed in waterproofs and boots but it would be easy to twist an ankle or sink up to the knees in a concealed gully.

We both fall silent and concentrate while hopping cautiously towards a pyramidal cairn of stones left by other walkers to show the point at which the path picks up again.

Below us, distant Finnverinnity looks as innocent as a child's model village, and across the sea Auchwinnie is just visible, its harbour crowded as a mall parking lot with boats, most of them idle yachts owned by city dwellers who work so hard to make the money to finance them that they rarely have the time to get up here for a weekend's sailing. Agnes takes another picture by the cairn and I dodge out of view again. Her father won't want a photo of me.

Ahead, the path looks badly eroded. I'm beginning to wonder if this walk was such a good idea.

'Better get on,' I say. 'Weather's changing. We might have a very wet picnic.'

Seconds later, a storm cloud above us unleashes its burden and we hurriedly put up our hoods and zip our jackets. It's impossible to talk as the rain noisily rattles our waterproofs. We're walking uphill again and a mist begins to swirl around us. Soon, the shower stops and it's as if we're moving through thick cloud. We stumble on in the eerie silence, unable to see more than two feet in front of us. Suddenly a dark shape materialises just ahead and advances towards us. Agnes squeals. A gust of wind clears the haze momentarily and reveals a young deer, as startled as we are, who takes off so swiftly across the hill that it seems he's in flight.

'Wow! Just like Bambi, only bigger. I should have taken a picture of him for Papa. But he was so quick. Do you think if we stayed very still for a while he'll come again?'

'Probably not.'

The rain returns, a sharp slanting sleet that stings the face, and I'm getting anxious. We should turn back. Agnes though is irrepressible, leaping from rock to rock like that young deer.

I call her back and stand to squint at the map, which is getting sodden in the rain. Unlike Marco I'm a poor orienteer, plus which I have mild vertigo; I can't judge from the contour lines just how steep this path might become.

'C'mon, Mom!' Agnes is off again.

As the trail rears upwards the stones are loose and water is falling in torrents. Even Agnes begins to falter as I struggle up behind her, panting. I ask myself whether my urge to turn back comes from maternal instinct or sheer self-preservation. But though Agnes is finding the going hard, she is determined. I take my lead from her.

Finally, both out of breath, we reach the top of the path and see a stone pillar, a cartographer's trig point, which tells us we've reached Mammor's ridge. And then we are rewarded. The sun returns, scattering the mist. Agnes spins round, arms outstretched, laughing and triumphant, taking in the panorama. I lean against the pillar to steady myself as I look down giddily on the tiny circuit-board cluster of Finnverinnity, with Auchwinnie across the sea and beyond it the mighty hills of the mainland. To our west stretches Lusnaharra's pale scimitar of sand while behind us, tethered to Fascaray by its strip of causeway, the green disc of Calasay shimmers under the perfect arc of a rainbow.

Agnes takes pictures and I set out our picnic – bread, cheese, apples, chocolate and a flask of tea – on a flat stone well away from the ridge's edge. But as soon as we sit on our waterproofs and raise the food to our lips a dark cloud sweeps over us. Midges. In October! Another effect of climate change. But we are prepared, thanks to my native pessimism. Marco would have scoffed but I made sure I packed the unseasonal midge hoods, along with ineffectual repellent spray, suncream – what was I thinking? – and a first-aid kit. We swiftly roll the khaki veils over our heads.

'We're beekeepers. Or aliens,' Agnes says. 'Is that a metaphor?'

At first, we try to continue with our picnic, sneaking our cheese sandwiches under our drapery, but the insects are fiendishly persistent and swarm on our unshielded hands. A few find their way inside our hoods and we make a comic turn of it, slapping theatrically at our faces. Then we give up and hurriedly pack the picnic away. Agnes reaches for my hand, threads her small fingers through mine and, laughing and breathless, we scramble down the hill together in our net shrouds.

BY THE LATE SPRING OF 1958 THE BIG HOUSE WASN'T THE ONLY place on the island where you could find a television set. Effie Morrison, now Effie MacLeod and mother of a four-year-old girl and two-month-old twin boys, had a brother who repaired sets for Rediffusion in Glasgow and had brought her one all the way up from Strathbungo as a birthday present.

The television didn't have an imposing wooden cabinet which concealed it when not in use, as in Finnverinnity House, but Effie's set seemed to fill one corner of the MacLeods' cottage and, in our interview, she told me of the night Shuggie first plugged it in, with newborns Barry and Kenny asleep, top-to-tail in their cradle behind the couch, and wee Moira struggling to escape her mother's lap. It seemed that half of Finnverinnity crowded in the house with them, while several 'strays from Lusnaharra' stood outside on tiptoes peering in through the window.

Sheena Macpherson was over from Balnasaig Farm with her husband Stevie MacEwan, showing off their own newborn, Innes, 'round and swaddled as a wee Eskimo doll'. But Effie's adult visitors were restless, doubtful about the merits of this newfangled machine, wondering if they were ever going to get a cup of tea, or something stronger, and they barracked Shuggie as he struggled to adjust the aerial, a plastic dome with two protruding wire antennae. 'It's like something out of Buck Rogers,' said Roddy McIntosh, a regular at the mainland picture house.

The snow on the screen finally cleared to reveal a snub-nosed man in a kilt bantering with a pair of handsome young guitarists, one fashionably bearded, the other whose severe Plantagenet hairstyle suggested to Effie that 'his mammy had cut it, using a skellet [saucepan]'. The programme was a variety show, the *White Heather Club*, and Andy Stewart, the chirpy master of ceremonies, was introducing a popular folk duo. Robin Hall and Jimmie Macgregor smiled shyly, fixed their eyes heavenwards with a gaze of secular piety, strummed a gentle three-bar intro, and launched into song.

Within seconds a thrilled silence gripped the room and outside the house, standing on tiptoe and 'keekin in through the windae', according to Effie, eight-year old Fergus McKinnon and his cousin Mikey gasped as the earnest crooning harmonies twined around a song of shocking familiarity – their song.

Hee-ra-haw, boys,
We're awa, boys,
Gangin hame
Tae Fascaray.

Meanwhile, seven and a half miles north in his Calasay croft, wearing beret and scarf against the chill, the poet was at work by the bilious light of a Tilley lamp, recording the nesting habits of the peregrine falcon, expressing trenchant views on the latest barbarities of Westminster, recalling the heroic, vainglorious and tragic history of Scotland, and reimagining classic verse into Scots, unaware that at that moment he had just been touched – scorched, he would later say – by the hot breath of fame.

A Granite Ballad – The Reimagining of Grigor McWatt,
Mhairi McPhail (Thackeray College Press, 2016)

Ode tae a Nichtingall

Ma hert yauks an a drousie dowfness pynes
Ma virr, as tho o hemlock Ah hae slocht,
Or whummelt some dreich opiate tae the sheuch,
Ane meenit syne, an lethe-wards Ah hae cowped:
It's nae fer eelist o yer cantie share,
But bein tae cantie in yer cantieness, –
That you, licht-winged Dryad o the trees
In some braw hinnied kailyard
O bonnie emerant, an shaidaes stentless,
Crood o summer in fu thrappled saucht.

Och, for a waucht o bevy! That hae been
Cuild lang syne in the deep-howked yird,
Gustin o heather an the emerant glens,
Reels, an waulkin songs, an lauchter shared!
Och for a quaich fu o oor michty Scotia,
Fu o the sonsie watter o aw life,
Its gowden promise glimmerin at the lip,
A douce ambrosial waucht;
That Ah micht drink an think o nocht,
An gie aw strife an fasheries the slip.

Grigor McWatt, efter John Keats, 1958[9]

9   From *Kenspeckelt*, Virr Press, 1959. Reprinted in *Warld in a Gless: The Collected Varse of Grigor McWatt*, Smeddum Beuks, 1992.

22 October 2014

I look up from my desk to see a figure lingering outside the window in the rain. It's Margaret Mackenzie. Our eyes meet and the postmistress dips her head and hurries away.

Johanna told me that locals call new arrivals to the island 'white settlers'. Who'd have thought, with my sketchy past, family disadvantages and genuine Fascaradian connection that I would be viewed as a colonial carpetbagger, patronising the natives and pillaging their assets?

For all his misanthropy, Grigor McWatt eventually had some success at integration here and his journal entries in *The Fascaray Compendium* show a curiosity about the lives of fellow islanders I could never share. Away from the edgy society of office life, I've never been much good at 'community'. As a child, I was always in permanent flight from family get-togethers of both sorts – visits with the disputatious, noisy Gallaghers or the silent McPhails imposed their own agonies. At St Maria Goretti's I had my small group of particular friends – there were four of us, intense, secretive girls with intellectual pretensions. My year at Turville Chantry consolidated my introvert tendencies; boarding school was a forcing house for cliques – passionate, self-sufficient and hostile to outsiders.

As an undergraduate in Toronto, grabbing at the chance to get away, I worked so hard (waitressing, bar work) to pay for my course and to get a good degree that I didn't – couldn't afford to – get swept up in student life. Which, as it turned out, was a blessing. Because when I finally looked up from my books and noticed what my peers were up to, when scholarship money delivered me as a postgraduate to New York and Europe, I took to the sybaritic life. I wasn't a natural. I had to work at it – even at play the ingrained work ethic had its place – and that's where the drink and drugs came in. Useful for blurring edges, eliminating inhibitions and anaesthetising private pain.

But I was always a weekend Generation Xer and when Hal died, and I decided it was time to get serious again, I quickly acquired a whole new set of friends – steady, interesting and sober – mostly through my work.

Off duty, I never liked to see them in groups of more than four; I got enough community in the course of my day job and by evening my small store of gregariousness was exhausted.

Agnes, who has none of her parents' failings and all of their strengths, is fine here in Fascaray, as she is fine in New York. She is an assiduous and generous friend yet content in her own company. She goes to school each day without complaint, her wide green eyes untroubled by anxiety.

I've sometimes flinched to see Marco so vividly in her, in her sudden enthusiasms and quick delight, her expressive hands and easy laugh, her reckless runs at life and her way of reading intently, cupping her sweet chin in her hand. From me, I suppose she has a certain focus and serious-ness, the iron will to see a task through to the end, no matter how dull (homemaking excepted). Her colouring – dark hair, the green eyes, skin that can take the sun (a trait that's wasted here) – she owes to both of us. But she is also entirely her own creature and surprises me every day with her difference. Where did this person come from, with her subtlety, her instinctive tidiness, her acute awareness of the feelings of others and a sometimes disabling desire to please? Not from me. Certainly not from Marco.

I seem to have spent my entire life aspiring to solitude; as children, my brother Aidan and I slept in bunk beds – I claimed the top on account of seniority – but I campaigned for years for a room of my own, not easily achieved in the small apartments my parents could afford. I didn't take easily to dorm life in Turville Chantry, though it did have the advantage of being thousands of miles from home. By the time my parents acquired a three-bedroom tract house and my wish for a room of my own could have been granted, I was out of the door, on my way to college.

At work, my ambition for promotion has never been primarily about salary or even responsibility; what I've always aspired to is an office of my own. I don't have a problem with colleagues, mostly, and I enjoy collective work and office banter, but I also prize the freedom to be able to walk away and focus on singular tasks in silence. I'm not greedy – a cupboard with a desk and chair would be just fine. All I want is a space where I can shut the door for an hour or two, sit down and hear nothing but my own sighs of relief.

Yesterday, in one of McWatt's notebooks I came across an old Scots word: 'katterzem'. He'd underlined it and written the definition in brackets – '(someone willing to go out dining at a minute's notice)'. It would never have applied to McWatt but it would work for Marco, who was incapable of being alone. 'I'm a social animal, a macaque monkey – we hang around in packs,' he told me. 'You're more of a solitary creature, a bear or a bobcat. You only meet up for mating and breeding.' I think it was meant to be funny. We would have been out every night of the week, seeing bad off-Broadway plays then downing compensatory drinks in bars or clubs or at crowded theatre parties, if he'd had his way. Well, he has his way now.

How did we ever think our relationship could have worked? We should have seen it coming and ignored those friends who reassured us 'opposites attract': his fearlessness balanced my timidity, and vice versa, they said; his reckless head for heights was tethered by my vertigo; his tendency to chaos balanced by my instinct for order. But opposites also repel. So I came to Fascaray looking for my own room once more, hoping to close a door on the clamour and disarray of my love life, gather strength in tranquillity and listen to the ocean surging and withdrawing in an amplified version of my own sighs.

Looking out at the sea's grey swell under the incessant rain, I know that John Donne was right – no man is an island – but he told only half the story; no island is an island either. Here there's no escape, no privacy. We're all sharing the same small space, the same room, encircled by the same uncompromising sea.

Tomorrow, once again, I'll abandon my daughter and flee the oppressive intimacy of Fascaray, seeking sanctuary in the anonymity of the mainland. Sanctuary, purely in the interests of work, of course.

Solitarnes

Tae dowp on crags, tae muse oer loch an glen,
Tae huily scart the forest's mirky deep.
Whaur things dae dwell forby oor narra ken,
An human fit is seendil tae be keeked.

Tae sclim the paithless mountain aw unseen,
Wi the wild deer stravaigin free;
Oer skooshin linns an steep ravines
Ah'm nae alane, perlustrin cantily,

Bletherin wi Naitur, nae alane
But corrieneuchin wi her chairms,
Far frae clannish meddlin an pain
Frae clashmaclavers an aw hairm.

Grigor McWatt, efter Lord Byron, 1950[10]

10 From *Kenspeckelt*, Virr Press, 1959. Reprinted in *Warld in a Gless: The Collected Varse of Grigor McWatt*, Smeddum Beuks, 1992.

24 October 2014

The address takes me to a fifties maisonette block, part of a dispiriting low-rise ochre project with a view of the town retail park. The woman who opens the door is, I guess, in her forties, thin and nervy with a badger-streak of white in her dark bobbed hair. Speaking in a whisper, she leads me into a small overheated front room where an elderly man sits in an armchair scowling over a crossword, one slippered foot stretched out on a low stool.

Transcription of interview with Donald MacInnes,
Taigh na Mara, Ballantrae Drive, Oban, 24 October 2014.
Conducted by Mhairi McPhail. Unedited.

'No. I'm sure it was tomorrow. I had it down in my diary as tomorrow. Flora? Flora! What did you let her in for? She's a day early. If she wants her interview, she'll just have to go away and come back tomorrow. I'm a busy man. I can't just drop everything because she's too gowkit to get the date right . . . Flora? . . . [INAUDIBLE] . . . A mix-up in my diary. Must have been Flora, my daughter. She took it down wrong. As usual. What's the point of keeping a dog and barking yourself? . . . No, no. You might as well stay, now you're here . . .'

'So it's Miss McPhail, isn't it, scion of Hector, one of the Five Immortals? I never met your grandfather – I was barely a year old at the time of the Land Raid – but Grigor will have known him. My late wife Nancy's family would have known him too. She was a Fascaradian, one of the Finnverinnity Campbells.

'You've one of those awful American accents though . . . Canadian? Same difference. A Yankee McPhail. Hector wouldnae have been too pleased about that. Nor Grigor. But it could be worse, I suppose. You could be English.

'You're not exactly a fair-skinned Celt "wi' the bloom of the gowan

220

on your haffet". I might have had you down as a "BWT" at first glance, no offence. A Bloody Wee Tally – that's what we used to call the Italians who came to the west of Scotland to run the ice-cream vans and chip shops. No?'

'Your mother was Glasgow Irish? Och, we're all Irish. The Scots were an Irish tribe who drove out the benighted Picts from ancient Alba. You could be Black Irish – a descendant of the Spanish sailors shipwrecked on Ireland's shores after the Armada. Or maybe one of our endangered aboriginals – a dark-browed Pict. Yours was a matrilineal tribe. Bold Macalpin's mother, from Fascaray herself, was the last of the royal line. Flora! Flora! Tea please. Now she's here, she might as well stay . . .'

'Aye, Miss McPhail, I can see it now, you're a throwback to the women warriors of ancient Caledonia – pirates and raiders every one . . .'

'McWatt? I'd say he had a strong streak of Pict, too. Maybe not in looks, but he was born to fight. Half Pict, half Viking – a proud berserker, as he liked to say. He was a fighter all right. But a dreamer, too, and a visionary. A *seannachie* – descendant of the bardic class of our Dal Riatan forebears over the water in what they now call Ulster.'

'No, he didn't have the Gaelic – always said that was another thing the English stole from him. But for me, a wide-eyed know-nothing boy, it was pure good luck that he didn't speak it and I did. That was a service I could perform for him.'

'. . . Flora! We'll take a jug of hot water too. This may take some time . . .'

'So, Grigor. Aye. I first came across him in 1959. I was a lad of fifteen, working for the forestry. We were up the woods by Kilgurnock Falls over towards Calasay and he came out to us – that collie of his, Luath, straining and snapping on the rope – to see what we were up to. When he established there were no Englishmen among us, and that we were not there at the behest of Montfitchett or his crew, he went back to his croft and returned with a bottle of whisky and some bannocks for

221

us. We sat on a felled tree trunk and talked. I could have listened to him for hours. I ended up listening to him for years. Thirteen years in fact. Thirteen long years. Aye, my meeting with Grigor McWatt was my awakening. My political awakening . . .'

'. . . You could say Grigor was what they cry a mentor. A father figure. And by God I needed one of those. My own father, a coal miner, was a clever man, eaten up by bitterness and drink. He'd been forced to leave the Highlands, like so many, and was driven underground like a rat to grub for money in the pits of the eastern flatlands. He'd no education, see. Education was for the well off. They liked to keep the working men stupid, stupid and docile so they'd put up with the miserable lives they had to lead in order to keep the wealthy warm in their big mansions and their London gentlemen's clubs. If my father had had an education, he could have made something of himself. But he had no chance.

'Some men in those situations tried to do it themselves – found a subscription library, filled the house with improving books, took evening classes and made damned sure their children got the education they were denied. My father, who had all the severity of Calvinism without the religious belief, went the other way. He saw books as a middle-class conspiracy, saw school as the Establishment's way of further oppressing the proletariat and he did his best to ensure we were as ignorant, illiterate and angry as he was.

'I couldn't get away from my family quick enough and the first time I left home, to work with the forestry, was a revelation. The freedom, the landscape – I felt an instant and ancient connection – the companionship of men who weren't always drunk or recovering from the effects of drink and didn't necessarily want to hammer the lights out of you for expressing an opinion contrary to their own.

'So when Grigor suggested I stay in Calasay and work for him as his "amanuensis", as he called it, I flew at the chance. I trailed round the island with him to the crofts and blackhouses, drinking tea with the old folk, listening to their stories, taking notes, interpreting and translating from the Gaelic for him when necessary. I also took care of the animals, helped with the crops, household stuff, general repairs, that sort of thing. Easy money, you could say. But there was no money involved.

He became my legal guardian and I was happy to sever ties with my own family. I got my keep, a roof over my head, food and a bit of change – pocket money – to spend in the shop and the pub, though I was never a drinker. I jouked that McWatt masterclass. I had my father's example to think of. And though Grigor liked a dram, he never turned violent on me. Well, maybe just the once . . .'

'I ken that to the modern way of thinking the arrangement was unusual – older man, teenaged lad, unrelated, living thegether in an isolated place. There was talk on the island too. There's always talk. You'd spit in the face of one Fascaradian and thirty would wipe their eye. I've lost count of the times I've had to tell smutty-minded interviewers – "no impropriety whatsoever took place". And in case you're still wondering, Miss McPhail, I repeat – Grigor McWatt never laid a finger on me. Not in that way . . .'

'He wasn't the easiest man, especially in drink, I give you that. But who is? And compared to my father, believe me, he was a model of douceness and sobriety. There was no badness in him. He looked out for me. Remembered me in his will, too, despite our falling-out. Enough to see me comfortably through to my own end, anyway, and my daughter . . .'

'Aye, I mind Lilias. I mind her well; heaven and hell in one neat wee package. As lovely a lassie as any you'd clap eyes on. She came over to Fascaray just the once. Grigor was all for sending her away the minute she arrived. She just turned up with her bags and a bottle on the back of Mikey MacRae's tractor, hair streeling in the wind, singing some raucous ballad. Worse for wear, I think. I made up a bed for her in the byre . . .

'She was a good-hearted lassie. Nice wee figure, too. But she could be tough. Knew what she wanted. Dug her heels in. Stayed for a fortnight, tried to make herself a fixture. She'd a good way with the animals, a dab hand. Patient and cheerful, when she wasn't creeping about, bluitert or reeling from the effects of the previous night's session. But she was never a nasty drunk. Not to me. She bubbled a bit – she was the greetin [weeping] kind of drunk. Tearful and affectionate. Hands everywhere . . . !

'She got stuck in with the chores too. Shared the burden of work with me. I got on fine with her . . . But she was no for Grigor. Too wild for Grigor. He could match her dram for dram – and he did most nights – but she was seeking some kind of rapture in the bottle and if rapture wisnae available, which it wisnae, oblivion would do the trick. Grigor, though, rarely lost control. He was cold, see. Fascaray, Scotland, they were his only real passions. Maybe it was his poetic calling, or his childhood, or his commando training or whatever terrible sights he'd seen in the war, but he was inward; a life-o-the-mind man. A stoic.

'She tried to stir him up, sunbathing on the brae in the scuddie – a fine sight, I tell you – chapping on his bedroom door in the wee hours more than once. He would shout at her tae clear off. I heard her greetin many a night. And then she took a shine to me. What healthy young fellow could resist?

'And that was when Grigor and me had our big fallout. It had been brewing between us for a long time. There were problems with the otters. Those craturs were wild, dangerous, should never have been taken into a domestic setting. They caused havoc, almost burned the place down twice and attacked me. Nearly had the leg off me. I could have bled to death. It was a doomed project and he didn't like me pointing it out. You can be sure that story never made its way into his columns, or his compendium. Didn't fit the myth.

'Lilias, that summer of 1972, was the breaking point. He found us, her and me, thegether in the byre one morning and it all blew up . . . He ordered her out of the house. Ended with me and him scrapping on the floor, tearing lumps out of each other, while Lilias stood wailin and greetin by the door, suitcase in hand. I walked her back over to Ruh where Mikey picked her up in his tractor and took her to Finnverinnity. That was the last I saw of her. And a week later I was gone from Calasay myself. Alec Campbell offered me a job on the boats and I made myself useful in Finnverinnity for a year or so. Grigor and me, we'd see each other around the island. We'd nod, be civil, but we never exchanged another word . . .'

'You're living in Fascaray now? So you can imagine how it must have been for a young man like myself coming up from one of the miserable mining villages of the south – lungs full of coal dust, heart full of hate – stepping off that boat at Finnverinnity. The curve of the harbour drawing you in like a welcoming arm, the surge of the sea, the hills, and mighty Mammor putting us in our place, reminding us of the pettiness of our problems and the fleeting nature of human life.

'It was a sudden admission to paradise and, to a young man hungry for knowledge as well as freedom, it was a chance to sit at the feet of genius. Everything I learned, I learned from McWatt. He opened his library and his mind to me. I was a daft boy, no idea what I was doing, where I was going. It was hard, often lonely work. But, whatever happened between us at the end, Grigor McWatt made a man of me.'

Gin

Gin you can dwaum – an no mak dwaums yer maister,
Gin you can think – an no mak thochts yer mynt,
Gin you can tryst wi Sonse an wi Mishanter,
An haunle thaise twa mak-ons jist the same . . .
Gin you can staun tae hear the trowth ye've spaiken,
Pirled by reivers tae mak a fank fur fuils,
Or watch the things you gied yer life tae, breuken,
An lootch tae build agane wi dashelt tuils . . .
Gin you can mak a bing o aw yer gettins
An chance it aw upoan a gem o cairts,
An tyne, an stert agane aw over
An nivir girn or show embdy yer feart.
Gin ye can gar yer hert an virr an smeddum
Tae ser yer shot lang efter they hae gaun,
An sae haud on whan there is naething in ye
Binna the wull that says tae them 'Haud on!'
Gin ye can gab wi thrangs an keep yer virtue,
Stravaig wi kings or fowk wi but a puckle
Gin naither faes nor louing pals can skaithe ye,
Gin aw men coont wi you but nane sae muckle;
Gin ye can colf the unforgeein meenit
Wi saxty saicants' wirth o hynie rin,
Yours is the Yird and awthing that's in it
An – whit is mair – ye'll be a Man, ma son.

Grigor McWatt, efter Rudyard Kipling, 1960[11]

11 From *Kowk in the Kaleyard*, Virr Press, 1975. Reprinted in *Warld in a Gless: The Collected Varse of Grigor McWatt*, Smeddum Beuks, 1992.

A real *Wicker Man* moment. I walk into the store on a busy Thursday morning – must be a dozen people in there, talking, confiding, laughing – and the whole place falls silent. Margaret Mackenzie eyes me shiftily as she serves me. I'm so weary of feeling that I have to justify myself here but my anger at this unspoken hostility to outsiders is matched by a corrosive sense that my silent accusers are right: I don't belong here. I've always been a fraud. I don't belong anywhere.

When I arrived at the age of five for my first day at convent school in Canada, I was asked to recite a nursery rhyme from memory. I meekly obliged and was puzzled by the response. This was the nursery rhyme that determined my fate:

> *Wee chookie birdie, lol, lol, lol,*
> *Sittin on a windie sol,*
> *The windie sol began tae crack,*
> *Wee chookie birdie, quack, quack, quack.*

The nuns treated me with kindly concern and arranged free elocution lessons. My Professor Higgins was Miss Garrahy, an Irishwoman with a gift for mimicry and an odd passion for English royalty. I learned to purse my lips as I spoke, eliminate my rhotic 'r's by taming my tongue, truncate my 'ch's into a hard click and stretch out those telltale vowels. Miss Garrahy taught me well. Too well, it seems, as I negotiate the hostile preconceptions of fellow Scots and the narrow-eyed exasperation of my egalitarian American daughter.

The language question set me apart from my own family – my parents retained their Glasgow accents and as I grew older I caught in my mother's flashes of impatience the sense that I had become the enemy within – a strange bird cuckooing away in a nest of doves, or doos as they would call them. My brother, who went to a co-ed high school and always saw himself as a straight-on uncomplicated Canadian – his classless North

American accent was acceptable to my parents – teased me without remorse for what he saw as my vocal affectation.

My newly acquired diction could be a source of entertainment, too. Home from a hard day in the steel mill, after a meal grudgingly cooked by my mother and eaten in silence, my father would hand me a copy of the *Globe and Mail* and ask me to read out news items I was barely old enough to understand. He would listen to me, ear cocked, with quiet attention as if I were the BBC World Service. He was much taken with a term of disapproval I picked up from some of the wealthier girls at school, and his impersonation of me became a family joke, especially relished by my younger brother. At news of some minor inconvenience or disappointment, our father would draw himself up, flutter his eyelashes and utter, in the manner of, say, Billy Connolly playing Lady Bracknell: 'How ghaaarstly!' He would drag out my extended 'a' for a full four seconds as if retching.

Three terms in Oxfordshire, England – I sat, and won, the scholarship in open defiance of my parents – completed the process. Surrounded by Henriettas, Serenas and Venetias, I couldn't join in their talk about ponies, or hunt balls, or skiing holidays with any confidence but I could mimic their accents. The mask became the face.

Vocabulary was trickier; it took me some years, weathering the confusion of friends and scepticism of strangers, before I could identify which word or phrase belonged at home and which in the wider world. At home, we 'got the messages', while my friends went shopping; my family 'redd the table', rather than cleared it; were 'scunnered', rather than sickened; I was 'thrawn', rather than stubborn; we were 'clatty' rather than untidy; we 'greeted' rather than wept. We ate 'champ' with 'sybies' (mashed potatoes with spring onions), 'pieces' rather than sandwiches; and the washroom, known by the nuns in Canada as 'the lavabo' and the girls at Turville Chantry as 'the loo', was called at home 'the cludgie'.

I had a 'spirit of the staircase' moment today when I read an entry in *The Fascaray Compendium* aimed at those 'gallehooing gowks, mostly – though not exclusively – non-Scots, who dismiss the Scots language as a regional dialect of English'. McWatt, making the case for Braid Scots in its Doric and Lallans forms, explained that it's 'no more a dialect than Catalan is a local variant of Castilian Spanish'. If only I'd read this before

I'd met Ailish, I could have countered her smug Hibernian certainties. Like Grigor McWatt's grandfather Aonghas, denied his Gaelic 'mither tongue', my education stifled my Scottish self and was the first stage of my long journey away from home. I lost my voice and became a permanent exile, internally as well as geographically.

Arriving in the teeming Babel of New York was liberating because no one, or almost no one, belonged there. It was as good a place as any for a confused, estranged itinerant like me to end up; everyone I knew, bar Marco, was a confused, estranged itinerant. We were all stateless orphans and here in this great city of self-invention, we could make ourselves up as we went along. Marco, of course, arrived in the world complacent and fully formed; the nearest he ever got to an identity crisis was when he mislaid his driver's licence. He describes himself unselfconsciously as an Italian-American, in that order, though he possesses little of his ancestral motherland's language and few of its culinary skills. 'You got to face it,' he said to me. 'Italy is a state of mind as well as a nation. It's about home and family and friends and food and *la dolce vita.* And Scotland? If your family's anything to go by . . . Plus, it's not even a nation. And don't get me started on the food.'

This Fascaray venture is my crack at proving him wrong and coming home. I may be an incomer, but many of the islanders today are incomers themselves and, as the child of Dougal McPhail and the granddaughter of Hector McPhail, I have as much claim to a place here as Margaret Mackenzie or any of them.

The Pirlin Scottish Road

Afore the Roman came tae Tyne or oot tae Falkirk strode,
The pirlin Scottish drunkart made the pirlin Scottish road.
A reelin road, a trinnlin road, or sae we've aften heard,
An efter him the meenister ran, the factor an the laird;
A blythsome road, a birlin road an such as we did tread,
The nicht we ganged tae Plockton by way o Peterhead.

Ah kennt nae harm o Bonaparte an plenty o the laird,
An fur tae fecht the Frenchman Ah widnae hae a care;
But Ah wid gie them laldie if ere they came arrayed
To straighten oot the creukit road a Scottish drunkart made,
Where you an Ah went doon the wynd, aw bevvied tae oor lugs
The nicht we ganged tae Clachtoll by way o Candleriggs.

His sins they were forgien him, or why dae flooers rin
Ahint him: an the bruim-buss aw strengthenin in the sun?
The skellum ganged frae left tae richt nae kennin which was which,
But the clonger was abuin him when they foond him in the sheuch.
God forgie us, nor gang by us; we didnae see sae clear
The nicht we ganged tae Arisaig by way o Ardersier.

Ma pals, we wullna gang agane or gamf an aunceant radge,
Or rack oor haulflin gowkerie tae be the sheem o age,
But we'll stravaig wi shairper een this paith that wandereth,
An see ungubbed in e'en licht the dacent howff o death;
For there is guid news yet tae hear an braw things tae be seen,
Afore we gang tae Paradise by way o Pittenweem.

Grigor McWatt, efter G. K. Chesterton, 1958[12]

---

12 From *Kowk in the Kaleyard*, Virr Press, 1975. Reprinted in *Warld in a Gless: The Collected Varse of Grigor McWatt*, Smeddum Beuks, 1992.

RUMOURS BEGAN TO CIRCULATE ON THE ISLAND IN THE LATE 1950s about McWatt's occasional 'lost weekends' in Edinburgh. He was said to spend his time there getting drunk with fellow poets in the cramped bars of Rose Street, arguing about prosody and Home Rule. He was also thought to be soft on a girl he had met. But on Fascaray he remained a solitary figure, tending his croft, reading his books and, as he said himself, 'writing, writing, writing. Only with a pen in my hand do I ever feel truly alive.'

To local children he was a wild-haired bogeyman, best avoided – especially when in drink. Young Fergus McKinnon once claimed he'd seen McWatt bite the head off an otter, a story which, according to Effie MacLeod, earned the boy a swift smack from his teacher, Miss Elspeth Millar.

'Oh, what a tangled web we weave, when first we practise to deceive, Fergus,' Miss Millar was said to have told the boy, before adding, by way of illumination, 'Scott. *Marmion.*'

McWatt's national fame – and notoriety – had another boost in 1959, the year he published his first collection of verse, *Kenspeckelt.* It was also, coincidentally, the bicentenary of the birth of Robert Burns.

Roy Fraser, editor of the *Pibroch*, planned to launch a Burns celebration in the area – Burns's great-aunt Isabella Blaine was said to have married a Fascaradian – and Fraser thought Fascaray's 'resident poet' might want to honour his predecessor.

'We'll have a Burns Supper at the Finnverinnity Inn and you could give a reading of his work. Perhaps "The Cotter's Saturday Night"?' Fraser suggested over a three hour lunch in the Fisher's Airms. 'We could also have a poetry competition and you could choose the winner.'

The poet described their meeting, and Fraser's proposal, in the *Compendium.* 'As is so often the prelude to questionable ventures, strong drink was taken,' he wrote. He declined the invitation to the supper, though he agreed, 'following several further persuasive rounds of whisky,' to judge the competition. After a week spent sifting through verse by local school-children and pensioners, McWatt declared in an intemperate column in the *Auchwinnie Pibroch* that all the entries were doggerel, unfit to be considered poetry. He went further, taking a sideswipe at the national poet – 'Burns was a man of contradictions, an egalitarian who courted elites, a fine lyricist and a cheap songster, aye trembling on the brink of a sentimental, dishonest tear. And let us not forget he made his money collecting taxes for the English.'

McWatt might have felt he had a supporter in his friend Hugh MacDiarmid, who consistently attacked the Burns cult for its reactionary kitsch and 'kailyard' whimsicality. It was, after all, MacDiarmid who wrote – '*You canna gang to a Burns supper even / Wi-oot some wizened scrunt o a knock-knee / Chinee turns roon to say, "Him Haggis – velly goot!" / And ten to wan the piper is a Cockney.*' But even MacDiarmid felt moved to defend Burns, while acknowledging his 'shortcomings' (among which MacDiarmid identified, somewhat contradictorily, 'a tendency to jeer at foreign things and express a sort of xenophobia'). The national poet, however, could not be blamed, MacDiarmid argued, for the 'Church of Burns', which 'denied his spirit to honour his name, denied his poetry to laud his amours, preserved his furniture and repelled his message'.

MacDiarmid did, though, endorse McWatt's view of the appalling standards of literary skill in contemporary Scotland: 'The horde of Burns imitators have . . . reduced Scots poetry to an abyss of worthless rubbish unparalleled in any other European literature,' wrote MacDiarmid. He exempted himself, and McWatt, from that abyss.

In London, the *Times Literary Supplement*, the *Listener* and the *New Statesman* reported the controversy with undisguised pleasure. But the support or condemnation of metropolitan English critics was of little interest to McWatt. A letter at that time to Lilias Hogg, to whom he had dedicated *Kenspeckelt*, suggests he was more concerned with news that his opinions and poems had received respectful attention in the Soviet Union, despite the fact that Burns was held in great esteem there as a poet of the people.

'Mother Russia seems to have taken me to her bosom,' he wrote. 'Oh, clever, lucky Mother Russia,' replied Lilias. McWatt's satisfaction in seeing his name in *Pravda* – an Edinburgh-based member of the Scottish

USSR Friendship Society sent the cutting and the translation – must have been tempered by the description of him in the article as 'the British folk singer Gringer McWat'.

A Granite Ballad – The Reimagining of Grigor McWatt,
Mhairi McPhail (Thackeray College Press, 2016)

She Gangs in Brawness

She gangs in brawness, like the nicht
O cloodless climes an starnlicht skies;
An aw that's best o derk an bricht
Meet in her coupon an her eyes;
Aw saftened tae that neshie licht
That heiv'n tae glormach day denies.

An oan her brou, an ower her een,
Sic douceness, man, ye've niver seen,
Her daizlin smouch it beirs the gree;
This paragon o womanhuid,
A mynd entranced by aw she sees,
A hert whase loue is nocht but guid.

Grigor McWatt, efter Lord Byron, 1959[13]

13   From *Kenspeckelt*, Virr Press, 1959. Reprinted in *Warld in a Gless: The Collected Varse of Grigor McWatt*, Smeddum Beuks, 1992.

AFTER FASCARAY, AND SCOTLAND — A LONG WAY AFTER, BY her estimation — Lilias Hogg was said by many to have been the love of Grigor McWatt's life. But, as she complained in one bitter letter to him in the seventies, 'I always thought I was a poor third, and I settled for that. Now I realise I was even lower in your ranking.' According to the feminist narrative, Hogg, creatively thwarted and romantically spurned, was driven to take her comforts where she could find them, among the poets in their hangouts in the smoky bars and rackety flats at the edge of Edinburgh's New Town. The poets, or makars, if they did not fall for her, were certainly charmed by her in the early years and she flits through their verse, evanescent, gay (in the old sense), sometimes unreachably sad, but always ornamental.

When describing her, admirers often alluded to masterpieces of Western art — 'A luscious Ingres on a bar stool', 'Manet's Olympia with a glass of malt', 'Botticelli's Venus in the crepuscular manly world of a Scots pub', or, according to Archie Aitken, 'in contemplation, and even in drink, possessing the luminous beauty of a Vermeer'.

In his frequently anthologised poem 'She Gangs in Brawness', McWatt described his first sight of Lilias Hogg in 1958 in the gloom of a Rose Street pub where the cigarette smoke swirled like dry ice: '*saftened tae that neshie licht / That heiv'n tae glormach day denies*'.

Hugh MacDiarmid hymned her eyes, '*dark as peat, bricht as the North Star*'. Norman MacCaig saw her as '*lonely and loveless as the moon*'. Sydney Goodsir Smith, when he wasn't talking poetry and politics with the men or running after his latest girlfriend, was all over Lilias, panting like a puppy. Ian Crichton Smith lent her money during hard times and never asked for it back, while shy, courteous George Mackay Brown delivered her safely home after several nights of barbarous drinking. Willie McCracken compared her to Millais' Ophelia — '*white gowan pale, as the ghaist o' loue*' — and broke the nose of Archie Aitken in Menzies' Bar over a disputed glance from 'Bonnie Lilias, the Flooer o Rose Street'.

She was, when she first came into their lives in the late 1950s, an auburn-haired beauty of seventeen, a warm-hearted, big-bosomed Edinburgh lass with an easy laugh, poetic ambitions and inchoate yearnings, enduring her secretarial course to appease her conventional family.

Taken by a racy friend to Menzies', where the poets presided like knights in a Caledonian Camelot, drinking competitively and jousting noisily over literature and politics, Lilias was drawn to them as to a blazing hearth in a northern winter. The racy friend – not a looker – fell away but Lilias became a regular, thrilled to be the lone girl, exalted, in the company of these bohemian alpha males, awed by their 'sublime blether'.

The artist Billy Drummond recorded one of those immortal evenings in a sketch-book and later painted the scene in oils from memory in the 1980s, long after the Menzies' Bar set had vanished, some to the 'ayebidin lock-in abuin', as McWatt put it. The finished canvas, an enormous work of 8ft by 6ft rendered in bold, Matisse-like colours, now hangs in Edinburgh's National Gallery of Modern Art.

The painting, called *Makars' Menzies'*, shows a group of ten men of various ages, formally posed in an ill-lit pub. Some are standing, others are seated on bentwood chairs. Seven are smoking (two pipes, five cigarettes), seven are holding pint glasses containing beer – 'heavy' – five have, alone or in addition, stubby glasses of liquor.

One poet, identifiable by his heroically jutting chin as the Orcadian George Mackay Brown, puffs at a cigarette and holds a pint of cream-topped stout while leaning in to listen to the central figure, a dark, wild-haired shaman who points skywards like an Old Testament prophet with his right index finger while his left grips a tumbler of what we assume is whisky. Grigor McWatt has taken the floor and is commanding the attention, if not the direct gaze, of his nine compatriots who seem to be caught in his force field. Directly facing McWatt stands a pipe smoker with small, terrier-like features and a lion's mane of white hair. This is Hugh MacDiarmid, 'looking like a Caledonian Einstein', according to McWatt. In the painting, MacDiarmid's face is creased in an attentive scowl as he listens to 'the Fascaradian in fu flaucht'.

Edwin Morgan, bespectacled, the collar of a flamboyant lime-green shirt visible under his dark jacket, sits in profile at the edge of the group, apparently reflecting on McWatt's words, and sips a glass of wine: a defiant double affectation in 1950s Scotland where, in the spartan, masculine world of the public house, to take one's alcohol – only beer or whisky permitted – sitting down was regarded as effeminate. English even. Long, lean Norman MacCaig, his sombre demeanour giving no hint of his warmth and humour, is drinking his beer in the acceptable male stance. He looms over McWatt but looks away, perhaps lost in thought, while Sydney Goodsir Smith, 'a degenerate cherub', according to McWatt, plump, ruddy-cheeked and glistening-eyed, is just behind McWatt, leaning towards him, mouth half open as if about to interrupt.

Two other figures in the picture, ascetic and drinkless, have been identified as Iain Crichton Smith and Sorley Maclean, while glowering at each other in the right foreground, fists bunched, 'twa pugilists in duffel coats', are Willie McCracken and Archie Aitken.

The only woman in the painting, a lambent beauty with smouldering eyes, stands to the left of the picture and is naked, save for a Saltire flag which covers her hips and thighs. Her breasts, 'perky as the Paps o Jura', according to Willie McCracken, are on full display. Continuing the mountaineering metaphor and in reference to the striking western peaks of Staic Pollaidh, Archie Aitken called her 'Oor ain Stacked Polly'. This is Caledonia herself, in the person of young Lilias Hogg. The poets, rapt in thought and argument, ignore her.

A Granite Ballad – The Reimagining of Grigor McWatt,
Mhairi McPhail (Thackeray College Press, 2016)

Hogmanay, 1958

Ah hae met thaim at the dit o day
Comin wi bricht coupons
Frae counter or lettern amang grey
Embra New Toon hooses.
Ah hae passed wi a nod o the heid
Or pit-on haiveless wirds,
Or hae daedled awhile an said
Pit-on haiveless wirds,
An thocht afore Ah hae done
O a jamphi yairn or a sneist
Tae cuitle a cronie
Aroon the gleed at the howff,
Siccar that they an Ah
Bided where mixter-maxter's worn:
Aw cheenged, cheenged thortout:
An unco brawness is born.

Tae lang in thrall
Can mak a chuckie o the hert.
Soond oot the bagpipes:
That is heiv'ns pairt, oor pairt
Tae hishie name onwith name,
As a mither cries her wean
When dowre at last has come
Oan skellum limbs.
Ah write it oot in varse —
MacDiarmid an MacCaig,
An Morgan an MacLean

Nou an in time tae be,
Whaurivir plaid is worn,
Are cheenged, cheenged thortout:
An unco brawness is born.

Grigor McWatt, efter W. B. Yeats, 1958[14]

14   From *Kenspeckelt*, Virr Press, 1959. Reprinted in *Warld in a Gless: The Collected Varse of Grigor McWatt*, Smeddum Beuks, 1992.

found a new job: 'a part-time, temporary arrangement that will not – not too much, anyway – interfere with my work at McDuff's. You're always telling me that I need to hold down a steady job so I will do as you say, my liege, even though I die of boredom each day. But this unsteady job is a bit of fun'. It was also, she said, her 'bid for stardom' after a chance encounter in Rose Street.

'I bumped into – collided with, really – the merriest bunch of fellows. They were travelling players up from London for the Fringe Festival, keen to the see the city's sights, so we trailed up and down the local hostelries, your Flooer a tour guide to four rampaging thespians. You should have seen the look Sydney gave them. Archie got gey obstreperous and was all for asking them to step outside to settle the matter with fists, but they administered copious quantities of whisky which took him over the threshold of rage to the vestibule of insensibility. I cannot tell you how I came to wake next morning in an unfamiliar flat in Stockbridge with a pneumatic headache and metholated breath in the (entirely innocent) company of two loons who, in the crisp light of an Edinburgh morning, were not nearly as witty, and certainly not so merry, as I remembered. But they did offer me a job!'

The director and leading actor of the Balham-based Catalyst Collective had invited her to appear in their experimental theatrical production over three nights at the Edinburgh Festival and her manager at McDuff's printworks was giving her two afternoons of unpaid leave for rehearsals.

McWatt's reply was laconic.

'If there is one thing worse than an Englishman it is an English actor – snobbery with an admixture of insincerity.'

Lilias, in a subsequent letter, was defiant.

'You always tell me I should find purposeful work. Everyone else of our acquaintance, it seems – yourself included – is permitted to swan around, playing languid martyr to his own genius. But I must pay my way with office drudge work. You say I'm a Muse. Have you noticed that this revered status is one consonant away from Mute? Well, here's my chance to shine and speak out – not literally, alas. Not yet. Mine is a non-speaking role in this production. A non-costume role too. But from little acorns . . .'

The revue, *A Masque for Calliope*, featured jazz scat singing, a mock crucifixion and satirical references to Harold Macmillan, Cyprus, the new sixty-mile M1 motorway, Margot Fonteyn's imprisonment in Panama, and the Aldermaston 'Ban the Bomb' march. The cast of fifteen performed in the nude. The production attracted some publicity, and a boost in audience figures, after outraged Edinburgh councillors and clerics tried to close it down on the grounds of indecency and blasphemy. The revue completed its three-night run before its cast and crew disbanded and journeyed southwards into obscurity and eventual respectability, leaving Lilias to return, chastened, to work. She expressed no further ambition to work in theatre, and never mentioned the experience again.

A Granite Ballad – The Reimagining of Grigor McWatt,
Mhairi McPhail (Thackeray College Press, 2016)

31 October 2014

A big day. For Agnes and for me. I'm making my maiden speech to the residents of Fascaray tonight. For her, the real event is Halloween.

'Ailsa said the Scottish people invented it. And we're just copying them,' she says, indignant, trusting I'll contradict her friend.

'Ailsa's right. But we gave the world Walt Disney.'

Her pride is restored. She's dressed in costume – an old cotton nightdress, hiking boots and a witch's hat (from the pound store in Auchwinnie). She hisses, waving her hands with their stick-on luminous talons (also from the pound store). Under her hat, she has painted her face white and rimmed her eyes with black. Though she wouldn't like to hear it, she makes an endearing ghoul.

'Scary!' I say.

'They call ghosts "bogles" or "bogies" here, and trick-or-treating "guising",' she says.

My own guise this evening is calculatedly conservative. Skirt, shirt and jacket – my unexceptional corporate threads – instead of my preferred uniform of jeans and sweater, and low-heeled pumps rather than sneakers; my Invisible Woman interview costume. I'm hoping no one will film my speech and post it online. Even under favourable conditions, with the most well-disposed audience, when I know my brief and have no fear of being exposed as a fraud, I'm a timorous public speaker.

While my Pygmalion transformation hasn't hindered my career, it's left me with a terror of addressing an audience, which has been something of a handicap. The most hostile crowd could never trash my performance as effectively as I do myself. I open my mouth to speak and, though to some I might sound plausible enough, if a little quiet, my inner Scot is hooting at my pretensions. I'm overcome by a sense of inauthenticity. With a concentration I imagine approaches that of a recovering Tourette's sufferer, I mentally rehearse each word, iron flat the relevant vowels and prune my consonants hard before I speak, and I enunciate just as Miss Garrahy taught me, forcing my mutinous mouth into the necessary cat's ass. I can 'do' Scots just as I can 'do' North American English, but I'd feel fraudulent. Face it, I'm a fake in both tongues, only truly myself when silent and alone in a closet with a laptop and a box of index cards.

Johanna and Ailsa (for some reason dressed as Batman – another American gift to the world) arrive to pick up Agnes and I walk alone through the rain to Finnverinnity Hall to address the islanders, three decades after McWatt first roused the fledgling Fascaray Preservation Society in the same small, shabby venue.

The hall is already dismayingly full and vibrating with animated talk when I arrive. Sparse fairy lights twinkle over the arch of the stage and tartan bunting is strung across the rafters. As I walk down the aisle towards the narrow stage, the din of conversation stops suddenly, as if there's been a power outage. McWatt received a standing ovation here for his stirring words in 1985 but the crowd tonight seems as welcoming as a Kuna raiding party.

I recognise, next to a piratical figure with a plaid bandana and grey bird's nest beard, Barry, the postman. There is Agnes's schoolteacher, Niall Kennedy, next to Margaret Mackenzie from the post office and Reza and Iqbal Shah from the store. Eck Campbell is there with Chic McIntosh and a bunch of pub regulars including Chic's grandfather Roddy, who must be in his late eighties – his survival, he claims, a testimony to strong drink. They might be under the false impression that the free refreshments promised after the meeting will run to more than tea. I scan the faces in the hall, searching for an expression of sympathy. Encouragement would be too much to ask. I'd be happy with neutral curiosity, though mild boredom would be acceptable.

Agnes had asked to come but I didn't want my little cheerleader to witness a public display of her mother's anxieties and humiliation. My socially adept daughter would have no trouble solemnly addressing a crowd of strangers on a subject in which she has some interest and little authority. Astronomy perhaps. Or Highland cattle and palaeontology. Or driftwood collecting. I wonder if she and her friends will have any luck with their trick-or-treating. Surely all the potential treat-dispensers are here in Finnverinnity Hall hoping, in sympathy with the season, to scare the hell out of this naive American interloper.

243

I make my introduction, explain, as if for a job interview, my 'vision', for the museum and the island, and describe briefly, and without overt sentimentality – Scots have little time for overt sentimentality, though the covert sort has its place – my family connection with the island. Their eyes seem to narrow in unison. Then I invite them to make suggestions for developing the museum.

No one stirs. No one speaks. I try again, my voice faltering.

'I really would welcome your views . . .'

Someone clears his throat in the lengthening silence. But I have something up my sleeve. (Tip to anxious public speakers: always have something up your sleeve. There is no shame in bribery.)

The Auchwinnie Development and Enterprise Board, tasked with overseeing McWatt's legacy to the Fascaray Trust, has, I announce, authorised an immediate grant of £100,000 to spend on community projects.

Surely this will warm them up. Silence. Not even a tentative cough. In another setting – a chamber-music recital, perhaps, or a funeral – this profound stillness might be welcome. I steel myself for a slow handclap and a hail of tomatoes.

'I wonder,' I ask, fighting a faint vocal tremor, 'if any of you might have any suggestions as to how we might use this extra cash.'

My words trail away in a whisper of defeat and I face the mortifying hush. Someone in the back row, one of the pub regulars, gets to his feet and asks me to repeat my last sentence. It's not a friendly question exactly, but it's a question, and for that I feel cravenly grateful. I say it again, 'I'm looking for any suggestions as to how Fascaray might use this extra cash?', with the over-egged declamatory style of an auditioning actress. A very bad amateur actress, playing Portia. 'The quality of mercy . . .'

In the front row a stout elderly woman raises her hand, setting off a wind-chime arpeggio of silver bracelets. Her wide face is framed by coiled braids of white hair, Swiss milkmaid-style, and she's wearing a garish voluminous robe that could have been crafted from several medieval jousting pavilions. She is flanked by two younger companions, a man and a woman, sombre as tomb carvings in their more muted linen drapery. His pink skull shines above a froth of grey hair like a hilltop breaking through a bank of cloud, while the younger woman might make a credible Cleopatra impersonator, late period.

'We would welcome the funds to extend Balnasaig Tower Room,' says the old woman in a voice more used to issuing commands than making requests.

She is unmistakably Home Counties English and for that I feel a wild sense of relief. My accent may be mid-Atlantic but my connection to this island is unassailably stronger than hers. Gathering strength, I remind myself that I'm more of a Fascaradian than most of them here tonight.

'It's too small for our Mindfulness workshops,' she continues, 'and we've had to hold our Sacred Dance Circles outside, which isn't easy with the weather.'

'It would be helpful,' I say gently and disingenuously (for who else could she be?) 'if we can all introduce ourselves – name, job, address – before making our suggestions.'

Evelyn Fletcher, *éminence grise* of the Balnasaig Seekers, announces herself, followed by her acolytes, Jeremy Gortz and Jinny Aubrey.

A middle-aged man, lean and rugged with a terracotta tan, wearing a sweater that might have been knitted from frayed rope, stands and introduces himself as Nigel Parsons. He is also English.

'The pier should be upgraded. Larger boats still have to anchor offshore in high tide and send out a tender,' he says.

Again, it's a command rather than a request.

A bearded man in wire-rimmed glasses and army fatigues stands now. He is Piers Aubrey – is it only the English who speak out at public meetings here? – and he makes the case for a permanent office for No Fascaray Array, the campaign against the Trondfjord wind farm. His partner Alison – ah, a Scot, at last – argues that the money could go towards setting up a weekly newsletter for the campaign. The first indigenous Fascaradian to speak is Margaret Mackenzie, who overcomes her reticence, or distaste, to press for a bench outside the store, 'and a wooden shelter, with a seat, to protect old folk and young families from the rain'.

Kenny MacLeod, landlord of the Finnverinnity Inn, suggests a music festival for the island, 'it'll bring in some custom to the pub', while Chic McIntosh argues that a new central heating system for the Bothy bunkhouse will bring in more tourists. When he is not working on the ferry, Chic McIntosh manages the Bothy. Niall Kennedy suggests that a computer in the school would benefit the children as well as their families, while Lorna McKinnon, a *soignée* nineteen-year-old redhead, briefly visiting her family from nursing training in Edinburgh, makes the case for a village defibrillator.

From the back of the hall, the haggard buccaneer shouts to introduce himself. He has the rasping voice of a heavy smoker – not necessarily tobacco, his get-up suggests – and his accent is German.

'Reinhardt Schneider. Finnverinnity House. Artist . . . I support Kenny's proposal for a music festival. We could do with some livening up in the village.'

Ve could do viff some life-ening up in the willage.

Two young guys standing near the door, both gangly and glowering, raise the question of the local fishing industry. They introduce themselves as Shonnie MacDonald, prawn fisherman and, I know from my research, great-grandson and namesake of the piper who died in World War II, and Donal MacEwan, who runs the local scallop-diving business. They're backed up by a voice from the front row; an older man, a hulking figure with weather-beaten face and faded knuckle tattoos, asks me if I can give any assurances about inshore fishing quotas. He expresses concern, as others nod their heads and murmur support, about the effects of the Fascaray Array, and any future marine renewable technology, on the fishing industry. He gives his name as Eck Campbell, owner of Fascaray Fish Farm.

This is way beyond my brief but I conceal my doubts, make bland and reassuring noises and turn to the next questioner, Kylie Macfarlane, a wispy brunette in her twenties wearing an oversized field jacket and combat boots, who wants more support for the pony-trekking business she runs with her brother Darren. I assure them all, as Nesbitt instructed me, that their fish, horses, rock festivals, Sacred Dance Circles, et cetera will be given serious consideration. As long as they think their personal projects stand a chance, they're on my side.

A woman in a yellow rain slicker, round and pink-cheeked as a matryoshka doll, stands to argue for a professionally designed website for the island: 'It would help us communicate better. We can notify each other of events and services and it could also be an advertising gateway, bringing more visitors to Fascaray.' She introduces herself as Dot McKerrill, co-owner and chef of Watergaw House Hotel.

It's not a bad idea. None of them are truly bad ideas – though I think the Balnasaig Seekers make enough money to finance the extension of their own Tower Room – but the truth is when it comes to distribution of funds, the Grigor McWatt Heritage Centre and Fascaray Museum will have to be my priority.

As I issue my final bland reassurances, Margaret Mackenzie and Reza Shah lay out tea and biscuits and the pub regulars slink away disappointed. Evelyn Fletcher and her assistants have brought their own herbal infusions, which they spoon into an earthenware pot, also brought over from Balnasaig.

Evelyn comes over to suggest that I might like to visit one of their Mindfulness workshops. I thank her for the invitation.

'We tend to be oversubscribed so you should book early,' she says.

'I'll bear that in mind. Thanks.'

Kenny MacLeod intercepts me, his teacup an absurd doll's-house miniature in his ham-shank fists.

'We don't see you much in the pub,' he says.

Ten years ago, it might have been the minister or the priest challenging me about my non-attendance at church. But the clergy have gone and any remaining practising Catholics and Presbyterians must travel to Auchwinnie for their services. Balnasaig is the only religious centre left on the island. Balnasaig and the Finnverinnity Inn.

'I'm not really a pub person,' I say.

'It's the heart of the island,' he says. 'The real community centre. You can't avoid it if you want to fit in here.'

'I'll bear that in mind. Thanks.'

I walk home to number 19 in the drizzle just as Johanna brings back Agnes, an hour earlier than planned. As I'd guessed, their guising hadn't yielded much bounty.

'No one was in. They were either at your meeting or just not answering the door,' said Johanna. 'It was raining heavily, too. But we had plenty of treats at home.'

Agnes is full of it.

'We did apple bobbing, only they call it apple "dooking". And we wore blindfolds and pinned tails on a paper donkey and told stories.'

'Agnes has a great imagination,' Johanna tells me. As if it will be news to me. 'She had them all going. I thought I should break it up before things got out of hand. How was your evening?'

'Let's just say apple dooking sounds more fun.'

As I prepare our supper, Agnes tells me more about her evening.

'Aaron Schneider says he has a ghost in his house. You know, the Big House? It walks down the corridor at night rattling its chains? But Oonagh says it's just the plumbing. Kirsty says there used to be ghosts on the island but they've all gone, like the fishing.'

I have a long way to go here, but my daughter's own programme of community integration seems to be coming along nicely.

Hallowe'en, the feast of All Saints' Eve, has long been a significant event in the local calendar. It owes its origins to our ancient Celtic autumn festival of Samhuinn, when, according to the Irish medieval manuscript, the Book of Lismore, 'from sunrise to sunset, all the gods of the world were worshipped on that day'.

The recently harvested fruits and crops were consecrated, great bonfires were lit to purify communities from evil influences and the dead awoke from their graves to consort with, or admonish, the living. Torch-bearers would process around houses in the *deiseal*, or right-handed direction, to protect property and prevent fairy thieves from snatching infants and replacing them with ugly changeling children.

Before the great fires were lit, small stones would be placed at their base to represent members of each household and the following morning the ashes would be raked and each stone carefully accounted for. If a stone was missing, that family member, it was said, would be dead before the kindling of the next Hallow-Fire. Futures would be told from stalks of kail pulled blindfold from the earth, from the riddling of corn and the burning of hazelnuts, and from the uncoiling of an egg white dropped in a glass of water.

The old folk on the island can still recite the invocations made in secret by lovers bestowing charms upon each other against malign forces:

> Seun roimh shaighead,
> Seun roimh chlaidhe,
> Seun roimh shleagha,
> Seun roimh bhrùdh 's bhàthadh,
>
> Seun roimh shìodhach,
> Seun roimh shaoghlach,
> Seun roimh bhiodhbhach
> Seun roimh bhaoghal bàsach.

Chairm agin arraes,
Chairm agin claymores,
Chairm agin schiltrons,
Chairm agin birses an drounin.

Chairm agin faerie bairns,
Chairm agin bogle bairns,
Chairm agin th'ill-kyndit yins,
Chairm agin the gloam o the deid.

Even now, in this post-war Jet Age, Hallowe'en remains for many Fascaradians a day of divination, and on the evening of 31 October a young girl will still stand before a mirror, cut the peel from an apple in a single strip, cast it over her shoulder and see in its fallen shape the initials of the name of her future lover. The guising and apple dooking that delight children today are benign remnants of the early festival, in which wild dancing and general drunkenness would take place round bonfires high as hayricks. By the end of the nineteenth century, Presbyterianism imposed its stern will on the practice and it was discontinued, though a bowdlerised version of the ancient customs of merriment and misrule was considered acceptable for schoolchildren.

Thus, today, we must be tolerant when confronted with excitable bairns in their tattered costumes who approach us demanding treats with menace. A handful of nuts or a boiled sweetie should suffice to keep any mischief at bay. We should be grateful that some remnant of one of our great traditions has not been entirely vanquished by the homogenising influence of our southern neighbours. Our exiled ancestors, cleared from the land by the lairds, took Samhuinn to America and Canada, where it continues to be observed today in a sanitised form and, in a reversal of the usual tidal flow of cultural imperialism, there is some evidence that a variant of our Hallowe'en rites has even been taken up in small pockets of England, surely the death knell of any tradition.

Grigor McWatt, 31 October 1958, *Auchwinnie Pibroch*

THE NAME OF THE BAR WHERE THEY FIRST MET, MENZIES',
usefully served the function of outing any infiltrating English, who gave
themselves away by pronouncing it phonetically, to rhyme with frenzies.
To the Scots, and those in the know, it was always 'Ming-us'.

At that first meeting in 1958, Hogg wrote, 'The constant din of the
place suddenly ceased, the crowd vanished as if by sorcery, the poets
turned to pillars of salt and only we two existed, talking and talking
through that first fond night.'

The following evening they met again at a late-night hoolie in Willie
McCracken's seedy flat in McEachen Place. 'I don't remember what we
talked about,' she wrote. 'Poetry must have played a part, I suppose – but
I remember the laughter, the sudden, conspiratorial, cataclysmic hilarity
that robs you of sense and dignity, makes your lungs ache and slicks your
cheeks with tears,' she wrote.

They saw in the dawn picking their way unsteadily across the cobbles
of Grassmarket in search of a store where they might buy her cigarettes.
By noon they were back in Menzies' – favoured for its brazen flouting
of Scotland's draconian licensing laws – and were inseparable until the
Tuesday train to Fort William.

Whatever McWatt's true feelings for Lilias Hogg – and it is hard
to imagine, given the paucity of female company on Fascaray, that her
rapture at that first meeting was not shared – the letters we have indicate
that from the start it was not an equal relationship. He seems to value her
admiration – what lonely bachelor poet would not be flattered by the
attentions of an adoring girl twenty years his junior? – and he uses her as
a sounding board for his ideas and his poems rather than as an intimate
friend. The more she moves towards him, the more he retreats. Her pain,
and her need for more, is all too evident in her replies.

In June 1961 he wrote to her, 'The seggie flooers are out, gilding the
shoreline and the sight of them has forced me to drop the history and
rhapsodise in verse:'

Stravaigin lanely as a clud,
That fleets on heich ower glens an braes
An aw at aince a daizzlin croud,
A thrang, o gowden seggie flooers
Forby the loch, aneath the firth
Flauchterin and birlin in the souch.

Her response followed swiftly:

'I loved your seggie flooers and how I wished I was wandering among them too. Such stravaiging need not be lonely. You only have to ask and I'll be over in an instant, ferry permitting.'

McWatt's reply, in July, changes the subject. He sends her his Scots 'owersettin' from the Latin of the 1320 Declaration of Arbroath. 'As lang as a hunder o us bide abuin the muild, niver will we be brocht ablo English owerins. In suith it's nae for glory, nor bawbees nor mense that we ficht but for freedom – for that alane, whilk nae aefauld man gies up but wi life itsel.'

In this context, it is hard not to read his Declaration as a call to freedom not just from southern tyranny but also from the shackles of love.

A Granite Ballad – The Reimagining of Grigor McWatt,
Mhairi McPhail (Thackeray College Press, 2016)

3 November 2014

'Mom . . . ?' Agnes asks, looking up from her end of the kitchen table, an improvised workstation strewn with paints, brushes, felt pens and coloured pencils. She's tackling a school project with her usual gravity.

Down at my monochrome end of the table are my laptop, draft chapters from my book and the forbidding stack of my typed pages from *The Fascaray Compendium* awaiting a final edit. I'm sorting through the latest batch of documents, lifting them one by one from the box at my feet and putting them in orderly piles. Letters from Grigor to Lilias. Lilias to Grigor. One from Grigor McWatt to Willie McCracken. No envelope. Written but never sent perhaps. One from McCracken to McWatt. Bills. Receipts.

'Mommy?'

'What is it?'

'How do you spell celebration?'

I tell her.

'You know, when we were living in Brooklyn . . . ?'

'Shh. Not now, honey. Mommy's working.'

In one of the new letters from McWatt, dated 1970 and returned to him by her, scored through with a red cross, he tells Lilias firmly that he can't join her on a weekend trip to London.

'You know by now, surely, that such a jaunt will never happen,' he says. 'It is not just the time away from work that I can ill afford, it is the place, and the people. Edinburgh remains as far south as I'm prepared to venture and I've a fresh head of steam on with my work right now, so I'm even reluctant to make that journey. Try Archie or Willie.'

England was hostile territory to my parents too. Along with my Scots origins and Fascaray roots, I have that much in common with Grigor McWatt. To my Glasgow-Irish mother, Dolores, England was a nation of snooty, deferential, Catholic-hating, Irish-persecuting Protestants. Scots Protestants were bad enough, but they were the forelock-tugging slaves of the English. Dolores of the Many Sorrows, as I've come to think of her, had defied her religious upbringing to marry my father but she nominally kept her faith – taking me and my brother to mass every Sunday, insisting on my convent education. In later life, I suspect she has come to regret her decision to 'marry out'.

For my father, Dougal, despite his lack of curiosity about his father's Fascaradian roots, ancient familial loyalties also ran deep, and while privately he may have thought that the English had got it right about the feckless Catholics and the Irish, he shared my mother's view that England was a nation of snobs and willing serfs. On that they could agree. And then, thanks to the nuns, their first-born child learned to speak 'Broadcast Standard US English', a fancy North American version of the enemy tongue.

We grew up in Canada with a sense of embattlement. Despite my parents' unsentimental natures and their reluctance to return to the homeland that had forced them into exile – rare family holidays in Scotland would be preceded by long campaigns of attrition – my brother, until he was old enough to physically resist, was made to wear a kilt to Mass each Sunday and we were sent to school wearing the little silver badge of the Scottish National Party, its blue loop like an inverted Aids ribbon, pinned to our blazers. It must have been some other, ideal Scotland, that they longed for, a Scotland free of family grudges and tribal hostilities, in which the only enemy was the country south of the border.

We committed McWatt-style acts of sedition at home, turning the English Queen on her head on all our mail, and knew more verses of the English national anthem than most monarchists, that the 'knavish tricks' the English were planning to 'frustrate' had originally been 'popish tricks', and that the final, rarely sung, verse called for the crushing of 'rebellious Scots'. Accordingly, we were taught never to stand for 'the Queen', which caused some awkwardness, particularly as we grew older, among commonwealth loyalists.

'Mom . . . ?'

My daughter, thankfully, like her father, has no struggle with identity. An early childhood in New York, city of immigrants in a country of settlers, must have built up her immunity to the cheap and illusory comforts of belonging. She is a happy outsider, delighting in the exoticism of her new life in a place with which she has only the most abstract connection.

'Do you ever miss *your* mom and dad?' she asks.

What trap is she setting me here?

'No. Not really. Grown-ups don't miss their parents.'

'Well, I'll miss you. Even when I'm an old lady.'

'That's nice, honey,' I say. I don't add 'Don't count on it'.

She has my attention now. Tomorrow, she tells me, she is going for tea at Ailsa's house, where they plan to boil some plants to make perfume.

'We're going to use the yellow broom. That's what Ailsa calls it. Like a brush, though it doesn't look anything like a brush. Have you smelled it? It's like coconut? It's all over the hills behind Lusnaharra. Finn calls it win, or whin, but he's Irish I think. And Henry Aubrey says it's gorse. But he's English. Mr Kennedy says it's called genista, like Jennifer, in Latin. But he's a teacher. What do we call it, Mom? . . . Mom?'

'Shh,' I tell her. 'Mom's working . . .'

Indulge me for a moment if I turn my fire away this once from our southern masters' many shortcomings and examine instead an area of weakness closer to home: our own *hamartia*, or tragic flaw, cringing in a cobwebbed corner of our psyches. Scotland is strong. Scotland has given, and will continue to give, much to the world. Scotland's claims to nationhood are unassailable. So, let us, as one English poet might have said, roll all our strength into one ball and tear our pleasures with rough strife through the iron gates of life . . . to independence, the natural state of our self-reliant people, and stop, once and for all, fighting amongst ourselves.

History tells us that our origins are various, that we contain, as the American poet Walt Whitman said of himself, multitudes, that we are, at the very least, Picts and Gaels with an admixture of Viking . . .

These days, though, it seems, we have but two tribes – Catholic and Protestant – mutually exclusive, with their own customs, culture and territorial claims. Across the Irish Sea, in Ulster, where the IRA have launched a military campaign on the border with the Irish republic, such religious affiliations could be a matter of life and death. On the mainland of Scotland, the religion of your birth can determine your name, your schooling, your friends and your career prospects. Sometimes, it gets nasty and on these occasions it becomes a playground fight between two child psychopaths asserting the supremacy of their respective imaginary friends. Blood – good Scottish blood – has been shed. Lives – good Scottish lives – have been lost. For what?

On my island home of Fascaray, the sectarian divide is exemplified in a generally benign but no less baffling way by our two main clachans or villages, Lusnaharra and Finnverinnity, and is most evident after major sporting fixtures in Glasgow involving Scotland's most famous football teams.

Three years ago it seemed, when we celebrated the first marriage across the divide, between Jessie Mackenzie, daughter of the kirk, and

Francie MacDonald, Catholic former altar boy, that the Big Thaw had set in and that such absurd and arbitrary religious divisions had been consigned to the past.

Sadly, the Big Thaw has been succeeded by an even Bigger Freeze as the old prejudices and patterns seem to have been hardened in permafrost.

Any first-time visitor to the island with the most rudimentary knowledge of Scottish football, will be able to tell on which side of the sectarian divide each village falls. West of our main harbour, the papists of Lusnaharra, who worship at the oldest extant holy building on the island, the former Teampull Beag, now the Church of the Sacred Heart and Immaculate Mary, festoon their homes with the green-and-white favours of Celtic, while to the east, Finnverinnity is gay with the cerulean colours of the rival team. Lusnaharrans refer to the Finnverinnitians as 'Huns' or 'Blue Noses' while Finnverinnitians, most of whom are nominally members of the 'Wee Free Kirk', call Lusnaharra 'the village without a Sabbath' and its inhabitants 'Fenians' or 'Taighs'. Abusive adjectival intensifiers are frequently used when drink is involved, which it usually is whenever the two teams clash in Glasgow, although a few devout Finnverinnitians share their minister's view of alcohol as the devil's work.

I like to remain provocatively even-handed, identifying with the football equivalent of the Scottish Liberal Party (which offers an option to those myopically disdaining nationalism but weary of the Labour–Conservative divide) by wearing the red, yellow and black scarf of Glasgow's other football team, the non-aligned, unofficially agnostic club of Partick Thistle.

Watching an Old Firm game, as these hot-tempered Celtic–Rangers clashes are known, is like witnessing a full scale re-enactment of the ancient wars between Ireland and England over ninety minutes on a two-and-a-half-acre field in Scotland. The Celtic fans, waving the tricolour flag, sing ballads celebrating the Irish rebellion of 1916 and denouncing the English Queen, while Rangers fans, flying a thousand Union Jacks, cast aspersions on the Pope, sing the English national anthem and make slighting references to the Irish famine.

Now this rivalry is plain daft, as well as grotesquely ahistorical. For Scotland, as any attentive student of our nation's history knows, takes its name from our country's founding tribe, the Scotti, who came from

Ireland; until the late Middle Ages the west of Scotland and Ireland fell under the same jurisdiction. These polarities, features of what my friend Hugh MacDiarmid has called the Caledonian Antisyzygy – the unity of contradictions that characterises the Scottish psyche – are but 'twa haffets o the wan bawbee' (two sides of the one coin).

It was Julius Caesar who wrote *divide et impera* – divide and rule – and it is a maxim that the English ken all too well. The tribalism of religion is a distraction and any Scot should put aside such infantile animosities and, regardless of affiliation, follow the example of his Irish cousins to pursue a destiny of mature self-determination.

Grigor McWatt, 1959, *The Fascaray Compendium*

Mr Kennedy has asked to see me after school. By the time I arrive, the other children have already left. He wants to speak to me privately so we leave Agnes alone in the empty classroom finishing her homework and we go outside to sit in the dusk, shivering in the sharp wind on a bench in the small play area behind the school.

Niall Kennedy looks tired.

'I'm a little concerned . . .' he says.

'Concerned?' I feel a throb of panic.

'She's a bright child, Agnes. How do you feel she's adapting to life here, away from her life in New York?'

'She's fine. Happy even. She likes nature, the outdoors. She's made some friends . . .'

'Well, forgive me . . . I don't mean to pry, but I gather there's been a recent change in family circumstances.'

I bristle.

'I don't see what my break-up has got to do with anything. My ex-partner and I have done all we can to protect Agnes from the fall out.'

'I'm sure you have, Miss McPhail.'

'Mhairi.'

'I'm sure you've done all you can. Mhairi.'

'It's not exactly an unusual situation. Or perhaps everyone you know is a member of a functioning two-parent nuclear family?'

He folds his arms and sighs.

'You'd be surprised,' he says.

Now we're both bristling. He tries another tack.

'Her father is Italian, I assume.'

'Italian-American. You worked that out from her last name? Bartoli? All by yourself?' I say, unable to restrain myself.

'Look . . . Mhairi . . . I've no wish to create problems for you, or to impugn your parenting skills. We're on the same side here. Agnes is our concern and she's been exhibiting classic symptoms of emotional distress.'

For a moment, I think there's been a mistake. He's talking about someone else's child. Not sweet, open Agnes. He holds my gaze. I am astonished and seriously alarmed.

'What symptoms?'

He answers my question with one of his own.

'Have you any idea where all the other children on the island are right now?'

'Not doing homework in the classroom while their mothers are interrogated by their teacher, that's for sure. At home with their parents, I assume.'

'No. You're wrong. They're all at a fireworks party – Aaron Schneider's party at Finnverinnity House. They've all been invited. Every child on the island, except Agnes.'

I am outraged. My poor, guileless, eager-to-please daughter, snubbed and excluded.

'That is so mean,' I say, tears of anger springing to my eyes. 'It's bullying.'

'Up to a point. We're very vigilant about bullying here, on the lookout for it. We aim to stamp it out at the first sign . . .'

'Well, you haven't done so well in this case, have you?' I say, turning to look through the window at Agnes, diligently bent over her books while the island's children make merry without her.

'It's not as simple as that,' he says.

'How complicated can it be? My daughter's been singled out and treated like a pariah. It's your job to do something about it.'

'As I say, she's been displaying symptoms of emotional distress. The other children find it hard to deal with.'

Are we really talking about the same child?

'What symptoms?'

'Exaggerating, fantasising, lying . . .'

This can't be Agnes he's talking about; sweet, transparent, pure-hearted Agnes.

'What lies?' I say.

'Well, she told the class her father was a cowboy, a rodeo rider . . .'

I rock back on the bench, incredulous.

'Is that it? Really? For chrissakes, she's a highly imaginative child. Give her a break.'

'Then . . .' He pauses, '. . . she said he worked for the Mafia.'

I laugh. The idea of Marco as a hit man is hilarious.

'Do you have something against imagination here?' I ask. 'It's story-telling. Simple storytelling. That's what kids do. Make stuff up – until humourless, conventional adults stamp it out of them.'

I've gone too far but instead of taking the bait and snapping back at me, he lowers his voice and talks in the slow, measured way of a therapist dealing with a volatile client.

'The class had a project. The theme was celebration and they were asked to write and draw scenes of family feasts and parties.'

Ah. The project she was working on the other night; another night in which I pored over letters and documents and wrote another chapter of my book while Agnes companionably got on with her schoolwork, the lamp illuminating her solemn, determined little face while I deflected her questions.

'Some chose the Auchwinnie Highland Games,' he continues. 'One boy chose his uncle's wedding in Lusnaharra. Finn O'Kane did St Patrick's Day. Ailsa, whose grandmother is Lithuanian, did St Casimir's Day and Aaron Schneider chose a music festival by Loch Ness. Agnes drew a rocket on the moon.'

I laugh.

'*The Little Prince* . . .' I say. 'Antoine de Saint-Exupéry. One of her favourite books . . . Is there a problem with that?'

He shakes his head.

'No. And yes. The project was supposed to be about family. She also told the class her father was an astronomer – she gave us a presentation about the night sky. And now she tells us he's an astronaut.'

'Right.' I put my hands in my pocket for warmth. It really is cold out here. 'So you have a problem with fantasy?'

'Not personally, no. But children are very alert to confabulation. Fibs. Whids. Lies. She won't make friends this way and it will lead to a further sense of isolation.'

He reaches for a stack of exercise books and hands one to me. I recog-nise Agnes's distinctive writing, a series of splayed verticals and jostling lassoes. Several phrases leap from the page – 'We waved goodbye to Dad and cryed, but not a lot.' And 'We doant know how long he'll be away but'. There is the rocket, nose deep in the pocked surface of the moon, and next to it a grinning figure in shorts and T-shirt, wearing a helmet like an upturned goldfish bowl, holds a purple suitcase. Below the picture, she has written 'Bye Dad!'

She must have shown the finished work to me that night for my approval. And, it occurs to me, I must have given it without even looking at the page – 'Very good, Agnes . . .'

I look up at Mr Kennedy whose head tilts inquisitively. I feel winded. All I want to do is collect my daughter and go home. He hasn't finished with me yet.

'Children who are unhappy, isolated, who are going through difficult times at home, often resort to fantasy. They can brag, exaggerate and sometimes create another identity entirely for themselves.'

'She's okay,' I say, rising from the bench. 'She needs to talk to her father, is all. She'll be fine.'

As I walk home with Agnes in silence, fireworks pop and flare over the night sky.

Sang o Solitude

Cantie the loon, whase cark an wiss
His kin's ain croft is tae him bliss,
Cadgy tae pech his hamelt air,
       In his ain hauch.
Whase kye gie milk, whase fairm gies breid,
Whase baurley fills his quaich tae brim,
Whase shaws in simmer gie him scug,
       In winter wairmth.
Seilie wha kens an disnae fash,
As oors an years gang douce agley,
A sonsie hert an saucht o mynd,
       Wheesht aw day,
Soond roo by nicht, his thochts his ane,
Thegether mixt wi naitur's chairms,
An solitude, alane at last,
       Awa frae hairm.
Sae lat me live, no seen, unkennt,
Sae ungrutten lat me dee,
Skyced frae the warld, and nae a stane
       Clype whaur Ah lee.

Grigor McWatt, efter Alexander Pope, 1960[15]

---

15 From *Kowk in the Kaleyard*, Virr Press, 1975. Reprinted in *Warld in a Gless: The Collected Varse of Grigor McWatt*, Smeddum Beuks, 1992.

'A PALL OF GREY SMOKE HANGS OVER BALNASAIG FARM,' wrote McWatt in *The Fascaray Compendium* in October 1960, 'as Tam Macpherson stokes the funeral pyre of his Galloway and Aberdeen Angus herds.' The island's cattle had been stricken by foot-and-mouth disease. 'The choking smoke is once again proof, if proof were needed, that our wee island sanctuary is not completely immune from the scourges that beset the wider world.'

Dramas at sea also provided McWatt with a regular harvest of stories, triumphs as well as tragedies, for his *Compendium* notebooks and *Pibroch* columns that year. The Scottish fishery protection cruiser *Thor* capsized in a November gale in 1960 off Mhor Sgheir reef with the loss of three lives, and two weeks later a Moray trawler, the *Finlay*, was lost in an easterly storm with all ten crew, despite the heroic interventions of the new Auchwinnie lifeboat, the *Morag May*, crewed by local volunteers including the Fascaray brothers Jamie and Francie MacDonald.

The week after the *Finlay* was lost, Francie was forced to brave wild seas in an open boat on a personal errand of mercy when his wife Jessie gave birth prematurely to their second child. Baby John-Joe weighed just three and a half pounds and a nurse, bringing oxygen and other equipment needed to ensure the baby's survival, was sent from Auchwinnie on the *Gudgie*. Fierce winds prevented the puffer from landing and Francie, with his younger brother Jamie, cousin Donnie, and Tormud and Alec Campbell, went out in the *Silver Darling* to meet the *Gudgie* by the uninhabited island of Plodda, where it had found shelter.

The transfer of the young nurse, Marsaili MacAskill, and her equipment was effected in appalling conditions. The *Morag May* lifeboat, whose coxswain was Marsaili's father Mungo, had been called out that morning – without the MacDonald brothers – to deal with a stranded tanker west of Auchwinnie, so it was down to the valiant little *Silver Darling* to save the day, and the baby. At times, the Campbells' small launch all but disappeared under the twelve-foot waves and on the journey back to Finnverinnity the outboard motor flooded. The MacDonalds and the Campbells took up oars, rowing against the fierce currents until the rowlocks broke within sight of the harbour. They were finally helped to safety by Roddy McIntosh and Joseph McKinnon, who braved the mountainous seas in small fishing skiffs to rescue them.

The following month Francie and Jamie joined the *Morag May* when it was called out from Auchwinnie to aid an Aberdeen trawler, the *Northern Quine*, which ran aground after a nine-day fishing trip and was flooded beneath the Calasay cliffs. McWatt watched the dramatic rescue operation – 'the very definition of seamanship and courage' – as the lifeboat plucked to safety all fourteen crewmen by 'breeches buoy' winches, 'only minutes before the *Northern Quine*, in full majesty, finally sank below the heaving sea'.

Mungo MacAskill was awarded the Royal National Lifeboat Institute silver medal for gallantry and his *Morag May* crew were given 'vellum commendations'; Jamie MacDonald, who went on to marry Mungo's daughter Marsaili, framed his citation and put it above the bar in the Finnverinnity Inn, where it still hangs today.

In his *Pibroch* column and in the *Compendium*, McWatt recorded lighter moments on the island that year, too. The hula-hoop craze reached Fascaray and a competition held in Finnverinnity Hall was won by a game young girl from Glasgow, Sophia McKinnon, over visiting Fascaray relatives during the city's annual 'Fair Fortnight' holiday, when all the factories closed. Concerns were expressed by church elders that 'unseemly gyrations' might corrupt the morals of the island's youth. McWatt expressed reservations about the importation of 'American fads'.

'We have, and only just, managed to resist complete cultural extinction at the hands of the English. How strange it is to see our young embrace inane Yankee ways at the expense of our own traditions of ceilidh music, dancing and storytelling,' he wrote for the *Auchwinnie Pibroch* in 'Frae Mambeag Brae'.

He set himself against local opinion by criticising new Department of Agriculture loans to crofters for housing improvements, which saw several Finnverinnitians constructing piping systems to pump water into their homes.

McWatt disapproved, writing in his column: 'We have a new status symbol on the island – the kitchen tap. Like all status symbols it is a triumph of vacuous consumerism over common sense. Here we have burns and buckets and the finest water on earth in its natural setting at our disposal. The arrangement was good enough for our ancestors. What need do we have of pipes and taps? If any of modernity's contrivances make a jot of improvement to our lives, I'll eat my bunnet'.

He did his best to hold out in Calasay but, ironically, it was his lyrical celebration of the island that ensured he could not entirely keep the modern world at bay. 'Hame tae Fascaray' had been recorded by the folk singer Ewan MacColl and the song was becoming a standard in the smoky cellar folk clubs of the UK. Occasional parties of bearded men, Scottish city-dwellers wearing fishermen's sweaters, would make pilgrimages to the Finnverinnity Inn to drink and sing the song *in situ*. Though McWatt was scornful of MacColl's credentials – 'He's an Englishman! A fake. His real name's Jimmy Miller!' – he did not return the royalty cheques that came in, along with regular letters from Lilias in Edinburgh.

She gave him news of the Menzies' set – 'George brought in his new fiancée (Sydney's old flighty-piece Stella C) and we circled each other, teeth bared, like lionesses. She's smart, has a fine head of hair, can hold her drink and will run rings round the Orcadian hermit.' Lilias herself had embarked on an affair with Archie Aitken. 'He's not you, but he'll do,' she wrote. Aitken's wife Meg, a bony, highly strung university librarian – described by Lilias as 'crabbit' – later retaliated by having an affair with Willie McCracken and within three months the love quadrangle span apart, culminating in an undignified scrap outside Menzies' which left all four bloodied, bruised and facing criminal charges for breach of the peace and assault.

Up at Calasay, Grigor McWatt, who was never given to open displays of emotion and shied from personal drama, must have felt glad to be out of it.

A Granite Ballad – The Reimagining of Grigor McWatt,
Mhairi McPhail (Thackeray College Press, 2016)

Spaes o Aefauldness

Tae see a warld in a puckle o saund,
An a heiv'n in a machair flooer,
Haud mairchlessness in your haun,
An ayebidin time in an oor.

The lairdie's robes an tinker's rags
Are puddock-stuils on miser's bags.
A truth that's tellt wi ill intent
Dings aw the whids ye can invent.

Joy an dule are brawly flaucht,
A fykie tweed for beekin thocht.
Ablo oor ivery dule an pyne
Rins threids o seil like gowden twine.

The hoor an gemmster, by the state
Appruived, swall up the nation's fate.
The limmer's yowt frae brae tae knowe
Maun flaucht auld England's winding sowe.
The winner's heuch, the loser's feuch,
For England's corpse will dig a sheuch.

Grigor McWatt, efter William Blake, 1962[16]

16 From *Kowk in the Kaleyard*, Virr Press, 1975. Reprinted in *Warld in a Gless: The Collected Varse of Grigor McWatt*, Smeddum Beuks, 1992.

'Get oot as early as ye can,' wrote the poet. I got out all right, fleeing family, class and culture. Out, and so far away I am comprehensively deracinated. So what have I become? A self-loathing Canadian? A bogus Brooklynite? Or just another counterfeit Celt? In a globalised age of dissolving borders, devolution, fabulous racial and cultural meldings, multiple identities and sometimes murderous alienation, I know my confusions amount to no more than a little local difficulty. Nothing to 'greet' about.

But then I abandoned my relationship too, fleeing all the way here, looking for a sense of connection that now seems spurious, the consequence of childhood bewilderment and a career spent sifting through dead people's garbage. I'm in danger of becoming a heritage apostate. I need to prioritise my present and my daughter's future, not the past of some misanthropic stranger.

Watching Agnes collect seashells on Lusnaharra Strand, humming quietly to herself, I feel a wounding guilt. We should have given her a sibling. She's such a reflective, inward child. The problem was timing. Marco and I wanted the same thing but not at the same moment. When I was broody, watching my friends with new babies, remembering only the blissed-out hyperspace that attended Agnes's arrival and forgetting the shock, chaos and sleep-deprivation, he was too caught up in his work and anxious about money. Or maybe he recalled all too keenly the shock and chaos and, perfectly reasonably, didn't want to go through that again. But when he felt more secure in his job and was ready to contemplate fatherhood once more, my career was lifting off and I was reluctant to take time out.

Even one brother or sister might have taught Agnes the true art of friendship, desensitising her in a useful way and showing her that it is possible to fall out with someone and still love them – though I have to face the fact that, even with the foil of Aidan, my good-natured, uncomplicated brother with whom I quarrelled on a regular basis, this might not have been a lesson I've learned so well myself.

Tonight, we'll Skype her father. Or rather she'll Skype her father. I have emailed him, polite but distant, and received a reply in the same tone. Agnes has installed the software. We'll check the connection and then I'll dress the set. The look I'm aiming for is happy, functioning, Appalachian Rustic Chic – a fire in the grate, Agnes's shell collection in prominent view, a duck-egg-blue mohair blanket over her chair and, I can't resist, a passive-aggressive vase of dried flowers, papery white discs, whose name, *Lunaria annua*, I didn't register until after I'd bought them at the Auchwinnie craft fair. Marco will recognise them straight off, and instantly summon their common name, honesty. With luck he'll wince, but I won't be there to see it. I'll transfer my centre of operations, my papers, to my bedroom, out of range of screen and webcam, and leave them to it.

The superiority of our educational and legal systems over those of our southern neighbour is widely known. So it is with our cuisine. These receipts, or recipes,[17] are the folk varse of our womenfolk, part of a long oral tradition that proves once more the distinctiveness and pre-eminence of Scottish culture, despite the suppressions and depredations following the Act of Union.

Athol Brose
black bun
clapshot
clootie dumpling
cock a' leekie
cranachan
crappit heid
Cullen skink
Finnan haddie
Forfar bridies
fruit pudding
guga
het pint
hot toddy
mealie creashie
neeps and tatties
nettle soup
oatcakes
pancakes or drop scones
partan bree
pea brae
roastit bubbly-jock

17 See Appendix I.

rumbledethumps
Scots broth
Selkirk bannock
skirlie
sowans
stovies
tablet
tattie scones

Robert Burns, to whose cult of personality I do not subscribe, did to his credit extol the virtues of Scottish fare, especially in relation to the cuisine of our European neighbours. He dismissed '*French ragout, / Or olio that would sicken a sow, / Or fricassee would make her vomit*'.

Robert Bird, writing in the nineteenth century, praised parritch and damned fancy foreign fare.

> *Gie France her puddocks and ragouts,*
> *Gie England puddings, beefs, and stews,*
> *Gie Ireland taties, shamrocks, soos,*
> *And land sae bogie,*
> *True Scotsmen still will scaud their mou's*
> *Ower Scotland's cogie.*

Close to my own home, the humblest provender has inspired the most lyrical varse: the wild carrot that grows abundantly in my far corner of Fascaray is the staple of many local soups and stews, and it is also the subject of a Gaelic praise poem (my owersettin follows):

> *Is e mil fon talamh*
> *A th' anns a' churran gheamhraidh,*
> *Eadar Latha an Naoimh Aindreadh agus An Nollaig*

> *Honey underground*
> *Is the winter carrot,*
> *Between St Andrew's Day and Christmas.*

The English – and here I feel a rare pity for our southern neighbours – have neither the tradition of praise poetry nor the cuisine that could inspire it. The cockney music-hall standard 'Boiled Beef and Carrots' simply makes my point.

As they say round here: 'Ken the scran, ken the man.'

Grigor McWatt, 1960, *The Fascaray Compendium*

PAIRT THRIE

Oor Ain Fowk

THERE WERE SUDDEN, SEISMIC CHANGES IN THE ISLAND'S PLACES of worship in 1962. Ranald Paterson's wife Wilma died in July, 'keeling over while tending the heathers in her rockery garden', according to McWatt in *The Fascaray Compendium*, and her grief-stricken widower left the manse and returned to Milngavie to live out his retirement with his niece.

In Lusnaharra Father Maclennan breathed his last during Benediction a month later, subsiding to the floor of the altar, McWatt wrote, 'in a heap of frayed ecclesiastical vestments after the Tantum Ergo'. The altar boys, Fergus McKinnon and Padruig MacRae, 'nudged each other and bit their lips to stifle their laughter before they realised that this collapse was not simply the stumble of an old man partial to whisky. Then they began to weep.'

Father Maclennan's wake at the Finnverinnity Inn was, McWatt noted, 'according to those few present who remembered it, a memorable affair', attended by drinkers of both persuasions and, as in McWatt's case, of none. As he recalled later in the *Pibroch*: 'We marked Father Col's death not with three minutes of silence but three days of mayhem.'

McWatt composed the memorial poem 'Coronach for Father Col' (based on the Gaelic dirge 'An Tuiream Bais'), which is now one of the most requested verses at Canadian and New Zealand funerals for those claiming Scots descent.

> *Yer awa hame this nicht tae yer hame o winter,*
> *Tae yer hame o hairst, o spring, and o simmer;*
> *Yer gangin hame this nicht tae yer ayelastin hame,*
> *Tae yer bed for ayeways, tae yer ayebidin dover.*

The requiem Mass at the Church of the Sacred Heart and Immaculate Mary was, by McWatt's account, 'beautiful and dignified', conducted by a monsignor from the mainland accompanied by Fascaray's new Catholic priest, 'a pale and watchful young man with an Irish name and a background in the coal fields of North Lanarkshire'.

The arrival of Ranald Paterson's successor, George Ferguson, 'a stout bachelor with a waxed moustache', wrote McWatt, prompted an unprecedented event – an invitation extended to the Reverend Ferguson and his congregation to a tea party on the lawn of the Big House. It was, according to McWatt's description in *The Fascaray Compendium* 'a balmy May day of blue skies and soft breezes. Unsmiling servants covered trestle tables with white linen cloths, on which were arranged urns of tea, rows of china cups and plates piled with sandwiches, buns and biscuits.'

Grigor McWatt, though not a member of the Free Church congregation, had been invited on account of his celebrity – the popular Scottish tenor Kenneth McKellar had recorded 'Hame tae Fascaray' on his new album, propelling the island from total obscurity to mere isolation and, according to Effie MacLeod, bringing in more envelopes to Calasay, 'a fair few of them containing cheques, as well as the odd bit of fan mail. Awful odd in some cases – they'd came up with the strangest names and addresses for him. I don't know how they found their way to Fascaray. He'd hand them back to Shuggie, "return to sender", without even opening them'. McWatt didn't return the laird's invitation and failed to attend the party, sending his young lodger, Donald MacInnes, in his place. Donald brought home to Calasay 'a handful of tea cakes and a firsthand account of the event', which McWatt recorded in the *Compendium*.

'The laird, in scarlet corduroys, walked round the garden, hands behind his back, making small talk with the men, "warm for the time of year . . . salmon biting yet? jolly good, jolly good . . ." while Minty Montfitchett asked Effie MacLeod for the recipe for black bun – "Is it like meat loaf?" asked Lady Montfitchett, "I can't abide meat loaf."'

The laird's sons, Clarence and Peregrine, 'shared cigarettes in the shrubbery with Mary-Kate and Shona McKinnon, lively Lusnaharra girls who had managed to sneak into the party despite their affiliations to the Sacred Heart and Immaculate Mary rather than the kirk'. Jamie MacDonald had helped Rab McNab over to the Big House and settled him into a wicker bathchair by the croquet lawn, 'from where the former landlord of our island howff surveyed the scene with a glazed and benign look, his mouth covered with cake crumbs.'

The hospitality that day at Finnverinnity House might have signalled a hopeful new era in Fascaray's feudal arrangements, a thawing of manners and mores reflecting the mood of what would be called down south the Swinging Sixties. But, as Lilias Hogg later tauntingly observed, 'apart from the weekend folk hoolies at the inn', the only thing that was swinging in Fascaray at that time was 'the laird's kilt at the Hogmanay ceilidh'. The Big House Tea Party of 1962 reflected change, certainly – the notion of the auld laird inviting the Finnverinnity hordes to break bread with him would once have been unthinkable – and events were to prove it was the first phase of the new laird's long farewell to the island. But the party, which had begun so well, was, according to McWatt, broken up by the arrival of 'a swarm of midges which sent the laird, his family and staff, shrieking indoors, arms windmilling, while the islanders, more inured to the native pests, made their way home after helping themselves to the remaining sandwiches'.

A Granite Ballad – The Reimagining of Grigor McWatt,
Mhairi McPhail (Thackeray College Press, 2016)

Many visitors ask me about the midge, the tiny flying insect (*meanbh-chuileag* in Gaelic, *Culicoides impunctatus* in Latin) with a bite that belies its size. It's a social creature and swarms in great enveloping cumulonimbi from late spring to late summer, turning the well-equipped visitor into a veil-wearing denizen of some Eastern harem. (By East, I am referring here to Constantinople, not Edinburgh.) We locals are constantly devising new ways to avoid their assaults. Some take up smoking, putting their faith in the repellent effects of nicotine. Others swear by a cheap face cream sold in the village store. I knew a priest at Glenfinnan who washed himself in paraffin in a bid to deter them. (This method also had the unexpected advantage of keeping his congregation at a distance.)

The midges certainly have their uses. Wullie Maclean from Killiebrae told me of a kindly uncle whose wife was afflicted in middle age by a sudden madness – fear of neighbours, of sheep, of wind and clouds, of portents seen in fallen leaves and blades of grass. Several times Donal Maclean found Annie-Kate roaming Doonmara cliffs barefoot with a wild look in her eyes, beating her breast and keening, and he had to steer her gently home.

Then one fine summer's day Uncle Donal was obliged to leave their isolated croft and go out on his boat to check his lobster pots. He didn't want to leave Annie-Kate unattended but he had no choice; he couldn't lock her in the house – then as now, home security was not a priority in the islands and she would have been out and off in a second. In desperation, he took her into their small field, tethered her with a long rope to a hawthorn tree, which would give her plenty of shade from the sun, left her with a pan of water and set out for his boat.

Once at sea, he found his creels had become entangled with a drifting buoy. To set them free again was slow and fiddly work. He was anxious about Annie-Kate but the job had to be done. Eventually, much later than he'd planned, he made his way to the shore and, now in a fever of anxiety, hurried back to his croft.

There he found his poor wife sitting under the tree, desperately batting at the cloud of midges which had descended soon after he'd left her. She was a changed woman. Aunt Annie-Kate had endured for hours the torment which many cannot thole for more than a minute – and the experience had driven her completely sane.

There is, however, no doubt that a haar of spiteful midges can spoil a summer's evening. But despite the inconvenience of these pesky creatures, I regard the midge as the Scotsman's friend. I have no wish to eliminate them, indeed I celebrate them, because they perform the useful service of repelling the English.

Grigor McWatt, August 1962, *Auchwinnie Pibroch*[1]

1   Reprinted in *Frae Mambeag Brae: Selected Columns and Essays of Grigor McWatt*, Stravaigin Press, 1985.

See Me

Ah handsel masel, an sing masel,
An whit Ah ken ye'll ken,
For ivery gru belanging tae me as guid belangs tae you.
Ah slinge an bid ma saul,
Dwaumin ower a straik o simmer gress.

Alane hyne awa in the hills Ah snoke. See me,
Stravaigin dumfoondert at ma ain lichtness an glee.
As gloamin faws Ah seek a siccar scug tae ware the nicht.
Kinnlin a gleed an sottlin the caller-killt meat,
Doverin ower the gaithert leaves, ma collie at ma feet.

Wha has done his day's darg an swallaed his tea?
Wha sees me, an seeks tae stravaig wi me?

Grigor McWatt, efter Walt Whitman, 1962[2]

---

2   From *Kowk in the Kaleyard*, Virr Press, 1975. Reprinted in *Warld in a Gless: The Collected Varse of Grigor McWatt*, Smeddum Beuks, 1992.

With the paucity of documents or photographs from McWatt's early life, I turn to the Internet. Broadband only came to the island last year and can still be maddeningly sluggish. I've set up my laptop on the kitchen table and, with Agnes's help, using a password and username provided by Ailish, log on to Scotia'sFolk, a genealogy website used mostly, I imagine, by fellow Canadians and New Zealanders agonising over which tartan they're entitled to wear at Burns Night suppers. The website gives access to digital scans of statutory birth, marriage and death records from 1855, old parish registers of baptisms, weddings and funerals, some dating back to the sixteenth century, as well as wills and censuses from 1841, all handwritten. Those Presbyterians were punctilious record keepers.

In 1850, the year of McWatt's grandfather's birth, the old parish records of Auchwinnie and Fascaray list, as far as I can make out (the calligraphy is challenging), several newborn McWatts, Macquats, MacWatties, McQhauts and MacWhitts – two Anguses (born in January and September), a Duncan, an Isobel, an Ishbel, an Elspeth and a Euphemia as well as a Mary (listed as 'Elizabeth Campbell and Archibald Macquat's natural child', meaning illegitimate; Mary would be destined to carry the stigma of sin for life). The fathers' occupations are given as crofter (four), fisherman (two) and 'gardner'. Their mothers' occupations – though even with newborns at their breast they would have helped with the fishing and crofting – were left unsaid. Using the five surname variants, I turn to the Glasgow census records for 1861, the first census for the city after the family's clearance from the island in 1853.

In the city parish of Barony, now known as Anderston, at number 3 Grace Street – a long-vanished tenement, I guess – an Aonghas McKwitt is listed as one of twenty-six residents. His age is given as eleven, his place of birth Inverness-shire, and his occupation 'scholar'. It seems a pretty good fit. But the birthplace of the head of the household, 'a shipbuilder's labourer' called Roderick McKwitt, presumably Aonghas's father, is listed as Enniskillen, Ireland. Roderick's wife, Margaret, whose occupation is given as 'an earthenware painteress' – city records were more scrupulous and less sexist than their rural counterparts – is also described as Irish by birth. Five other children are listed in the family – from eight months to seventeen years old – which definitively rules out a Grigor McWatt connection. He was, he said famously, 'a Scots singleton, from a long line of Scots singletons'.

I search the register of Glasgow deaths, now using the five surname variants and two forename variants of Aonghas. Nothing comes up, though I note in passing that Roderick McKwitt, widower, ended his days in the Barony workhouse and died of 'senile decay', that Archibald Macqhuatt, an unemployed iron planer, aged fifty-six and single, died of 'asphyxiation by suspension' – the poor guy hanged himself – and on the same page, William McWhittie, aged seventeen, described as a coal miner, is recorded as dying of 'inflammation of the bowel', while two and four pages on, the causes of death of Helen MacWat (aged two) and Margaret McQuitt (aged nine – Agnes's age) are listed, respectively, as 'croup' and 'acute lobar pneumonia'. So much tragedy – it reads like the outline of a Zola novel.

I turn to the statutory register of marriages for the city hoping to find a little cheer, as well as a few facts. I'm searching for the late-nineteenth-century marriage of a McWatt, Macquat, McQhaut, MacWhitt or a McKwitt to a McDougall. Or possibly a MacDougal. Or even a McDugel. No luck and little cheer – I'm distracted by the number of couples whose names are signed with an 'X – his/her mark'. The statutory birth record for Ossian should be more fruitful – it's an unusual name with few possible spelling variations. Using Grigor McWatt's chronology, it seems his father was probably born around 1885, but again, with a ten-year time frame, using all the surnames, I find not a single match, nor any name that comes near to it. And of Grigor's own birth in November 1921 there is no trace.

I feel the familiar welling despair and self-loathing generated by too much Internet activity – I've just spent ninety minutes exhuming fragments of dead strangers' pasts and, apart from illuminating the general misery and deprivation of earlier generations of Scots, all it has revealed are the idiosyncrasies of spelling, the comparative unreliability of record keeping and the infinite variety, and frequent illegibility, of nineteenth- and twentieth-century handwriting. I log out.

Good timing. At that moment, my present and my future walk through the door. Agnes is wearing one of her secret smiles, which gives her face a pixieish cast.

'Can I Skype Papa again?' she asks.

She has her own more pressing genealogical quest to attend to.

THE LOCALS DIDN'T LEARN OF THE LAIRD'S SALE OF BALNASAIG Lodge until the arrival on the pier, shortly after the 1962 Big House Tea Party, of three English visitors wearing what McWatt described in the *Compendium* as 'ill-fitting oilskins'. Neville Booth, 'balding, long-nosed and mild in appearance and manner – a nervy oystercatcher of a man', fussed over their suitcases with Evelyn Fletcher while his wife Althea, 'an aloof heron to Fletcher's bustling puffin', gave orders.

They didn't look like the usual visitors to the island. In the early 1960s, apart from the laird's shooting parties and inspectors from the Fisheries Board, the only outsiders who came to Fascaray were occasional parties of venturesome birdwatchers, or archaeologists, sent by the Museum of Scottish Antiquities to scratch away at the soil above Lusnaharra and exult over mud-caked fragments of Neolithic pottery. Among the numerous bags of the Booth party, no guns, binoculars or spades were on view.

It soon emerged, as the trio squeezed into Francie MacDonald's Ford Anglia with their luggage, 'that they were not visitors but new residents, having taken possession of Balnasaig Lodge at a knock-down price; a consequence of Torquil Montfitchett's recent embarrassments at the baccarat table'.

They planned, they told Francie on the drive north, to set up a 'study centre' in the Lodge. Asked what subject they would be studying, the visitors exchanged looks that Francie described to McWatt as 'gey shifty'.

McWatt recorded Francie's account in the *Compendium*:

It was Neville Booth who finally spoke.
'We're here to pursue the study of truth,' he said.
'Aye, right.[3] Aren't we all?' said Francie, as they rattled along the potholed track to the Booths' new home.

3   Scots double positive denoting scepticism.

Althea Booth felt that more explanation was needed. Her spirit guide, she said, had brought them to 'this ancient place of mists, myths and mountains in search of ancient wisdom'.

'If it's wisdom you're looking for, your best bet is the Finnverinnity Inn,' Francie told them as they pulled up outside the grey crenellated bulk of Balnasaig. 'You'll find plenty of ancient spirit guides there, dispensing wisdom every night for the price of a decent dram.'

The most generous Fascaradians regarded the island's first permanent English residents as harmless but dotty curiosities – 'bampots', who, it was thought, wouldn't stay long but in the short term might bring some welcome revenue to local business.

Cynics, chief among them McWatt, regarded the new occupants of Balnasaig with open hostility as incomers, the enemy within, threatening island traditions with their bizarre Sassenach ways. 'They are English,' he wrote in the *Compendium*, 'which is bad enough, but also pan-loaf English, and unlike their compatriot, coeval and vendor Lord Montfitchett, they do not have the ameliorating virtue of spending two-thirds of the year in England.'

Even among the more easy-going islanders, the Balnasaig Seekers' quest to return to 'ancient truths and certainties' elicited bafflement. The real struggle for Fascaradians was to overcome the ancient certainties – feudalism and a creaking infrastructure that hadn't changed since the Middle Ages – and enter the modern world.

Joseph McKinnon, lobster fisherman and father of seven from Lus-naharra, proved to be a pioneer in this respect. With a new Department of Agriculture grant, he installed a septic tank and built a generator shed from railway sleepers taken from the recently closed Auchwinnie East station. McKinnon seemed to have provoked a brief island rage for home improvement. Cottages and blackhouses were re-roofed with slate, leaking byres were patched up and several old Nissen huts that had housed the lower-ranking soldiers at the Big House during its SOE days were retrieved from a dump east of Finnverinnity House and redeployed as grain stores and piggeries.

Even McWatt, who a decade earlier had railed against the disappearance of vernacular architecture and the 'restless urge to modernise' and only two years before had questioned whether any of 'modernity's contrivances make a jot of improvement to our lives', was stirred to upgrade An Tobar and finally replace his corrugated-iron roof with slates, install a fireplace with a flue, pipe water from the burn into the house, glaze windows, put in stairs to a new attic bedroom and take delivery of a newfangled compost toilet. But these changes were, as he noted in the *Compendium*, superficial. Fascaray remained – to the satisfaction of McWatt as well as the incomers of Balnasaig – an island 'bound by ancient tradition to our ancestors who lived here at the dawn of human history'.

A Granite Ballad – The Reimagining of Grigor McWatt,
Mhairi McPhail (Thackeray College Press, 2016)

For centuries male Fascaradians have sailed in the autumn, at the time of the ripe barley and the fruiting buckthorn, to hunt the plump young solan geese or gannets – the guga – near their nesting sites on the uninhabited rock pinnacles of Plodda and Grodda. No true Fascaradian can suffer vertigo since the scaling of these granite towers is done without the aid of mountaineers' crampons or picks. Using long poles we prise the birds from the nest, kill them instantly with a rock, then remove their heads and pluck them. Peat fires are lit and any remaining feathers are scorched from the skin. We split the carcasses with a knife, gut them, rub them with salt, stack them up in tall broch towers and cover them with tarpaulin until we have sufficient pickled meat[4] – usually about two thousand birds in all – to see us through the winter.

One distinguished visitor to these islands, the clergyman Donald 'Dean' Munro, observed this practice in the sixteenth century with a commendable even-handedness that our censorious southern neighbours would do well to emulate today.

> Be sex myle of sea east from Fasquarhay lye two iles callit Ploethe and Groethe, ane myle lang, without grasse or hedder, with highe blacke craigs, and black fouge thereupon part of them. This ile is full of wylde foulis, and quhen foulis hes ther birdes, men out of the parochin of Lusnaharra and Finnverinnitie will sail ther, and stay ther seven or aught dayes, and to fetch hame with them their boitt full of dray wild foulis, with wyld foulis fedders.

Squeamish southerners of the sentimentalist tendency, including recent arrivals at Balnasaig, might baulk at this ancient practice, but their domestic cats kill many more birds than the most accomplished team of Fascaradian guga hunters could ever hope to in a lifetime. The solan goose population is

---

4   See Appendix I for recipes.

thriving and the guga hunt fosters a greater sense of community, history and a link with landscape than does the breeding of flightless birds for ritualised killing on the laird's moors, the mass slaughter of our stags by public-school types in tweed trews, or fox hunts led by tally-hoing scurryvaigs from the English shires.

Strange to think that just as Scotland's movement for political independence begins to grow, Fascaray should be infested by a new gang of colonialist relics: the English occultist bampots of Balnasaig Lodge.

Grigor McWatt, 1964, *The Fascaray Compendium*.

9 November 2014

New York may have felt more like home than any other place I've lived but I could never truly pass as an American. Marco spotted it straight away. It wasn't so much my accent; what gave me away as an incomer, or an outsider, was my habit of self-deprecation.

Marco insisted, though I have no memory of it, that on our first date, when he complimented me on my hair – then long and comparatively lustrous – I told him I had a bald patch; I even went to pains to point it out, he said, though when he looked he failed to find it.

Any dress I wore that he liked I would dismiss, citing its thrift-store provenance and price or pointing to a poorly repaired zipper or a moth hole. At first this beguiled him. Later it irritated him, along with my general wariness.

'Relax, can't you? Just this once? Can't you take a compliment with good grace? Do you have to smack it right back in my face? It's an insult to the complimenter, another form of poor mouth, this habitual public self-laceration. It's modesty to the point of grandiosity.'

My trait did not serve me well in job interviews. Asked to outline my strengths, I preferred to elaborate on my weaknesses. The fact that I did so in a patrician accent may have neutralised the effect, but then, bolstering the negatives, there was the public-speaking problem. I don't suppose Karmic Kate had difficulty accepting admiration or addressing her class in anything but tones of silvery self-confidence. Nor can I see her admitting to a bout of flatulence during her morning's sun salutation or confessing to a debilitating outbreak of athlete's foot or thrush.

'What's wrong with a bit of modesty?' I asked Marco, before I pushed it too far. 'You should try it sometime. The trouble with you and your friends, with all Americans in fact, is you suffer from self-loathing deficit disorder.'

At that point he reminded me: my daughter is an American too – blithe, confident up to a point but never bumptious, generous, concerned for the welfare of others and optimistic, she is a living rebuke to all stereotypes.

Today, Agnes has asked if she can Skype her grandparents in Toronto. I mask my reluctance and get through to my brother, who is as blithe and unsurprised to hear from me as if I were living in the next street, and he agrees to set up a call.

My mother and father sit uneasily side by side on their couch, a webcam version of Grant Wood's farmer painting, without the pitchfork. Canadian Gothic says it all. Their distance seems defensive. Since my teens they've always circled me cautiously, as if I were a primed grenade. Then Aidan leans in and waves, softening the mood, and Agnes does the rest. After twenty minutes of her excited chatter – '. . . and we went into this cave where a harper disappeared and then we saw Great-Grandpa McPhail's house in Killiebrae . . .' – we're all smiling. We agree to be in touch again soon.

There seems to have been some sort of rapprochement between Agnes and the other kids. She had a sleepover last night with Ailsa and Oonagh, and on Friday, Mr Kennedy arranged an outing to the pool in Auchwinnie followed by a matinee at the cinema (Disney. But what do I expect? Werner Herzog?). Apparently Aaron and Finn fought to sit next to Agnes on the ferry.

There's also been a rapprochement of sorts between me and Niall Kennedy. Last night while Agnes was over at Ailsa's we met for a drink in the Finnverinnity Inn. The decor was not nearly as brutally butch as I'd imagined, the restroom was acceptably clean and the music – fishermen Shonnie MacDonald and Donal MacEwan playing uilleann pipes and accordion – was surprisingly good.

Niall asked me how I thought Agnes was doing.

'You tell me,' I said. 'She always seems fine to me.'

'She's a lovely child,' he said. 'I don't know what's happening at home but she seems much more at ease at school now and the other children have picked up on that.'

'I must be getting something right, for a change.'

He ignored the barb and asked me about my work. He knew McWatt slightly, he said, and had visited him in Calasay.

'We would play chess and he liked me to read to him. Mostly poetry. *Palgrave's Golden Treasury*. Yeats. Especially Yeats. He liked to hear my

Irish accent, even though Yeats himself had the most aristocratic Anglo intonation. Have you heard the recording of him reading "Lake Isle of Innisfree"? Hilarious.'

I asked him what he'd thought of McWatt.

'A cantankerous old man, sure. But he had great integrity and he was passionate about the island. There are some from round here who wouldn't hear a bad word about him.'

I've yet to meet them, I said.

'You will.'

As for McWatt's poetry, Niall was circumspect.

'I'm no judge. I'm more of a down-the-line Heaney man myself. But I admired his commitment to his art and his tenacity.'

He offered to help with the museum – 'any labouring, transporting, cajoling. You've got a big job there but this could be the best thing that's ever happened to the island.'

I thanked him. Too curtly, perhaps. For me, there's always been a difficult line between a simple acknowledgement of kindness and an undignified display of tail-wagging. Gratitude – something else I've never been much good at.

Lin

Whit is this life wi worries cowpt,
We hav nae lin tae bide an gowp? –

Nae lin tae bide aneath the boughs,
An gowp as lang as coos an yowes:

Nae lin tae see, when shaws we pass,
Whaur wee cons dern their nuts in gress:

Nae lin tae see, in braid daylicht,
Burns fu o starns, like skies at nicht:

Nae lin tae birl as Brawness keeks,
An watch her pirl, on dinkly feet:

Nae lin tae wait till her gab can
Braiden that smile her een began?

A puir life this if, wi worries cowpt,
We havnae lin tae bide an gowp.

Grigor McWatt, efter W. H. Davies, 1959[5]

---

5   From *Kowk in the Kaleyard*, Virr Press, 1975. Reprinted in *Warld in a Gless: The Collected Varse of Grigor McWatt*, Smeddum Beuks, 1992.

AFTER YOUNG DONALD MacINNES ARRIVED IN CALASAY IN 1959, McWatt was freer to spend time in Edinburgh, knowing that back home the earnest lad – he was fifteen, but the concept of teenagers had only recently been invented – had proved himself a fit custodian of An Tobar, happy to run the house, till the soil, tend the animals and ensure that the place was clean and relatively dry when the poet returned home, 'begrimed with soot, deafened by city noises', as McWatt wrote, his ears ringing from the competitive chatter of poets in drink.

McWatt had a love-hate relationship with the nation's capital that had once been, as he liked to point out, the hub of the European Enlightenment. But by the middle of the twentieth century, after the adversity of war and economic hardship, it had become an inward-looking and unforgiving city. 'It's no surprise,' he wrote, 'that Edinburgh is the most English of our cities. In this huddle of architectural conceit and squalor, chilly commerce, Presbyterian rectitude and middle-class conformity strive to ignore the adjacent misery of its pitiful slums.'

The city earned its nickname, Auld Reekie, as smoke from thirty thousand coal fires – 'black pennants streamin frae heich lums', McWatt wrote – mingled with the stench from the breweries and turned the air yellow. 'Sometimes the smog is so thick, I cannae see ma ain haun in front o my coupon,' McWatt complained in a letter to Hogg in 1963. In such a city of perpetual night it was inevitable that men and women – though it was mostly men – would gather for comfort in the intimate warmth of a public house.

McWatt's journey to the capital, first by foot, bicycle or tractor, then ferry and rail, was usually made in high spirits as he anticipated the cheer of good company and stimulating talk after months of silence – when Donald arrived on the island, he was instructed to 'speak only when spoken to' – broken occasionally by 'Fascaradian blether' at the inn. One of McWatt's best-loved translations, 'Tae a Wee Bauchle', was written on the steam train from Auchwinnie to Fort William, en route to Edinburgh in 1965.

Och why do you daunder throu glens in gluives
Missin sae much an sae much?
Och pudgetie wee bauchle wham naebdy loues
Why do you daunder throu glens in gluives,
When the heather's as saft as the diddies o doos
An chitterin douce tae the touch?
Och why do you daunder throu glens in gluives
Missin sae much an sae much? [6]

In the early years of McWatt's relationship with Lilias Hogg, he spent several nights at her flats and bedsits (she moved four times in the first five years of their friendship), but we have no account of their precise sleeping arrangements. In his bet-hedging biography, Knox-Cardew high-mindedly refuses to speculate as to whether their relationship was ever consummated: 'Theirs was a complicated love, a mutual passion for their native land and its history, a loathing for its enemies, and a shared spiritual yearning at once encompassing and transcending the physical.' In other words, he found no definitive evidence of intercourse.

The couple spent a weekend at an inn in the Campsie Fells together – the plan was to hike the hills but because of 'foul weather and strong drink', they didn't stray far from bar or bedroom, though it seems they had separate quarters. Two decades later, he was to write about the trip in one of his best-known and most poignant poems, 'Strippin the Willow', which is the only indication from him that their bond had ever been sexual as well as intellectual and emotional.

The correspondence we have from the early sixties points to a generalised frustration on Hogg's part: wanting, wishing, never quite achieving. McWatt, when he isn't rhapsodising about nature or history or ranting about politics and England, can be playful and flattering. But the pattern is established – the closer Lilias moves towards him, the further he retreats.

'Shakespeare – or was it his simpering Juliet? – got it wrong. Parting

6   Grigor McWatt, efter Frances Cornford, 1965. (*Kowk in the Kaleyard*, Virr Press, 1975. Reprinted in *Warld in a Gless: The Collected Varse of Grigor McWatt*, Smeddum Beuks, 1992.)

is such bitter sorrow,' she wrote on 23 September 1964. 'There's nothing sweet about it.'

She seemed to take as compliments his complaints about the journey back to Fascaray from Edinburgh. 'It's hard, I know,' she wrote, 'but we must both be strong, Griogal Cridhe, until we can meet again . . . Just say the word and I'll join you. I have all the time in the world these days since Beattie gave me the heave-ho.'

The kindly manager at McDuff's had retired and his replacement, who took a dim view of Lilias's absences and unpunctuality, had summarily fired her one morning when she had arrived for work half an hour late.

'Can you believe it? Half an hour?' she wrote. 'And for the first time in my working life I had a genuine excuse – my bus had broken down. The old bastard was longing to get shot of me.'

She was given a pay-off of £17 – a week's wages – and spent it over six days in Menzies'. 'Bugger the job. The wee windfall helped ease the separation pangs.'

But McWatt's letters suggest that it was not the sorrow of parting from Lilias that made the homeward journey so miserable. 'I was done,' he wrote to her on 29 September 1964. 'Talked out, social energy exhausted, hangover stupendous. I sat scowling on the train to Fort William in a cold carriage reeking of cigarettes, urine and stale beer. Then on the Auchwinnie branch line train I saw Effie and Shuggie MacLeod get on with their twins, a pair of blooters in short trousers with scabby knees, wee fat hands ramming sweeties into pudgy faces. The last thing I wanted was an hour of their company. I nodded and got back to my book.'

Waiting for the *Gudgie* at Auchwinnie, he kept a distance from the MacLeods and paced the harbour, wincing at the shrieks of the seagulls which, he wrote to Lilias, seemed to mock his mighty hangover. There was more discomfort to endure once he boarded the puffer which, 'stout as a child's bathtime boat, bounced mercilessly over the waves, with both MacLeod lads boaking – one on each side of the boat, Kenny port, Barry starboard – all the way to Finnverinnity Pier'.

McWatt was the first to alight, 'jostling the MacLeods aside and scrambling onto the pier, to freedom'. On dry land he 'sniffed the air, sighed deeply, turned my face from Finnverinnity and skiltered [scurried] up to Calasay to stare in grateful silence at the indifferent sea and resume my work'.

A Granite Ballad – The Reimagining of Grigor McWatt,
Mhairi McPhail (Thackeray College Press, 2016)

Strippin the Willow

D'ye mind thon wee howff,
Melinda?
D'ye mind thon wee howff?
An the pou'in and the spreidin
O the scrimpet auld beddin,
An the midgies that bite in the high Campsie Fells,
An the whisky that garred us tight?
An the gallus keelies makin gowks o theirsels
Chappin aw nicht on the bedroom winda?
D'ye mind thon wee howff,
Melinda?
D'ye mind thon wee howff?

Grigor McWatt, efter Hilaire Belloc, 1981[7]

---

7   From *Wappenshaw*, Virr Press, 1986. Reprinted in *Warld in a Gless: The Collected Varse of Grigor McWatt*, Smeddum Beuks, 1992.

McWATT HAD HIS CRITICS; CHIEF AMONG THEM THE DUNDEE professor Alastair Galbraith, who wrote in the Edinburgh literary magazine the *Quill & Thistle*, in May 1964, that 'McWatt was always a good hater and he turns his hates into political ideology and literary theory. He doesn't much like the English (did some cheeky Sassenach keek up his kilt as a boy, perhaps?) so he celebrates the blowing up of post-boxes bearing the insignia of England's Queen, seeks to cut Scotland painfully adrift from its southern Siamese twin and promotes a bastardised invented language – a sort of Woolworths Pick'n'Mix assortment of half-remembered barely spoken words from innumerable incompatible dialects across Scotland (and, though it would cost him dear to admit it, some northern counties of England) – in place of the beautiful, organic, globally recognised language of Shakespeare.'

McWatt, in the *Auchwinnie Pibroch* the following month, returned the compliment and went some way to proving one of Galbraith's points by denouncing the Dundee professor as a 'a quisling . . . a collaborator . . . a hireling, and a man so devoid of cultural and poetic sensibility that one has to assume that this rogue has fully renounced any claim to Scottish nationality. Galbraith is clearly an Englishman under the skin . . .'

In his *Pibroch* column of 15 September 1964[8], McWatt revisited the subject, after Galbraith made another slighting reference to him, as 'the kilted curmudgeon who hates the people of England so much he has devoted his life to kidnapping, torturing and killing their poetry', in the *Quill & Thistle*. McWatt wrote:

Literary criticism is rarely a theme for discussion on this island.
The weather, the brewing and abating of storms, winchings and wanings [romance and illness], the price of fish, ditto of liquor, the iniquities of feudalism, the wanderings of cattle and sheep and

8   *Frae Mambeag Brae: Selected Columns and Essays of Grigor McWatt*, Stravaigin Press, 1980.

the depredations wrought on hens by foxes are all regular subjects for consideration by our panel of experts at the Finnverinnity Inn. As to academics down south and their axe-grinding views on poetry, here, as a topic, they rarely come up.

It is to the inhabitants of my tidal isle that I turn to for wisdom on such small but occasionally irritating matters. Last Monday, Shuggie the Post delivered the miscellany of second-hand books, small magazines, press clippings and bills that make up my regular mail delivery. My eye fell on a self-styled literary journal whose name suggests a public house in Edinburgh of the sort frequented by tourists. In it, a critic with a Scots name and an English sensibility was once more, and for reasons that only Sigmund Freud might guess at, taking issue with my verse. He questioned my right, as a dispossessed and drouthie Scot – denied autonomy, language and respect – to dip my simple quaich [cup] into the brimming well of English verse. Did I wish to dignify his insult with a defence? In Calasay there were more pressing matters to attend to. It was a beautiful day and the lobster pots needed checking.

I was out on the boat beyond the skerries with my able young assistant when the sharp-eyed lad alerted me to an agitation on our starboard bow in the otherwise placid sea. It was an improbably large and muscular cat, swimming desperately towards us, back arched and tail high out of the water. It had the variegated fur of a tabby, but it was definitely not of the domestic variety. It was in fact a wildcat kitten (*Felis silvestris grampia*) and how it got there we could only speculate, although it is not unknown for wildcats to take to the water when survival demands it. Donald swiftly managed to get a hand to it without so much as a scratch and dumped the writhing creature in a lidded creel by the tiller.

As we made our way back to the shore the wildcat, whose comparative meekness we had ascribed to gratitude, was reverting to type and emitting the warning yowl of an air-raid siren while hurling itself at the lid of the basket with impressive ferocity. I was aware of the species' reputation for savagery but, as readers of this column know, I always relish a challenge.

I kenned too that our existing menagerie – one collie dog, two pine martens, an otter and a recently rescued fulmar – might be more sceptical about this new arrival, a lacerating, spitting, howling coil of muscle and fur, with steel-trap teeth, claws like sprung-tine harrows and the manners of a Glasgow corner boy with a fistful of razors and a grudge.

So it was decided that night that I would leave my bedroom, which was easiest to secure against ingress and egress, to the reluctant house guest, whom we had christened Attila. I placed a skellet of milk and three opened cans of sardines by the creel, loosened the lid a little, ran for it and bolted the door behind me.

My night downstairs in the sleeping bag by the fire was not the most restful, disturbed as it was by hectic scamperings and knockings and strange rendings upstairs. But by dawn all was quiet and, wearing falconer's gauntlets, I tiptoed into my room to find a scene of utter desolation. Shredded curtains, a disembowelled armchair, trashed bedding, papers and letters reduced to sodden confetti and on my bed the Edinburgh literary journal, open and unread as I had left it the previous day. Now it would never be read because Attila the Wildcat had delivered his own damning and extremely foul-smelling verdict on Professor Galbraith's criticisms.

Attila and I, I then knew, were going to get along just fine.

There was a more harrowing incident involving the menagerie around that time, which McWatt never referred to in his *Pibroch* column. He continued to promote in public the narrative of Calasay as a paradise in which man and wild beast lived together in mutual understanding and respect. I found a truthful account in anguished journal passages, dated November 1964, in *The Fascaray Compendium*, later confirmed in my interview with Donald MacInnes. That month, one of McWatt's two new otters, Darnley and Mary, bit through a cable and caused a fire that burned out An Tobar's kitchen. Grigor was in Edinburgh but Donald, who had been down in Finnverinnity with the Campbells getting supplies, returned in time to fight the fire with buckets of water filled from the burn.

Darnley, enraged when Donald climbed a ladder to unseat Mary from the crossbeam in the byre, savaged the young man's leg, nearly cutting an artery, and bit clean through the boot of his right foot, severing three of his toes. An emergency crossing to Auchwinnie Infirmary on the *Silver Darling* failed to save the digits. It was 'the end of the days of freedom for the otters, who [had] become so aggressive that they [had to be] confined to a cage', wrote McWatt in the *Compendium*.

But in the *Pibroch*, McWatt continued to write his charming accounts of otter, wild cat, pine marten and man living companionably in harmony and freedom in their Calasay Eden. Donald MacInnes, who was left with a permanent limp after the incident, was 'a stoic', according to McWatt in the *Compendium*. He refused to be drawn on the subject in private or public, until my interview with him in 2014.

A Granite Ballad – The Reimagining of Grigor McWatt,
Mhairi McPhail (Thackeray College Press, 2016)

balg-buill: ball bag, in which witches were said to keep balls of twisted wool used for raising storms. The most famous Fascaray folk tale involved the witch Gormshuil (Gormal) Mhòr na Mòighe who was said, at the bidding of Alisdair McWatt, to have thrown the balls which conjured the storm that wrecked Cromwell's English fleet in 1653. Today, in especially wild weather, Fascaradians will say, 'The balg-buill is empty . . . Gormshuil's no knittin the nicht.'

ballan-buaile: the wooden tub suspended from a pole in which milkmaids carried home the milk from the herd to the clachan. The milkmaids marched in step and sang a milking ballad, 'crònan-bleoghainn' (my owersettin below).

> Bò lurach dhubh, bò na h-airidh,
> Bò a' bhàthaích, màthair laogh,
> Lùban sìomain air crodh na tìre,
> Buarach shìod' air m' aighean gaoil.
> Ho m' aghan, ho ma' agh gaoil.

> Bonny broon coo, pride o the sheilin'
> First coo o the byre, mither o braw calves,
> Wisps o straw roond the coos o the townland,
> A fetter o silk roon my beloued heifer.
> Ho my heifer, ho my douce heifer.

bòrlanachd: twenty-one days of free labour once exacted from tenant crofters on the 'king's highway' on the mainland by the factor, or bailiff, even though the only time most Fascaradian crofters set foot on the 'king's highway' was when they were obliged to go to Auchwinnie to mend it. The most infamous factor on Fascaray to exact this 'statute labour' was Red Roderick of the Hens, about whom a Gaelic satire was written (my owersettin below – Black Donald of the Whids, or lies, is another name for the devil).

> *O gun robh do spiorad fiar*
> *Gu sìorraidh a' ruith nan cearc!*
> *Agus Dòmhnall Dubh nam breug*
> *Gad riasladh air sliabh nam peac!*
>
> *May your camsheuch saul*
> *Chase the teuk fur aye!*
> *And Black Donald of the Whids,*
> *Rive you abreed oan the Ben o Sin.*

dùthchas: the native system of land tenure by which clan members are entitled to occupy their ancestral land; the place of birth, spirit or blood, in which one is engaged in a mutually respectful relationship with the land.

Grigor McWatt, 1964, *The Fascaray Compendium*

THE PACE OF CHANGE ON THE ISLAND ACCELERATED, WITH or without the assistance of its absentee landlord. Calor gas cookers were installed in the humblest kitchens and by the mid 1960s the old black ranges had mostly fallen out of use, while septic tanks and inside toilets were no longer regarded as the costly affectations of a privileged few. External television aerials were seen for the first time, sprouting from the 'lums' of the modernised cottages in Finnverinnity (though reception remains bad to this day). But the population had sunk to a new low – sixty-eight adults and twelve children – with an exodus to the mainland not seen since the nineteenth-century clearances. Peigi MacEwan died in her sleep in Doonmara – her neighbour Hamish McIntosh was alerted by the clucking of her hens anxious to get out of her house in the morning – and the clachan of Killiebrae now stood empty after the death of Wullie Maclean and the emigration of his children and grandchildren to a newly built town, certain work and uncertain futures in what McWatt described as 'the badlands of central Scotland'.

Those who stayed, however, seemed determined to make a go of it and the fad for home improvement, often with poor materials and improvised skills, continued. At Balnasaig Farm, Tam Macpherson, now a rheumatic 63-year-old, badly hit by the foot-and-mouth outbreak five years earlier, reluctantly accepted that there was little money in cattle, sent his remaining herd away to the mainland abbatoir – the bellowing of the cows could be heard all over the island as they were loaded onto the *Gudgie* in three separate journeys – and acquired a large flock of sheep whose wool would service the mainland tweed industry.

While the farm's fortunes declined, the Seekers were expanding operations at Balnasaig Lodge, restoring the house and garden and hosting visitors from England who had been alerted to the centre's existence by an article in *Serenity Times*. This London-based alternative magazine, whose interests included complementary medicine, conspiracies and UFOs, had described Balnasaig as 'a visionary community, based in an ancient land where the spirits make their presence felt on a daily basis'.

The visitors to Balnasaig were, wrote McWatt, 'often dressed in bright mixter-maxter [motley], patchwork, fringing, beads and other embellishments rarely seen on the island, so that when one large boatload of glairily [gaudily] costumed Seekers was disgorged at the pier, a rumour went round Finnverinnity School that the circus had come to Fascaray – which, in a way, it has'.

Some visitors to Balnasaig Lodge paid for their bed, board and twice-daily 'spiritual cleansing and calisthenics' with Neville and Althea by working in the house, plastering and painting walls, cooking and cleaning. Others paid in cash for their stay and rates were said by islanders to be the price of a three-star hotel in Edinburgh.

'All that money tae bide in the cold wi a bunch o bawheids,' said Effie MacLeod.

Evelyn, who had recently discovered what the Seekers described as 'her gift of communicating directly with plant yakshas [angels]', was making the garden her own domain, supervising volunteer teams of visitors who toiled away in the mud hoping to make their own divine connection with the presiding spirits of potatoes, peas and turnips.

Most islanders shared Effie's view of the Seekers but some, including Hamish McIntosh and the Campbells, who were employed respectively as builder and carpenters at Balnasaig, saw that there was money to be made from these interlopers.

'Their cash is as good, or as bad, as anyone's,' said Hamish, who now had three children to feed.

'The wunds o cheenge are blawin,' wrote McWatt in the *Compendium*. 'An it's gettin awfie oorit [cold] roon here.'

Even the immutable seascape faced drastic alteration when, in 1965, substantial deposits of oil were discovered in the Clinch Straits off Plodda and Grodda and the Westminster government announced that the seabed in the Fascaradian archipelago would be opened up for exploration by global oil and gas companies. The island's peace was disturbed, wrote McWatt in the *Compendium*, 'by the constant clatter of helicopters ferrying Americans in sharp suits and cowboy boots on brief fact-finding trips', causing a surge in takings at the store and inn and rumours of new local jobs in the burgeoning industry. In 'Frae Mambeag Brae', however, McWatt sounded a warning against 'the exploitation of our resources by Yanks as well as Sassenachs and the desecration of the beauties of our landscape'.

In both the *Compendium* and his *Pibroch* column he gave accounts of more drama at sea, when lifeboat coxswain Mungo MacAskill was called out on the *Morag May* from Auchwinnie and was joined by the Fascaradian MacDonald brothers to search for a missing fishing boat from their own island. Joseph McKinnon's son Fergus and his friend Alec 'Wee Eck' Campbell, son of Alec and grandson of Tormud, were feared lost in the ferocious gale. Joseph, Tormud and Alec risked their own lives by joining the search on the *Silver Darling*, which was by now considered barely seaworthy even in the calmest of weather.

'It was a vicious night of clooring wind and endless rain that would wash away your very soul,' wrote McWatt in an article for the *Pibroch*, later reprinted in the *Scotsman*. 'And into the mouth of this hell, the men of Fascaray launched their frail vessels, pitting kinship and friendship against the barbarous might of nature.'

The *Silver Darling* almost capsized several times during the night, and from the bridge of the *Morag May*, Mungo MacAskill and the MacDonalds watched its unsteady progress and muttered that Tormud, Joseph and Alec would soon be in need of rescue themselves. In the blessed calm of a clear, windless dawn, as the lifeboat rounded Lusnaharra Point with the plucky *Silver Darling* swaying in its wake, they found the boys' fishing boat adrift and deserted.

'Their agony was beyond the reach of words,' wrote McWatt, but it did not last long – sharp-sighted Jamie spotted two figures waving from the skerries. Fergus and Eck were safe and well, though cold, wet and hungry, having found shelter overnight on a rocky islet after sixteen hours adrift in the storm. 'In the end,' wrote McWatt, 'simple human virtues were aided by pure luck.'

'Saw your article,' wrote Lilias, who was struggling to hold down a job in the soft furnishings department of Goldbergs department store. 'Glad to read the surly troglodyte of Calasay celebrating friendship and kinship. Might we raise a glass to the "simple human virtues" when you're next in Edinburgh?'

A Granite Ballad – The Reimagining of Grigor McWatt,
Mhairi McPhail (Thackeray College Press, 2016)

Today I receive a deputation from Balnasaig. Evelyn Fletcher sweeps in with her two assistants, Jinny Aubrey and Jeremy Gortz.

She tells me she has 'received a sign' that the Seekers should become involved in the Heritage Centre and Museum.

'It came to me in my morning communication with the plant yakshas,' she says. 'They told me this will be another way of spreading the influence of the spirit kingdom and promoting the energies of nature for the good of mankind.'

I smile politely. Jinny takes a velvet pouch from her belt and casts an assortment of small rocks on my desk.

'Healing crystals,' she explains.

'From Balnasaig,' adds Jeremy.

I touch them lightly, knowing from my dealings with Agnes and her collections that my job is to admire them.

'Beautiful,' I say.

'We can sell them in the museum gift shop,' says Jinny. 'Along with our organic herbal infusions.'

'We haven't really got to the gift-shop stage yet,' I say. 'But when we do, I'll be in touch. Locally grown dried herbs, attractively packaged, might well appeal to visitors but –'

'The crystals,' Evelyn reminds me. 'Harnessing all that positive energy . . .'

I riffle through the pile of dusty stones and put them back in Jinny's pouch one by one.

'Rose quartz, granite, fool's gold . . . yes, a really interesting proposal. Thank you for dropping by. I appreciate it.'

Evelyn, undeterred by my brush-off, enquires about the Trust's funding for the Balnasaig Tower Room, receives another polite brush-off, and invites me over to the centre for a Past Lives workshop. I tell her I'll let her know when I'm free. She is so supremely confident that I imagine nothing will shake her self-belief, or the belief of her followers. I watch them make their way back to their Land Rover and it occurs to me that Evelyn and I are both in the past lives business.

As they drive off, I notice Margaret Mackenzie loitering on the beach across the road. She sees me watching her and hurries off. That's all I need. A Fascaradian stalker.

I go to the shelves and take down the two Balnasaig books. Evelyn's *The Wisdom of the Wilderness Within* and her former partner Neville Booth's *Reflections from the Pilgrim Path: The Balnasaig Story*. Her book was written in 2007 – with, I see in the acknowledgements, the help of Jeremy Gortz – the year after Neville had fled the island on a permanent detour from the Pilgrim Path. I skim through Evelyn's self-regarding froth about visions, yakshas and spirit communications to get to the facts – here was another woman dumped by another faithless man. How did she get through it? Her unwavering egomania must have helped.

'Neville had been straying from the path for a long time, forsaking the spiritual for the corporeal as the plant yakshas had warned me. I needed to grow and expand, establish my identity fully as the pure channel for the spirit world, and he was holding me back. It was necessary and purging to let him go.'

We all tell ourselves consoling stories. When I realised Marco was having an affair, my first response – before the landslide of rage and despair – was a thrilling sense of liberation, a giddying lightness. He had set me free. I could do whatever the hell I liked, with whomever. I was single again.

Single. With an eight-year-old child and a live-in nominal partner who slept in the spare room, when he slept in the apartment at all, who mumbled a curt apology when his hand accidentally brushed mine over the coffee machine in the morning. Agnes's face, pale and tremulous, tethered my helium elation. How did I think this could possibly work?

It couldn't, of course. I barely slept, agonised as I heard him leave the apartment at midnight, lying rigid and alert till early morning, straining to hear him return. I yearned, pitifully, to hear his footsteps falter outside the bedroom door, then a soft knock that would signal an end to misery. I also longed to lay waste to his new pinball machine with a crowbar. Four excruciating months later it was over with Kate. Marco was abject and mortified, or he said he was. 'I don't know what I was thinking.

I was crazy. I'm so very sorry.' But it was too late. By then I'd met Pascal and hurled myself into an affair of my own which, apart from the obvious pleasures, provided an excuse for satisfying tit-for-tat elusiveness – 'Where are you going?' 'Out . . .' 'Who with?' 'Never you mind.' My rage at Marco, nursed during all those sleepless nights, mutated into ravening lust for Pascal. The deeper my anguish about Marco, the wilder the sex with The Other. The father of my child may have dumped me for a skinny contortionist, but this beautiful boy finds me attractive, therefore I'm attractive. I fuck therefore I am.

I should have seen it coming. Two woozy months later, the beautiful boy, like once-loyal, personable Marco before him, began to tire of me. Not of my company, it seemed – Pascal didn't seem embarrassed about introducing me to his friends (decorative dullards) and was happy to have me round backstage at his gigs, or to hang out with me at his place, that unexpectedly glitzy loft, watching black-and-white movies and picking desultorily at the vegan takeouts I brought over. It was my body he tired of. We were like a gender-swapped fifties comedy couple, sulking in bed; Desi Arnaz and Lucille Ball between the sheets, with Desi excusing himself from conjugal duties on account of a headache and mad-for-it Lucille folding her arms in a huff.

Was a pattern emerging here? To be cheated on by one man may be a misfortune, but two? In succession? Carelessness couldn't explain it. Pascal reassured me; there was no other woman. No man, either; good to get that clear. He loved my energy, my life force, he said. He even maintained that 'we were meant to be. I knew it the moment I saw you. I felt this spiritual connection.' I winced, but let it pass. He wasn't interested in other women, or men, that was the thing. He adored me. Loved my body. He'd been sick, low-level stuff, a virus, and hadn't got the energy for sex right now. It happened. We had a great relationship, didn't we? Wasn't it worth weathering this awkward patch?

'Only after Neville left,' wrote Evelyn Fletcher, 'once I was truly alone, as my plant yakshas had counselled me, could I focus on my work, truly achieve transcendence and lead others unencumbered towards the light.'

Transcendence, alas, is not an option for me. All I have is my work.

We Scots are modest types. We cringe at the first blast of a boastful blowhard's trumpet and the cold brass of the instrument of self-praise rarely grazes our lips. But the question does comes up: Big England – our southern master – would like to know by what right does Wee Scotland claim nationhood and independence. Who, they wonder, do we think we are and by what means do we imagine we can successfully go it alone?

Where do we start? Our self-evidently superior legal system? It's not evidently superior enough to the purblind Sassenach. Our more rigorous and egalitarian education system? It doesn't cut much ice or pierce the cerebral permafrost down south either, where egalitarianism is seen as akin to Bolshevism. Our natural resources? Our oil? The black stuff gushing from our north-eastern seabed is, as far as Westminster is concerned, Their Oil. Our majestic landscape of hill and loch? The insipid Sassenach, apparently, prefers the pretty and pastoral; give them nature tamed in mild fields and trimmed hedges over true wilderness any day. Apart, that is, from the few weeks a year they like to travel up here and slaughter our wildlife.

Perhaps, in response to their question – who do we think we are and by what means do we imagine we can successfully go it alone? – a better starting point would be our native riches; our people, who have given the world, among many things, anaesthesia, the aeroplane, the bicycle, cordite, canals, kaleidoscopes, cotton reels, colour photography, the electric clock, economics, fingerprinting, fridges, lawnmowers, light bulbs, logarithms, marmalade, the mackintosh, postage stamps, penicillin, the piano footpedal, radar, the steam engine, steam hammers, steamboats, syringes, tarmac, telephones, television, tyres, toasters and flush toilets, down which we can consign the patronising assumptions of the English. Our ingenious indigenes were the first to come up with the theory of electromagnetism, to measure the distance to a solar system outside our own, to identify a cell's nucleus, to discover a vaccine for typhoid fever and track down the cause of malaria.

We created the Bank of England (an act of perversity, I grant you) as well as the Bank of France, we can claim responsibility for the prototype police force of the Pinkerton National Detective Agency in America as well as the American navy, and it was a Scot, the Aberdonian Thomas Glover, who was behind the industrialisation of Japan.

Let us not forget the Enlightenment, which the English like to lay entirely at the door of the French. The writings of the great David Hume, Scots born and bred, champion of philosophical empiricism and scepticism, celebrator of liberty and social progress, was inspirational to colonists in the New World whose struggle with their English masters overseas sparked the War of Independence in 1775, the year before Hume's death.

And so, if you'll forgive me as I rehearse my embouchure once more and raise the trumpet to my lips for a final fanfare, it was the Scots who came up with what has arguably been the most influential invention of all – America. And it is America which rules the waves these days; not Britannia, and certainly not England. Thus, when the question of nationhood arises, north of the border we find ourselves asking, who do the Sassenachs think they are and by what means do they imagine they can successfully go it alone?

Grigor McWatt, November 1965, *Auchwinnie Pibroch*[9]

9   *Frae Mambeag Brae: Selected Columns and Essays of Grigor McWatt*, Stravaigin Press, 1985.

THOUGH HE RARELY LEFT FASCARAY (HE MADE THE JOURNEY TO Edinburgh perhaps seven times a year) and never Scotland – he said he would never travel abroad until his homeland was free and his passport bore no reference to an English queen – his reputation was becoming global. A photograph, in a May 1965 edition of the *Auchwinnie Pibroch*, shows a delegation to the island, organised by the Scottish USSR Friendship Society, which seemed to have overlooked McWatt's Burnsian solecism. The visitors were led by a dough-faced woman swaddled in a large overcoat, a Mme Kropotskaya, described by the *Auchwinnie Pibroch* as 'a teacher of Russian residing in Edinburgh'. Also in the party were several trades union delegates, the Russian novelist Boris Polevoi and Professor Samuel Marshak, the Russian translator of Robert Burns.

McWatt's correspondents included Ezra Pound, whose poetry he admired (though there is no record of his views on Pound's dalliance with fascism). In 1960, the American poet, newly released from a Washington psychiatric hospital, set up home in Italy and busied himself by catching up with the further reaches of European poetry. He had somehow got hold of a copy of McWatt's first collection, *Kenspeckelt*, and was drawn to the Scottish poet's outsider status. Seeing McWatt as a fellow 'prophet pariah', Pound invited him to Rapallo.

McWatt made polite noises – 'Thank you for your invitation. It's a long way from my little northern island of Fascaray to Genoa in terms of miles, but poetry makes close neighbours of us' – and turned him down.

In 1965, Pound tried again. He was coming to London to attend T. S. Eliot's funeral. Might he see the great Scottish poet there? McWatt was polite. 'I fear not. London is in enemy country. I wish you well for your journey. Condolences to the widow. I didn't see eye to eye with Eliot, particularly on the matter of religion. But he had the virtue of not being English, which showed in the best of his verse.'[10]

10 Correspondence held by Yale University Library.

McWatt also failed to take up an invitation to visit Bertolt Brecht in Berlin, though the politics of the German writer were closer to McWatt's own. In 1973, Ted Berrigan, the New York School poet, then visiting professor at an English university, sent McWatt a letter asking if he would give a reading in Colchester. In the letter, Berrigan expressed admiration for McWatt's 'pugnacious, polychromatic language'. There is no record of any reply in Berrigan's papers at Syracuse University or UC San Diego but the invitation was not sufficiently enticing to lure McWatt across the border.

Nearer home, he had a brief correspondence with Douglas Young, former chairman of the SNP and translator of Aristophanes into Scots, but the letters dried up in 1967 when Young moved to take up a teaching post in Canada. There is a collegiate exchange with Professor Alexander Gray, translator of German and Danish verse into Scots, and a polite but terse postcard from William Laughton Lorimer, best known for his translation of the New Testament into Scots.

Of more general interest are letters from Ted Hughes (1960) and Seamus Heaney (1975) thanking McWatt for copies of his collections *Kenspeckelt* and *Kowk in the Kaleyard* respectively. Hughes's typed acknowledgement is politely distant – it's unsigned and may have been written by his publisher's secretary. Heaney's reply is handwritten, warm and encouraging: 'You are a poet and will go where you decide.'

A Granite Ballad – The Reimagining of Grigor McWatt,
Mhairi McPhail (Thackeray College Press, 2016)

Another tug-of-love evening. My book? More work on the *Compendium*? The letters?

Agnes, uncomplaining and absorbed in artwork at her end of the table, doesn't get a look-in.

Yale University Library has just agreed to lend McWatt's correspondence with Ezra Pound to us for the museum opening. A bit of a coup, I thought. The letters are of interest to academics, literary biographers and, incidentally, to me, and will – properly exhibited – help to bulk out the display. The Auchwinnie Board, however, was not impressed. 'They won't exactly draw in the day trippers, will they?' said Gordon Nesbitt, who made it clear that we'll need more pop culture – 'accessibility', he calls it – for any box-office success and, by implication, for any guarantee of future funding; the museum, and my job, depends on it.

There is a letter from the publisher of Silver Key Comics (1963) who wanted to produce a weekly comic strip based on 'the adventures of Looa [*sic*] the sheep dog, Marty the Pine Marten and Otto the Otter, as recounted in your newspaper column in the Achwinnie Peabroch [*sic*]'; another from the Children's Film Foundation, which in 1965 sought permission to make a film 'using the lively characters from your private zoo in a short feature for our Saturday Morning Pictures' audience'; and one from a London advertising agency seeking permission in 1970 to use the song 'Hame tae Fascaray' in a TV advertising campaign for a new oat-based breakfast cereal.

Permission in the first two cases was refused in one dismissive line. In the case of the director of the London advertising agency, the poet went further, sending him a Gaelic incantation – *Is mairg do 'n dual am poll itheadh. Is fhèarr am bonnach beag leis a' bheannachd, na 'm bonnach mór leis a' mhollachd* – which McWatt also translated: 'Pity him whose birthright is to eat dirt. Better a wee bannock wi a blessing than a big yin wi a curse.'

As far as Gordon Nesbitt is concerned, the prize exhibits so far are a request from Albert Grossman, then manager of Bob Dylan, for permission to record 'Hame tae Fascaray' on Dylan's 1964 album *The Times They Are A-Changin'* and one from Columbia Records twelve years later for clearance to include McWatt's song on Dylan's live album *Hard Rain*. Permission was brusquely denied for the former and granted for the latter.

In fact, the bulk of McWatt's letters comprise denials and refusals and, in the case of his correspondence with Lilias Hogg, evasions. I'm speaking against my job here, and I would never admit it to Nesbitt and the board, but it is the story of the thwarted lover, Lilias Hogg, that intrigues me most of all. Her letters, full of such bravado, anger and defiance, also have a quality lacking in much of McWatt's correspondence – emotional authenticity.

Niver gie aw the Hert

Niver gie aw the hert fer loue,
Wull barelins seem wirth weenin o
Tae tapteed weemen gin it seem
Siccar, an they niver dwaum
It dwynes frae smeeg tae smeeg;
For aw that's bonnie's nocht
But swith, dwaumy couth delicht.
Och niver gie the hert ootricht,
For they, for aw sneith mooths can reel,
Hae gien their herts tae whumgee spiel.
An wha could spiel it weel eneuch
Gin deif an dwm an blyn wi loue?
He that writ this kens it aw
Syne his hert wis brak in twa.

Grigor McWatt, efter W. B. Yeats, 1965[11]

---

11 From *Kowk in the Kaleyard*, Virr Press, 1975. Reprinted in *Warld in a Gless: The Collected Varse of Grigor McWatt*, Smeddum Beuks, 1992.

McWATT CONTINUED HIS DIVIDED LIFE – POET-ANCHORITE OF Fascaray and 'rairin gadgie' of the howffs and inns of Edinburgh – throughout the sixties. Not all of these visits to the capital ended well. There are eyewitness accounts of evenings turning bitter, of a cursing McWatt 'black affronted', storming from the pub, often with Lilias running after him calling soothing words.

The occasion of these rages would be well-meaning young people who, recognising The Poet, would break into song. That song. The popular folk singer Hamish Imlach recorded 'Hame tae Fascaray' in 1965 and, along with 'The Wild Rover', it became the most requested ballad in cellar bars and clubs throughout the UK. In one letter to Lilias, dated 14 June 1965, McWatt is scathing about Imlach – 'He was born in Calcutta. He's as Scots as Mahatma Gandhi.' For McWatt to hear his own words bawled by drunk youths – often university students, some of whom had the temerity to be English – was enough to drive him instantly 'hame tae Fascaray'.

The letters at this time reveal a man consumed by passion, for poetry, landscape and nationhood – 'our first victory since Bannockburn!' he wrote in 1967 after the election of Scottish National Party candidate Winnie Ewing as MP in Hamilton. But he is mute on the subject of love. When, if ever, he found time to kindle his relationship with 'Jean' is not known. His 'consuming ambition', he wrote to Lilias, was to 'build a bridge of words across the Clinch Straits, tae heal my family's breach with oor ancestral hame and scrieve [write] Scotia back tae hersel'. He warned Lilias: 'You must understand. This project is not a negligible undertaking and leaves little time for the smaller business of the human heart.'

Many of Lilias's letters to her 'Griogal Cridhe' in the mid-sixties seem to have been composed at the speed of thought. The handwriting is slapdash, an ink-spattered spree of loops and dots. It took me some time to decipher one scrawled letter, dated August 1966, which was written after a drinking session with Sydney and Archie:

After another heavy hoolie, seeing in the dawn in silent, bluitert awe, we found ourselves blinking against the daylight, away from our usual beat, as the unco guid, conscientious types in suits and secretarial mufti hurried to work. We hurried ourselves, to the nearest pub, an unfamiliar, cavernous joint. We breenged up to the counter and some snooty barmaid recoiled as we went to order a round. 'It's a bank, not a pub,' she pointed out with unnecessary hauteur.

Hogg emphasises again and again in the sixties just what a good time she is having, as if to say to McWatt: 'Look what you're missing!' She is sacked from Goldbergs for, she says, 'liberating' some of the exotic birds kept in a cage in the department store's rooftop cafe, and she makes a joke of it – 'Billy the parrot flew the coop. Then I did too.' – though she must have been worried about money and security. Underscoring all her letters is a sense of honest anguish. Like McWatt, she is engaged in a lifelong search for connection, but for Lilias people took precedence over place.

'I feel strongly that in some way you and I are the same – lost souls spinning wildly, rogue planets in an alien universe,' she writes in April 1968. Unlike McWatt, who dips in and out of the vernacular, Lilias rarely uses Scots, except in jest. After immersion in McWatt's Doric and Lallans (some of which, wrote Alastair Galbraith, 'would bamboozle Burns'), Hogg's sparky English can come as a relief. A fragile hope is in evidence – hope of love, perhaps, stirred by a too-personal reading of McWatt's verse.

It would be hard for a romantically inclined young woman, infatuated by poetry and convinced that it is a communicable gift, to read some of McWatt's verse as anything other than a direct come-on.

In one letter from Calasay, dated June 1968, he wrote to her: 'I've been working up some metaphysicals. What do you think?'

> *Gin we hae warld eneuch an time,*
> *This erchness Lassie, were nae crime.*
> *We wid sit doon an think whit paith tae tak*
> *An pass this lang loue's day.*

You wid stravaig by the Watter o Leith
While Ah hung aboot oan Mammor's lanely heath.
Ah'd loue ye ten years afore the warld wis raw
An you could, if it pleases you, say naw,
Till England richts its wrangs an tyrants faw.

But jest ahint Ah hear the soond
O time's auld tramcar gangin roond
An thonder aw aheid us lies
Muckle deserts bidin aye.

Let us pirl aw oor poost, an aw
Oor douceness intae wan baw.
An rive oor pleasures wi roch strife
Ben the airn yetts o life.
Sae tho we cannae mak oor sun
Staund still, yet we will gar him run.[12]

Hogg's reply, from her basement flat in a decaying New Town terrace, was unequivocal:

'As to your metaphysical urgings, I can only, like Molly Bloom, exclaim "Yes! Yes! Yes!"'

A Granite Ballad – The Reimagining of Grigor McWatt,
Mhairi McPhail (Thackeray College Press, 2016)

---

12 'Gin We Hae Warld Eneuch', efter Andrew Marvell, 1968. *Kowk in the Kaleyard*,
    Virr Press, 1975. Reprinted in *Warld in a Gless: The Collected Varse of Grigor
    McWatt*, Smeddum Beuks, 1992.

15 November 2014

'Hurry, Mom! He's waiting.'

It's one of those fine winter days that give summer a run for its money – cloudless sky, amber sunlight, cleansing cold and a gentle breeze ruffling a sea blue as a Hollywood pool. We're going on a boat trip round the island with Niall Kennedy. My contribution is a picnic. Agnes is bringing our waterproofs, a plastic container for shells, and a tablecloth. She wanted to film the trip for her father but I persuaded her to leave her phone behind, arguing that it might get swamped by a wave.

We walk down to the harbour where, instead of the sleek fibreglass yacht I was expecting, we see a small open wooden boat with a single red sail. It is, Niall tells us, a traditional fishing skiff, used on the island up to the beginning of the last century. Not much bigger than a kayak and as apparently seaworthy as a bathtub, it might explain the historically high attrition rate in the fishing industry.

Agnes steps sure-footedly into the boat and immediately volunteers to help sail the thing. I follow more hesitantly, hoping Niall knows what he's doing. There's no cabin in which to shelter should the weather turn. Where are the lifejackets? I feel faintly nauseous and, remembering our first ferry trip to the island, hope that Agnes's nonchalance and my limited reserves of maternal patience won't be tested by another bout of her seasickness.

He starts the outboard motor and we head straight out towards Auchwinnie. Agnes stands in the back of the boat, her hand shading her eyes in salute, hair streaming in the chill breeze, an elfin figurehead. She points out number 19, the school, Ailsa's cottage, the Campbells' place, the Big House, as Finnverinnity shrinks into the horizon and Beinn Mammor, with a scattering of snow at its peak, dwindles to a hillock.

'The snow's like doughnut sugar!' says Agnes, then turns to Niall to explain: 'That's a metaphor.'

'No, honey,' I tell her. 'That's a simile – another figure of speech, like a metaphor only different.'

We head west, past the twin rock bird colonies of Plodda and Grodda on our left, crowded and noisy as a nightmare housing project. Niall shuts off the engine and Agnes scrambles to help him tighten the sail.

'The important thing,' he tells her, 'is to work out the direction of the wind. You can't sail directly into it.'

'Why not?'

'You just can't do it,' he says. 'The game would be up.'

She nods, enthralled by the possibility of peril. I, meanwhile, silently rejoice in the calm sea and the gentle wind that is just strong enough to stiffen the sails.

Once we've left the citadels of screaming gannets behind, a soothing silence washes over us. Soon we pass the creamy strip of Lusnaharra beach on our right or, as Agnes now knows to call it, starboard.

'So Finnverinnity, our port, is on our starboard side now and the bird islands were on our port side?' she checks.

Niall nods. 'You've got it,' he says.

The ridged earthworks of the Neolithic village above Lusnaharra are plainly visible from the boat, and we can just make out the scaffolding round the former Catholic church and ill-fated Tempull Beag Arts Centre and Tea Room, which has just been bought by a Danish retail magnate. He plans to set up a micro-distillery and, in a nod to island history, he told the *Auchwinnie Pibroch* he will call the single malt 'Father Col's Special Reserve'.

Agnes points out Oonagh's farm.

'The sheep look like spilled popcorn or something on the hill from here,' she says. Then she turns to me. 'Another metaphor? Right, Mom?'

'Another simile. If it uses the comparing words "like" or "as", it's a simile.'

Niall hands her the tiller.

'So I just steer straight on?' she checks.

'Yes. Keep her steady. I'll let you know when we have to change our course.'

She frowns, transfixed by responsibility.

'What's that orange ball in the water?' she points.

'It's a buoy,' I say.

'Why's it a boy and not a girl?'

I'll save the spelling lesson for later. Agnes isn't pressing for an answer because there's a new and exciting distraction. A sleek, moustachioed grey head has popped up by the side of the boat.

'Wow! A seal! He's so cute. Like a little puppy. Can we feed him?'

'Not a good idea,' says Niall, taking over the tiller. 'We don't want to teach them bad habits like begging. They should get their food in their own way.'

She reddens as if rebuked.

We're rounding the headland past the mouth of the Cannioch River – Invercannioch the map says – and heading north now, following the line of the coast to the mighty Doonmara cliffs where more birds, seagulls and solan geese, wheel above us and call from their rocky perches.

Further north, out to sea, there is a distant agitation in the water and a faint, ominous roar. The Carracorry whirlpool.

'It's the fourth largest whirlpool in the world,' Niall tells us. 'Geologists say it's caused by the tidal race running over a large underwater chasm and several basalt pinnacles rising from the seabed. Folklore says it's caused by the old goddess of winter, Cailleach Bheur, washing her enormous kilt in the sea.'

'Folklore's so dumb,' Agnes says.

'Maybe. But these are stories people told themselves before science was invented to explain the world. They have value too.'

'Okay,' she concedes. 'It's dumb, but it's kind of fun.'

Niall drops the anchor and ties up on a spit of rock under the Calasay cliffs. Somewhere up there is McWatt's grave, marked by a driftwood cross. We clamber ashore on the strip of machair and Agnes spreads out the hideous teddy-bear tablecloth on the beach, smoothing it carefully.

'Do you think your poet picnicked here?' she asks me.

'What do you think, Niall? You knew him,' I say, setting out the food.

'Well . . . I don't think he was much of a picnic man.'

We eat – oatcakes, cheese, fruit and chocolate, the best I could do from Finnverinnity store – in contented silence, looking out to sea. Once we've packed away the remnants, shaken the tablecloth and cleared away the last scraps of orange peel, Agnes gets out her plastic container and goes off in search of some fresh shells for her collection.

Niall and I watch her skip through the grass to the water's edge and our talk turns personal. He asks about Marco and I give what I hope is a wry haiku account of our courtship, parenthood and break-up. Wry but acid-free, is the intention. Bitterness, hard to avoid, is so unattractive.

'He's a good person. Hard-working. Loves his daughter. Loved me. Once,' I say with an even-handedness that almost persuades me. 'I loved him. It just didn't work out.'

Then it's Niall's turn. He talks about his partner, currently based in Auchwinnie for work, and I manage to conceal my frisson of disappointment.

'We've been together for two years,' he says. 'We hope to live together on the island eventually but it's difficult. We can only manage a weekend a month at the moment.'

'What does she do?' I ask.

'He. He's an archaeologist.'

We look up as a shadow passes over us, cast by a huge bird.

'*Iolar mara.* Sea eagle,' says Niall.

It gives me time to recover. How did I not guess? Most kind, attentive, halfway presentable men of my acquaintance are gay. Most of my male friends. What happened to my New Yorker's infallible antennae? Did I honestly think there were no homosexuals in Fascaray?

'Interesting work,' I say. 'Especially round here. I hope I get to meet him.'

'You will.'

If Niall has noticed my discomfort, he isn't letting on.

Agnes calls to us: 'Mom! Mr Kennedy! Look!'

She points towards the horizon where two dark crescents rise and fall through the waves, stitching the sea.

Dolphins.

'They're playing!' she shouts.

We watch, entranced, until they're out of sight, then she races back to us, rattling her box of shells.

'I got a pink razor clam, like a witch's fingernail,' she says.

Niall unties the boat, pulls up the anchor and we set off for home. The sea is restless as we pass the Ring of Drumnish, its standing stones gaunt and jagged against the scudding clouds.

'Broken teeth, Mom? Right?'

'Right.'

She turns.

'Look, Mom!'

She is pointing out to sea towards a cluster of eight large circular tanks ringed by rails.

'Merry-go-rounds for mermaids,' she laughs.

This metaphor kick has got to stop.

It's the Fascaray Salmon Farm, set up by Eck Campbell a decade ago with his wife Isa and son Andy. It's a small-scale business compared to the vast industrial fish tanks out beyond Plodda and Grodda that are owned and operated by a Norwegian corporation.

We get closer and see geysers of spray spouting over the tanks as threshing fish, large and muscly as wrestlers' forearms, leap vertically three feet out of the water, twist in the air and crash back down before repeating the display seconds later.

'Are they playing?' asks Agnes.

'Not here. No,' says Niall. 'They like leaping when they're free, but here, because they're living in such a small space, they all get fleas, which drive them mad with itching.'

'So they're jumping in the air all the time to get rid of the fleas?'

'That's right.'

'But they never will?'

He shakes his head. 'No.'

She bites her bottom lip. 'That is so sad.'

'Not so sad, maybe, as all the fishermen who used to die braving rough seas to put fish on our plates,' he says.

That night as I set out supper – grilled salmon – she tells me she can't eat it.

'I'm a proper vegetarian now,' she announces. 'No meat. No fish. Just vegetables.'

cod: known as coddie, shingle, stockfish, slink or soushler. A large cod is called a keelin while a young cod is called a cabelew. A poor specimen, usually thrown back in the water by disappointed fishermen, is a drowd. Boat fishing north of Mhor Sgheir reef can produce good catches with crab and mussel baits.

dab: lang fleuk. Flatfish, found near Calasay and Lusnaharra strands.

dog fish: sea dug. Aggressive feeder, responds to crab and fish baits.

flounder: craig fleuk. Found from early spring at the mouth of the River Lingel.

haddock: haddie, cameral. Identified by 'thumbprint' mark behind head. Abundant, particularly in the island's western waters.

hake: gairdfish. Predator, with a sharp set of teeth found in deeper waters towards Plodda and Grodda.

herring: herrin or sgadan. The silver darlings of song and legend.

lesser-spotted dogfish: Blind Lizzie. Always keen to take the bait off Calasay.

plaice: plashock or beggar fleuk. Bright orange spots. Abundant from early spring and summer, especially off Calasay, where they feed on crabs.

turbot: the bunnet fleuk. A flatfish, abundant around Fascaray.

Grigor McWatt, 1967, *The Fascaray Compendium*

THE FISHING INDUSTRY, THE HEART OF FASCARAY'S ECONOMY for centuries, was in serious trouble. One spring weekend in 1968, the men put out to sea as usual and came back five hours later, empty-handed for the first time in living memory. There was much discussion in the inn: tides were normal and the winds were moderate – none of the harsh easterlies that could be the bane of the fleet. 'The sea has fallen silent,' wrote McWatt in *The Fascaray Compendium* in May 1968, 'and a sense of terrible foreboding pervades the island.'

For ten days, the fishermen ventured out in hope and returned in despair, then one day the fish were back, island life resumed and within days the 'vainishin' was forgotten. But by the end of the following month it happened again; after a day at sea the fishermen returned to the island with empty creels and nets as light and clean as they had been on departure. In the inn there was much dark talk and head-shaking, according to McWatt. Some older fishers blamed the oil exploration going on in the Clinch – a 5,000-ton converted barge with a helipad, living quarters and a steel tower, visible from Finnverinnity and Lusnaharra, was drilling for oil east of Plodda.

'I wouldn't fancy that carry-on myself if I was a fish,' said Francie MacDonald.

Others attributed the barren catches to supernatural forces. Some argued that Seonaidh, the sea god, had not been appeased in the traditional manner for some years, while the righteous of the Free Church suggested it was punishment for recent lax observance of the Sabbath and the absence of morals among the young. The new dance, the twist, had come to Auchwinnie and by all accounts this 'unwholesome craze' – the 'work of Satan' and an inevitable consequence of the hula-hoop fad – was in danger of crossing the water to Fascaray.

The prosaic truth was revealed by an unexpected source. After an all-night hoolie in Finnverinnity, Murdo 'the Fiddle' McIntyre was returning uncertainly to his cottage in Doonmara by flashlight in the early hours of the morning along the cliff path when he made out the menacing hulk of a big boat, its navigation lights turned off, surreptitiously trawling the inland waters of Fascaray. Some doubted Murdo's account at first – 'a man who spends all his waking hours in the company of a whisky bottle might not be the most reliable witness', wrote McWatt – but the following day the fish had gone again.

After midnight that night, Tormud Campbell, with his son Alec and grandson Wee Eck, launched the *Silver Darling* from Finnverinnity and steered her round the island until, just as Murdo had said, the outline of the phantom boat loomed ahead in the darkness. Tormud turned off his outboard engine and they rowed up to the behemoth – more than 900 gross tons, with a low-slung rail and high bulwarks – where they saw that its name, number and builder's plate had been obscured by paint, its bell had been shrouded by cloth and the crew were masked as they hauled in their catches onto the open foredeck. They were masked but they weren't silent and their northern English accents were unmistakable.

This was poaching on an industrial scale, stealing from impoverished locals rather than wealthy lairds. Islanders were enraged and furious representation was made to Auchwinnie Council, the port authorities and the owners of the big commercial fleets on the east and west coasts, in England as well as Scotland, reminding them of the statutory limits protecting local fishing. The interlopers were, it transpired, from Fleetwood in Lancashire and a fine was eventually imposed on the boat's owners. But it was only a quarter of the value of the illegal catch, which had long been sold to Billingsgate market in London and dispatched in the usual way.

This was, as McWatt wrote, the start of the 'fishers' faw'.

Meanwhile the seas around the island were despoiled in another way by the arrival of yet more unsightly drilling rigs. 'Sea-girt pylons, spewing monsters, the de'il's brochs', McWatt called them.

Their profileration, at a time of change and uncertainty, when the fishing industry seemed gravely imperilled, gave an undeniable boost to the nationalist movement. In the 28 September 1968 issue of the *Auchwinnie Pibroch*, the headline on McWatt's 'Frae Mambeag Brae' column read: 'FASCARAY'S OIL FOR THE FASCARADIANS'.

A Granite Ballad – The Reimagining of Grigor McWatt,
Mhairi McPhail (Thackeray College Press, 2016)

The Sang o Stravaigin Aengus

Ah ganged oot tae the hissel wid,
Acause a gleed wis in ma heid,
An cut an pilked a hissel scob,
An cleeked a brammle tae a threid.
An when white mochs were flichterin roon,
An moch-like starns were blinterin oot,
Ah drapped the brammle in a burn
An claucht a braw wee siller troot.

When Ah had set it oan the groun
Ah went tae blaw the gleed alicht
But somethin reeshelt oan the groun,
An sumbdy cawed ma name aricht,
It had become a gliskin quine
Wi aiple flirry in her hair,
She cawed me in a vyce sae fine
Then dwimisht throu the brichtenin air.

Nou Ah'm auld an hae stravaiged
Thro glens an michty mountain launs,
I'll scart her doon tae where she's pugged
An pree her moue and clesp her hauns;
An gang amang lang dappelt gress,
An pouk tae time itsel is done
The siller aiples o the muin
The gowden aiples o the sun.

Grigor McWatt, efter W. B. Yeats, 1969[13]

13 From *Kowk in the Kaleyard*, Virr Press, 1975. Reprinted in *Warld in a Gless: The Collected Varse of Grigor McWatt*, Smeddum Beuks, 1992.

A CRAVING FOR REASSURANCE BECOMES APPARENT TOWARDS the end of the sixties in Lilias's self-deprecating humour and the madcap accounts of late-night escapades, mishaps with drink and ruinous romantic adventures.

> A stramash with Syd last night – Stella came to claim him, again – somehow ended in a bleary breakfast with Archie (I was too scunnered to face his clootie dumpling and fried-egg special) and a livid Rothkoesque bruise on, of all places, the big toe of my right foot. The administration of Johnnie Walker, topical and oral, did not help and Archie took me to the infirmary, from which I emerged on crutches, bandaged like a cartoon gout victim.

Alluding to the colloquial designation of Protestant and Catholic, she added 'my Episcopalian granny would be mortified to know I am now, officially, a left footer'. Despite the merriment, even in the dewy glory of her twenties, when she was still McWatt's 'lanely, anely Flooer o Rose Street', there were signs of encroaching mental distress and it is hard to avoid the sense that her stories of reckless nights spent in the company of other men were at that stage part of a desperate ploy to make McWatt jealous and bind him to her.

She had taken a job, temporarily she insisted, in a betting shop.

> The owner, a madly uncultivated bear of an Irishman, has a fondness for me and guesses, rightly, that I am reasonably numerate and that gambling is the one vice I do not possess. The customers are all desperate men, squiffily handing over pay packets or broo [dole] money each week in hope of the life-transforming Big Win. Now I think about it, I'm not so very different. I squandered everything, gambling on the Big Love that would transform my

life. The odds were rotten and I lost the lot. Still, like them, I continue to live in hope . . .

Her subtle reproaches were still leavened by memories of the best of their affair and a sense that even now, ten years after their first meeting and their happiest times, their love might be revived.

'Oh, Grigor,' she wrote in 1969, 'if only you and I had been French . . . We could walk barefoot in the sand in St Tropez like Bardot and Delon, and toast our happiness in champagne. Instead we're cursed with the ayebidin dusk of cold Caledonia and drink McEwan's and Johnnie Walker. Come and keep me warm! How darkness descends here. The nights draw in – and so do I.'

A Granite Ballad – The Reimagining of Grigor McWatt,
Mhairi McPhail (Thackeray College Press, 2016)

I've hit a wall here. I still have little on the poet's early life, less on his time with the SOE and nothing at all on Lilias's rival, to whom McWatt's biographer makes only the briefest reference: 'there were other loves, chief among them the elusive Jean'. Knox-Cardew enlarges on Lilias's caustic comparison between Grigor McWatt's Jean and Robert Burns's wife, Jean Armour – the 'Belle of Mauchline' and 'the lassie I loue best' – but doesn't provide further details. Knox-Cardew had no luck in tracking down Lilias's rival either.

Unless I make some kind of breakthrough, *A Granite Ballad* is going to look like a feeble rehash of Knox-Cardew's chapter, with a few documents and quotes thrown in.

I keep despair away by diverting myself back to the letters, the poetry and the *Compendium*. I've plenty of material, I tell myself. It's just a matter of putting it in the right order. And then there are the lexicons and inventories, with incantatory echoes of those oddly soothing prayers we were made to learn at school: the Litanies of the Blessed Virgin Mary and the Litanies of the Saints.

'St Mary Magdalene – Pray for us . . . St Lucy – Pray for us . . . St Agnes – Pray for us . . .'

No St Jean. Nor St Lilias. And I might as well be asking McWatt's birds, or seashells, or mammals for divine assistance with this project.

Order, Lipotyphla. Family, Talpidae:

mole (*Talpa europaea*, L.): mowdie, mowdiewort, mowdiewarp. Said to have been accidentally introduced into the island in the early nineteenth century in a boatload of top soil from Mull that was destined for the walled garden of Finnverinnity House. Now common, sighted most recently (July 1972) in author's vegetable patch in Calasay.

Order, Carnivora. Family, Mustelidae:

marten (*Martes martes*, L.): tuggin, mertrick, mairtin. Once common, now rare. Can be lured by a 'piece and jam', ie a jam sandwich. Four rescued and reared as household pets by the author. The species is referred to in the place names Suidhe an Taghain (Marten Den) and Lèana an Taghain (Marten Meadow) in Calasay.

otter (*Lutra lutra*, L.): formerly common, now rare. Author and ornithologist Murdoch McMurdo, in his *History of the Fascaradian Archipelago* (1886), recorded that two had been seen 'disporting themselves' on the banks of the Cannioch 'after an apparent absence of almost half a century'. Five cumlins rescued and reared as household pets by the author.

polecat (*Mustela putorius*, L.): fozel, thulmard, thoomart. Dean Munro, the sixteenth-century cleric and travel chronicler, who called the creature 'foulmart', observed its abundant presence on his visit to Fascaray in 1548. Now rare, though its existence is reflected in the place name Lag nam Feocullan (Polecat Hollow), near Tilliecuddy Burn.

common seal (*Phoca vitulina*, L.): selch, selkie. Relatively rare, though Murdo McIntyre, musician, claims to have seen a family of them basking off Doonmara Cliffs.

grey seal (*Halichoerus grypus*, Fab): selch, selkie. Once rare, now common. Breeds in the autumn, frequently seen on rocks just above high water off east coast of Calasay. Young sighted by author as early as the second week in August. Enshrined in local folklore as the selkie 'seal women' who lured many sailors to their death.

Grigor McWatt, 1972, *The Fascaray Compendium*

THE *GUDGIE*, THE OLD COAL-BURNING PUFFER, SERVED THE ISLAND
for forty years and inspired McWatt's famous *cinquain* verse, 'Cargoes'.[14]

> *Clatty Scottish puffer wi a smuired smoch lum,*
> *Breengin up the Clyde in a pit-mirk haar*
> *Wi a cargo o Shotts coal,*
> *Gartcosh fire clay,*
> *Cattle feed, fishmeal an claggie tar.*

The boat was finally sent into retirement in 1970, along with skipper
Ali Hume and first mate Malkie McTavish, and replaced by a new diesel-
fuelled cargo vessel. The *Bonxie*, 132 feet long, 'neat as a trivet' according
to its new captain, Pat Boy Cairns, was equipped to carry cargo, cattle and
a dozen passengers. Chic McIntosh, son of Hamish and Sarah McIntosh,
'a tall, streichly [straggly] laddie', according to McWatt in *The Fascaray
Compendium*, was taken on as deckhand.

But within months the new boat was already too small to accommodate the increasing numbers of visitors to the island. Flotillas of small
boats and rubber dinghies from Fascaray and Auchwinnie began to
operate as private water taxis to and from the mainland.

The spirit of romantic nationalism, the growing fashion for folk
music and developments at the Balnasaig Centre were bringing new visitors hame tae Fascaray. The 'big bearded men in fishermen's sweaters'
were gradually supplanted at the Finnverinnity Inn, wrote McWatt in
the *Compendium*, by 'fey youths with long hair', some of them carrying
guitars or banjos for music 'sessions'. They were often accompanied by
'silent girls, with longer hair and secretive smiles', who wore blue jeans so
tight that George Ferguson was moved to deliver a sermon denouncing
their 'unwholesome dress'. The Seekers set tended to be older and

14 Efter John Masefield, 1969. *Kowk in the Kaleyard*, Virr Press, 1975. *Warld in a
Gless: The Collected Varse of Grigor McWatt*, Smeddum Beuks, 1992.

quieter, shunning the noisy bacchanals of Finnverinnity for sedate group chanting at the Balnasaig Centre.

In the pub, the young 'folkies' would sit in a haar of cigarette smoke and sing McWatt's song, which had recently been recorded by the musician Donovan Leitch and sold in sufficient numbers to enter the Top 10 pop charts. It must have generated welcome income up at An Tobar but this new version of 'Hame tae Fascaray', with its heavy use of sitar and triangle, was thought 'too psychedelic' for some purists and in the Finnverinnity Inn in 1970, the song was still sung with eyes closed, in reverent voices 'of varying pitch and uncertain musical quality', according to McWatt, to a simple strummed chord accompaniment.

Jamie MacDonald and his wife, Marsaili, got permission from the laird to take over a derelict byre on the outskirts of Finnverinnity, gut it, run a hardboard partition down its centre and equip it with rudimentary bathroom facilities and a dozen bunk beds. The Bothy, as it became known, 'allows the hippy boys and their girlfriends to spend a night or two on the island and extra money in the pub', wrote McWatt.

'The narrow bunk beds and the partition, with its painted signs indicating which side belongs to the "lassies" and which to the "laddies", is said to ensure that there will be no opportunity for any of what is called round here "hochmagandy".' The MacDonalds also gave an undertaking that there would be no singing on a Sunday. 'George Ferguson and the church elders are pacified, for the moment.'

It is telling that, in his columns for the *Pibroch* at this time, apart from a satirical piece about the Balnasaig Seekers, McWatt makes little mention of these island developments and instead uses 'Frae Mambeag Brae' to publicly rail against plans for the decimalisation of currency – 'an English plot to raise prices and rents' – and writes about the latest losses and additions to his menagerie (two new pine martens, an otter, a pair of mating wildcats, and four seabirds incapacitated by an oil leak from a passing cargo ship).

He also records in his column the heroic rescue by the *Morag May* lifeboat of the fifteen-man crew of the Grimsby trawler *Fleet Flourish*, which ran aground on a reef west of the Doonmara cliffs in a fierce blizzard. Water was pouring into the engine room and the vessel had begun to 'rock like a pendulum', according to the *Fleet Flourish*'s skipper Albert

Smart, who managed to send out a Mayday message as he and his men clung desperately to the pitching boat.

The *Morag May* reached the scene in an hour and battled to secure her anchor in white-out conditions before a rocket line attached to a life raft could be fired onto the stricken trawler. 'The first eight trawlermen managed to jump into the rolling life raft which was pulled back towards the *Morag May*, hand over hand, by Mungo MacAskill, his Fascaradian son-in-law, Jamie MacDonald, and Jamie's brother Francie. Waves swamped the raft twice but the crew of the *Morag May* managed to haul the men to safety before the exercise was repeated and the remaining seven men were rescued,' wrote McWatt.

For his part in plucking the trawlermen from certain death in the most perilous conditions, Mungo MacAskill was awarded another RNLI medal while the MacDonald brothers and the other eight *Morag May* crew members added to their collection of vellum commendations. In his *Pibroch* column, McWatt reflected that there was irony in the fact that brave local fishermen had risked death to rescue the very men – 'trawlermen on the big boats from distant ports who prey on our precious resources' – who would rob them of their livelihoods.

Meanwhile, in the *Compendium*, McWatt noted that the Balnasaig Seekers had expanded their operation 'after reports of a personal encounter with the god Pan in Evelyn's healing flower patch'. Neville Booth and a team of volunteers, from mainland Europe and America as well as England, began constructing a 'hydroponic nursery to grow exotic vegetables and fruits' while his wife Althea now offered 'Rebirthing and Past Lives Therapy' to growing numbers of pilgrims lured by articles in esoteric magazines and 'the endorsement on a TV chat show of an actress who had, before joining an ashram in India, once played Doctor Who's sidekick'.

The Seekers were picked up at the harbour by Balnasaig's new assistant, Izzy Wallop, described by McWatt as 'a loud, hearty blonde – a young Margaret Rutherford without the charm or subtlety – from Berkshire, England'. She was a former chalet girl who was said to have undergone a mystical awakening in Gstaad 'after overdoing the schnapps'. She drove the new pilgrims in a Transit van over the rutted track to the Lodge, where, according to an advert in the 'Mind & Body' pages of *Time*

Out magazine, they would have enjoyed 'a macrobiotic supper, a Tarot reading, collective chanting and guided meditation before a week of intense spiritual parturition in a magical glen'.

A Granite Ballad – The Reimagining of Grigor McWatt,
Mhairi McPhail (Thackeray College Press, 2016)

The folk at Balnasaig have been at it again. Readers will be acquainted with the antics of the community, some call it a cult, which has taken over the old Balnasaig Lodge. Their members' common-sense-to-cash ratio errs towards the monetary and they spend most of their time engaged in 'workshops' communing with spirit guides, extraterrestrials and what I assume must be their own inner demons.

They were drawn to our island firstly, I suspect, because no one else would have them. And then our folklore – stories of second sight, of sidhe fairies, of kelpies and bogles – sealed it for them. The self-described Seekers say they feel a kinship with 'our spirituality', overlooking the fact that our stories were devised by a people enduring lives of harshest poverty, subject to the caprices of climate and challenges of terrain, whose folklore sought to explain the whims of nature and the transience of life and had the additional purpose of entertaining them during long hard winters. The spiritual tourists appreciate our isolation in Fascaray and the sublime emptiness of the landscape, failing to recognise that if it hadn't been for brutal absentee lairds, who found sheep, deer and grouse more profitable than human tenants, our clachans and glens would be peopled with thriving communities.

But the enlightened interlopers of Balnasaig intuit that they know us better than we know ourselves. They like our sense of tradition, up to a point. They oppose the ancient practice of guga hunting, disdain the local pub, have little interest in the local 'unenlightened' folk and would, if they could, shrink us to the status of harmless elves capering among the standing stones of Drumnish. Only last week, I returned from a morning's fishing to find a party of Seekers, dressed in exotic robes as if performing a Christmas pantomime, standing in a circle in my back field holding hands with their eyes closed. I went up to their leader, Neville Booth, a villainous Abanazar in his embroidered fez, and asked what they were doing. He released one hand from an earnest-looking Widow Twankey on his left, put his fingers to his lips – I was interrupting an important meeting – returned his hand to his partner and began to hum tonelessly.

I turned away, puzzled, and went to attend to the goat, whom I'd tethered in the next field. By the time I had fed Puck her scraps, the humming had stopped. Neville Booth hurried over to me to explain.

'Wonderful news!' he said. 'I was leading a party on a walk to the Calasay cliffs and I came across this! Your croft is a place of special enchantment!'

He indicated the area in the corner of the back field where he'd been conducting his ceremony.

'Look!' he said.

I looked.

'Don't you see it? The fairy ring!'

He pointed at a patch of flattened grass, a perfect circle, two and half feet in diameter.

I shook my head and led him to the next field where Puck was tethered to her post, around which was another perfect circle of flattened grass, trampled and cropped by the goat since I'd moved her from her previous patch in the back field that morning.

Neville Booth swiftly moved his party on in search of the next place of enchantment, leaving me to reflect on an old Scots saying – of the Balnasaig Seekers and their ilk, it can be truly said they are 'away with the faeries'.

Grigor McWatt, July 1970, *Auchwinnie Pibroch*[15]

15 Reprinted in *Frae Mambeag Brae: Selected Columns and Essays of Grigor McWatt*, Stravaigin Press, 1985.

Yink

Ma first an hinmaist handsel,
Ah yink this toosht o sangs,
The anely plack Ah hae,
Jist as they are, tae you.

Ah speak the suith, ungubbed,
Ah'd raither licht a gleed in yer bricht een,
Had raither hear ye ruise
Ma bosie fu o sangs
Than that the hale warld, in wan vyce,
In an ayebidin queir o cheers,
Skinks ower ma hummel haffet
Splairges o fleech fer aw ma years.

Ah pen this end agin ma hert,
Ma loue's bonailie an her tuim.
Here the road pairts an we maun gang
Oor separate weys till crack o doom.

Grigor McWatt, efter Robert Louis Stevenson, 1971[16]

16 From *Kowk in the Kaleyard*, Virr Press, 1975. Reprinted in *Warld in a Gless: The Collected Varse of Grigor McWatt*, Smeddum Beuks, 1992.

IN EDINBURGH, LILIAS'S EXTENDED SUMMER OF LOVE WAS GIVING way to an autumn of anxiety. With little comfort in her personal life, hard drink was an anaesthetic and a solace.

'Oh, Grigor,' she wrote in November 1971, 'it seems so long ago when you and I rampaged through the streets of Edinburgh, inflamed by love and poetry.'

She had fallen out badly with her boss at the betting shop.

'He sacked me for being drunk on the job. Drunk! Like him and all his customers. The real reason, of course, was I wasn't up for any of the old hochmagandy. Not with him, anyway.'

She could no longer afford the rent on her apartment and, humiliated, had gone back to live with her parents.

'They see my temporary retreat to Liberton as the return of the bloody prodigal daughter. They're bursting to declare, through their sanctimoniously pursed lips, "We told you so!"'

She was hurt to learn that Grigor had left the island to join the strikers at the Upper Clyde shipyard and hadn't troubled to make the extra hour's train journey to see her.

'Jimmy Reid's a handsome fellow. Nae doot. Charismatic too,' she wrote. 'But I can't believe that you would entirely forsake your Flooer for him? And now you're back in your island sanctuary, stomping the hills alone like a Fascaray Heathcliff.'

He may have repented of his distance from her and, the following spring, they were both part of a Menzies' Bar 'works outing' that travelled to Aberdeenshire for a reading and rally by MacDiarmid and McWatt. Willie McCracken, Sydney Goodsir Smith and Archie Aitken came too and they stayed at the Monymusk Inn. There is no information about the sleeping arrangements that night but whatever happened between McWatt and Hogg, she always looked back on the trip with pleasure as well as sadness. 'Do you remember Monymusk?' she wrote at the end of one anguished letter the following August, a month after her disastrous visit to Fascaray. 'A whole sea of bad blood, most of it mine, has welled up between us since then. Will you ever forgive my grievous carnaptiousness?'

His reply was elliptical, and in verse; a reimagining, later published in *Kowk in the Kaleyard* and reprinted in *Warld in a Gless*,[17] of Edward Thomas's more famous poem 'Adlestrop'.

> *Aye, Ah mind Monymusk.*
> *The name, acause wan efternuin*
> *O leep, the fest train poued upby,*
> *Unettled. It was ahint Juin.*
>
> *The steam fuffed. A fellae redd his thrapple.*
> *Naebdy left and naebdy came*
> *On the bare stance. Whit Ah saw*
> *Wis Monymusk — anely the name.*
>
> *An widdies, widdie-yerb, an reesk,*
> *Queen o the meidae, an hayrucks freuch,*
> *Nae whit less lown an lanely braw,*
> *Than the heich wee cloods i the sky.*
>
> *An for that glisk a merlie sang,*
> *Naurhaun, an roon him, haarier,*
> *Faurer an faurer, awra birds*
> *O Aiberdeen an Morayshire.*

> *A Granite Ballad – The Reimagining of Grigor McWatt,*
> Mhairi McPhail (Thackeray College Press, 2016)

17 Virr Press, 1975. Smeddum Beuks, 1992.

19 November 2014

Niall walks Agnes over to my office after school. They find me in a state of agitation — my laptop has frozen and I fear I've lost a day of work. I try to appear calm but I feel hysterical. Niall makes tea while Agnes deals with the problem — a frown and five keystrokes restore everything.

They go into the museum to tackle the last of the MacRaes' junk, leaving me to get on with my typing. The door is open and I tune in and out of the music of their conversation and laughter.

I'm envious of their easy relationship and wonder whether, surrounded by all this documentary evidence of blighted love, I've 'caught' Lilias's misery. Coupled with my pre-existing *Morbus Fascariensis*, the prognosis is not good.

I'm avoiding emails from friends — I've had two from Hobi and three from Pilar, all unanswered. Marco's emails have become more expansive, actually asking me how I am. I only answer his questions about Agnes.

I've tinkered with a telegraphic email template — 'Hi, all well here in the ancestral land, weather not withstanding. Work absorbing. Agnes content. Fuller email soon. How you?' — but even that sounds inauthentically cheerful.

A more truthful template might read: 'What the hell am I doing here?' It could, I realise, have come straight from the pen of Lilias Hogg.

EMBOLDENED, PERHAPS, BY THEIR TRIP TO MONYMUSK, LILIAS made a surprise visit to Fascaray in the late summer of 1972, arriving on the *Bonxie*. The new puffer was carrying a cargo of alabaster that had covered boat, crew and passenger with a coating of fine white dust.

Pat Boy Cairns and ship's mate Donnie MacDonald were both flushed through their frosty pallor as they handed a giggling, unsteady Lilias, white as a marble nymph, down the gangplank. She had paid for her passage with a bottle of whisky and it had been a merry voyage. Young Chic McIntosh gingerly set down her scuffed vinyl suitcase on the quay and tried to dart away, but she was too quick for him and gave him a theatrical kiss on the cheek, which he never lived down. She was a 'game lassie', he said later, 'but we were awful glad to see the back of her. She'd make trouble at a kirk purvey [church tea].' Until he could stand up for himself, McIntosh became known as Chic the Pòg. *Pòg*, of course, is Gaelic for kiss.

Lilias booked to stay in the Bothy that first night – it was too late to travel on to Calasay. She had a bath there, left her bags with Jamie and Marsaili MacDonald and went out to the Finnverinnity Inn. The next morning, the bunk she'd paid for had been barely slept in. She spent much of the night at the pub, where she must have hoped to run into Grigor. He never appeared but she didn't waste time in morose reflection. She was a roaring girl on a spree and matched the regulars drink for drink. Accompanied by Murdo McIntyre on fiddle, she sang ballads bawdy and sad into the small hours. A party of visiting folk-music fans, including a journalist writing up their journey for the *Scots Magazine*, thought the striking girl with the 'ready laugh and lovely voice' was a 'marvellously authentic Fascaradian, a daughter of those braw, bawdy fisher lassies who once travelled the coasts of the north in search of seasonal work'.

She hit it off with Mikey MacRae and the next morning when the tide was out he took her over to Calasay on his tractor. We have no record of the poet's reaction when he opened the door to find the Flooer o

345

Rose Street temporarily transplated to his native soil. Donald MacInnes, by then a restless, lanky 27-year-old with a pronounced limp, was out collecting wood at the time, and when he returned to An Tobar, he opened the door to 'a hostile silence' and found Grigor sitting opposite his surprise visitor 'with the look of a caged man, rattling at the bars'.

Lilias had been crying, Donald thought.

'I made them tea,' he recalled in 2014 in his interview with me. 'She smiled bravely at me, emptied the dregs of a half-bottle of whisky in her mug and knocked it back. Made small talk, about the journey, her impressions of the island, asked me questions about myself. And all the while Grigor was glaring. He couldn't wait to get her out the door.'

Under instruction from McWatt, Donald made up a bed for the visitor in the byre. She had planned to stay for two weeks. McWatt told her it was impossible but she insisted that she wouldn't get in his way. 'You owed me that much,' she wrote later, 'considering all the hospitality, corporeal and otherwise, I extended to you over the past dozen years.'

'It wasn't all bad,' said MacInnes. 'I got on fine with her. Took her out walking. Showed her the special places around. She was interested. She cooked a couple of times, things out of tins mostly, and managed to get the odd conversation and even a rare smile out of Grigor. But he didn't like the way she was getting on with me. To be honest he was jealous. They had a terrible falling-out towards the end of the second week – we all did – and he ordered her out of the house.'

Lilias's visit may have been a final attempt to reignite her romantic relationship with McWatt. If so, by the time she left Calasay her hopes were ashes. In the byre, under a stack of books, she had come across a letter to the poet written in an unfamiliar hand on peach notepaper.

'A billet-doux from your fancy's flight,' Lilias wrote to him from Edinburgh, still fuming, three days after she finally left Fascaray. 'Your own bonnie bloody Jean.'

According to Lilias's account, he had snatched the letter from her hand before she had time to read anything other than the signature – 'Yours, Jean' – and he refused to be drawn on its contents or its author.

'You simply wouldn't talk about her. I take that as final confirmation that I can never truly claim your heart. Never could. Well, you took your time to tell me. Dragged it out and dragged me down.'

After McWatt banished her from An Tobar, she stayed on the island for another three days. She was said to have spent one night in Murdo McIntyre's disordered hovel in Doonmara and passed the remainder of her time in the Finnverinnity Inn, until Mikey MacRae gently escorted her onto the *Bonxie* back to the mainland.

'She was a cracking lassie,' MacRae told Knox-Cardew over the phone from Pictou, Nova Scotia – one of the few first-hand interviews conducted by the biographer. She outdrank several of the fishermen, including MacRae, who, aged nineteen in 1972, was twelve years younger than Lilias. He told Knox-Cardew that he had to restrain her from loudly singing 'Hame tae Fascaray' outside the pub at 3 a.m. on the Sabbath and 'knocking on the manse window in the scuddie' (which Knox-Cardew helpfully defines as 'unclothed').

In a letter to McWatt from Edinburgh, dated a week after her visit, Lilias wrote: 'Now, as the foreign tourist in Edinburgh might say, I am understanding. The haar has cleared. You are as loyal to Your Jean as Burns was wedded to his Jean Armour. Why settle for prosaic Lilias when you could have poetic Jean? If only, though, you could have *told* me.'

The sole reference we have from McWatt to Lilias's unexpected visit is a perfunctory postcard – a picture of Burns's cottage in Alloway – that accompanied a parcel sent to her in Edinburgh a month later.

'Here are your pawkies [mittens] and gravat [scarf] which you left behind,' he wrote on the back of the card. 'I'm sure they'll be of more use to you in Edinburgh. Work on the *Compendium* progresses. Tremendous storms here over the last few days. Sea black and boiling. You're well out of it. Aye, Grigor.'

A Granite Ballad – The Reimagining of Grigor McWatt,
Mhairi McPhail (Thackeray College Press, 2016)

Niall offers to accompany me to Calasay to search the library for more material. We take the quadbike and I ride pillion. In our down jackets, beanies and walking boots we make comic bikers – Auchwinnie's Angels – as we rumble across the strand. I call in at An Tobar to pick up the four volumes of *Jamieson's Dictionary*, put them in a waterproof box which Niall straps to the back of the quad bike, then we cross the yard to the byre.

It's two months since I've been here but Johanna has been checking the building weekly and it still seems watertight. A beam of light slants through the west window and for the first time I appreciate what a pleasing space this is. All these books, all this quiet order. I could move in here right now and shut out the noisy chaos of the world for good.

Under the west window is history – 900, according to Dewey – with Toms Devine and Nairn heavily represented, as well as Fraser Darling, Smout, Mackie and a four-volume set of *The Edinburgh History* series. Opposite them is the *Carmina Gadelica*, the six-volume facsimile; my tidy mind – rigid, uptight, according to Marco when he was still enthralled by Karmic Kate – takes pleasure in the fact that the series has been correctly labelled, 398, under folklore.

Niall has climbed one of the ladders and is standing on a platform, three loosely jointed planks, above biography (921) where I find Alan Bold on Hugh MacDiarmid, Antonia Fraser's life of Mary Queen of Scots, studies of William Wallace, Robert the Bruce, James Hogg, Mackay Brown, Robert Burns and several editions, hardback and paperback, of McWatt's own two volumes of memoir, *Forby* and *Ootwith*.

Next to the anthologies of English verse and selections of Keats, Wordsworth, Shelley and Clare, and taking twice the shelf space, are collections of verse by MacDiarmid, Mackay Brown, Goodsir Smith, Norman MacCaig and Sorley Maclean as well as scores of copies of McWatt's own collections. Here his personal filing system departs from Dewey. In libraries they would be numbered, like the *Palgrave's*, the

Quiller-Couch and Keats and co., under 821 – 'English and Old English literatures'. Here McWatt classifies Scots poetry under 890 – 'other literature.'

Shuggie the Post was right. He took better care of these books than he did of himself in his frugal home next door. Better care than he took of his friends too. I think of Lilias nursing her thwarted love in her squalid basement in Edinburgh. Inevitably, she quarrelled with her parents when she returned from her calamitous trip to Fascaray. She signed on at the Labour Exchange and moved into two rooms owned by Archie Aitken in a condemned tenement building in Bedford Street.

How Lilias would have loved to have been permanently filed here in this beautiful place by her 'Fascaray Heathcliff'. On the shelf, but in the best possible way. Cherished and classified: 152 (psychology, perception, emotions) perhaps, or better still 808.80 (erotic literature). And always with the consoling prospect that some evening he might choose her from all the others, bring her out, run his finger down her spine, and sit quietly alone with her for a few hours. She didn't ask much. 'And she got nothing,' I hear her sister's reproach.

I step back, taking in the scale of the library. I can't decide whether it represents the collection of a scholarly completist or the hoard of an acquisitive monomaniac with pretensions. Either way, the Grigor McWatt library is worth preserving, and he knew it. But I need more than books to furnish the museum in Finnverinnity and flesh out the narrative of his life.

The only furniture in the room is a single cane-seated chair, a rosewood desk – its drawers are empty – and a swan-necked brass reading light. No obvious place for hiding treasures.

'Ah!' Niall calls from his perch above me. 'Might this be of use?'

He reaches precariously above the top shelf and prises from the space between bookcase and rafter a brown attaché case that, a billowing cloud of dust suggests, has been crammed in there for some time. Coughing, he descends the ladder gingerly and hands me his find.

It's locked, of course. And the chances of locating the key must be zero.

Niall produces a penknife.

'A little light breaking and entering, in the interests of poetry?' he says. 'Or maybe, in the interests of Fascaray?'

'Okay, but try to minimise the damage.'

With a deft twist of the blade he opens the case.

I'm about to ask him jokily if he'd ever tried his hand at burglary when I'm stopped in my tracks.

Inside, tied in two neat bundles, are dozens of papers and documents secured by rubber bands. My eye is drawn to a handwritten note on the top of the smaller pile. The paper is peach-coloured and the signature, plain and childishly round, reads 'Yours, Jean'.

Aw naitur haes a feelin

Aw naitur haes a feelin; firth, hauch an ben
Are vieve ayebidin: an in seelence they
Speak cantieness ootwith the sillereds' ken;
There's nae thing mortial in them; their mozin
Is the grein vieve o chynge; bygae awa
An come agane in bluims floorishin.
Its howdiein, afore oor day, was auncient,
Its stay ayebidin, wi sun and muin,
Lang past oor nicht that comes tae suin,
Aneath the michty unforgien skies abuin.

Grigor McWatt, efter John Clare, 1972[18]

---

18 From *Kowk in the Kaleyard*, Virr Press, 1975. Reprinted in *Warld in a Gless: The Collected Varse of Grigor McWatt*, Smeddum Beuks, 1992.

THERE WAS A DEGREE OF RECONCILIATION BETWEEN HOGG AND McWatt. He returned to Edinburgh twice in the winter of 1972 to meet up with the poets and, the letters indicate, with Lilias in Menzies'. But he stayed with Archie Aitken and his wife in Gilmore Place or in a cheap bed and breakfast close to Waverley Station. Lilias had found temporary work in August handing out leaflets for the Edinburgh Festival's fringe shows but she was 'back on the booze', as she admitted, and essentially unemployable. She was now living in a room in a Leith hostel, where her domestic set-up had become too chaotic for the increasingly fastidious McWatt.

'Lilias, Lilias,' he scolds in one letter dated 18 December 1972, 'at the risk of sounding bourgeois, I was alarmed to see you in that state. Even the lowest beast does not foul his own nest. I do not expect to find the Flooer o Rose Street blooming on a midden.'

Increasingly, an unattractive note of bitterness enters Lilias's letters – 'and how is Bonnie Jean? Is it, after all, *her* stieveness [firmness] that maks your circle suith? Is it Jean who makes you "feenish whaur ye stairt"? Daft thing is, I thought it was all about me!' she wrote in January 1973. 'Tell me, does she ever come across with the goods or is she too perjink [fussy] for all that farmyard stuff? Well, if she won't, you can tell her that others will. Though maybe you think me too old for all that now.' Lilias was thirty-two.

We can only guess at his response. By the time he received this last letter, he, and the rest of Fascaray, would have had bigger tragedies than mere heartbreak to address.

On Tuesday 13 March 1973, in a force-ten south-easterly gale, the Auchwinnie lifeboat was called out to assist a Panama-registered 1,800-ton cargo ship, the *Lara*, which was in severe difficulties west of the Mhor Sgheir reef. The *Lara*'s Greek captain had radioed for help and fired distress flares that were seen all the way up to the northern isles. Lifeboat coxswain Mungo MacAskill launched the *Morag May* from Auchwinnie with five crew. On their way to the stricken vessel they picked up two further hands, Fascaradians Jamie MacDonald, Mungo's son-in-law, and Jamie's brother Francie, two of the most experienced lifeboat volunteers in the region.

But as the *Morag May* made her way towards Mhor Sgheir, a rescue was already underway. The *Lara* had foundered just offshore by Doonmara Cliffs and Tormud Campbell's *Silver Darling*, aided by a flotilla of smaller fishing vessels, was able to help the crew of sixteen, mostly Filipinos and Portuguese, across the rocks to safety. Two months later Tormud was to receive an award for his courage from the owners of the *Lara*, but by then there was little appetite for honours or awards of any sort.

As the storm worsened that night, the *Morag May*, intent on its mission, buffeted by hundred-mile-an-hour winds and tossed by sixty-foot waves, lost radio contact. By 9.30 p.m., as the crew of the *Lara* and their rescuers were recovering from their ordeal, drinking tea and huddling under donated blankets in Finnverinnity Hall, the lifeboat was last sighted by Duncan Maclean, keeper of the Fascaray Head lighthouse.

During the long night that followed, coastguards desperately tried to make radio contact with the *Morag May* but she remained silent. Three bigger lifeboats, from the west coast and the northern isles, joined the search backed by two RAF planes and a helicopter. It wasn't until noon the following day that the *Morag May* was seen floating, hull upturned, out beyond the Carracorry whirlpool. All hands were lost.

Six women were widowed and thirteen children were left fatherless by the *Morag May* disaster. Jamie MacDonald's widow Marsaili, eight months pregnant with their third child, also lost her father, Mungo MacAskill. Francie MacDonald's widow Jessie, mother of three, also lost her brother, lifeboat bosun John Donald Mackenzie, father of seventeen-year-old Margaret, who worked in Finnverinnity post office.

Mourners of all denominations attended the MacDonalds' requiem Mass at the Church of the Sacred Heart and Immaculate Mary in Lusnaharra, where seventeen years earlier, in the face of snowstorms and defying sectarian hostility, Francie and Jessie had received a marriage blessing from Father Col. Among the congregation at the funeral was Albert Smart, captain of the *Fleet Flourish*, the Grimsby trawler that, three years earlier, had been saved by the *Morag May*. Smart, in conjunction with the Seamen's Union, launched a nationwide disaster fund to help the bereaved families of Auchwinnie and Fascaray. Tormud Campbell donated the £500 he received for his part in the rescue of the *Lara*.

A black border was printed around the front page of that week's *Auchwinnie Pibroch*, which carried an interview with Marsaili MacDonald. The new editor of the paper, a Skye man with a strong feeling for the fishing community, conducted the interview himself. Marsaili told him that there was great sadness but no bitterness among the bereaved families. 'We know those happy days of our family life are over but we can't regret that our men died trying to help others and that the crew of the *Lara* were saved.'

In McWatt's column for the *Pibroch* that week he honoured the widows as well as their husbands for 'selfless stoicism in the face of such personal catastrophe'.

Three weeks later, on 2 April, Marsaili gave birth to her third child, a boy. She named him James Francis MacDonald.

A Granite Ballad – The Reimagining of Grigor McWatt,
Mhairi McPhail (Thackeray College Press, 2016)

Fur the Fawen

They ganged wi sangs tae their baits, they were braw,
Sonsie, stalwart an strang, wi youthie lowe ableize.
They were stieve frae end tae wynd an braved the maw,
But fell in wild rumballiach seas.

They'll niver lauch wi pals agane,
Nor see kenspeckelt sichts o hame;
In daily darg they shallna jyne us;
They dover forby Scotland's faem.

They shallnae dwyne as we that bide shall dwyne:
Age shallnae forfecht them, nor the lang years duim.
At the gangin doon o the sun an in the mornin
We wull aye mind them.

Where oor whumleeries an deepest thochts,
Rin like a dern burn datchie frae sicht,
Tae the howie hert o their ain laun they are kennt,
As the starns are kennt tae the Nicht;
As the starns that wull be bricht when we disemberk,
Ootower the braid skies they glaister an glide,
As the starns that flichter in the days o oor mirk,
Tae the end, tae the end, they bide.

Grigor McWatt, efter Laurence Binyon, 1973[19]

---

19 From *Kowk in the Kaleyard*, Virr Press, 1975. Reprinted in *Warld in a Gless: The Collected Varse of Grigor McWatt*, Smeddum Beuks, 1992.

Agnes is asleep upstairs as I sit at the kitchen table at 2 a.m. sifting through the latest documents retrieved from Calasay. I've sorted them into two bundles now, one of them archivist's gold (or this archivist's gold): letters from the elusive Jean.

There is the faintest tremor in my hands as I finally unfold the paper carefully. Though the salutation cannot compare to Lilias's Griogal Cridhe, 'Dear G' strikes a hopefully familiar note. Excitement – professional pride tinged with a cheap jolt of voyeurism – turns to dismay. That they are all undated and the address is simply given as Abbotsford Drive is disappointing enough – the Walter Scott echo a coincidence McWatt surely wouldn't relish – but it's the content of these letters, written in royal-blue ink on lined peach A5, that truly vexes: the prose is uniformly pedestrian.

Reports on the weather – 'mild for the time of year', 'raining stair rods', 'a glimpse of sun at last'; developments in the garden – 'the first snowdrops', 'putting the bedding plants in', 'lobelias and narsissi [*sic*] in my hanging baskets'; and what seem to be veiled requests for money – 'the conservatory extension is costing more than we planned. It seems we must hope for a pools win to complete the building work. How are you fixed at the moment?'; 'We had so hoped to take a little foreign holiday this year after my mishap with my leg. Majorca looks particularly appealing but things are tight and we cannot run to it ourselves. Heard your song again on Radio 2. You must be raking it in.'

This is not the stuff of high romance. Or any romance at all. I can't possibly include these letters in the exhibition. That McWatt favoured dull Jean over wild, witty Lilias hardly suggests sound poetic judgement. Jean must have had something, I guess. She could have been a remarkable beauty but that alone, so we're always told, would hardly be enough to sustain a long-term passion. She might have been a powerhouse in the sack, but there's little evidence of sensuality here. Perhaps McWatt was simply seeking an antidote – Jean's stability against Lilias's volatility. The headlong stampede to self-destruction, exhilarating to watch until the chasm yawns, rarely coexists with a fondness for hanging baskets.

I'm unreasonably annoyed with Niall for finding these letters. Far better if they'd remained where they were, if Bonnie Jean had remained a cipher, the enigmatic Dark Lady of McWatt's sonnets. Exposed, her trite correspondence will undermine our story. Of course I'll do my duty and catalogue them; to do otherwise would be a grossly unprofessional act of deception, to which Niall would be a witness. Again, I feel a prick of irritation. Why hadn't he kept out of it? The letters will have to be made available to any PhD students or future biographers. But unless I can turn up McWatt's replies to Jean's mind-numbingly mundane letters, at least placing them in context, I'll make sure this half of the correspondence is consigned to storage. And I won't be quoting them in *A Granite Ballad*.

I turn with relief to another of yesterday's finds. Two acrostic poems by McWatt and Hogg; his, with excisions and emendations, is clearly a draft.

> *Love breenged*
> *In. Ah gawked,*
> *Like aw the rest,*
> *In this moment*
> *At this oor,*
> *Saw naebdy but*
> *Her. She o the russet hair*
> *O the faithomless een,*
> *Guidness in a gowen fair*
> *Gladdened ma hert ayont repair.*

I hope he sent Lilias the finished poem. It would have made her happy. Hers to him – both poems are undated but I'm guessing hers was written after the ill-fated visit to Fascaray – might have been a direct reply.

> *Give me.*
> *Render me.*
> *I'm yours for the taking,*

357

Gleeful and quaking.
Or would you forsake me?
Redact me. No faking.
Make me.
Collate me.
When do we start?
All right – here's my heart.
Take it. Don't break it.
Too late – it's apart.

Perhaps I should draw up a proposal for a Lilias Hogg Heritage Centre. We might pull in the contemporary art crowd with a faithful recreation of squalor and squandered dreams, with added poetry, in a dim and airless basement flat.

INVENTORY OF SCOTS WORDS AND PHRASES
DESCRIBING GLOOM AND DESPAIR

dour
douth
dowie
dreich
dule
glunch
gowstie
gurrie
hasnae sorraes tae seek
hert-sair
hert-scaud
if it's no clegs, it's midgies
if it's no scab, it's skitter
manefu
mirk
misfeuchal
misfure
misglim
mougre
sair-aff
stoom
syte
wae
wanhowp

Grigor McWatt, 1973, *The Fascaray Compendium*

Grigor McWatt's birthday. He would have been ninety-three. The Scottish government has chosen today to announce plans to memorialise him on the Parliament building's Canongate Wall. Tipped off by Ailish – 'Yes,' I fudged, 'of course I know. I'm on my way' – I go to the post office to buy all the newspapers for the office. McWatt's grim face, briar pipe jammed in bristly undershot jaw, is pictured on the front page of the *National*, the new pro-independence newspaper. All the Scottish press feature the story inside, with the quote that will be engraved on the wall in a slab of Fascaray granite – 'Wha loues the laun, awns the laun, an the laun awns him' – alongside lines by MacDiarmid (on Lewisian gneiss), Norman MacCaig (Bressay sandstone), Robert Burns (Ardkinglas) and John Muir (Ross of Mull granite).

The press reports include several mentions of the Grigor McWatt Heritage Centre and Fascaray Museum – which will please Gordon Nesbitt and the board – and the *National*, in a 'souvenir double-page spread', runs two poems in full, 'The Pirlin Scottish Road' and 'The Paith No Taein', and retells the story of Lilias Hogg, 'the love that never died'.

Also rehashed in all the Scottish papers is the referendum debate. The birthday of the dead nationalist poet has given them an opportunity to air the arguments all over again. Come on, I want to say, it's over! Let it go! Move on!

I wish I could move on myself with this project but I feel truly stuck. Bonnie Jean continues to elude us, despite Ailish's efforts. I press on through Lilias's love letters – arranged chronologically they describe a perfect arc from hopeful youth to embittered age, prefigured by the sour quatrain, written in Scots, that she sent McWatt in May 1973.

> *Frae goddess tae gargoyle in three easy stages:*
> *One: faw for a fella who aye disengages.*
> *Twa: faw for the joy-juice, which ayeweys says yes.*
> *Three: count on Bitch Time tae accomplish the rest.*

A year later she wrote to him again, a single sentence in large red letters, underlined on a sheet of old aerogram paper: 'You fake. You ruined my life.' No address. No salutation. Ugly.

I feel a shameful pulse of recognition; some of my later emails to Marco and to Pascal weren't exactly pretty. No matter how justified, no matter what outrageous treachery has been perpetrated, bitterness always poisons the betrayed rather than the betrayer.

Grievously wounded by Marco's affair – though he was still living in the apartment, sharing parenting, we had never been more distant – and bent on a mad pursuit of revenge, I was determined to make things work with Pascal. At first I tiptoed round the feelings of my delicate lover. He may have been sick, there was no denying it, and he had a hacking cough to show for it. He was post-virally exhausted and his only response to my most selfless attempts to arouse him was mild exasperation.

After another night of sexless affection, I began to wonder again whether Pascal was gay. Finally, rebuffed once more, I asked him. He reacted with a vehemence that didn't reassure me and which nearly undid us altogether. What was the point of a sexless affair? I asked. If I'd wanted to do without sex altogether I could have stuck with Marco. As soon as I'd spoken I felt guilty. What could be more unmanning than to challenge a lover on his performance, or non-performance? He was vulnerable and hurt, and had an artist's susceptibility to depression. *Morbus Williamsburgensis*, perhaps.

He told me he'd been going through something I couldn't understand. Try me, I said. So he tried me. There had been problems with the promised recording deal. Money was tight. The manager of their club residency hadn't paid up in a month. The band was falling apart. He didn't know how he was going to pay his rent. He wept. So I got out my credit card, comforted him, mothered him, while three miles away, across the bridge in the next borough, my real child sat waiting for me, patiently colouring in until I could find the time to come home with my unmet needs and my resentments.

It wasn't until it all fell apart, with Pascal, then with Marco again, that I realised the basest treachery was mine. My hunger for sexual love, for intimacy, had caused me to sideline my love for my daughter. Maybe – suggested one therapist I was once talked into seeing briefly – my own

361

mother hadn't provided such a great blueprint for maternal affection. For this insight I paid $220.

I've always believed, unfashionably, that there's a statute of limitations on blaming your parents and it kicks in at about the age of twenty-one. Agnes still has a few years to run. Bringing her here was partly an attempt to make amends: to have another go at motherhood, resit the exam and maybe scrape a pass this time. Life on a small island in the far north, with no distractions and few comforts, seemed the perfect clinical condition for the experiment. But, as I let my problems with my work overwhelm me, I fear I'm in danger of failing Agnes yet again.

THE FIRST SERIOUS CONCERNS ABOUT LILIAS'S HEALTH BEGAN TO sound in June 1973. She had always been a heavy smoker and suffered regular bouts of bronchitis, but early that month she was diagnosed with pneumonia and pleurisy. Against her doctor's advice she continued to drink while taking prescribed medication. On 15 June she was found unconscious in Thistle Street and admitted to the Royal Infirmary. In a self-mocking note to McWatt written from her hospital bed, she said, 'I had followed the unsmiling Dr Smilie's orders to a T. No drinking. Thus no tea, coffee, water, milk, Irn-Bru, Cremola Foam or any other liquid passed my lips while I was on the wee blue pills. But surely, I thought, to avoid total dehydration, I was allowed a wee drop of whisky?'

McWatt wrote to Willie McCracken, now teetotal and running a small poetry magazine in Leith, asking him to 'look out for our fragile Flooer. Her appetites could be her undoing. She is an unhappy lassie who is looking for some kind of salvation and I fear I cannot provide it.'

McWatt continued to visit Edinburgh but avoided her. It was fortunate for him, and perhaps for her, that she had been barred from Menzies' after another of what she called 'my nights of shame'.

Edinburgh was changing; the old printing and manufacturing industries were failing while the festival and attendant tourism were beginning to rival banking and insurance as the city's chief source of income. With the annual northern transhumance of bohemian southerners the grey, close-mouthed city metamorphosed each summer into a month-long Mardi Gras of music and make-believe. Even outside the festival, the old poets had been unseated from their strongholds, 'replaced', wrote Lilias, 'by long-haired students, lads and lassies dressed like medieval mummers, playing their cat-screech jukebox music and talking not of poetry or national identity but of Vietnam, South Africa, Greece, Thailand. Any damned far-flung place but here, right under their noses. It's all fashion, not passion, for them.'

A Granite Ballad – The Reimagining of Grigor McWatt,
Mhairi McPhail (Thackeray College Press, 2016)

Ah'm!

Ah'm — yet whit Ah'm nane gies a damn or kens;
Ma pals forhou me like a mindin tyne:
Ah'm the sel-devoorer o ma dules —
They heeze an mizzle in unkennin thrang,
Like shadaes in loues doistert stychelt thraws
An yet, Ah'm, an leiv — like fungit haar

Intae the naethiness o geck an squall
Whaur there is nawtherane sinse o leif or joyes,
But the muckle schipwrak o ma leif's emprise;
E'en the dawtiest whase loue Ah crave
Are antrin — an mair antrin than the lave.

Ah lang tae be whaur loons hae niver trod.
Whaur sneuterin quines hae nivver dabbed their eyes,
Wi Naitur tae the cantie end Ah'll dod.
An like a dirrin bairnie doucely nod,
Unfashin naebdy an unfasht whaur Ah lie
Ablo the gress, abuin the vowtit sky.

Grigor McWatt, efter John Clare, 1973[20]

---

20 From *Kowk in the Kaleyard*, Virr Press, 1975. Reprinted in *Warld in a Gless: The Collected Varse of Grigor McWatt*, Smeddum Beuks, 1992.

Just over a month to go before the museum opens on 31 December and Johanna breaks the news that she has to leave the island. Ailsa's father, an offshore oil worker based in Aberdeen, has been injured in a rig accident.

'I'm so sorry to let you down,' Johanna says. 'But Ailsa needs to see her daddy.'

I reassure her, dishonestly, that I'll be fine.

'Just go,' I say.

I call Gordon Nesbitt, asking for help. As I feared, he cites financial constraints.

'I'm afraid you'll have to go it alone, Mhairi. Don't worry. I'm certain you can do it.'

I envy his certainty.

Niall says he would help out but he is leaving tomorrow for a long-planned trip with his boyfriend; a supply teacher from the mainland is booked to cover at the school for the week.

'I can't undo the arrangements now. It's a family obligation, took months to clear with the school board. I'd let too many people down if I cancelled,' he says.

Now I'm really alone.

'Don't worry. I'll be okay . . .' I say, lying for the second time that day. 'Where are you going anyway?'

'New York.'

New York! My home! Familiar setting of my triumphs and tragedies; Agnes's birth, friendships, purposeful work, love, and the death of love. I'm felled by an irrational sense of injustice, that he should be going there and I should be stranded here.

'Take me with you,' I say, mocking my real desperation.

He laughs.

'We'll be back on Sunday week. You can hold on till then. We'll both do whatever we can. I really want you to meet him, anyway.'

I go home to an empty house. Tonight, Agnes is having a sleepover at the McAllisters' before Ailsa and Johanna catch the morning ferry to the mainland. Will both girls talk of their fathers, I wonder? What secrets do they share? I hope they don't talk of their mothers. In any maternity duel, Johanna would win hands down.

I've done a bit of nurturing, sure, but not always to Agnes's advantage. I mothered Marco after a fashion, until we both tired of the arrangement, and I mothered Pascal when he was going through his crisis; I might as well have been Pascal's mother for all the sexual gratification I was getting. When he told me about his money worries, I paid his rent that month (and the next) and also gave him money to buy food, see off his creditors and get round town. He accepted my offer with extravagant gratitude, told me he adored me, couldn't do without me, without my life force and my energy and our ancient spiritual connection, and in the early hours of the morning, as dawn broke over the Manhattan skyline, in the cavernous gloom of his apartment, we made love for the first time in weeks. There wasn't the same savage desire or disabling release but it was tender and honest, or so I thought. Blinded by need, I knew as much as Lilias Hogg about honesty.

She finally found the truth about her lover in a letter; I found it, five weeks after I'd bailed him out, in a gum wrapper. I'd come round to tell him, in the nicest possible way, that our relationship was over. I spared him the announcement that Marco and I were back together, instead wheeling out the usual kindly lies – I need space; it's not you, it's me; I'm just not ready. He took the news annoyingly well. Then I went to the bathroom and found the charred gum wrapper resting by the sink. Next to it was the empty casing of a ballpoint pen. Of course. It made sense straight away. Heroin. He'd been smoking it; chasing the dragon. Pascal, my so-called lover, ex-lover, was a junkie. And cool, experienced older woman that I was, I'd never even noticed. Now I understood the crashed libido, the hacking cough, the poor health, the lethargy (he was high, not depressed), the crankiness (he was waiting to get high). Now I understood the money. I'd been subsidising his addiction.

It was 'only a small habit', Pascal told me.

'No more than a bag a day. No big deal,' he said.

Neither was the money I'd lent him to finance this insignificant peccadillo, he insisted, suggesting that there was something vulgar in my line of questioning.

'Look, if it's money you're worrying about,' he said, 'my folks will give me a cash advance. I don't like asking them – they're so anal about money – so I thought it would be easier to borrow from you. A friend. At least I thought you were a friend.'

Now, incredibly, he was sulking.

'Did you use needles?' I asked coldly.

'Oh, so you want all the gory details, huh?'

'I'm asking again – did you use needles?'

He turned away before conceding an answer, defiant as a bratty teen.

'I had a little spike now and again. So what?'

'So what? I'll tell you so what – how about HIV, for starters? Or hepatitis?'

He was indignant.

'I'm not some street junkie. It wasn't that often. I used clean equipment. From trusted friends.'

'Trusted friends. Like me you mean? Friends you lie to? Steal from? Those kind of friends?'

He was kidding himself, with his little habit, his trusted friends. But how had he concealed the track marks on his arms?

Then I realised. I hadn't seen him fully naked, in daylight, for two months. He may have been kidding himself, but in my rush for revenge and eagerness for intimacy, I had cast this empty, pretty boy in a role he could never play. I was the real sucker.

Eariwigged oan a Gullion

Sidhe, sidhe, whit are yer purls?
Haw gless, kelpie. Why dae ye gowk at them?
Gie thaim me.
Naw.
Gie thaim me. Gie thaim me.
Naw.
Then Ah wull yowt aw nicht in the coolks,
crooch in the crochan an yowt fur them.
Kelpie, why dae ye loue them sae?
They are better than starns or wattir,
Better than mirkest nicht's brichtest gleed,
Better than any loon's bonnie dauchter
Yer haw gless purls oan a siller threid.
Wheesht. Ah sniggt them oot the muin.
Gie me yer purls, Ah wint them.
Naw.
Ah wull yowt in the jubest hoob
Fur yer haw gless purls, Ah loue them sae.
Gie thaim me. Gie thaim.
Naw.

Grigor McWatt, efter Harold Monro, 1974[21]

21 From *Kowk in the Kaleyard*, Virr Press, 1975. Reprinted in *Warld in a Gless: The Collected Varse of Grigor McWatt*, Smeddum Beuks, 1992.

THE ISLAND'S FISHERMEN WERE, BY THE MID 1970S, BECOMING 'as obsolete as the old farm horses', wrote McWatt in *The Fascaray Compendium*. He also compared them to the 'purefinders who, in the nineteenth century, scoured the banks of city waterways for dog excrement, which they sold to the leather-tanning industry. Mechanisation saw off the horses – the infernal noise of Tam Macpherson's first tractor engine at Balnasaig was their death knell – just as changes in the tanning process, and the first stirrings of the hygiene movement, put the purefinders out of business. It is the urge to modernise, backed by government grants, that has done for Fascaray's fishermen.'

Loans were given to upgrade the UK's fishing fleet and, inevitably, as McWatt wrote ruefully, 'micht was richt'. Only the big companies benefitted and gradually the steam-driven wooden trawlers were replaced by hulking steel vessels with sophisticated electronics systems. Ships owned and crewed by Englishmen and foreigners began to loiter brazenly in the bay. What chance had Fascaray's little boats, minnows guided by native guile and serendipity, against these gargantuan whales with echosounders capable of pinpointing the slightest movement of a distant shoal of fish?

The three-mile limit was forgotten, quotas were brought in and local marine traditions gradually eroded. Soon, with a new fisheries policy imposed by Britain's recent entry to the European Common Market, the old way of life, governed by tides and seasons, by an instinctive respect for the capricious power of the sea, would vanish. Young men had to go to the mainland to join the big lads on the big ships or find some other means of earning money. Too often, defeated, they turned to the 'broo' – social security – and took their consolations at Finnverinnity Inn where, in bitterest of ironies, the day trippers and weekenders from the mainland and the south would sit in their fishermen's sweaters singing sea shanties.

Meanwhile, in Edinburgh, Lilias's bright pluck was draining away.

'I'm sick, Grigor. And afraid,' she wrote in June 1975. 'The swallae has done for me. *Uisge beatha*, the water of life, could turn out to be my water of death.'

A Granite Ballad – The Reimagining of Grigor McWatt,
Mhairi McPhail (Thackeray College Press, 2016)

Whan Ye're Auld

Whan ye're an auld grey bauchle doverin ower,
An noddin by the gleed, tak doon this beuk,
An huilie read, an dwaum o the saft luik
Your een had wanst, an o their sheddas deep;

Hou mony loued yer glisks, ye gledsome doll,
An loued yer brawness wi loue fause or leal;
But wan man loued yer douce stravaigin saul
An loued your coupon, flochtersome or dule.

An bouin doon forby the glowin gleed,
Souch, a wee bit oorie, hou loue fled
An spanged onwart the braes abuin,
An dernt his gizz amang a thrang o starns.

Grigor McWatt, efter W. B. Yeats, 1975[22]

---

22 From *Wappenshaw*, Virr Press, 1986. Reprinted in *Warld in a Gless: The Collected Varse of Grigor McWatt*, Smeddum Beuks, 1992.

As Lilias waned, Grigor waxed. His public profile was growing, largely due to his song, which had recently been recorded in a shouted, satirical version by the Sensational Alex Harvey Band, whose lead guitarist wore full-face white make-up – 'Like that French fool Marcel Marceau,' wrote a contemptuous McWatt. But there were no financial penalties for satire and the record appeared in the singles Top 50 charts, bringing in more cash to Calasay and generating a new interest in McWatt's writing.

In the evening, after a day of physical labour at the museum, I put the Alex Harvey track on in the kitchen while I make dinner. Agnes gets up from her chair, throwing out her arms, and pirouettes manically around the table, laughing and shouting along with the chorus.

'Hey,' she says, breathless when it's over, 'I kind of like that. Maybe the song's growing on me?'

She goes to Skype her father in the sitting room while, in the kitchen, I put on Alex Harvey again – his 1973 album, *Framed* – at full volume and clear away the dishes. Marco might hear the background blare and wonder what the hell is going on. 'Giddy Up a Ding Dong'. Improbably, many years ago, in another universe, Dolores Gallagher and Dougal McPhail might have had their first dance to this crazy music at Green's Playhouse in Glasgow. It's an unsettling thought.

'Mom!' Agnes opens the kitchen door and shouts to be heard over the music. 'Papa wants to talk to you.'

'Tell him I'm working. He can email me.'

Am I imagining it, or does Agnes slam the door with unnecessary force?

After she finishes her call and goes up to bed, I return to silence, the sobering letters and the *Compendium*.

In 1974 McWatt made several trips to Edinburgh to give readings and meet publishers but he had moved on from sofa beds in fellow poets' flats and austere bed and breakfasts. He would stay in a two-star hotel with a licensed bar off the Royal Mile, and visit the Rose Street pubs where Maclean, MacCaig, Mackay Brown, Crichton Smith and Morgan could still be sighted, usually, these days, singly or in pairs. The poets, whose raucous repartee once commanded the bar, now had to fight their way through thronging students and festivalgoers to get served and, wrote McWatt in the *Compendium*, 'we had to yell till we were hoarse to make ourselves heard over the racket of the jukebox'. Lilias, 'the fiery comet', according to McWatt, 'had crashed to earth' and was no longer welcome in the old haunts.

Inevitably, she came to hear of these visits after he'd left and in several letters expressed her hurt and anger at the snub. She wrote, as a post-script to a congratulatory note sent to him after he'd won the 1975 Kerr-MacDonald Award for Poetry in Edinburgh (prize: £80 and publi-cation of a single poem in the *Scotsman*): 'I wouldn't expect you to ask an old boiler like me to put on my sad glad rags and be your date for the evening. You must have younger, more pleasing fish – a whole shoal of silver darlings – to fry these days. And then there is the sainted bloody Jean. But I can't deny I was pained to learn that after your stuffed-shirt celebratory dinner you slunk away back to your island holt without paying a call on your Former Muse, who would have raised an unre-proachful glass to your genius.'

That note of bitterness again.

It's after midnight. I stretch out on the couch, put in my earbuds and select one more Alex Harvey track. An insinuating song, in the style of Kurt Weill, about another Isobel, Goudie not Grant; not a twentieth-century Scottish museum curator – history's blameless handmaiden, whose story brought me here in the first place – but a seventeenth-century Scottish witch, according to her confession exacted under torture. Another wronged woman, looking for love in the wrong place. It didn't end well for Isobel Goudie either.

THE OIL INDUSTRY'S INTEREST IN FASCARAY SUDDENLY CEASED in 1975, when it was finally established that the water around the island wasn't deep enough to accommodate a pipeline.

'No more hovering helicopters making an infernal racket over our heads, no more sharp suits in cowboy boots demanding custom in the inn,' exulted McWatt in the *Pibroch*. 'Our geology, which threatened to be our undoing, has saved us.'

Attention had switched to the mainland coast off Auchwinnie, where a 200-acre parcel of farmland had been allocated for a terminal to house four vast storage tanks, each the size of an ocean liner and capable of holding 500,000 barrels of oil. The march of modernity seemed unstoppable but for now it had taken a detour round Fascaray.

Up at Balnasaig, where Pan, the stars and all the plant spirits had been enlisted in the fight against the oil giant, the Seekers saw the scrapping of the island pipeline as a personal triumph. But their celebrations were short-lived; Althea and Evelyn fell out badly, and in the struggle that followed, Althea's past-life expertise was no match for the combined forces of Evelyn's plant yakshas. 'Althea, accompanied by an Australian devotee fourteen years her junior who goes by the "spirit name" of Dzaq, has moved back to the mainland where they plan to set up a commune in the Borders,' wrote McWatt in the *Compendium*. Evelyn, he recorded, 'has moved into Neville's bed'.

1975 was also the year the island became the site of one of Britain's first experiments in fish farming when Alec Campbell and his son Wee Eck (whose nickname, innocently conferred in childhood, now seemed a sardonic reference to his impressive height and girth) received grants from the Highlands and Islands Development Board and Auchwinnie Council for two floating cages containing turbot.

'It reduces fishing to a fairground game, or dooking for apples,' wrote McWatt in the *Auchwinnie Pibroch*. 'Like colour television, it's expensive, no great improvement on the existing arrangement, no one needs it and it'll never catch on.' On one issue only, McWatt was avid for change: 'The island must and will shake off the yoke of foreign oppression.' But, even as he engaged with politics, local and national, the poet never forgot his 'first duty', as he reminded himself in *The Fascaray Compendium* in December 1975 – 'to immerse myself in the pleasures of the natural world and the music and discipline of poetry'.

A Granite Ballad – The Reimagining of Grigor McWatt,
Mhairi McPhail (Thackeray College Press, 2016)

Tae Hairst

Season o haars an maumie fruitfu'ness
Close bosie-pal o the mucklin sun
Colloguin wi him how tae laid an bliss
Wi fruit the brammles that sae fykie rin,
Tae swell the marrae, pluff the puddock stuils,
Tae boucht wi apples crofters' foggie trees,
Tae fill wi kernels douce the hizzel huils
An gie bouquets o flooers tae eydent bees,
An fill aw fruit wi ripeness tae amaze,
Enchant the eye an set the whin ablaze,
Untae we ween sic days will nivir end,
For simmer's gien us bounteous dividend.

Grigor McWatt, efter John Keats, 1975[23]

23 From *Wappenshaw*, Virr Press, 1986. Reprinted in *Warld in a Gless: The Collected Varse of Grigor McWatt*, Smeddum Beuks, 1992.

AS PROFESSOR ALASTAIR GALBRAITH OBSERVED, McWATT, LIKE MacDiarmid, was always good at grudges. And both poets didn't confine their contempt solely to the English. So it was inevitable that when the two fell out, neither went quietly.

What appears to have triggered the row was MacDiarmid's abandonment of the poetic language he had once approvingly termed 'Synthetic Scots' – his experimental linguistic synthesis of Scotland's vernacular variants, ancient and modern, largely gleaned from dictionaries of the old tongue. Instead, in his verse, MacDiarmid had turned to English, and an English rich, some said clotted, with modern scientific terminology. McWatt, in his *Auchwinnie Pibroch* column of 1 September 1975,[24] accused MacDiarmid of 'wilful obscurantism and a shameful betrayal of our language, our land and our people'.

MacDiarmid, inevitably, did not take this accusation lightly, dismissing McWatt in the letters page of the *Scotsman*[25] as a 'penny balladeer and composer of jingles for the wireless'. The insult was reciprocated in the *Glasgow Herald*[26] – 'Although his long-suffering friends and supporters have forborne from saying it, the truth is that the self-styled Hugh MacDiarmid, has not written a decent poem since 1933' – and returned again, in the same newspaper[27] – 'How odd it is to see McWatt, this passionate defender of the Scots tongue, crouched over his desk by the spectral light of a Tilley lamp spending all his time rewriting, like a schoolboy at his lines, with varying degrees of success, the literature of the enemy.'

That week, McWatt devoted all six hundred words of his 'Frae

---

24 Reprinted in *Frae Mambeag Brae: Selected Columns and Essays of Grigor McWatt*, Stravaigin Press, 1985.
25 *Scotsman*, 5 September 1975.
26 *Glasgow Herald*, 8 September 1975.
27 *Glasgow Herald*, 10 September 1975.

Mambeag Brae' column[28] to the feud. 'It seems that, in politics as in poetry, Hugh MacDiarmid has lost the heid. He has sacrificed his lyrical, nimble native tongue for the kind of recondite English terminology that seems to have been cribbed from a Porton Down laboratory report and this former scourge of Empire now defends the coloniser's right to appropriate the riches of the earth. Why should England have it all? I have, in my small way, devoted my life to a literary Land Raid, seizing a few acres of the abundant miles of English verse, staking them off, recultivating them and returning them to the people of Scotland.'

MacDiarmid's response was printed in the *Scotsman*.[29] 'The day Grigor McWatt, the Harry Lauder of letters, writes anything beyond the banal and derivative is the day I throw my principles to the wind and cast my vote for the Conservative and Unionist Party. Until then, I have no wish to hear his name or renew our slight acquaintance.'

McWatt, however, had the last public word on the subject. 'Our Sassenach enemies have dismissed our magnificent vernacular verse as "doggerel in dialect". But, to quote the linguist Max Weinreich: "A language is a dialect with an army." I am a proud conscript to the commando division of that army, ready to do battle for the cause of our great tradition. MacDiarmid, or Grieve, has proved to be in this, as in so many other areas of life, a feartie conscientious objector and a collaborator.'[30]

The press, in England as well as Scotland, made much of the spat, and in 1976 Bowster Books brought out a chapbook, *The Flyting of McWatt and MacDiarmid*, anthologising the poets' mutual insults and placing their hostilities in the context of Scotland's medieval tradition of poetic sparring. Alastair Galbraith, writing in the *Quill & Thistle*,[31] dismissed the book – and the quarrel – as 'the unedifying spectacle of two kilties fighting over a sporran'.

Several friends, among them Lilias Hogg, attempted to effect a

28 *Auchwinnie Pibroch*, 13 September 1975. Reprinted in *Frae Mambeag Brae: Selected Columns and Essays of Grigor McWatt*, Stravaigin Press, 1985.

29 *Scotsman*, 17 September 1975.

30 *Auchwinnie Pibroch*, 20 September 1975. Reprinted in *Frae Mambeag Brae: Selected Columns and Essays of Grigor McWatt*, Stravaigin Press, 1985.

31 'It's Square Go the Poetry Men', Alastair Galbraith, *Quill & Thistle*, October 1976.

reconciliation but both men were implacable and when MacDiarmid died two years later, in 1978, McWatt marked the event in his *Pibroch* column[32] with two brief sentences, in which he referred to the poet by his real name, Christopher Grieve: 'So MacDiarmid is silent at last. Grieve not.'

McWatt also fell out with George Mackay Brown, 'the papist of Papa Westray', over his conversion to Catholicism; with Ian Crichton Smith, 'mild as milk', over his refusal to take sides in the argument with MacDiarmid; with Sydney Goodsir Smith, 'the English public schoolboy and kilted kiwi', for not being sufficiently Scottish; and with Norman MacCaig who, in an unguarded moment, questioned the 'exhumation of obsolete Scots words' for poetic purposes, and, fatally for his friendship with McWatt, described vernacular verse as 'a queer marriage . . . of the dying with the dead'.

A Granite Ballad – The Reimagining of Grigor McWatt,
Mhairi McPhail (Thackeray College Press, 2016)

32 *Auchwinnie Pibroch*, 16 September 1978. Reprinted in *Frae Mambeag Brae: Selected Columns and Essays of Grigor McWatt*, Stravaigin Press, 1985.

Tae a Laverock

Hoy tae thee, blythe bogle!
Wee chookie birdie thou werenae,
That frae Heiv'n, or naur aboots,
Skinkest thy fu hert
In routhie strains o unettled ert.

Abuin aye and abuin
Frae the yird thou lowpest
Like a smuir o gleed;
The blae howe thou wingest,
An bayin aye dost brall, and brallin aye bayest.

Grigor McWatt, efter Percy Bysshe Shelley, 1978[33]

---

33   From *Wappenshaw*, Virr Press, 1986. Reprinted in *Warld in a Gless: The Collected Varse of Grigor McWatt*, Smeddum Beuks, 1992.

FOR FASCARAY, THE 1970S ENDED ON A DISSONANT CHORD OF optimism, frustration and anger, which, in some cases, resonated all the way down to Westminster.

Nationally, the promise of a referendum on Scottish devolution had brought heady new hopes for the future; hopes that were eventually dashed in what McWatt called 'a humiliating victory'. Fifty-two per cent of Scots voted in favour of greater independence, 48 per cent against. But, McWatt wrote in the *Auchwinnie Pibroch*, 'Once more the English establishment has set us up, massaging the figures. It's another fix.' Westminster had ruled, late in the day, that the referendum results were to be adjusted to reflect turnout, 'making fifty plus two equal thirty-two' by stipulating that a minimum of 40 per cent of the electorate had to exercise their vote in favour of devolution before any constitutional change could take place. 'The English didn't just move the goalposts, they dug them up, rolled up the pitch, dismantled the stands and took the whole stadium back to London,' McWatt wrote.

And so it was, by the law of unintended consequences, that after furious Scottish Nationalist MPs withdrew support from the Labour government, a general election was forced and a Conservative government, headed by the first woman to lead a UK political party, was returned with little support in Scotland. As McWatt wrote, the new prime minister's 'ill will towards Scotland has not been seen since the Butcher Cumberland rode into Culloden'. His choleric post-election column appeared in the *Pibroch* under the headline 'MAGGIE THATCHER: MY PART IN HER ASCENT'.

Locally, news that the nationalised ferry operator Caledonian MacBrayne proposed a regular passenger service between Auchwinnie and Fascaray was welcomed by everyone except the laird, who, writing from his London town house, opposed the idea of a regular link with the mainland, on the grounds that it would 'destroy the character of our paradise island' during his annual six-week visits. The ferry proposal was scrapped by the Westminster government's Scottish Office and islanders suspected that Lord Montfitchett's close friendship with the flamboyant Scottish Tory MP Nicholas Fairbairn, a confidant of Margaret Thatcher, played a key part in the decision.

At Balnasaig Farm, Tam Macpherson finally ceded the reins to his grandson, Innes, a cheerful, leonine twenty-year-old. Tam had, at seventy-six and despite ill health, fought retirement desperately, resisting all pressure from his daughters Maggie and Sheena. But once the resourceful Innes was installed, Tam seemed reinvigorated in his new role as Farmer Emeritus, dispensing agricultural and horticultural advice at the Finnverinnity Inn to anyone who asked for it, 'and a fair few who didn't', McWatt wrote in *The Fascaray Compendium*.

While Balnasaig Farm made a graceful transition to new management, over at Balnasaig Lodge the Seekers were in turmoil. Evelyn Fletcher had uncovered evidence of Neville Booth's affair with their administrator, Izzy Wallop, and turned them both out, denouncing the lovers, as she wrote in *The Wisdom of the Wilderness Within*, for 'deception and coarse venality which contravened the spirit of Balnasaig'. Izzy had fled the island but returned a week later and moved into Alec Campbell's old caravan behind the herring sheds. Neville checked into the Bothy for three lonely nights before Evelyn forgave him, blaming 'dark forces' which had identified Balnasaig Lodge as a target and were working to tempt him from the Path. Perhaps it was in the spirit of reconciliation, or as a simple diversionary tactic, that Neville ordered the felling of an ancient stand of Caledonian pines behind Balnasaig Lodge to 'vanquish the darkness, bring in the light and await the arrival of sensitives from other realms', as he wrote in his own memoir, *Reflections from the Pilgrim Path*.

A Granite Ballad – The Reimagining of Grigor McWatt, Mhairi McPhail (Thackeray College Press, 2016)

It's Sunday. St Andrew's Day, Agnes tells me.

'He's the patron saint of Scotland. He died on a cross shaped like an "X". You know, like a kiss. And that white kiss on a blue flag, the Saltire, that's St Andrew's cross.'

'Great,' I say, looking up from my end of the kitchen table, which is heaped with typed pages from my book, the latest edited sections of *The Fascaray Compendium* and an unsorted batch of letters from Lilias Hogg. Over at my daughter's end, she's working on another school project.

There's a ceilidh tonight in the village hall and she wants me to go with her. Twenty years ago, the idea of a Sabbath ceilidh would have been unthinkable in Finnverinnity. In my present mood, my sympathies are with the old-school Calvinist grouches.

'Please, Mom! There's going to be dancing and bagpipes and everyone on the island will be there.'

How could she know that her three arguments for going to the ceilidh are precisely my three reasons for staying away? Plus the work, of course.

'Sorry, honey, I'm busy. You go with Oonagh and her mom. You'll have a great time.'

I wave them off and get back to my evening's tasks. Sixteen letters from Lilias. Two replies from Grigor. Early in 1980, after suffering a number of dizzy spells, Lilias was admitted to hospital and diagnosed with polyneuropathy, or 'not-so-pretty polyneuropathy' as she wrote, brought on, said the doctors, by alcohol abuse.

'Very sorry indeed to hear about your bad turn,' Grigor wrote in February. 'Is it too much to ask that you might start taking care of yourself and forswearing old pleasures that now bring only harm?'

After two weeks in hospital she returned home and resolved to stay dry. But the damage had already been done.

'I'm a husk,' she wrote to McWatt, 'trembling in the slightest breeze.'

In response to her request for a loan, McWatt sent her money to pay the rent arrears on her bedsit in Cowgate. She wrote to him a week later:

'I used your money wisely, if not well. We always abhorred the property-owning classes so instead of shelling out to my Edinburgh Rachman I decided to hand the lot to landlords of another stripe, revisiting old haunts and raking over old passions. The Menzies' barman was new, a guiless lad who kennt naught of my reputation and served me till the lights went out. Of the old passions, I saw only ghosts and instead of all our brave talk of poetry, politics and art, the air was shrill with the idle chatter and inane jukebox music of the young.'

Two weeks later, on 23 May, she wrote again to Grigor: 'Your Flooer is not just sick now. She's blown and blasted, a rank weed. Destitute.'

Not so destitute that she had given up entirely on the possibility of love, or the comforts of sex and affection. She resumed her affair with Archie Aitken, who was by then drinking heavily himself and remained unhappily married to Meg, the short-tempered university librarian.

Reeling from this close attention to someone else's domestic disasters, I hear a gentle knock at the door. I have a visitor. Surely everyone is up the road at the ceilidh. It's Margaret Mackenzie, sheepishly holding a plastic grocery bag.

'I've something for you,' she says, reaching into the bag. 'For the museum.'

She hands over a brown paper package. It's surprisingly heavy. I unwrap it and inside is an irregular rectangle of red and black metal, embossed with letters and a Roman numeral. E II R.

'It's from the old pillar box, outside the shop. The one he blew up. Or they said he blew it up. McWatt. If you had any interest in it . . ?'

She smiles uncertainly.

I examine it more closely.

'My grandfather, Donald John the Shop,' she continues hesitantly, 'retrieved it the day after the explosion and gave it to my father. After he died on the *Morag May* it was passed on to me. But if it's no use to you . . .'

I turn it over in my hands. It's a curio. Part of the island story. Following the independence referendum, it has some topicality and would make a good illustrative footnote to Minka Redpath's timeline.

'We can definitely find a place for it,' I say. 'Thank you.'

More valuable to me than this sixty-year-old chunk of shrapnel is the fact that Margaret Mackenzie, my erstwhile stalker, is here in my home and bears no ill will towards me. In fact she wants to help.

'If there's anything I can do,' she says. 'It's just what the island needs, the museum. There's so much history in a place like this and if we're not careful it'll be forgotten. I've seen you working so hard at it. Late into the night.'

I thank her.

As she steps out into the night, bagpipe music, a wild reel, drifts down from the village hall.

'Aren't you going to the ceilidh?' I ask.

She laughs.

'Och, I'm no really one for the dancing.'

Me neither. Chastened – another case of serious misreading on my part; I'm beginning to wonder if I'm emotionally dyslexic – I get back to the certainties of work and to the unfolding catastrophe of Lilias's life.

'Would you believe it?' Lilias wrote to Grigor. 'The Flooer o Rose Street is now a kept woman, *une grande horizontale*. I'm rather taking to it. Archie's a funny fellow, carnaptious and daft with jealousy in drink, but it's a nice change to be the object of, rather than consumed by, desperate passion.'

Aitken had had some financial success co-writing a TV detective series and he set Lilias up in a bedsit round the corner from his house by the Union Canal.

'Note the new lodgings – 5a Rope Walk. Smart address, don't you think?' Lilias wrote. 'Perfect for a hangman, or a suicide. In fact you'd be spoiled for choice as a suicide. What's it to be? The canal or the noose?'

Her letters fill me once more with a creeping sadness. All her life Lilias Hogg saw love where there was none and then, too late, realised her mistake.

I got out just in time. In a fever of passion I bloomed under the intensity of Pascal's gaze. Only later did I realise he had been staring into my eyes like Narcissus, admiring his own reflection.

Fareweel Fause Loue

Fareweel, fause loue, the howdie o aw whids,
A deidly fae an enemy tae roo,
An eelist loon frae wham aw braibit flaws,
A bastart qued, a tirran birsie baest,
A miskennt paith, a kirk that's fu o traison,
In aw pasments thrawartlie untae rizzon.

A pushion sarpent happit ower wi flooers,
Mither o souchs an murtherer o saucht,
A sea o grothoes draikin dreichest shours
Bedewing ilka waeful dool that cooers;
A school o slig, a mash o joukerie,
A gowden cleek that hauns a pushiont bait.

Syne yer flums ma callant days begowkt,
An fer ma fegs, unthankitness airts oot,
An syne Ah've swithered oan the cutty-stool,
An pruived masel tae aw wha ken a fool,
Fause loue, ettlins an puchritud, adieu,
Deid is the ruit where whigmaleeries grew.

Grigor McWatt, efter Walter Raleigh, 1980[34]

34 From *Wappenshaw*, Virr Press, 1986. Reprinted in *Warld in a Gless: The Collected Varse of Grigor McWatt*, Smeddum Beuks, 1992.

WITHIN A YEAR, LILIAS WAS HOSPITALISED AGAIN AFTER A SERIES of falls. She was referred to a psychiatrist, who diagnosed depression as well as alcoholism and prescribed electroconvulsive therapy.

'They're not sure how it works,' she wrote to McWatt, mustering some of her old cheer after her first session, 'but apparently it's like taking a bowl of porridge, throwing it in the air and seeing where it falls. The hope is the porridge – the brain – lands in such a way that the whole arrangement becomes more congenial. Sunny side up. It seems to work, for a week or two at least, though the memory's shot.'

She had broken acrimoniously with Aitken after another drunken row. His marriage was back on – he had been diagnosed with kidney disease and his wife Meg was a more capable nursemaid, and certainly a better housekeeper, than Lilias. Meg would also be harder to shake off. Lilias was homeless again and her parents told her they were too old to cope with the burden of her illness and would not be able to offer her a room.

'As if my illness was *their* burden,' she wrote.

Her sister Dolina, who had 'made a good marriage and moved to the prosperous south neuk of Glasgow' was, according to Lilias, 'too dour and nebby, too plain embarrassed, to care for her troublesome older sister'.

Edinburgh social services found Lilias digs in Marchmont – 'awfie clatty, even for me', she told Grigor, and, encouraged by a hospital art therapist, she took up painting, covering random pages of old newspapers with smears and daubs of colour. 'Mixed media,' was how she described this new enthusiasm in perky letters to Grigor. She sent him an early effort rolled in a cardboard tube, a series of khaki streaks with an emerald swirl painted on the classified ads section of the *Scotsman*. *Island Idyll*, she called it.

McWatt was not persuaded. In a letter to Willie McCracken, McWatt wrote: 'the painting looked like something she'd cleaned her brushes on – a dispiriting mess. Like her flat. Like Lilias herself, alas.' To her, though, he dissembled. 'I always knew you were an artist,' he wrote. 'Stick at it.'

But her capacity for adhesiveness was limited. What she did 'stick at' was the drink. Although the old crowd of poets had scattered – those who'd survived had become bored by the same old talk and the same old hangovers – and although she was intermittently barred by landlords weary of the sporadic tears and the shouting, Lilias couldn't keep away from the pubs of Rose Street. Grigor, visiting the city in the winter of 1980, was said to have exited Menzies' swiftly one Saturday night when she stumbled in, singing. But they continued to exchange letters.

'It seems I have been summoned all along not by Apollo, dreamboat god of poetry, but old red-nosed leering Dionysius, god of bevvy,' Lilias wrote. 'And I, his polyneuropathic nymph, limp gamely after him.'

The new landlord of Menzies', an ex-soldier from Yorkshire, finally lost his patience and called the police after Lilias took a walking stick to the pub jukebox. She was kept in a cell overnight and appeared in court the following morning charged with vandalism. Grigor paid the fine.

'I tried to explain to them,' she wrote. 'I was defending the honour of a dear friend and great poet.'

Before she 'whacked the lights out of the jukebox', it had been playing Alex Harvey's version of 'Hame tae Fascaray'.

McCracken, who had moved to the Borders where he was running a bookshop, found himself in Edinburgh on business in late 1981 and called round to see Lilias. 'I knocked on the basement door and there was no answer. I waited five minutes then, thinking no one was in, I walked back up the steps to the street with – I'm ashamed to admit – a sense of relief. It was then I heard the door below open and saw a stooped old woman looking out, grey hair awry, leaning on a Zimmer frame. I was about to apologise and say I had the wrong address. And then I realised. It was Lilias.' She had just turned forty.

A Granite Ballad – The Reimagining of Grigor McWatt,
Mhairi McPhail (Thackeray College Press, 2016)

Bygane Times

Bygane times when Ah loued ye,
Then Ah wis kennt as braw
An they blethered o my guidness
An spake o me wi awe.

Noo the whigmaleerie's ower,
An naethin bides the same,
An aw aroon they glower,
An there's anely me tae blame.

Grigor McWatt, efter A. E. Housman, 1985[35]

---

35 From *Wappenshaw*, Virr Press, 1986. Reprinted in *Warld in a Gless: The Collected Varse of Grigor McWatt*, Smeddum Beuks, 1992.

McWATT FOUND A NEW OUTLET FOR HIS ENERGIES CLOSER TO home when he launched a campaign against the Conservative government's forestry policy, which was giving grants in the form of tax concessions to investors wishing to plant tracts of fast-growing Sitka and lodgepole pines. Among these investors was Torquil Mere-Stratton, Lord Montfitchett and Laird of Fascaray, and a consortium of his business associates, who brought in English contractors to clear vast tracts of bracken and heather in Finnverinnity Glen and plant a monolithic twelve-acre block of pine trees.

The consortium also had designs on Mammor moor as a suitable site for a lucrative plantation. 'It is nothing less than desecration of our land by our Westminster rulers and their cronies, motivated by pure greed,' McWatt wrote in 'Frae Mambeag Brae' in 1982. 'The moorland west of Beinn Mammor is one of the largest areas of blanket bog in the world, with a unique ecosystem of plants, insect and bird life. It is essential to sustain populations of Arctic skua, dunlin, greenshank, golden plover and other endangered birds. And the laird and his pals would render this landscape dark and silent, sealing it forever under acres of toxic Axminster, carpeting it with those alien, light-excluding nutrient-leeching trees which are of no interest to anyone except tax evaders.'

McWatt's campaign was backed by most islanders, including the Balnasaig Seekers, although, as he pointed out in 'Frae Mambeag Brae', the Seekers' support was 'somewhat at odds with their decision two years ago to cut down a magnificent stand of Caledonian pines to facilitate the landing of flying saucers'.

The coalition between the islanders and incomers would always be uneasy, but the campaign against the pine plantations proved to be the first salvo in the battle for the soul of Fascaray.

Izzy Wallop, the former administrator at Balnasaig Lodge who had been exiled from the Seekers after her affair with Neville Booth, was now renting Donald and Morag MacEwan's old cottage in Finnverinnity. She had, according to McWatt in the *Compendium*, 'a freakish appetite for the tedium and intrigue of committee meetings, a small private income and time on her hands', and nominated herself for the post of secretary of the newly established Isle of Fascaray Residents' Association.

There were murmurs of dissent among indigenous islanders, echoed by recently settled Fascaradians from mainland Scotland: Wallop was a blow-in, another 'white settler', and an English one at that. But, in her favour, she had no difficulty expressing her views at length in public and seemed to enjoy regular correspondence with Auchwinnie Council, not just about pine plantations but also about rubbish disposal, the need for better access to medical services and for adequate housing, plumbing and sewage systems. Plus which, no one else was interested in taking on the job.

'Any army must accept the assistance of mercenaries,' wrote McWatt in a letter to Lilias dated June 1983, 'though we are not obliged to welcome them warmly. Izzy Wallop is a bore, and an English bore at that. But for the moment, as secretary of the Isle of Fascaray Residents' Association, she is *our* bore and the hope is that she might bore Auchwinnie Council into submission.'

Within nine months, following representations to Auchwinnie and Westminster – the local Liberal Democrat MP backed his island constituents – and many passionate columns by Grigor McWatt in the *Auchwinnie Pibroch*, Mammor bog was declared a Site of Special Scientific Interest, along with Calasay and Doonmara cliffs. Montfitchett's plan for the Mammor pine plantation was scrapped.

A Granite Ballad – The Reimagining of Grigor McWatt,
Mhairi McPhail (Thackeray College Press, 2016)

Our woods are so much part of our psyche that the names of the letters of the Gaelic alphabet are taken from trees.

ailm – elm
beith – white birch
coll – hazel
dair – oak
eadha – aspen
feàrn – alder
gort – ivy
h-Uath – hawthorn
iogh – yew
luis – rowan
muin – vine
nuin – ash
oir – spindle
peith – downy birch
ruis – elder
suil – willow
teine – furze
ura – heather

INVENTORY OF THE NATIVE TREES OF FASCARAY, WITH LATIN, SCOTS AND GAELIC NAMES

birch – *Betula*, birk, beith
Caledonian pine – *Pinus sylvestrus*, bunnet fir
hazel – *Corylus*, calltuinn, hizzle, coll
mountain ash – *Sorbus aucuparia*, rowan, luis
oak – *Quercus*, darach, aik, dair

Norway spruce – *Picea abies*
Sitka spruce – *Pinus sitchensis*

Percentage of Fascaray's land covered by native trees in the seventeenth century: 50

Percentage of Fascaray's land covered by native trees in 1975: 5

Number of insect species supported by native trees: 423

Number of insect species supported by introduced trees: 17

Grigor McWatt, 1983, *The Fascaray Compendium*

1 December 2014

My work, the Zen pleasures of systemisation, used to keep me going when all else was falling apart but now, with Johanna's departure, my editor at Thackeray pressing for more pages of *A Granite Ballad*, McWatt's Jean proving so elusory that I'm beginning to wonder whether she was a fictional construct devised to keep Lilias at bay, and the deadline for the museum opening looming, work seems to be the only problem in town.

Today I'm sustained by two things – Agnes, and the decency of strangers. For strangers, read Margaret Mackenzie. This morning she came into my office with a tin of scones she'd baked for us. I showed her around the museum, such as it is. The MacRaes' junk has been cleared and the cobwebs have been removed but the whole place needs to be cleaned, swept and painted and I've yet to fill the clusters of empty display cabinets. There are still letters to go through, choices to be made. Minka Redpath's frieze is up round the walls and has been wired in, its LED lights winking scornfully at me over significant dates, demanding attention, and the 'Hame tae Fascaray' jukebox has been delivered but lingers in a corner, still partially wrapped. The museum now looks dauntingly large, its emptiness a mockery of my own mental void. But Margaret is enthusiastic.

'You've done wonders!' she says. 'And all on your own.'

'Johanna did her share, before she went away. And Niall Kennedy has been great.'

'But Niall's away too. You can't do all this by yourself. You need some help.'

I feel like weeping. Instead I shrug and tell her I'll be fine. She leaves and I get back to the letters, attempting to immerse myself in someone else's problems.

Another begging letter to McWatt from Lilias, dated June 1985. She signs off with a tercet that could be read as an intimation of approaching death, or a suicide threat.

If Ah maun dee,
I wull meet mirkness as a quine
An tak her tae ma bosie.

Emotional blackmail was, I guess, the only hand she had left to play.

Pascal too. He proved to be a grandmaster at it. He finally took the blood tests, on condition that I paid for them, and when I phoned him from the street outside our apartment to hear the results he was angry. *He* was angry.

'You've put me through this,' he said. 'What do you want to hear? No HIV? That's what they said. Hepatitis though. Check. Hepatitis C. I got that one. Liver disease. Cancer. Death. Happy now?'

As it happens, I wasn't. A week before I learned the truth about Pascal, Marco and I had negotiated an uneasy peace. He'd wanted another chance.

He didn't want to know about my affair.

'Spare me the details. We both know it means nothing, just as my dumb interlude with Kate meant nothing. We're the main event. You, me and Agnes. Let's wipe the slate clean and start over.'

He had even used the M-word.

'Stop right there,' I said, palm out like a traffic cop. 'I absolutely rule out make-up nuptials. Not now. Not ever.'

Sex, though, was another matter.

I was vulnerable. My financial rescue package for Pascal had failed to rescue our physical relationship. It had been a while. Marco and I raced to the sack and for a couple of heady nights I cheated on my boyfriend with my ex, before I returned to Pascal's apartment, intending to let him down gently, and found the scorched foil. More terrifying than the possibility that I'd contracted the virus myself was the thought that, since my reconciliation with Marco, I could have passed it on to him. I could orphan our daughter.

Infection, Pascal grudgingly assured me, was not inevitable.

'I'm the one with the diagnosis here,' he said. 'Why does it have to be about you?'

I didn't bother to argue. I had to have my own blood test to check whether my fetching young lover had left me with a toxic parting gift.

*

My office door swings open. It's Agnes, pink-cheeked and giddy, on her way round to Kirsty Campbell's. School finished early today and Kylie and Darren Macfarlane are taking them pony-trekking with Aaron Schneider.

'They really liked it!' she says.

'Great!' I say, stalling.

Who 'they' are and what 'it' is should become clear if I let her keep talking. But my daughter, too subtle for me, guesses my confusion and bears me no grudge.

'My project!' she says. 'They really liked it. All the kids and the teacher. I got to read it out and it was passed round the school and everything.'

She takes the folder out of her bag and dumps it on my desk before running off to join Kirsty outside.

'See you later, Mom! Love you!'

In the folder are eight pages of unlined A4, taken from a spiral-bound sketchbook, held together with a single pink paper clip.

On the cover is a drawing of a mountain, Beinn Mammor, a green cone with a tiny Saltire flag on the peak. At the base of the mountain are the words, in purple felt tip, 'My Hero – Hector McPhail'. Inside is the story of the Fascaray Five and of 'my great-grandfather – my mom's grandpa – who fought from [sic] freedom on Fascaray'. There is a painting of the Big House, a sinister grey hulk with smoke curling from its many chimneys, and one of a thatched blackhouse with a family – mother, father and small boy, all wearing plaid – at the door with a caption: 'Hector's house in the clackan [sic] of Killiebrae'.

There is a battle scene of soldiers in trenches, their guns spouting tongues of flame, in a landscape whose gentle hills, umbrella pines and piercing blue sky tell us that this is Italy, not Scotland. Then we're back in Scotland again, under thick grey cloud, with five men in kilts wielding spades – 'The Famous Five of Fascaray, who staked their claim to the land'. On the facing page is a suited figure with a monocle and a panto-mime-villain moustache – 'Laird Montfitchett, who hated the people of Fascaray but was a friend of Hilter [sic].'

The biggest image, painted with great care in small strokes of muddy greens, greys and browns across two pages, is an empty glen – Killiebrae reduced to rubble.

Under it, she has written 'The Five Men lost in the court case and it was like a giant stomped his way across the island, flatening [*sic*] houses, and familys [*sic*] and cows.'

The last page echoes the cover, with a close-up of a tiny bearded man in kilt and bunnet waving a Saltire.

'But even though he's dead, my hero great-grandfather Hector McPhail won his battle in the end.'

I return to my work, and to Lilias Hogg's battle, in which there were no heroes and no victors.

WRITTEN IN HER INCREASINGLY SHAKY HANDWRITING, LILIAS'S letters to Grigor in the mid eighties are full of sadness and regrets, as well as recriminations.

'When you and I were young . . . Maybe if we'd stayed the course, if bloody Jean hadn't bewitched you, we would have had a couple of bairns by now. They'd be going to the Big School in Auchwinnie and I'd wave them off on the boat on Monday mornings and welcome them home on Fridays. I'd keep house for you all in Calasay, feed the hens, make pancakes and clootie dumplings and give you warm company in bed. You could "scrieve tae yer hert's delicht". Paradise it seems now. But I was foolish and madly jealous and I failed you.'

He doesn't get drawn on the subject and instead writes to her about his work, sending her drafts of his latest verse.

'Real narrative drive,' she writes, 'thrilling pulse, with the horses' hooves thundering through the cadence. Knocks old Rabbie B into a cockit hat. And gosh, what woman wouldn't want to be Bess the tapster's dochter, with her crammasie loue knot and her dashing whilli-wha [highwayman].' Lilias is pleased to be invited in, to participate, however tangentially, as 'a grateful geisha, happy to serve the grand project'. But she can't resist a sarcastic aside, asking 'if Jean has much to say on the subject of the lyric arts. How is she on the villanelle, or is she more of a terza rima quine?'

In another letter from this period Lilias writes, 'I did think you and Bonnie Jean would be shacked up by now, cooried in, enjoying cosy conjugality in Calasay. Maybe you are, and you're keeping it from me for fear of breaking my heart. Dinnae fash yersel – the heart's lang gone.'

Her anger at this point is reserved for her parents – 'the heartless, soulless Hoggs who surely got me into this mess in the first place, with their life-denying strictures and bourgeois shame. How else could I have turned out?'

McWatt, perhaps sensing that if weren't for her parents some of this anger would be heading straight for him, is unusually frank and stern.

'Your parents might have made a guddle of your childhood. I don't doubt it. But, *pace* Larkin, I think, though yer maw an paw may fuck yer heid, when we reach adulthood it's over to us. We become the authors of our own lives, and with our brief first chapter as a given, we can make a comic novel of it, or a beautiful haiku, a Gothic horror story, an exalted tale of high romance or a shabby little penny dreadful. What's it to be, Lilias? It's not too late, midstream, to switch genres. What about a redemption story?'

She doesn't answer him directly and instead writes back that he 'was aye the diffident one. The others would be sparking and fizzing, rapping the table to make their point. You could outquote and outbluster any of them when roused, but many's the time you'd sit there with an enigmatic smile and a distant look in your eyes, a look that I could only describe as longing. I fancied, hoped, that the longing was for me but I soon learned that, though you enjoyed your Edinburgh gilravages [romps], you were certainly yearning – yearning not for me, not even for Jean, but for home. For Fascaray.'

A Granite Ballad – The Reimagining of Grigor McWatt,
Mhairi McPhail (Thackeray College Press, 2016)

The Whilli-wha

The win wis a scriddan o mirkness amang the blashy trees,
The muin wis a bogle birlinn fung ower gruggie seas.
The road wis a rebin o muinlicht athort the pairple mair,
An the whilli-wha cam ridin —
　　Ridin — ridin —
The whilli-wha cam ridin, up tae the auld howff door.

He'd a cockit-hat on his forebree, a toosht o lace at his chin,
A coat o crammasie velvet an breeks o broon buckskin.
He wis snoddit in his guid claes, a braw an bauld-daur coof,
An he rode wi a gillum glaister,
　　His gun it was a-glaister,
His sgian-dubh a-glaister, ablow the gillum sky.

Ower the cobbles he brattled an clished tae the mirk howff yird.
He chapped at the widden shutters, but aw wis lockit an baured.
He sowfed a tune tae the windae, an who should be bidin there
But the tapster's dark-eed dochter,
　　Bess, the tapster's dochter,
Braiding a crammasie loue-knot intae her lang daurk heir.

Grigor McWatt, efter Alfred Noyes, 1985[36]

---

36 From *Wappenshaw*, Virr Press, 1986. Reprinted in *Warld in a Gless: The Collected Varse of Grigor McWatt*, Smeddum Beuks, 1992.

WITH A TORY WOMAN PRIME MINISTER INSTALLED IN WESTMINSTER, governing Scotland with little electoral support from the Scots, Fascaray went through what came to be known as the Corporate Era. After Torquil Montfitchett, Laird of Fascaray, died of cirrhosis in a Swiss clinic in 1985, Clarence, Montfitchett's first-born son, inherited the estate. Unfortunately Clarence had also inherited another family weakness and, within months, he lost the island in a gambling debt. The servants were dismissed overnight and left on the next afternoon's mailboat.

Fascaray was bought by a City consortium, Sapphire Holdings, which installed a factor from London to oversee the estate and a ghillie from Devon to facilitate recreational shooting breaks for the company's international clientele.

At first, life seemed to carry on much as before for the islanders; the factor, an impatient cockney, made it plain that his brief did not include management of Fascaray's tenanted properties, and he left them alone except when rents were overdue. The Big House stood empty and shuttered, as it had been for years until the start of the season. Temporary staff were shipped in to clean the house, greet and cater for the new shooting parties up from London – City brokers and Wall Street types, loud and emphatically cheerful in their expensive field coats, multi-pocketed vests and twill breeks. They pacified locals with thick wads of banknotes, with which they bought drinks 'on the house' in the Finnverinnity Inn.

Bigger changes were on their way, however, and when news broke of Sapphire's longer-term proposal for the island it was greeted with incredulity. The company was planning a 'large-scale job-creation scheme' for Fascaray. Good money, too. The young folk would no longer have to sail to the mainland to secure their futures; the island's economy was about to receive an unprecedented boost thanks to Sapphire, which was going to open a quarry on the island.

But the Fascaradians soon learned that there was to be a cost. The quarry would, in fact, be a 'superquarry', based in the green core of the island. Beinn Mammor was to be blasted and scooped out to provide a mountain of stone chips to aid the construction boom and road-building programme down south.

'Once more the future of our beautiful island sanctuary is in jeopardy for the sake of the City boys' bawbees,' wrote McWatt in the *Pibroch*. 'To destroy Beinn Mammor would be a monstrous disfigurement which, if we agree to it, will call to mind Mother Abbess Ulla's horrific self-mutilation a thousand years ago in the face of another barbarian invasion. The difference is, she saw off the marauders with her desperate act. We are inviting the pillagers into our home and offering them our treasures to despoil in whatever way they please.'

The economic arguments were, however, irresistible to 95 per cent of the islanders – what else could a fisherman do in these hard times? Fascaray needed jobs, argued Paddy and Mikey MacRae in a Residents' Association meeting in the village hall. Nearly three decades later, in 2014, Effie MacLeod gave me her account of that acrimonious evening. Jobs apart, Sapphire's scheme would bring extra business to the island, the MacRaes said. 'We needed to move with the times or die,' Effie told me, paraphrasing the cousins' argument.

The superquarry would also bring custom to the shop, the inn and the MacRaes' fledgling Museum of Island Life. 'They said it was only incomers like McWatt and the Balnasaig bampots who opposed it.' McWatt did not attend the meeting and could be safely criticised. Ignoring the hostility of the MacRaes, Neville Booth spoke out, making the case that Mammor was 'a sacred site whose primal energies have drawn us here . . . It cannot, must not, be defiled in the name of worldly gain.' An embarrassed silence greeted his speech, according to Effie. 'For most islanders, worldly gain was the reason we got up and went to work each morning.'

Up at Calasay, McWatt, who made no claim for the sacred status of Beinn Mammor, studied Sapphire's plans closely. Then he travelled to Auchwinnie to make use of the Carnegie Library for further research and finally, forcefully, presented his case not in a Residents' Association meeting in Finnverinnity Hall but more publicly, in a fiery 'Frae Mambeag Brae' column in the *Pibroch* on 11 January 1986.

His column (printed in full below), with its devastating conclusion, received national and international attention, but more importantly it persuaded most Fascaradians that Sapphire's superquarry, whatever short-term financial security it might bring to the island, would be disastrous. He became a figurehead for the opposition to the scheme and found himself, once more, in uncomfortable concord with the Balnasaig Seekers and with Izzy Wallop, who now employed all her energy, derived – she maintained – from Mammor itself, to overturn Auchwinnie Council's approval of plans for the superquarry.

A Granite Ballad – The Reimagining of Grigor McWatt,
Mhairi McPhail (Thackeray College Press, 2016)

PAIRT FOWER

Haste Ye Back

First there was Beinn Mammor, and then there were the Himalayas, the Alps and the Rocky Mountains. What claim, faithful readers of the Auchwinnie Pibroch might ask, even those of a justifiably chauvinistic bent, can our Fascaradian molehill make over the mighty mountain ranges of the Himalayas, the Alps and the Rockies? Bear with me and I will show that in matters geological, as in so much else, Scotland leads the world.

Our story, known in scientific circles as the Highland Controversy, involves nineteenth-century skulduggery, vainglory, scientific enterprise and valour. The cast comprises moustachioed, frock-coated geologists slugging it out in scholarly papers over the age of the origins of the Moine rock that makes up much of our region of Scotland.

In one corner was Sir Roderick Impey Murchison, a Scots-born, English-educated geologist, a London resident and president of the Royal Geographical Society, who looked at samples of rock layers from Beinn Mammor and concluded that the mountain was a comparatively recent feature of Highland terrain.

In the other corner were geologists Benjamin Neeve Peach, an Englishman (though in this context we can forgive him that), and John Horne, from Glasgow, who took the trouble one hundred years ago to actually travel to our island to investigate further. After a sojourn in the Finnverinnity Inn and days of fieldwork at the base and north face of Beinn Mammor, sketching the enfolded rock formations flecked with the glinting pyrite known as fool's gold, they discussed their findings over copious drams at the inn and came up with the radical theory of the Moine Thrust, in which the earth's movement in certain conditions can result in older rock being pushed on top of rock of a more recent vintage. Their conclusions, recorded as an addendum to their seminal book *The Geology of North-West Scotland*, revolutionised global understanding of the subject, established Scotland as a key site in its study, and, incidentally, made the case for thorough field-mapping, as opposed to abstract speculation, as a tool for research into tectonic movement.

Eduard Suess, the famous Alpine tectonicist, remarked that the work done by Horne and Peach on Beinn Mammor 'had made the mountains transparent'. Transparency. Lucidity. This is a service we Scots can perform.

But now, on Fascaray, we have another Highland Controversy as Sapphire Holdings threaten to dynamite our mighty mountain, our fulcrum, and to our great shame, a majority of Auchwinnie councillors and a few unprincipled islanders – a 'parcel of rogues bought and sold by English gold' – have supported the company's bid for the superquarry.

My research shows that over the proposed forty-year lifespan of the superquarry, Sapphire will be dropping on the Friendly Isle the equivalent of almost five times the amount of explosives used on Hiroshima. The peace of the island would vanish and birds and wildlife would flee as fifteen tons of dynamite would be expended weekly, finally reducing Fascaray's highest peak to a 'rubble-filled hole' several hundred feet below sea level. The English have bled us dry for years. Now the southern vandals want to bomb us, blast out our heart and leave us for dead. Though turncoats might make their accommodations, true Fascaradians will not stand idly by.

Grigor McWatt, January 1986, *Auchwinnie Pibroch*[1]

---

1 Reprinted in *Wittins: Mair Selected Columns and Essays of Grigor McWatt*, Stravaigin Press, 2011.

Bainisht

Sairchin ma hert for its suith sorrae,
This is the thing Ah find it tae be:
Ah'm forfauchelt by blether an fowk,
Scunnert by toun, glaggin for sea.

Glaggin for the claggie, saut douceness
O smattert skoosh an the wind's wild pech;
Glaggin for the lood rair an the saft skirl
O muckle waws that gurge an brek.

Lang syne Ah sprauchelt the waws in the mornin,
Shoogelt saund frae ma shoon at nicht
An noo Ah'm fankelt by tenements,
Stricken wi din, doitert wi licht.

Gin Ah could see the machair strand,
Stravaig the cliffs o Calasay,
Hear agane the sea's ayebidin souch
An the birdies' cruin oothro the day.

Ah should be cantie, that wis cantie
Aw the while in Fascaray.
Ah've a yen tae haud an haunle
Shells an jetsam in braw saut spray.

Ah should be cantie, that am cantie
Niver at all since Ah cam tae toun.
Ah'm too lang awa frae watter.
Ah need the sea an Ah need it suin.

Grigor McWatt, efter Edna St Vincent Millay, 1964[2]

2   From *Kowk in the Kaleyard*, Virr Press, 1975. Reprinted in *Warld in a Gless: The Collected Varse of Grigor McWatt*, Smeddum Beuks, 1992.

McWatt's new and very public life.

'All is sere, dry and silent here,' he wrote to her in 1985. 'I sit at my desk in Calasay and work because that is all there is.'

Perhaps he is exaggerating the loneliness of his life to cheer her up in her misery. It's also possible that he's simply trying to get her off his back. Lilias's letters were increasingly ugly and importuning. In a note from that period, scrawled on the back of a milkman's bill, she asks if he can spare some money for household repairs.

'The bathroom has sprung a leak. And so have I. I'm up to my oxters in domestic catastrophe. Fifty pounds would do it.'

The following week she tries again. The faulty plumbing isn't mentioned. Now the problem is a broken bedroom window.

'Twenty pounds is all I ask. Don't tell me you can't afford it. Your Flooer is so dreadfully cold at night and without a poet to warm her she shivers and wastes away.'

Four days later, presumably having received a negative response from McWatt, she abandons any pretence.

'I'm broke and I'm thirsty and I need a drink. Buddy, can you spare a dime?'

By 1986 she was in hospital again and her letters refer to his frequent visits to the city. 'Back in Auld Reekie, making a stir, I see,' she wrote in May. 'Saw you on the telly in the patients' day room. You've moved onwards and upwards and you've clearly no time for old muckers, let alone makars, these days. But I'm pleased for you, Griogal Criodhe. Honest I am. I hope you beat the bastards.'

The three-and-a-half-year campaign against Sapphire Holdings, from 1985 to 1988, now cited as an inspirational forerunner of successful community action and environmental lobbying, was said to be have been launched by Grigor McWatt's column in the *Auchwinnie Pibroch* in January 1986. His call to arms was picked up by the *Scotsman*, then by all the Scottish papers before the London press got in on the act. 'SAPPHIRE FACES A WHISKY GALORE! UPRISING' recorded *The Times*. 'RECLUSIVE ISLAND BARD TAKES ON SAPPHIRE' was the *Guardian* headline, while 'THE BATTLE OF BRIGADOON' was the *Daily Telegraph*'s take on the story.

By the time the officially constituted Fascaray Preservation Society (secretary: Izzy Wallop) had amassed sufficient funds, some diverted from the island's Residents' Association (secretary: Izzy Wallop), to print posters, flyers and a small booklet of photographs of the island, arrange transport and accommodation and hire the Assembly Rooms in Edinburgh, all the TV networks were in the city to film McWatt's speech. The footage shows him transfigured by rage, his hair a silver starburst, jabbing his finger towards the audience.

'Our wee hill, Beinn Mammor, has been so long above the sea it makes johnny-come-latelies of the Alps,' McWatt thundered. 'And these avaricious Sassenachs want to reduce Beinn Mammor to dust, simply to line their bulging pockets. They value Mammon above Mammor.'

Despite the island's now-unanimous support for the Fascaray Preservation Society, it was not an entirely harmonious forum. How could it be? There were serious divisions over presentation and aims – Izzy Wallop and the Balnasaig Seekers attempted to push through a motion banning the traditional guga hunt – and in 1987 McWatt threatened to resign after the Seekers invited a reporter and photographer from a Sunday supplement to attend a weekend vigil at the foot of Beinn Mammor, 'with sacred drumming, spirit channelling and vegan food'. The resulting article, with references to 'the reclusive Bard of Fascaray' and 'his famous pop song', was not sympathetic.

Deputations of indigenous MacDonalds, McKinnons and Campbells eventually persuaded McWatt to continue his association with the society but there was another flashpoint the following year when a short documentary for a TV news programme about the Sapphire campaign was screened. McWatt had agreed, reluctantly, to be interviewed on condition that filming would be brief and the documentary would focus on the Fascaray Preservation Society and its aims, rather than on him. The journalist and cameraman were duly swift and respectful but when the edited film was broadcast in May 1988, McWatt was incensed; the backing track to the film was provided by an aural collage of cover versions of 'Hame tae Fascaray', including the recent spoof recording, with manic accordion and rapping vocals, by a Dundonian punk band.

A Granite Ballad – The Reimagining of Grigor McWatt,
Mhairi McPhail (Thackeray College Press, 2016)

A Jaikit

Ah made ma sang a jaikit,
Happed wi browstary
Oot o auld yairns
Frae fit tae gizzern;
But the gowks claucht it,
Wuir it in the warld's een,
As if they'd wrocht it.
Sang, let them hae it.
Tae hell wi it,
Ah'd raither gang naikit.

Grigor McWatt, efter W. B. Yeats, 1988[3]

3   *Warld in a Gless: The Collected Varse of Grigor McWatt*, Smeddum Beuks, 1992.

IN 'FRAE MAMBEAG BRAE', IN THE *AUCHWINNIE PIBROCH* OF 10 June 1988,[4] McWatt grimly reflected on the the fact that Auchwinnie Council, backed by Westminster, continued to stand firmly behind Sapphire's plan. For the first time, he seemed to accept defeat.

Our many failures have defined us as much as our victories. All good Scots bairns know the story of William Wallace and his Davidean victory over the English Goliath at Stirling in 1297. Fewer Scots know of Fascaray's part in the battle in which three of its sons – Andrew and Grigor McWatt and Robert McDonald – formed part of the *schiltron*, circle of bowmen, that left five thousand English soldiers dead at Stirling Bridge. Wallace's defeat by the Sassenachs at Falkirk the following year and the death in that battle of our Fascaradian forebears does not detract from their heroic status.

The valiant struggle which ended in Wallace's torture and execution in London in 1305 was not in vain. Nine years later, in 1314, under the stewardship of Robert the Bruce, the Scots army decisively defeated the English at Bannockburn and settled the question of self-determination for four centuries.

Despite many setbacks, political, economic and cultural, the spirit of Wallace and Bruce is alive today – even here in our wee northern fastness of Fascaray, where the continuing struggle for liberty and dignity goes on. We may have lost the battle but the war continues. My hope is this: that in a quarter of a century's time, when we celebrate the seven hundredth anniversary of Bannockburn, it will be with our heads held high as citizens of an island owned by its people and as part of an independent sovereign nation once again.

4   Reprinted in *Wittins: Mair Selected Columns and Essays of Grigor McWatt*, Stravaigin Press, 2011.

The following month, in a surprise move, the Westminster government bowed to the pressure of publicity and launched a public inquiry into the Sapphire plan, to which McWatt was invited to submit his arguments. International figures – ecologists, academics, a pop group from Glasgow with a reputation for political activism and a Hollywood actor who claimed a Fascaradian connection (his stepfather's great grandmother was a MacQuitt) – were recruited to the cause. In propaganda terms alone Sapphire, represented by a City lawyer spokesman in a charcoal suit, 'a pinstriped popinjay' according to McWatt, could not compete.

Finally, after close questioning by a journalist from the *Auchwinnie Pibroch*, the managing director of Sapphire revealed that one of the longer-term plans for the 'Mammor hole' would be as an international dump for nuclear waste, and any remaining local support for the superquarry drained away. As McWatt wrote: 'If the arguments for the superquarry were purely economic – putting aside the health and welfare of Fascaradians and ignoring for the moment the island's natural beauty and unique biodiversity – it stretches credulity to think that boatloads of high-spending tourists will flock to take their holidays on a radioactive wasteland.'

After a catastrophic drop in Sapphire's share price, attributed to adverse press reports, the company abandoned its plans for the island in August 1988. Once more, Fascaray was up for sale.

A Granite Ballad – The Reimagining of Grigor McWatt,
Mhairi McPhail (Thackeray College Press, 2016)

Nae Waffin but Drounin

Naebdy heard her, the deid quine,
But still she ligged, greetin:
Ah wis muckle faurer oot than you thocht,
An nae waffin but drounin.

Puir lass, she aye loued daffin,
An nou she's deid.
It maun hae bin tae cauld for her her hert gave oot,
They said.

Och, naw, naw, naw, it wis too cauld aye
(Still the deid wan ligged greetin)
Ah wiz ower faurer oot aw ma days,
An nae waffin but drounin.

Grigor McWatt, efter Stevie Smith, 1988[5]

5   *Teuchter's Chapbook*, Smeddum Beuks, 1998.

IN LILIAS'S LAST LETTER TO McWATT, WRITTEN IN AN ERRATIC hand with many crossings-out and arrowed additions, she congratulates him on defeating Sapphire – 'you were always good at routing the enemy, as I know only too well' – and signs off with a couplet, a wry translation of the golden lads and lasses/chimney sweepers song from *Cymbeline*:

> Gowden loons an quines nae doot,
> As aw lum-scutchers come tae soot.

Aye, Lilias

We'll never know whether she received his reply, sent to her hospital ward three days later.

Dinnae Gang Saft[6]

> Dinnae gang saft intae thon guid nicht,
> Auld age maun scaum an feuch at dit o day;
> Feuch, feuch forenenst the dwynin o the licht.
>
> Tho cannie fowk at tail-end ken the mirk is richt,
> Acause their wirds had fowed nae fire-flaucht they
> Dinnae gang saft intae thon guid nicht.
>
> Gurly loons wha claucht an crood the sun in flicht,
> An leirn, ahint, they maned it on its airt,
> Dinnae gang saft intae thon guid nicht.

6   Grigor McWatt, efter Dylan Thomas, 1988. *Teuchter's Chapbook*, Smeddum Beuks, 1998.

And you, oor pal, upby your dowie hicht,
Winze, fair faw us wi your rammish hert,
Dinnae gang saft intae thon guid nicht
Feuch, feuch forenenst the dwynin o the licht.

The next day, while Fascaray was still celebrating its victory over Sapphire, Lilias Hogg, the Flooer o Rose Street and Muse o Menzies', whose youthful charm had bewitched and inspired a generation of poets, was dead, aged forty-seven, of bronchial pneumonia exacerbated by cirrhosis of the liver.

A Granite Ballad – The Reimagining of Grigor McWatt,
Mhairi McPhail (Thackeray College Press, 2016)

2 December 2014

It was drugs, not drink, that did for my own coterie. First there was Hal and then there was Pascal, born in the indecently recent year of 1987, long after flower power had shrivelled in the icy blast of seventies real-politik. Yet Pascal saw himself, spiritually speaking – and there was way too much spiritual speaking from him – as a child of the sixties.

Surely anyone who's ever popped a party Quaalude knows that recreational drugs aren't necessarily a gateway to enlightenment. Peace and love? The stoned hippies may have have been stardust and golden but ungilded soccer hooligans now smoked weed to prep for mass brawls.

The legacy of the surviving *soixantes huitards* was expressed in that excruciating catchphrase: 'Let it all hang out.' 'No! No,' I feel increasingly, 'put it away! No one wants to see it.'

In this respect, as Marco liked to needle me when our relationship disintegrated, I'm more Scots than North American. I would retaliate: 'Bigots might attribute your poor time-keeping and loud voice to your Italian heritage but I don't deal in cheap national stereotypes.' When I first knew him I marvelled at his emotional expressiveness – I'd never known a heterosexual man who wanted to talk about a relationship as a work in progress that could be tweaked and recalibrated on the move – but I never had him down as a Woodstock warrior. Then again, I never reckoned on the intervention of Karmic Kate.

Now Marco's out of my life, there's no need to be defensive. I can face it and finally come out: give me Caledonia over California any day. I admire dourness and the stiff upper lip, favour the Protestant work ethic over the pagan shirk ethic, and I'm coming round to the case for dutiful repression over self-pleasing self-expression. Yes, I'm uptight and proud. It was the sixties that gave moral authority to appetite and encouraged the view that passion and impulse are nobler than drab old rationality, that every itch must be scratched, that at the merest hint of boredom we must jettison existing relationships and move on to the next. It's bad enough that we do this to each other, but what are we doing to our children?

After a week of unexpressed terror, my blood tests came back. We – Marco, Agnes and I – were in the clear. With that good news it should have been easy to start over, take another tumble in the Super Kingsize, forgive past misdemeanours, get reacquainted. It would have made Agnes happy. I had to spoil it though. I had to tell the truth.

I knew that Marco would be hurt to hear details of my affair – though he had no right to be. I also thought he might be jealous – again, that prerogative was surely mine. I thought he might share my concern and relief about the blood tests. But no. He was outraged.

'A kid? A dumb junkie kid? What the hell were you thinking? Was that your idea of revenge? Were you trying to get us killed?'

HERS WAS A SMALL, HURRIED FUNERAL HELD IN A PITILESS RAINSTORM. Of the old Menzies' crowd, only Willie McCracken attended. McWatt chose to stay in Fascaray for the funeral of Tam Macpherson, who had died, aged eighty-six, in his sleep at Balnasaig Farm. From Edinburgh, McCracken wrote to McWatt that evening giving him an account of the day's sad event. Lilias's surviving relatives – sister Dolina, her husband and son, and an elderly cousin from Berwick – hung their heads, dry-eyed throughout the service in Liberton Kirk, 'conducted by a minister who had clearly never met Lilias – all that empty talk about resurrection and eternal reward – and wouldn't have approved of her if he had'. Lilias Hogg was buried in a plot next to her parents; 'reunited at last', wrote McCracken, 'how she would have hated that!', within sight of the Braid Hills – 'at least she could turn her back on her parents and gaze on the hills'. There were no speeches; no wake or purvey and no drinks for the mourners either. 'The final indignity. Lilias would have hated that too,' wrote McCracken.

From Calasay, McWatt arranged delivery of a wreath of lilies and wrote a valedictory poem.

Elegy fur Lilias[7]

Her quinie's bluim wis but a dowie cranreuch,
Her foy o joy an ashet pan o pain,
Her crop o barley but a midden hauch,
An aw her guid wis vauntie howp o gain.
The day's awa, an yet she keeked nae sun.
An nou she pechd, an nou her pech is done.

She socht release, and foun it in the drink,
She leukt for loue an airt oot anely scorn,

7   Grigor McWatt, efter Chidiock Tichborne, 1988. *Teuchter's Chapbook*, Smeddum Beuks, 1998.

She trod the yird an ceilidhd tae the brink,
An nou she dies, and nou she wis but born.
Her gless wis fu, and nou her gless is drunk,
An' nou she lives, and nou her sun is sunk.

His poems, rueful but curiously detached, are the only testimony we have of Grigor McWatt's response to the death of Lilias Hogg. But, given the couple's shared history, he would have been a rare, cold man, far along the spectrum as psychologists would say, if her sad end didn't stir up bereavement's usual anguished aftermath – guilt, self-reproach and the hopeless yearning for another chance to start over and get it right.

A Granite Ballad – The Reimagining of Grigor McWatt,
Mhairi McPhail (Thackeray College Press, 2016)

THE ISLAND WAS IN LIMBO FOR SIX MONTHS, AFTER SAPPHIRE'S defeat in 1988, as Fascaray's fate was haggled over in the auction houses of London. Limbo was not a bad place to be. There was no one to check the poaching, no one pressing for the month's rent and the feudal dues. It was a fertile time for Grigor McWatt's work too. He retreated to Calasay, to the *Compendium* and his 'reimagined' poetry, content to live up to his reputation as a recluse. In the *Auchwinnie Pibroch* in October that year he wrote:

As readers of this column know, I have on occasion taken issue with the English tax collector Robert Burns. His whimsical bent gives me, as my friends at the howff like to say, the dry boak. But he did get a few things right, among them the fact that fame, celebrity, whatever you like to call it, is the most bogus of achievements.

The 'tinsel show' of false regard and the 'ribband, star' of mob worship demean the famous and the fan alike. To be 'recognised' by unlettered schoolchildren and housewives is an excruciating humiliation. To be pointed at and stopped in the street by strangers is an affront and an intrusion. The letters – some of the begging variety – are an irritation to me and a burden to our long-serving postie.

Fame, so often won for the mildest of accomplishments, is a curse. In my case, a life of quiet toil in the service of Scots poetry goes unacknowledged by the general, but a simple song, cast long ago in a few bevvied minutes in my local hostelry, has doomed me to exist in the scorching heat and glare of public renown. If I could unwrite it I would.

My island home, I would like to tell my unasked-for admirers, is not for me a dull way station, a temporary halt on the journey to mass adulation and a busy social life. I am not here because I have somehow lost my way en route to the abundant pleasures of the metropolis. I am here because I choose to be alone.

Without an owner, corporate or private, Finnverinnity House was decaying further and its disintegration was, on a magnified scale, surpassing that of the island's crofts and cottages. Fascaradians were used to applying corrugated-iron patches to the leaking roofs of their former blackhouses and polythene sheets to cracked windows. Who was going to perform that service for the Big House, whose roof tiles were disappearing at a shocking rate?

Many suspected that wayward teenagers were responsible for the house's broken windows and smashed fanlight but no one was going to call the Auchwinnie police to investigate. Even if the 'polis' were to be summoned, would they bother to make the journey across the Clinch to protect a property with no owner?

As for the Big House garden, the lawns – unmown for years – were infested with molehills, all that remained of the first Lady Montfitchett's Elizabethan knot garden was a clump of blighted box hedging, and the overgrown shrubbery had become a trysting place for local youths and, judging by the empty bottles in the rhododendron bushes, an al fresco saloon bar for underage drinkers. The island's resident moral arbiters, priest and minister, had long gone and their homes, the simple presbytery cottage in Lusnaharrra and the imposing manse in Finnverinnity, were also empty.

The congregations of both denominations now had to travel to Auchwinnie for services but, since sabbatarian tradition prohibited Sunday sailings, the devout would cross the Clinch to attend special masses and services on Saturday mornings, return in the afternoon and spend Sabbath's Eve and the Lord's Day at home in private reflection and prayer.

The empty kirk in Finnverinnity was bought by a couple from London who turned it into a pottery workshop and gift store. But, wrote McWatt in *The Fascaray Compendium*, locals, Balnasaig Seekers and the occasional visiting hikers, 'showed little interest in Fauvist teapots, humorous knitwear, tartan aprons and thistle-shaped bookmarks'. The couple parted eighteen months later and sold the building at a loss to an Auchwinnie developer, who went bust within months of the sale. Empty once more, the kirk was, wrote McWatt, 'a silent, mouldering rebuke to consumerism and avarice'.

The Church of the Sacred Heart and Immaculate Mary was also derelict and, in *The Fascaray Compendium*, McWatt reflected that it would 'soon revert to its Neolithic state as the roofless pagan shrine of Teampull Beag, decaying with the rest of Fascaray as a reproach to our criminally negligent lairds'. Evoking Shelley's Ozymandias, McWatt saw the decay of Finnverinnity House, once a 'monument to vanity and greed', as a symbol of the systematic neglect of Fascaray by its absentee owners: '*Forby bides naethin. Aroon the clatty murl / O thon undeemous midden, mairchless an scabbit / Streeks oor disjaskit isle, far oot ayont their ken.*'

And then came the news, in early 1989, that the island had been sold; Fascaray had a new laird. Ozymandias was back.

A Granite Ballad – The Reimagining of Grigor McWatt,
Mhairi McPhail (Thackeray College Press, 2016)

3 December 2014

My first row with Agnes. I'm in shock.

She asked if she could Skype her father and I told her it wasn't convenient. I had some work to do — more, no doubt false, leads to pursue on Bonnie Jean — and I needed my laptop.

Thackeray Press are pushing for another chapter of *A Granite Ballad*, there are many more pages of the *Compendium* that need typing up and I need to transcribe some of the letters.

She stood her ground.

'But I said I'd speak to him tonight,' she said.

'Sorry, honey. It'll have to be tomorrow. Mommy has to work.'

Then there was the *Exorcist* moment, when my biddable child metamorphosed horribly: her face contorted, her cheeks reddened, her eyes narrowed and she shouted — Agnes shouted! — at me:

'Why is it always all about you? What *you* want? Can't someone else have a chance?'

She ran upstairs to her room, slamming the door so hard that the picture of the Highland cattle fell off the wall. I picked it up. In the circumstances, the corny portrait of a big-eyed calf with its mother has never looked more ironic.

She's still up in her room and I'm sitting at the kitchen table with the *Compendium* notebooks, my typed-up pages, my book, the letters, fending off the thought that Agnes is uncannily re-enacting my own adolescence five years ahead of schedule, and I'm doing the only thing I know how to do when faced with turmoil: working.

What am I actually good at? Not relationships. Certainly not motherhood. But sitting quietly alone in a room with a stack of thin sheets of pulped wood incised with symbols, methodically trying to make sense of someone else's messed-up life; maybe I'm okay at that.

Mindin

They rin frae me, wha bytimes did me seek
Wi scuddie fit, stalkin ma chaumer.
I hae seen them cannie, saft an douce,
Wha noo are camsteirie, an dinnae mind
That wance they risked a killie-shangie
Tae tak breid at ma haun; an noo they gang
Aboot, seekin the new-fangle.

Ah thank braw fate that lang
Syne, Ah had ma oor, and wance
In scrimpet duds, efter a cantie spiel,
Her gowen fawen frae her shouder,
She claucht me in her spirlie wee airms
An preed me doucely, speirin saft,
'Don't haud back, pal. Dinna be sae daft.'

Ah wasnae dwauming; it wasnae happenstance.
But time is rinnin too, Ah had ma chance,
Ah watch ma furmer hinnie jyne the dance.
An nou the warld has birled, Ah've been forsook.
It's time tae pack ma bags an sling ma hook.
She's turned awa tae sonsier, newer loues
An Ah maun gang an seek anither muse.

Grigor McWatt, efter Thomas Wyatt, 1989[8]

8   *Teuchter's Chapbook*, Smeddum Beuks, 1998.

THE NEW LAIRD OF FASCARAY, BARON GILES DE UYTBERG (pronounced Witberg), a short, plump man in his late forties, 'slick as a seal in a Savile Row suit', according to McWatt in the *Compendium*, had 'a brusque manner, Belgian name and English background'. Though de Uytberg traced his title back to the First Crusade, most of his money, like that of his corporate predecessor in Fascaray, was earned in the City of London, 'if "earned" is the word for it', wrote McWatt. Baron de Uytberg (named 'Witless' by McWatt) was a commodities broker, trading in 'futures'. There was some question, McWatt noted, 'as to whether he could bring any expertise to bear on the future of Fascaray'. But, triumphant though bruised by their recent battle with Sapphire, many islanders – McWatt was not among them – were willing to give Baron de Uytberg the benefit of the doubt. There was also some curiosity about his wife, his third, Claudia, who had once worked as a hostess on a television game show.

By the summer, after a frenzy of renovation and redecoration by a team of English staff supervised by de Uytberg's personal assistant, 'a bossy lassie in breeks', according to McWatt, the Big House was ready to receive its new owners. A poster appeared outside Finnverinnity Hall advertising the 'Inaugural Fascaray Highland Games', to which all islanders were invited.

There was already a traditional local Highland gathering – the long-established Auchwinnie Highland Games. Most Fascaradians took the ferry to the mainland each August bank holiday to watch, and occasionally participate in, the contests for caber tossing, hammer throwing, stone putting, tug-of-war, hill racing, bagpiping and Highland dancing. More popular attractions included food stalls, a subsidised bar and an evening ceilidh. But de Uytberg's Games promised 'new and innovative competitions celebrating Fascaray's rich history' on the Big House croquet lawn.

The poster stipulated that 'only those wearing full Highland dress will be admitted', but those without the requisite costume could hire it from Finnverinnity House, 'free of charge. Apply to Miss Chetwynd, PA to the Laird, rear door, stables.'

Though McWatt was the only islander at that time to possess – and routinely wear – Highland dress, he rejected this invitation from the new Laird of Fascaray. 'I have a more pressing engagement that day; mucking out my byre,' he wrote to de Uytberg.

McWatt's report of the event in *The Fascaray Compendium* was taken from eyewitness accounts recorded in the Finnverinnity Inn that evening. The best first-hand narrative we have of the games is from Effie MacLeod.

'The noise was something terrible,' she told me. 'All they helicopters bringing in the laird's guests for their weekend house party. You couldnae hear yourself think. But we all went along anyweys. We were curious, see.'

It was a day of fitful sunshine and a queue of Fascaradians, 'frae weans tae auld wans', assembled outside the stables of the Big House where they were handed flimsy costumes by 'a snooty besom in a trouser suit', de Uytberg's assistant Marina Chetwynd. There were kilts, blue bunnets, ginger wigs and swords for the men; ankle-length skirts, plaid shawls and wicker baskets for the women. The costume sizes were approximate and the effect, as the islanders filed out of the stables towards the croquet lawn, was, as McWatt wrote in the *Compendium*: 'of a comic, mismatched tartan rabble'.

De Uytberg had shunned the island's resident piper, Sorley MacDonald, fisherman grandson of the late bagpiper Shonnie MacDonald, and instead, according to McWatt, 'employed a multi-instrumentalist cockney from Mile End who had once served with the Argyll and Sutherland Highlanders'.

'We were all hangin aboot, eyein the tables piled high with food and drink, when suddenly there was this yell,' recalled Effie. De Uytberg, who had been hiding in the ha-ha, scrambled onto the lawn with his male house guests, dressed in the red uniforms of Hanoverian soldiers and carrying plastic blunderbusses and high-powered water pistols.

It was, de Uytberg explained later to a reporter from the *Auchwinnie Pibroch*, 'a re-enactment of the Battle of Culloden, meant to be a bit of fun'. Those islanders who tried to make their escape found exit routes blocked by Land Rovers and sandbags as around them whooping Redcoats took aim with jets of freezing water. It was a rout.

'After twenty minutes of pandemonium, the islanders staggered from the battlefield sodden and shivering and were directed to the stables, where they were handed towels and given a glass of ginger [soda] and a biscuit before they changed into their own, dry, clothes, and were sent on their way,' wrote McWatt. 'Never mind Culloden. It was Flodden, Falkirk, Pinkie Cleugh and Darien, combined.'

The only islander to emerge with any credit from the Inaugural Fascaray Highland Games was young James Francis MacDonald, described by McWatt as 'a gentle and mannerly youth', Marsaili MacDonald's son, who was helping his widowed mother run the Bothy before starting his studies at Glasgow University in September. 'In the heat of battle, under intense provocation, Jamie showed himself to be a man of mettle. He wrested a garden hose from a Redcoat and scored a direct hit, knocking the tricorn hat from de Uytberg's head and sending him staggering back into the rhododendrons.'

That night, and every subsequent night for the next two months, James Francis MacDonald, now known as Jamie the Hose, was given a hero's welcome in the inn.

A Granite Ballad – The Reimagining of Grigor McWatt,
Mhairi McPhail (Thackeray College Press, 2016)

Lines on the Finnverinnity Inn

Poets o the firmament,
Whit Elysium hae ye kennt?
Distant Edens, beauties far,
Choicer than oor island's bar?
Hae ye bevvied till yer stocious
In a howff mair perspicacious?
Are the fruits o Paradise
Doucer than those mutton pies?

Grigor McWatt, efter John Keats, 1989[9]

9   *Teuchter's Chapbook*, Smeddum Beuks, 1998.

IT SOON BECAME CLEAR, AS McWATT WROTE IN THE *COMPENDIUM*, that 'de Uytberg's flaws as Laird of Fascaray extended beyond a taste for humourless high jinks'. The island was one of his many playthings and his scant interest in it, dormant most of the year, was reawakened only during his infrequent visits. 'Ootta sicht, ootta mynd,' McWatt wrote, describing the period of de Uytberg's ownership as a regime of 'malign neglect'. The new factor, a retired policeman from Margate, was another part-timer, mostly based at the laird's southern pile – a pink stucco Beverly Hills-style mansion commanding a wooded hillside in Buckinghamshire, with a garage full of vintage cars, a reconditioned Spitfire plane and a state-of-the-art wine cellar.

It was said that Claudia de Uytberg had taken against Fascaray. 'She's no doubt troubled by the lack of shops, and the midges that, on the rare occasions when it is dry enough to sit outside, make it impossible to enjoy champagne on the terrace,' reported McWatt in a wry entry in the *Compendium*. During the laird's long absences from his northern seat, Finnverinnity House was looked after by a surly Welsh caretaker, Llew Evans, who lived in the former nursery, repaired the roof, glazed broken windows, checked for burst pipes and scared off any local youths trespassing in the gardens. He also began a furtive relationship with Izzy Wallop, occasioning late-night and, according to Effie MacLeod, 'rambunctious' visits to Wallop's cottage in Finnverinnity.

This relationship, according to McWatt, accounted for the 'unusual reticence of both the Isle of Fascaray Residents' Association and the Fascaray Preservation Society to pursue the laird for improvements to the island's shaky infrastructure and housing stock'. All requests from islanders for regular water and electricity supplies – those lucky enough to be wired up to the generator only had power between the hours of 8 a.m. and 9 p.m. and many Fascaradians still had to walk a mile to get their water from a well – as well as repairs to leaking roofs, installation of inside toilets, assistance with plumbing emergencies or for help with tackling the rising damp which jeopardised the health of children and pensioners, were ignored.

Above Lusnaharra, the MacRaes' old community golf course among the dunes, machair grass, wild orchids and sea pinks, was bulldozed and the fairway disappeared under a runway for the laird's twin-engined plane. At first local protests were quelled by assurances that what the laird called Fascaray Airport – a strip of tarmac and a windsock – would benefit the island: well-heeled mainland weekenders would bring custom to the inn, shop, the Bothy and the former Temperance Hotel, now renamed the Fascaray Hotel. Miss Geddes' severe rooming house had been transformed by its new owner, an antiques dealer from Kirkintilloch, who had decorated it in dark baronial style with antler trophies, four-poster beds, suits of armour and stuffed animals, and, as McWatt wrote in the *Compendium*, 'in a development that would have scandalised its former proprietor, he has equipped the residents' lounge with a mirrored art deco cocktail cabinet, fully stocked'. Naturally, the hotelier, who had use of a business partner's Cessna, welcomed the laird's airstrip.

Fascaray Airport would also be an amenity for ordinary islanders, argued Izzy Wallop; they would no longer have to rely on precarious sea passage or costly helicopter journey in medical emergencies. Grigor McWatt was unconvinced – 'this is no more a community airport than Finnverinnity House is a community centre', he wrote in the *Pibroch* – and he was once more proved right. The runway was used four times a year and, apart from the hotelier's occasional joyrides, the sole passengers were de Uytberg and his friends.

As in the days of the Montfitchetts, attention was only given to Finnverinnity House, and to Fascaray, the week before the laird arrived for the shooting and fishing in the summer and for the Hogmanay house party. His ghillie – another Englishman – would arrive a week before the laird and the factor to check the fishing equipment and guns while housekeeper and maids – a fresh batch every season, usually from Eastern Europe – would be drafted in to clean and air the place, and descend on Fascaray along with Marina Chetwynd, whose brief, wrote McWatt in the *Compendium*, 'was to ensure that her master's eye would not be offended by any unsightliness in the vicinity of the Big House, or when en route to the hills and rivers to slaughter stag and salmon'.

433

Sheets of iron and rolls of plastic, used for roofing and window repairs and usually stacked outside islanders' homes, had to be concealed in byres and sheds, along with sacks of manure, tangled nets, rusting tricycles, old prams and other clutter of crofting, fishing or family life. On Finnverinnity shore, the Campbells' old boat, the *Silver Darling*, was deemed to be an eyesore and was ordered to be hauled in and concealed behind the fish-drying shed before being broken up for firewood.

Meanwhile, in the *Pibroch*, McWatt reported the plight of Bernadette McKinnon and her husband Joe MacRae, who were living in a caravan with their three children on the beach – 'their cottage in Lusnaharra having become uninhabitable on account of damp'. During one fierce storm, an empty caravan nearby was hurled into the air and smashed against rocks. 'During the gales the noise is something terrible,' Joe MacRae told McWatt. 'The caravan shakes like a can of stones. The children cannae sleep. Whenever the wind turns, we're all living on our wits. The worry's something terrible.'

Davy McIntosh, Hamish and Sarah's youngest son, 'despairing of ever getting decent living conditions on Fascaray', wrote McWatt in 'Frae Mambeag Brae', moved to the mainland with his young family in search of work and social housing in the council flats on the edge of Auchwinnie.

In the *Compendium*, McWatt noted the departure of other islanders who headed south. The school lost half its pupils and there were fears it would have to close, while the new leaseholders of the island store, the Macfarlanes, lived 'in daily fear of bankruptcy'.

The empty homes soon reverted – moss crept over roofs, ferns unfurled from walls, rot devoured windows and door frames, birds and mice moved in, and finally the buildings, as if sighing with relief that the struggle to remain upright was over, collapsed back into the land. To an outsider, this dereliction could seem picturesque. After all, as McWatt wrote, 'the silent empty Scottish landscapes so beloved of charabanc-party romantics, testify as much to the human cruelty and tragedy of the clearances as to nature's magnificent artistry'. Less attractive were the heaps of primary-coloured plastic washed up on the shore at Lusnaharra and Finnverinnity – empty milk and detergent bottles, orange floats, mayonnaise cartons, the occasional sinister single trainer, discarded or lost from passing ships. Once, locals had taken it upon themselves to collect and dispose of ugly debris but now they left it to pile up in tangles of rotting seaweed. Neglect could be contagious.

A Granite Ballad – The Reimagining of Grigor McWatt,
Mhairi McPhail (Thackeray College Press, 2016)

Bryophyta:

Sphagnum acutifolium, Dill. Sphagnum cymbifolium, ehrh. Found near Loch Och, in Lusnaharra, Finnverinnity and Doonmara, growing on stone from abandoned, cleared crofts.

Weissia:

Pellucidum. Found on moist ground and stone in Calasay.

Pottiaceae:

Barbula. Usually grows on limestone walls in Killiebrae clachan but is also found on Lusnaharra Strand, growing in loose sand comprising pulverised seashells.

Flexicaule. Grows in crevices on rocky shoreline north of the Slochd caves.

Grimmiaceae:

Lycopodiopsida, club moss, garbhag. One of the fern allies, found in boggy sites by Mammor, or in sandy, acidic uplands including Balnasaig. Local associations with good fortune. Said to have protective qualities. Subject of an ancient Gaelic incantation, or *ubag,* given here with my reimagining below.

Zygodon viridissimus. Grows in semi-darkness in Clochd cave, along with **Eurynchium pumilum**, which is also found on the slippery rock at the side of Doonmara Falls and in the tributary of Cannioch River by Heuchaw.

Garbhag an t-slèibh air mo shiubhal,
Chan èirich domh beud no pudhar;
Cha mharbh garmaisg, cha dearg iubhar mi
Cha reub griannuisg no glaislig uidhir mi.

See me? See the club moss in ma haun?
Nae hairm can come tae me;
Nae fairies can slay me, nae neds can chib me,
Nae kelpies or bangsters can skelp me.

Grigor McWatt, 1990, *The Fascaray Compendium*

4 December 2014

I'm distracted in my office by another email from Marco.

'Are you okay?' he asks. 'I'm missing you both and wondering what we're doing. Does it have to be like this? Is there really no way back?'

The door opens and I look up from my laptop. Margaret Mackenzie has arrived with cleaning equipment and a delegation. There is Kenny MacLeod from the pub, holding a mop, which he raises in mock salute; Eck Campbell, from the fish farm, pushing an industrial steam cleaner; Chic McIntosh carrying two ladders and a bucket; and Reza and Iqbal Shah, who've brought a vacuum, dusters and a broom.

They all get to work in the museum, insisting I stay at my desk.

'Och, you've got enough to sort through there,' says Margaret, nodding at my piles of papers.

I'm tempted to reread Marco's email and toy with an answer but I resist and get back to work. Two hours later they call me in. The museum is as clean and light as a Scandinavian beach house. They've unwrapped the jukebox and moved it into the centre of the space and arranged all the display cabinets around it in two concentric circles. It looks magnificent. Now, all I've got to do is get the walls painted, hang some pictures and fill the cabinets. My eyes well and I laugh as Kenny MacLeod plugs in the jukebox, presses a button and Robin Hall and Jimmie Macgregor reprise their 55-year-old duet of 'Hame tae Fascaray'.

Eck Campbell is going to paint the place tomorrow with Shonnie MacDonald and Donal MacEwan while I go over to Calasay to sort through McWatt's collection of farm implements. Kenny and Chic insist on coming with me to help.

'A wee lassie like you can't be shifting all that big stuff herself,' says Kenny.

I overlook the patronising tone and accept gratefully. Before they leave, Eck takes me aside.

'I've got something you might be interested in,' he says. 'For the museum. Come round to my house tomorrow night when you get back from Calasay.'

I'm unused to all this goodwill – Agnes is in an equally merry mood when she returns from a playdate with Oonagh – and I find it oddly unsettling.

After supper she Skypes her father, who's staying with Nonna Lucia in New Jersey. He doesn't ask to speak to me.

In bed, just like old times, Agnes asks me to read her a story. She chooses *The Treasure Seekers*. My daughter, a digital native, my inhouse IT specialist, has become obsessed by this Edwardian morality tale of an impoverished but jolly family whose world is so different from her own; full of characterful siblings, a widowed father, a busy schedule of home-made low-tech fun undercut by a sobering strain of tragedy. She loves it but it brings me out in hives. I can't refuse, especially after yesterday's outburst. I take a deep breath. But then we're both spared.

'Look!' she says, throwing back her blankets and pointing at the window. I turn to see a vast green veil of light swirling across the night sky.

The aurora borealis.

Awestruck, we watch the display in silence.

'Wow!' Agnes finally says, taking my hand.

She's forgiven me. I got my girl back.

'That's way, way better than any crummy firework party,' she says.

Vita Summa Brevis

They arenae lang, the lauchter an the greetin,
Loue an ettle an laith;
They've nae pairt in us efter,
The gemme's a bogey. Life's fleetin.

They arenae lang, the days o flooers an bevvy,
Oot o a dwaumin haar
Oor paith shines clear alang the levee,
An noo it's derk, an noo it's au revoir.

Grigor McWatt, efter Ernest Dowson, 1997[10]

10   *Teuchter's Chapbook*, Smeddum Beuks, 1998.

EVENTUALLY DE UYTBERG'S INDIFFERENCE TO THE ISLAND TOOK a more sinister turn. An eviction notice was served on one crofter, John-Joe MacDonald, in February 1997, two weeks after he failed to run to open a gate to let through the laird's Land Rover, and in Lusnaharra crofters were shocked to receive a sizeable bill for the seaweed that they had, like their forebears since time immemorial, collected from the strand for free to fertilise their vegetable plots.

'The lairds would impose feudal dues for the oxygen we breathe, if they could get away with it,' wrote McWatt in the *Compendium*. 'It seems de Uytberg has a Crusoe complex and would prefer it if the Isle of Fascaray were uninhabited.'

The Auchwinnie Scottish National Party candidate lobbied Westminster's Scottish Office in March 1997 on behalf of John-Joe MacDonald and the Lusnaharra crofters. The official reply was that 'this is a private matter between island tenants and their landlord and as such does not fall within the purview of the Secretary of State for Scotland', a response which, wrote McWatt, 'would have satisfied the Duchess of Sutherland as she prepared to clear the benighted Highlanders from their land in the nineteenth century'.

John-Joe MacDonald had no inclination to fight and left the island with his family to look for work in Aberdeen. 'More than three decades ago, it seemed that fate and the elements were conspiring to snuff out the flickering spark of life in Jessie and Francie MacDonald's baby son,' reflected McWatt. 'Brave men and women battled sea, storm and cruel nature to save the newborn John-Joe. Now he is a fine man, with a family of his own to protect, and the caprice of a wealthy Englishman is casting him out of his island home.' Soon, John-Joe's empty croft went the way of all the other empty crofts.

But, as McWatt wrote in the *Pibroch*, 'It wasn't all bad news this year.' In Westminster, the Conservatives were ousted and the new Labour government set in motion plans for a fresh referendum on Scottish devolution.

This time, no finagling of figures could dispute the result – 74.3 per cent of Scottish voters backed the creation of a Scottish Parliament. In the 12 September issue of the *Pibroch*, McWatt was triumphant but still not entirely satisfied.

'So, Scotland is about to turn its back on shameful servitude and take its place once more among the nations of the world. This proposed Wee Pretendy Parliament is surely the first step towards full sovereignty. Now, what about independence for Fascaray?' he wrote.

Students of modern Scottish history still argue about the turning point, the moment when Fascaray finally shrugged off its feudal past. The Land Raid of 1946 was pivotal, certainly, but after the raiders' defeat in the Court of Session, when they were forced to leave the island, the spirit of the Fascaray Five slumbered for half a century as the island struggled on under what McWatt termed 'the Sassenach yoke'.

The decline in fortunes of the Montfitchetts and their class, the discrediting of corporate power and the personal eccentricities of de Uytberg, undoubtedly also played a part in the political awakening of Fascaray. And, while some give credit for the island's radical transformation entirely to McWatt, as the public face of the movement, it is generally agreed that one of the most significant events in the timeline of Fascaray's 'liberation' was what came to be known as the Battle of Fergus McKinnon's Bonfire or, as McWatt named it, the War o the Muckle Midden.

'It was trash,' McWatt wrote later, 'that permitted us to bid good riddance to bad rubbish.'

Islanders, used to fending for themselves and paying for the privilege, had disposed of their own domestic refuse since the days when their Mesolithic ancestors buried their food scraps in the caves of Slochd and Clochd. In the twentieth century, for as long as anyone could remember, garbage had been collected by island volunteers, shovelled onto fishing boats and buried at sea. But by the late 1990s, there were few available fishing boats and new EU rules forbade dumping in inshore waters. As a result, the islanders' heaps of waste were growing alarmingly – 'Soon those intrepid hikers in sturdy boots will be scaling our midden mountains with crampons and ropes,' wrote McWatt – and there was an infestation of rats in Lusnaharra and Finnverinnity.

A site at the base of the caves north of Lusnaharra Point was identified by islanders and, bypassing Izzy Wallop, Fergus McKinnon and Hamish McIntosh requested permission from the laird to use it as a community rubbish dump. He refused, via a one-line fax sent through to the post office. Locals had no choice but to burn their rubbish.

In May 1999, the veteran nationalist MP Winnie Ewing stood before the new assembly in Edinburgh and declared, 'The Scottish Parliament, adjourned on the 25th day of March in the year 1707, is hereby reconvened.' McWatt celebrated the event in the *Pibroch*, writing, 'after 292 years . . . better late than never. Though this is only the beginning of our march to self-determination and freedom.'

That summer, there was a quality of 'festive defiance' to the regular blazes which lit up Fascaray, 'like Norse funeral pyres', wrote McWatt. But when the English factor arrived with Marina Chetwynd to prepare for de Uytberg's visit and told the Fascaradians that there were to be no more bonfires, even the most quiescent islanders were roused to indignation.

Up at Calasay, McWatt – a scrupulous conservator who was also remote enough from the Big House to evade surveillance – continued to torch his small heaps of refuse. It was, though, the brazen bonfire of Fergus McKinnon which was said to have been the beacon that finally lit the new land reform movement in Fascaray. Within a week, Fergus McKinnon, along with his wife Maggie and their six children, received an eviction notice. The laird, the factor informed him, had identified McKinnon's Lusnaharra croft, the house where he'd been born and raised, which his father Joseph had worked so hard to improve, as the ideal site for a community garbage dump.

'As Scotland looks ahead to a bold future of autonomy, Fascaray seems to be retreating once more to the servitude of the dark ages,' wrote McWatt in 'Frae Mambeag Brae' in December 1999.

A Granite Ballad – The Reimagining of Grigor McWatt,
Mhairi McPhail (Thackeray College Press, 2016)

I've met members of the laird class and their henchmen many times. That is the tragedy of life in Scotland: it is not possible to tramp the hills between the months of June and September without running into the hee-hawing English classes and their shooting parties.

The old Fascaradian joke often comes to mind:

Q: How many Englishmen can you fit in a shooting brake?

A: Twenty-one. You call one the laird and the other twenty will crawl up his bahookie.

It was some years ago that I had my most memorable encounter with one of the breed. I was with Dougal Mackenzie, the fine pub baritone, an indispensable farmers' 'orraman', and one of the best poachers I ever knew. He could kill a stag and net a prize salmon in a single night and once famously carried an 18-stone stag, its fourteen-point antlers vast and unwieldy as the old Big House chandelier, a full mile, dodging the most vigilant factor and ghillies.

After a few stiffeners at our local howff we made our way into nearby woods. He was armed with his .22 and we soon found ourselves in possession of some handy birds for the pot.

By the time we made our way out of the clearing towards the clachan where Dougal lived with his wife and two children, we found our way blocked by a shooting brake driven by a scowling factor in cloth cap. In the back seat a wee fellow in saffron tweeds was smoking a pipe.

'Where are you going with those birds, my man,' said the wee fellow, whom I recognised as the infamous, Nazi-loving local Laird Montfitchett.

Before Dougal could reply I spoke for both of us.

'I am heading for the warmth of my friend's hearth after a successful excursion in these woods. And, for the record. I am not your man. And neither is my friend.'

'These woods,' replied the wee man, levering himself out of his seat, 'I'll have you know, are *my* woods. As are these hills, this island and every creature in it. I take a very dim view of poachers.'

444

'And how,' I asked with what I like to think of as beguiling inno-cence, 'did you come by these woods and hills?'

Unsure as to whether I was impudent or merely stupid he shook his head and answered: 'I bought them of course, along with the rest of this island.'

'And how did you come by the money to buy Fascaray?'

He stabbed the end of his pipe towards me.

'I inherited it from my father, in the time-honoured fashion.'

'And how, could you tell me, did *he* come by it?'

He was beginning to lose patience.

'From his own father, my grandfather, of course.'

'And how –' I began. He cut me short.

'Look here,' he said, opening the car door and stepping out to give us the full benefit of his five foot-four-inch stature. 'The Montfitchett estates have been in my family for five hundred years.'

'And how did the Montfitchetts come by their wealth five hundred years ago?'

By now he'd concluded that my cheek had got the better of my idiocy.

'You may be unfamiliar with English history but the Montfitchetts were granted our title and lands for services to the king on the battlefield. They fought for it!' he said.

'So,' I said, taking off my jacket, 'I'll fight you for it . . .'

Grigor McWatt, 17 December 1999, *Auchwinnie Pibroch*[11]

---

11 Reprinted in *Wittins: Mair Selected Columns and Essays of Grigor McWatt*, Stravaigin Press, 2011.

I spend the day with Kenny MacLeod and Chic McIntosh in the cart shed on Calasay going through McWatt's collection. We start early and they insist on doing all the heavy lifting. I'm left with the light work of issuing orders, recording McWatt's labels, identifying and relabelling where necessary, and making a start on the inventory. Any small pieces of interest can be added to the museum but we'll leave the larger artefacts in situ and the board can make a decision about their future. They might keep it all here to add value to the An Tobar site when they decide what to do with it, or it might be transported to Am Fasgadh, the Highland Folk Museum, now in Newtonmore, created by Isobel Grant, my spinster nemesis.

Kenny and Chic are tireless and cheerful workers – sanguine about the fossilised rats uncovered in the cab of the old Balnasaig tractor – but they have distinctly opposing views on the value of the collection. Kenny describes himself as a 'modern man', and says 'if it was down tae me I'd chuck the lot', whereas Chic who, like Marco, is prone to whistling, handles every object with reverence. 'All that history!' he says, gently wiping a wooden head yoke as if it were a Michelangelo bronze. Chic, also like Marco, has all the traits of an incipient hoarder. I compile my inventory, gritting my teeth at his chirpy trilling and feeling a professionally improper sympathy for Kenny's position.

It's a long day. Chic has brought some portable lights and a generator so we can work on after dusk, or the gloamin as he calls it. Agnes is having a sleepover with Aaron and Oonagh at Finnverinnity House so I can stay as long as I need to. In the end we leave at 8.30 p.m., before the evening high tide kicks in, making our way back to Ruh and home on Kenny's truck, driving across the strand through a foot of surging sea.

'You can't go home to an empty house without some food in you,' says Kenny. He insists I come into the pub for a meal.

'On the house, like. And there's a bit of a session planned with some of the local musicians.'

First I have to call round to Eck Campbell.

His wife Isa answers the door, wiping her hands on a dish towel.

'He's just finished his tea,' she says.

'I can come back later. Or maybe tomorrow?'

'Not at all! Come away in out of the cold. He's been looking forward to your visit, like a wee boy at Christmas!'

Kirsty, Eck and Isa's youngest grandchild, is there and she joins us as we walk out through the back door and across the yard to a large shed. It's almost as big as their cottage. Eck unlocks the double doors and pulls them open with a flourish.

I peer through the gloom, unable to make out what I'm meant to be looking at.

Eck turns on a flashlight and plays it over a large wooden structure which fills the shed. I'm still not sure what it is. He shines the beam over one end, picking out some faded lettering in flaked red paint: S . .v. . D . rl . ng.

'The *Silver Darling*!'

'You know about her? My grandfather's old herring drifter? Built in 1903 by Forbes of Sandhaven as a two-masted lugger. A beauty.'

My eyes have adjusted to the gloom and now I can see it clearly. Eck strokes the peeling wood lovingly.

'Saw some action, too,' he says.

'Yes, I've been reading about it.'

Kirsty pats the stern with a fond proprietorial air, as if it's a family pet.

'The last laird, de Uytberg, ordered my father to burn it,' explains Eck. 'Said it was an eyesore. But we couldn't do that to her, not after all she'd done for us, for Fascaray, so we hid her in here. I always thought I'd restore her if I ever won the lottery.'

'Well,' I say, 'maybe you just have.'

Ferguson TE20 Tractor – *c.*1947, donated 2011 by Innes MacEwan, grandson of the late Tam Macpherson, formerly of Balnasaig Farm.

head yoke – 2ft 10in, Found in Mammor bog by Calum Donald 'the Plough' MacEwan in 1968. Oak, with a large central rectangular opening set against a narrow comb. At each side of the neckpiece is a broad groove to which horn restraints would have been attached.

bow yoke – withers yoke for draught oxen, 3ft 8in long, with tubular iron semicircular shafts. Retrieved by author from Peigi MacEwan's byre in Doonmara, 1954.

flauchter spade – for turf cutting. Unearthed by author in Calasay on the banks of Loch Aye, 1972.

bog butter keg – made from alder wood, found by Rab McNab in Killiebrae, 1954. Radiocarbon dating to come.

clibber – wooden saddle, donated by Joe Macphee of Lusnaharra in 1947.

kishie – straw peat basket, made and donated by Wullie Maclean of Killiebrae, 1957.

seaweed sickle – bought from Joseph McKinnon of Lusnaharra in 1950.

boulsgan – a holed handstaff for threshing, made from two partly peeled branches hinged with leather. Mid nineteenth century. Found by Tam Macpherson, Balnasaig Farm, 1980.

self-acting back-delivery reaper – Scotia model, horse- or oxen-driven, with manual reaping and mowing attachments, 1855. Retrieved by author from Auchwinnie scrapyard, 1994.

iron laundry mangle – c.1905, donated by Jessie MacDonald, 1973.

copper laundry tub – c.1882, donated by Marsaili MacDonald, 1973.

diesel generator – Muir & Sons model, c.1968. Used to provide electricity to Finnverinnity 1975–2001.

THE SETTING UP OF THE FASCARAY TRUST, WHICH BECAME KNOWN as the 'Militant Tendency' of the Fascaray Preservation Society, could not have come at a better time in terms of political will and public opinion. McWatt, too, seemed to be ready for another fight and threw himself into public life with relish. At the organisation's inaugural meeting in Finnverinnity Hall he quoted his own 'reimagining' of Jean-Jacques Rousseau's *Discourse on the Origin of Inequality*:

The first loon wha fenced the laun and thocht o sayin 'This is mine', an found fowk gowkit enough tae trowe him, was the suith high heid yin o civil society. Frae how many crimes, wars and murders, frae muckle grue an mishanter micht Jock Tamson's bairns hae been saved, by pouin doon the fence, an yollerin: 'Dinnae mind this mak-on: the fruits o the earth belang tae us all, an the Yird itsel tae naebdy.'

Rousseau, McWatt told the local crowd, swelled by a few activists from the mainland, was writing in 1754 from France at a time when, across the water from continental Europe, on the islands of Britain, fresh horrors and misfortunes were being visited on the other half of the Auld Alliance by the English landowning classes who had begun to drive local inhabitants from vast tracts of the Scottish Highlands.

Here, on Fascaray, the island of the great Land Raid of 1946, we have long been Monsieur Rousseau's children. We know the full truth of this: 'Wha loues the laun, awns the laun, an the laun awns him.' Let us pay homage to the philosopher and honour our forebears – McNeil, MacEwan, McPhail, McPhee and MacDonald – by launching our own Reverse Highland Clearance, defending Fergus McKinnon's right to remain with his family on the island of their birth, and finally driving the southern tyrants from Fascaray.

450

It was clear to the islanders that their skirmishes over the Mammor pine plantation and the bigger battle against Sapphire's superquarry a decade earlier had been mere test runs for the all-out war to come. This time, though, they had tactical expertise and an army of supporters to draw on. 'All we had to do was push a button,' wrote McWatt in the *Compendium*, 'and the whole thing went off like Stephenson's Rocket.'

Llew Evans, caretaker of the Big House, had returned to his family in Pontypridd, and Izzy Wallop – 'roused by the new millennium', as she told a news reporter from the *Auchwinnie Pibroch* – volunteered as secretary of the new organisation. Once again, no one publicly stood in her way, though, wrote McWatt in the *Compendium*, 'there were some concerns about her recent performance on behalf of islanders'. The school's head teacher, Wilma Macmillan, was appointed press officer of the Fascaray Trust, and Netta 'the Shop' Macfarlane took on the role of treasurer. In a shrewd political move, Izzy Wallop nominated Hamish McIntosh – one of the oldest and more sceptical indigenous Fascaradians – as chairman of the management committee. He was elected unopposed.

Using the list of addresses harvested during the Sapphire years, they sent out mailshots to potential supporters and within a month had raised the £2,000 needed to register the Fascaray Trust as a charitable fund, produce a manifesto and call a press conference in Auchwinnie.

Pictures were taken by the *Pibroch* photographer of the McKinnon family (the youngest child, Lorna, a pretty six-year-old putto with red curls, was strategically placed in front of her less favoured older siblings), standing in the flickering shadows of a bonfire which blazed outside their croft. Despite the heroic improvements a generation ago by Fergus's father, Joseph, the house now looked serviceably (for the purposes of the campaign) decrepit. The photograph was used by the *Guardian* as the centrepiece of a double-page spread on 'the iniquities of Scotland's land laws'.

Even the *Daily Telegraph*, whose natural sympathies were with the feudal overlords rather than their serfs, and who failed to send a reporter to the press conference in Auchwinnie, felt compelled to use the photograph, albeit with a brief caption: 'The McKinnon family on the Scottish island of Fascaray: their eviction notice has prompted a local rebellion. Baron Giles de Uytberg, Laird of Fascaray, who has plans to modernise the remote island, has hit back at "socialist hotheads fomenting trouble". The island's most famous export is the hit song "Hame tae Fascaray", composed by local poet Grigor McWatt.'

This time, the campaigning islanders had a new ally – the World Wide Web. Izzy Wallop arranged a dial-up Internet connection in Finnverinnity. There were some teething problems, and the service was erratic, but when it worked, word of the islanders' cause spread around the globe almost at the speed of light. A dedicated bank account was set up to accommodate donations sent in from all over the country, as well as from Canada, New Zealand, America and Ireland. Famous and would-be famous personalities from the world of television, film and radio queued to join the cause.

A London chef with two Michelin stars and a Scottish grandmother devised a dish, the Fascaradian Fish Supper, to lend his support. Sean Connery was said to be interested in the campaign, as were a championship golfer, an Olympian cyclist and two Scots Premier League footballers (one dedicated his hat-trick at Hampden Park 'to the people of Fascaray'). A Hollywood leading man volunteered to be the 'face' of the Fascaray Trust but, for the first time in his career, didn't even get a screen test: the role was already taken. The unmistakable, wind-blasted features of Grigor McWatt, grimacing under a beret, briar pipe clamped between his teeth – 'The Popeye of the North' as the *Daily Telegraph* unkindly called him – conferred what the marketing men called 'brand awareness' on the cause.

Izzy Wallop, unconventionally telegenic with her wild hair and Gypsy Rose Lee style, was regularly interviewed as 'island spokeswoman' on the regional television news, although her patrician manner and 'booming English accent' continued to jar with some islanders.

But when she received an eviction notice from de Uytberg's factor, the island united behind her and even McWatt took up her case, overlooking Wallop's origins and inveighing in the *Auchwinnie Pibroch* against 'a southern carpetbagger who, in a grotesque replay of the infamous clearances of the last century, would, on a whim, turn Fascaradians out of their homes to survive as best they can against the harshest elements'.

De Uytberg, 'provoked beyond endurance', as he told the *Scotsman* and the *Daily Telegraph*, issued eviction notices against Wilma Macmillan at the schoolhouse, the Macfarlanes at the shop and Hamish McIntosh, whose well-situated croft on the Doonmara cliffs had been, according to the factor, 'earmarked as a pied-à-terre for de Uytberg's assistant Marina Chetwynd'.

More sensationally, and counterproductively, notice to quit was also served on Grigor McWatt. The development was described in the *Herald* newspaper as 'the biggest own goal since Tom Boyd handed one to Brazil in the opening game of the World Cup'. Once more McWatt's portrait graced the papers and the TV news, alongside pictures of Bob Dylan, Rod Stewart and other famous interpreters of 'Hame tae Fascaray'.

Despite the outcry, de Uytberg refused to budge. Hamish McIntosh, now widowed and increasingly infirm, had no appetite for the fray and moved to a residential care home in Auchwinnie. The other eviction notices remained in place. And so did Fergie McKinnon, Izzy Wallop, Wilma Macmillan, the Macfarlanes and Grigor McWatt.

A Granite Ballad – The Reimagining of Grigor McWatt,
Mhairi McPhail (Thackeray College Press, 2016)

Sang tae the Men o Scotland

Men o Scotland, why d'ye scodge
Fur the lairds who keep ye laich?
Why d'ye fash yerselves tae steek
Thon tyrant's fancy duds an breeks?

Why d'ye feed an cleid an hain,
Frae the cradlie tae the tuim
They unthankit bummers wha
Wid sook yer sweit an waucht yer bluid?

The seed ye sawed, anither hairsts;
The gowd ye find, anither reives;
The plaid ye flaucht, anither wears;
Yer ain claymore, anither bears.

Wi pleuch an pattle, howe an luim,
Scart yer graff an mak yer tuim
Flaucht yer shroud – an you maun learn,
That Scotia braw will be yer urn.

Grigor McWatt, efter Percy Bysshe Shelley, 1999[12]

TWO TENSE MONTHS PASSED AND THERE WAS NO SIGN OF A BAILIFF or the factor and no further communication from the laird or his lawyers.

'We have invited de Witless to choose his second for a duel and have yet to hear a peep out of him,' wrote McWatt.

It finally emerged that de Uytberg had been fighting a more bitter battle closer to home and it was this, rather than the local stramash in his northern seat, that finally dislodged the latest Laird of Fascaray.

His wife Claudia, who had recently learned of de Uytberg's affair with his personal assistant, had moved out of their Buckinghamshire mansion, set up home in their Monaco apartment, and was demanding a large sum in alimony.

News of the marital break-up leaked out in one of the newspaper gossip columns down south, and by the time it had been confirmed in the *Herald*, it was as a footnote to the even bigger news that de Uytberg had put Fascaray up for sale to pay for the divorce. 'You could say,' McWatt wrote, 'that every Claudia has a silver lining. De Uytberg's personal embarrassments might mean a bright new future for Fascaradians. At last we have a real chance of wresting our land from distant despots and becoming masters of our own destiny.'

The brochure produced by a plutocratic estate agency in London was, wrote McWatt, 'as monumental as the Book of Kells' and full of shiny photographs of the island's beauty spots – Beinn Mammor, Loch Och, Lusnaharra, the Lingel, Kilgurnock Falls, Doonmara cliffs – 'taken at crafty angles to avoid inexpedient images which might suggest that people, as well as stags and salmon, actually live here'. There was an aerial shot of the Big House, 'providing a necessary distance on some of the external dilapidation, which any prospective buyer might rightly infer promises greater dilapidation within'.

The pictures were all taken in blazing sunshine and under cloudless skies – such a rare meteorological occurrence on the island (the last spell of continuous good weather had been two days the previous May) that, according to McWatt, technologically savvy Fascaradians put the Aegean gloss down to 'digital trickery'.

Whatever the provenance of the photos, the island looked ravishing. The asking price was £1.5m, preposterously high to the islanders, even with the steady stream of donations, but well within the budget of the average oligarch looking for an amusing hideaway. It seemed, however, that the oligarchs were holding back. It was a jittery time in the world financial markets and, with all the publicity generated by the Fascaray Trust, any potential owner seeking a quiet retreat on a secluded island for a couple of months' fishing and shooting a year might reasonably decide to look elsewhere. It was impossible to ignore the fact that there were natives on Fascaray. And they were restless.

A Granite Ballad – The Reimagining of Grigor McWatt,
Mhairi McPhail (Thackeray College Press, 2016)

Ma Hert it Pines

Ma hert it sairly pines
Fur pals wha've ganged tae soon,
Fur aw the rose-lipt quines
An mony a licht-fit loon.

By burns tae braid fur lowpin,
The licht-fit loons lie now,
The rose-lipt quines are doverin
In glens whaur roses dowe.

Grigor McWatt, efter A. E. Housman, 2000[13]

13   *Thoog a Poog*, Smeddum Beuks, 2010.

There is no Abbotsford Close near Abbotsford, Walter Scott's country mansion in the Borders, but there are three Abbotsford Drives in Fife and one in East Dunbartonshire. The electoral registers yield no further leads so Ailish, at my insistence, spends a day driving round housing projects within two hours of Glasgow, asking puzzled residents for sightings of McWatt's Jean.

'Jean? Is it a Jean you were looking for? There's nane in oor street but there'll be a fair few of them aboot the toun. It's no exactly an unusual name,' one old ex-miner told her. 'But I doot any Jean roon here wid be pally wi a poet.'

There is a hint of triumph in Ailish's voice as she phones me with news of her failure. There were Jeans all right, Ailish tells me, but they were either long-dead great-grannies decades older than McWatt, or Jeans and Jeannies way too young to fit the story. After a period of obscurity, the old-fashioned names are coming back. I guess Agnes is part of that demographic.

Ailish's time was wasted, as was my money – her expenses' invoice includes the cost of two meals, petrol and 'wear and tear' to her car. The Auchwinnie Board, which has agreed to cover the cost of restoring the *Silver Darling*, is leaning on me about the project's budget. I ignore Ailish's petulant tone. It's not going to be easy, I agree. But in an age of surveillance, no one can hide forever. Jean, McWatt's lost love and agent of Lilias's destruction, could have married, divorced, changed her name several times over, emigrated, I concede. She could be dead. But for the sake of our project, for McWatt's legacy, for Fascaray, we've got to keep trying.

'Your job, my job too, depends on finding out more about this woman. Just do it,' I tell her.

Then this afternoon, I turn up a clue myself. It is in the 328-page supplementary volume to *Jamieson's Dictionary*, which I idly open to check a reference. The word I am looking for, 'schirryve', was used as a mystifying sign-off by McWatt in a 1969 letter to Goodsir Smith ('frae aine schirryve tae anither') that turned up at the National Library in a box of miscellaneous documents salvaged from an Inverleith house clearance.

There it is, on page 214 of McWatt's copy of the *Jamieson's* supplement; 'schirryve: a poet, form of schryve, to shrive, used by Dunbar in his Tabill of Confessioun'. There also, pressed between pages 214 and 215, is an envelope, peach-coloured, open and empty. The address on the front – 'McWatt, Calasay, Fascaray, Scotland' – is written in the same blue ink, and in the same handwriting, as the surviving letters from Jean. The postmark, dated 30 May 1971, reads 'Woking, Surrey'.

Woking, an Internet search confirms, is a large town in the south of England, part of the London commuter belt. Bonnie Jean could, of course, simply have been visiting the town in 1971, but the Wikipedia entry suggests it's an improbable holiday destination. A further search reveals an Abbotsford Close in the town. This has to be more than coincidence. It never occurred to me to look for McWatt's Highland Muse south of the border. There will be time for questions about her flight from the north later. For now, at last, we're on her trail.

Hame Thochts frae Abraid

Och, tae be in Fascaray
Noo that April's there,
An wha stravaigs in Fascaray
Sees, wi oot compare,
That the bonnie broom is in fu bloom
While the lintie sings on the rowan bough
In Fascaray – the nou.

An efter April, follaes May,
An the laverock nests, an the swallaes play,
An the haw-buss by the drystane dyke
Hings oer the gress an chucks its flooers
Like faws o snaw neath buchtit bouers.
The canny throstle gies an encore,
In case ye think he minds nae mair
That first braw fashless boch!
Though the hauch looks coorse wi cranreuch dew
It'll luik sae cantie when the sun gilds new
The gowan, flooer o blythesome herts
– Brichter than flooers frae furrin pairts.

Grigor McWatt, efter Robert Browning, 2000[14]

14 *Thoog a Poog*, Smeddum Beuks, 2010.

HISTORY WAS ON FASCARAY'S SIDE. IN LATE MAY 2000, THE NEW Scottish government passed a bill abolishing feudal tenure and set up a fund to help communities buy out their land. Word was that the MSPs down in Edinburgh would match whatever sum the Fascaray Trust managed to raise. The fight for the island moved to a new stage. Publicity attracted by the highest profile supporters (a Harry Potter star and a James Bond villain threw in their lot with the islanders) drew in thousands more individual donations, mostly from Canada and New Zealand, amounting to a total of £520,000.

A logo for the Trust was designed – two linked circles in green and blue representing an aerial view of the island, with a splash of red in the top right to denote Calasay. Mugs and posters were produced and T-shirts, with slogans including 'Fascaray Freedom Fighter' and 'Nae Lairds Here!', were printed. Demand for the mail-order merchandise was so high that the abandoned Fascaradian Museum of Island Life was co-opted by the Trust and volunteers worked for three weeks sorting, packing and dispatching the items. It was the nearest Fascaray had ever known to full employment.

One T-shirt bearing a quote from McWatt, 'An End tae Clearance and Interference', became a global bestseller after it was worn by an American rock star at the Glastonbury Festival in June. It raised £4,000 for the Trust in two months before it became a victim of its own success; pirated copies were made and a few could still be found for sale on stalls in Argyle Street, Glasgow, Canal Street, New York, and Petticoat Lane, London, long after Fascaray finally faded from the news.

There were benefit concerts in Auckland, Sydney and Toronto, and nearer home, as part of the Celtic Connections Festival in Glasgow, a distinguished roster of Scottish musicians including Dick Gaughan, Michael Marra and Shooglenifty 'sang out for Fascaray', along with the Chieftains from Ireland, harpists from Brittany and a group of Canadian step dancers. Van Morrison was busy but sent a message of support and

461

rumours that Bob Dylan was going to turn up at the festival and perform – 'paying his dues' for 'Hame tae Fascaray' – were useful for ticket sales but proved unfounded. Even without Dylan, however, the Celtic Connections concerts raised a further £13,700 for the Trust.

On the morning of 12 September 2000, as the sale of Fascaray was taking place in London, islanders ventured out in a rainstorm to gather in the village hall where they would learn their fate. The estate agents were accepting bids over the phone but Izzy Wallop had gone down to the Knightsbridge auction house to guarantee fair play – and additional publicity – for the Fascaradian cause.

In Finnverinnity Hall, the focus of attention was not on Fergus McKinnon, who stood tense and alone on stage, but on the satellite phone in his hand, which would ring as soon as the result of the sale was known. The main competitor to the Trust's bid was a property tycoon from Qatar with, it seemed, unlimited funds. In the tense silence of Finnverinnity Hall, the phone rang. It was Izzy. The tycoon had abruptly pulled out of the auction.[15] Fascaray was now owned by the people of Fascaray.

The community buyout was marked that night by a raucous session at the Finnverinnity Inn and the following week by the erection of a new standing stone – the Clach na Saorsa, or Freedom Stone, engraved with the names of the Fascaray Five – on Mammor's slopes, launching four days of drinking, dancing, feasting and fireworks that would not have disappointed the most dissolute Viking marauder. A flotilla of boats sailed to and from Finnverinnity over the next two weeks, disgorging high-profile supporters, members of the Scottish Parliament and Westminster MPs getting in on the act, folk from neighbouring islands and the mainland who didn't often get the chance of a good hoolie, as well as journalists who came to file stories and ended up partying with the rest of them, staying on in the Fascaray Hotel. Like its owner, the hotel was getting increasingly seedy but the art deco cocktail cabinet remained well stocked and prices were still advantageous for expenses purposes.

15 Thierry Malouf, owner of Severine Investments, later revealed in an interview with the *Herald* that he had been misinformed about Fascaray's location and on learning, mid-bid, that the island was in the inhospitable north rather than the Mediterranean, and that in the milder months 'small biting insects known as midges swarmed to such an extent that protective clothing had to be worn', he withdrew his offer.

McWatt was the man of the hour and only mildly protested when he was cheered at the unveiling of the Clach na Saorsa and presented with a parchment scroll from the Trust which declared him a 'Freeman of Fascaray'. That evening, for the only time on record since the 1960s, the poet sat without protest as visitors, islanders and press roared out all five verses, with choruses, of 'Hame tae Fascaray' in the Finnverinnity Inn. It was even reported that a triumphant smile flickered briefly over the poet's otherwise impassive face.

The anthem was sung so loudly it was said that the dolphins fled the bay, the guga abandoned their nests on Plodda and Grodda, and over in Auchwinnie, children were woken in their beds by the din of celebration carried by the steady westerly wind over the water from the newly liberated island.

A Granite Ballad – The Reimagining of Grigor McWatt,
Mhairi McPhail (Thackeray College Press, 2016)

Tae Saorsa

We kennt ye of auld,
Och Saorsa sae bold,
By the licht o oor eyes
An the stories we told.

Ye've been exiled a while,
Frae Scotia sae puir,
We've waited sae lang,
Fur this happiest oor.

Och, slow brakt the day,
An naebdy cried oot,
Fur the dead hand o tyranny,
Claucht at oor throat.

But then ye returned,
Wi tears doon yer face,
When you saw oor oppression
An England's disgrace.

Frae the tuims o oor deid
Yer smeddum inspires,
Nae mair English scoonrels
Can smuir oot oor fires.

Grigor McWatt, efter Rudyard Kipling, 2000[16]

16   *Thoog a Poog*, Smeddum Beuks, 2010.

Forty years ago, in these pages, I wrote: 'If any of modernity's contrivances make a jot of improvement to our lives, I'll eat my bunnet.'

Well, dear reader, it is time for me to remove my titfer, present it on a platter, apply knife and fork, chew vigorously and swallow it. For I have been persuaded finally by the enthusiasm of fellow islanders that modernity has its place, even here, on our wee island of timeless wonders.

Recently, on a glorious September evening when the rain had cleared, the wind was just brisk enough to keep the midges away and the setting sun was bruising the sky behind Beinn Mammor, a group of locals stood at the head of Finnverinnity Glen silently gazing towards a view in which I have long exulted.

Chic McIntosh was the first to speak.

'Will you look at that . . .' he said.

'Superb,' said Fergus McKinnon.

'Takes the breath away,' added Kenny MacLeod.

'Aye,' agreed Eck Campbell. 'Fantastic. Makes a hell of a racket but, by God, it's worth it.'

The object of their admiration was not the evening flight of the corbies towards the mountain, which reared majestically against the spreading contusion of the sky, but a noisy metal drum housed in a wooden shack below Kilgurnock Falls. The new island hydro turbine plant, bought and installed twelve months after the buyout with a loan from the recently-elected Scottish Parliament, has given Fascaray its first island-wide supply of electricity. Last month, when the hydro was switched on, the old generators were moved into storage and the newly rewired lights remained on in the inn, it was the occasion of another celebratory party that saw in the dawn. And I rejoiced with them, washing down my old bunnet with an emollient dram.

Grigor McWatt, October 2001, *Auchwinnie Pibroch*[17]

17 *Wittins: More Selected Columns and Essays of Grigor McWatt*, Stravaigin Press, 2011.

He Wisses fur the Cloots o Heiv'n

Gin Ah'd the heiv'ns browstert cloots,
Enwrocht wi gowd an siller licht,
The blae an the mirk an the daurk cloots
O nicht an licht an the gloamin,
Ah wud spreid the cloots aneath yer feit:
But Ah, bein skint, hae anely ma dwaums;
Ah hae spreid ma dwaums aneath yer feit;
Stramp doucely fur ye stramp oan ma dwaums.

Grigor McWatt, efter W. B. Yeats, 2001[18]

---

18 *Thoog a Poog*, Smeddum Beuks, 2010.

A YEAR AFTER THE BUYOUT, FASCARAY WAS LOOKING IN BETTER shape than it had done for centuries. The new hydro plant was up and running, providing twenty-four-hour power to the island for the first time in its history, essential repairs had been carried out, crofts and cottages were restored as new residents arrived – romantic idealists and borderline survivalists escaping cities, former lives or encroaching doom, or pragmatists in search of cheap housing, new lives and business opportunities. An extension was built at the school to accommodate the surge in pupil numbers, a new system of rubbish disposal was put in place with a landfill site behind Lusnaharra Point, the plastic debris washed up on the shore was regularly cleaned by parties of schoolchildren and adult volunteers, and the Scottish government had agreed to underwrite the cost of a new pier, which would allow bigger boats, with facilities for cars, to visit the island.

De Uytberg's Finnverinnity Airport now had a passenger lounge – a recommissioned bus shelter – and GaelAir had begun to run chartered flights, in an eighteen-seat De Havilland Twin Otter, from the mainland. The herring-packing shed became the permanent office of the Trust with Izzy Wallop retaining her post as full-time, salaried secretary.

It seemed fitting that, while the islanders were enjoying the benefits of self-determination and sprucing up their homes, the Big House was crumbling further. Apart from its leaking roof, collapsing chimneys and broken windows, burst pipes had brought down ceilings, wrecked rooms and covered walls with a stinking slime. The Trust had investigated the possibility of applying for government money to restore it and turn it into a community centre or a hotel – the former Temperance Hotel was up for sale again (the owner had gone bankrupt) while Marsaili MacDonald was struggling to keep the Bothy going. But that was a grant too far. There were other demands pressing in on the new parliament and the Big House had to be sold.

Occasionally a helicopter would bring in parties of potential buyers attracted by the notion of being 'a genuine Scottish laird'. But none returned for a second viewing. The title of laird was now only honorary – instead of the entire island, the new owners of Finnverinnity House would be acquiring an impenetrably overgrown nine-acre garden and an enormous, ugly shell of a house in need of urgent repair.

Finnverinnity House was eventually sold in 2002, at a third of its asking price, to Reinhardt Schneider, a German wholefood entrepreneur turned artist. Schneider had seen a photograph of the island in a Sunday supplement and flown in from Hamburg with a chequebook. Proceeds of the sale would go towards repaying the government loan for the hydro plant. Schneider planned to turn the stables into a studio while Greta, his third wife, a former dancer, wanted to create a 'sensory garden' in the shrubbery.

Schneider was said by McWatt, writing in a May 2002 entry in the *Compendium*, to have 'cut a flamboyant figure with his ponytail, earrings and blue tartan suit, when he first entered the Finnverinnity Inn. But Fascaradians, by now used to the idiosyncratic costumes of the Balnasaig crowd, turned to stare only when Schneider asked the barman, Kenny MacLeod, for "a Perrier vater".'

Schneider told the silent drinkers that he and his wife planned to live full-time on Fascaray with their three-month-old daughter. 'The city is finished,' he said. 'The pollution, the vibrations. All wrong. Here we can be free.'

He explained that he had Scottish roots – 'the first wife of his mother's great-grandfather had once been married to an Armstrong. Hence the tartan suit.'

According to McWatt, 'the new laird claimed he had "grown up with the great Walter Scott and Bobby Burns", pronouncing Walter as Valter. He then raised his glass of Irn-Bru (no Perrier to be found) in a toast to "Ivanhoe! Auld Lang!"'

A Granite Ballad – The Reimagining of Grigor McWatt,
Mhairi McPhail (Thackeray College Press, 2016)

INVENTORY OF SCOTS WORDS
DESCRIBING FINE WEATHER

daak – a lull in bad, windy weather

deow – gentle rain

gludder – fleeting sunshine between showers

Maag's thirl – light in the south-west after storm indicating clearer weather

maumie – soft, mild

pet day – day of fine weather in the midst of a long spell of bad weather

roosie – glint of light through clouds, portending storms

soneblenk – a short spell of sunshine, usually followed by showers

Tormud's thirl – brief interval of fine weather before heavy rain

Grigor McWatt, 2002, *The Fascaray Compendium*

WITHIN THREE YEARS OF THE COMMUNITY BUYOUT, DIVISIONS were beginning to emerge and Fascaray was showing signs of descending into what McWatt later termed 'uncivil war'. There were four main factions: English incomers, Scottish incomers, Balnasaig Seekers (past and present) and the natives, among whom was counted McWatt, whose ancestral connections, fame and more than sixty years' residence had finally conferred on him indigenous status.

Among the new English contingent were the Taylors, Dick and Sandra, a couple of empty-nesters from Hampshire who planned to use their savings, his construction skills and her culinary artistry to open a tea room and B&B in the old Finnverinnity kirk, while Nigel Parsons, a retired naval officer from Wiltshire, bought two neighbouring fishermen's cottages which he was converting into a single home with his wife Gill. As McWatt noted in the *Compendium*, both couples unwittingly offended local sensibilities within a month of their arrival; the Taylors by hoisting a Union Jack flag above the kirk and the Parsons by letting slip their plan to operate a private ferry service on Sundays to and from Auchwinnie. By now, few Fascaradians who identified themselves as religious, Catholic or Protestant, made the journey across the Clinch to attend church services on Saturdays, settling instead for twice-monthly prayer meetings led by a peripatetic preacher in Finnverinnity Hall or monthly Masses in Fergus McKinnon's converted byre in Lusnaharra. But old sabbatarian habits died hard and in many Finnverinnity households, work, or play – as well as running, humming or whistling – were still forbidden on the Lord's Day and any incomer careless enough to peg out their laundry on a clothes line on a Sunday could expect a stern reprimand from church elders.

The Lusnaharra population was boosted by the arrival of a young Scots family from Edinburgh. Ben and Alison Guthrie moved into Father Col's old presbytery cottage with their three children and planned to turn the derelict Church of the Sacred Heart and Immaculate Mary into an arts centre, restaurant and pottery workshop – 'Just what the island needs: more damned pottery!' wrote McWatt.

Balnasaig Sanctuary had expanded further and, to create overspill accommodation for the influx of visitors, the Seekers acquired fifteen acres from Tam Macpherson's old farm to create a 'tepee campsite'. Several Balnasaig pilgrims went on to become permanent residents, moving into the old servants' quarters of the Lodge to assist with the burgeoning business and set up a print workshop to disseminate the teachings of Evelyn Fletcher and Neville Booth to a wider audience.

McWatt noted in the *Compendium* that there were also several 'outliers' on the island: new residents whose uncategorisable origins meant that 'all factions are equally cordial, or equally hostile, towards them'. This party included Mr Kennedy, the head teacher at Finnverinnity Primary, 'a young Irishman who keeps a diplomatic distance from the fray'; the Schneiders, 'whose free-ranging transcendental inclinations are not to the taste of the Seekers and whose fondness for tartan and commitment to their indefinable art perplexes the Scots'; and the recently arrived van Donks, a Dutch couple, 'aloof introverts in their forties', who were running an Internet company selling wild-flower plug plants from their nursery garden and polytunnels on Peigi MacEwan's old croft in Doonmara. McWatt reported that the van Donks were never seen in the pub or shop and avoided any contact with locals, making trips on their speedboat to Auchwinnie for supplies.

At first, as Trust secretary, Izzy Wallop was a popular figure around the island with those residents, mostly English incomers, whose kitchen extensions and double-glazed conservatories she offered to finance, and her release of a grant to assist the construction of a series of 'eco cottages' at Balnasaig finally healed her thirty-year rift with Evelyn over the affair with Neville.

But native Fascaradians and Scots incomers were less successful with grant applications to the Trust and, wrote McWatt, their scepticism became mutinous when funds were allocated to restore the derelict manse in Finnverinnity and, once building work was completed, Izzy herself moved in. Wallop had, noted McWatt in a *Compendium* entry in January 2003, earned 'the unique distinction of making enemies among all parties on the island'. She had become increasingly eccentric and indiscreet, describing the indigenous Fascaradians in one newspaper interview as 'ungrateful aborigines'. (Her defence was that she had thought this part of the interview had been 'off the record'.)

Her final fall from grace came after a profile in a weekend newspaper interview, which described her appearance ('as if one of Macbeth's witches had been cast as Titania') and her home ('a version of Doctor Who's Tardis in which the exterior gives no clue to the dispensation within; this handsome Georgian house proves to be a shambolic five-bedroom landfill site on which Izzy Wallop perches, a prattling Winnie from Beckett's *Happy Days*'), and the heap of discarded bottles at the bottom of her garden ('to achieve "spiritual equilibrium", she tells me, she meditates three times a day. There is evidence that the regular application of Sauvignon Blanc also plays a part in her personal path to enlightenment.').

'She has', wrote McWatt, 'held the island up to ridicule,' and her attitude and presentation were not going to help Fascaray's future applications for government funding. Izzy Wallop had become a liability. McWatt argued in his *Pibroch* column of 18 October 2003: 'The sooner a certain blow-in blows out of Fascaray, the better it will be for all of us. This is not so much a case of the merchants in the temple as the bampots in the basilica. I hesitate to say that one yearns for the return of the Montfitchetts but there is no doubt that, after all our struggles for self-determination and justice, the dignity and peace of our lovely island have been severely compromised by the antics of recent incomers.'

A Granite Ballad – The Reimagining of Grigor McWatt,
Mhairi McPhail (Thackeray College Press, 2016)

Calasay

In ma gab is ma hend.
Ane efter th'ither
Hooses heeze an faw, crottle, are eiked,
Cleared, malafoustert, sturkened, or in their steid,
Is bog, midden, bungalow or gowf links.

Auld stane tae new schemes, auld wid tae new gleed,
Auld gleed tae yask an yask tae yird
Which is awready flesh, fur an keech,
Bane o man an beast, windlestrae an leaf.

Hooses leeve an dee: there's a time fer biggin
An a time fer leevin an fer breedin
An a time fer wind tae crack the lowsin windae
An tae shoogle the skiftin where the mousie pugs
An tae shoogle the loorach hingins braidit wi seelent ensenzie.

Grigor McWatt, efter T. S. Eliot, 2003[19]

19   *Thoog a Poog*, Smeddum Beuks, 2010.

For a recluse, McWatt seemed better attuned to the island scuttlebutt than I could ever be. In this he is like my daughter, whose curiosity about people is limitless. We are both at work at our respective wings of the kitchen table – she is setting out paints, brushes and a jar of water – and I'm tuning out her chatter about the latest insights and revelations from school. 'And then Finn said . . . So Kirsty told him . . . And Henry butt in . . . But Oonagh . . . And Mr Kennedy . . .' Gradually, it fades to distant generic birdsong, of the soothing, non-territorial kind.

The *Compendium* entry for 2006 is particularly detailed: a sign, perhaps, that after more than six decades McWatt had finally fully integrated on the island. Or maybe it's just that more happened that year.

'The blow-in has finally blown out, taking another long-standing settler with her,' he wrote. Evelyn Fletcher was apparently stoical when Neville Booth failed to return from his evening's meditation by the standing stones of Drumnish.

Nor did Fletcher flinch 'when it emerged the following morning that Neville had picked up a suitcase, packed and secreted in an empty tepee the previous week, and left the island at midnight with Izzy Wallop on a chartered speedboat from Auchwinnie'. The pair were said to be heading, via Glasgow Airport, to a Cycladic island in Greece to found a new community 'based on love and light' and funded – 'though the police could never pin anything on the pair' – by donations diverted from the Fascaray Trust.

Agnes interrupts: 'You know Nigel who does the boat trips?'

'Hmm . . .'

'Well, Kirsty said he saw some sharks. Just near Fascaray? Like *real* sharks, only this kind don't have teeth so they won't bite you?'

'Imagine that!' I say, too preoccupied to imagine anything. With all this documented reality to contend with, I've no time for speculation.

In the *Auchwinnie Pibroch*, McWatt recorded another, sadder departure from the island – Marsaili MacDonald, widow of the *Morag May* hero Jamie, mother of three and plucky owner and manager of the Bothy hostel, died of cancer aged sixty-eight. Relatives flew in from England, Canada, America and New Zealand for the requiem Mass, held in Auchwinnie's Catholic church before a 'sombre sea crossing' for a blessing at Fergus McKinnon's byre chapel and burial next to the grave of her late husband Jamie in Lusnaharra churchyard. 'It was', wrote McWatt in the *Auchwinnie Pibroch*, 'the nearest thing Fascaray has had to a state funeral.'

The same year also saw the death of the island's former postman, Shuggie MacLeod. McWatt was a pall bearer at the kirk service in Auchwinnie, 'at which', he wrote, 'we delivered our beloved postie to the final sorting office'.

Another family of what McWatt called 'Sassenach dreamers' arrived, 'threatening to destabilise our cultural ecology further'. Piers Aubrey, a former probation officer and local councillor from London, and his partner Jinny, a homeopath, moved into the old McGregor croft in Tilliecuddy with their daughter Seren and newborn Henry.

Aubrey, 'rangy, raw-boned and earnest', wore 'wire-rimmed glasses of the type popularised by John Lennon', devoted himself to the restoration of the croft and cultivation of organic vegetables and, McWatt noted disapprovingly in the *Compendium*, was 'rarely seen in the pub and has made it plain that he disapproves of our guga hunt'.

As the Aubreys arrived, the Taylors left – 'signalling, I hope, the start of an English evacuation', wrote McWatt – selling up their kirk B&B and moving to Gibraltar where 'presumably they'll find the politics as well as the climate more congenial'. In September that year there was more sensational news of an 'island flitting' that made national headlines after a midnight police raid – 'the first time the polis have been seen on the island since the postbox explosion of 1953', according to McWatt. Following a local tip-off, a team of policemen arrived at Doonmara at midnight from the mainland on a fleet of inflatable boats and, after a thorough search of their premises, escorted the van Donks from Fascaray in handcuffs. The couple had, it emerged, been selling not cornflowers and cowslips grown in their polytunnel nursery but marijuana.

'If only they'd been more respectful of local traditions and customs, these Dutch incomers might still be flogging their exotic wares on the quiet from Doonmara and the authorities would be none the the wiser,'

McWatt wrote in 2007, when the van Donks' case came to trial. 'After all, in this part of the world we have an ingrained suspicion of authority and regular recourse to mind-altering substances, in the form of a warming dram or two at our local howff. But there is a lesson here for all incomers: whatever their origins, ambitions and inclinations, Fascaray must come first. More than eight thousand years of community and culture cannot be ignored and overridden by money-grabbing outsiders with their own agendas.'

Local news, national news, history, polemic, but no mention of Jean here nor, as far I can see, in the whole of *The Fascaray Compendium*. I must phone Ailish. Time is running out.

Agnes, brushing a watercolour wash over a new page in her sketchbook, is still at it: '. . . and then Kirsty's grandad, you know, Eck? They call him Wee Eck even though –'

'Sorry, honey. Mommy's got to work.'

Ah Mind, Och Aye, Ah Mind

Ah mind, och aye, Ah mind,
The huis whaur Ah wis born,
The booral windae whaur the sun
Cam keekin in at morn;
He niver cam a prink too rath,
Nor brocht too lang a day,
But hou Ah aften wissed the nicht
Had wheeched ma pech away.

Ah mind, och aye, Ah mind,
The clonger crammasie,
The cuckoo-brogue an lilikins,
That grew alang the wynd.
The laylock whaur the rabbin bigged
An whaur ma faither sheuched
The rowan on ma birthday
Ah scrieve ablo its beuchs.

Ah mind, och aye, Ah mind,
Whaur aince Ah used tae swee,
An thocht the air maun breenge as fresh
Tae swallaes flichtin free;
Ma smeddum flew in fedders then,
That is sae wechtie nou,
An simmer burns could barely cuil
The fiver oan ma brou.

Ah mind, och aye, Ah mind,
The bunnet firs sae heich;
Ah used tae think their spirlie taps,

Were scuffin up the sky:
It wis a bairnie's fancy,
An noo it gars me pain;
I'm faurer nou frae paradise
Than when Ah wis a wean.

Grigor McWatt, efter Thomas Hood, 2008[20]

20   *Thoog a Poog,* Smeddum Beuks, 2010.

THE ISLAND FACED A BIGGER CHALLENGE FROM 'PROFIT-SEEKING outsiders' in 2009, when Archie Tupper, a billionaire leisure-complex magnate from Atlanta, Georgia, alighted on Calasay as a perfect location for his most northerly golf resort. Tupper, whose great-grandmother, a Maccree, was said to be distantly related to the Lusnaharra MacRaes, finding himself between divorces, had visited the region in May 2009 on a sentimental journey by private plane, landing at an airstrip near Auchwinnie (Fascaray Airport runway was too small to accommodate his luxury executive jet). He travelled on to the island by speedboat on a midge-free day of remarkably fine weather, was amazed by the sapphire seas and alabaster beaches and decided that the island's satellite islet, Calasay, was the perfect location for a Tupper Links Leisure Resort.

'This place beats the Caribbean,' he told a reporter from the *Auchwinnie Pibroch*. 'It's a real peach, waiting to be plucked. A world-beater.' He planned to build a causeway and bridge across the strand from Ruh and a clubhouse with 'five-star boutique hotel facilities' on the cliffs. He didn't mention directly the inconvenient presence of An Tobar, its land and ancillary buildings, but made a passing reference to 'a few tumbledown shacks'.

The Fascaray Trust rejected the plan outright, but Tupper, undeterred, applied to Auchwinnie Council, which had a veto over development in the region. Despite the promise of new jobs and the ancillary benefits of high-spending tourism in the area, Auchwinnie Council bowed to pressure from local lobbyists – and several impassioned columns from McWatt in the *Pibroch* – and also turned down Tupper's plan.

Celebrations in Fascaray were short-lived. The tycoon, aided by his Wall Street law firm, was used to getting his own way and appealed directly to the Scottish government, now installed in its expensive new Parliament building in Holyrood. To the dismay of many and the outrage of McWatt, the national government acceded to Tupper, citing progress, and the jobs and revenue the development would bring to the region.

'Calasay's protected status as a Site of Special Scientific Interest has proved to be as much use as a caunle in a hairiken,' wrote McWatt in the *Pibroch*. Once again, he cited Burns, adapting the famous 1791 poem to read: *'We're bought and sold by Yankee gold / Such a parcel of rogues in a nation!'* The islanders of Fascaray faced a new fight and their own devolved national government, Scots to a man and a woman, had sided with the enemy.

To McWatt it was a shocking paradox that while Holyrood had given a green light for the desecration of Calasay, it was an Englishman who came to their aid. *'Tapsalteerie is lowsed ootower the warld,'* McWatt wrote in the *Compendium*, quoting his own 1946 reimagining of Yeats.

Piers Aubrey, according to McWatt, 'exudes the kind of agonised middle-class asceticism associated with Anglican vicars'. But when Holyrood overrode local protests and gave the American billionaire the go-ahead for a golf resort on Calasay, Aubrey, despite his ethnic disadvantage, showed a steely determination and ingenuity 'worthy of Wallace himself', wrote McWatt.

A Granite Ballad – The Reimagining of Grigor McWatt,
Mhairi McPhail (Thackeray College Press, 2016)

fertiliser: ESCO Iron (Agri-Plex)

fungicides: Dithane F-45, iprodione, carbendazim, chlorothalonil, gamma-HCH, chlorpyrifos, carbaryl

herbicides: Princep Caliber 90, Scott's Fungicide VII Bentgrass Selective, KERB 50-W, Scott's Goosegrass-Crabgrass, Trimel Bent, Surflan, pendimethalin, Simazine Pre-Emergent, MSMA – Bulgrass Formula, IMAGE, LESCO Three-Way Selective, Ronstar G, Scott's Fluid Broadleaf, 2,4-D/dicamba, 2,4-D/mecoprop; fluroxypyr/mecoprop-P

insecticides: Orthene R 75 S and 90 S, Triumph 4E, Sevimol 4C, Dursban 2-5-6, Crusade 56

in addition: bleach 'to burn off algae'

Analyses taken from a US Office of Public Health report, based on samples taken from a single golf course in the American south, and from the UK Department of Environment, Food and Rural Affairs' Central Science Laboratory study of 650 golf courses.

'Of the pesticides applied,' according to John Burnside, writing in the *Guardian* on 28 July 2001, 'carbaryl is considered moderately to very toxic; it can produce adverse effects in humans by skin contact, inhalation or ingestion. Direct contact with the skin or eyes can cause burns, while inhalation or ingestion damages the nervous and respiratory systems, resulting in nausea, stomach cramps and diarrhoea. Though the herbicides, mecoprop and mecoprop-P, have long been used in agriculture and amenity horticulture in the UK, the Danish EPA considers them "seriously damaging" to health, the environment or both, and has placed bans or severe restrictions on both. The US Institute of Medicine's study, *Veterans and Agent Orange: Health Effects of Herbicides Used in Vietnam*

481

(National Academies Press, Washington DC, 1993) has linked exposure to 2,4-D/mecoprop with incidences of non-Hodgkin's lymphoma, and soft tissue sarcoma.'

Grigor McWatt, 2009, *The Fascaray Compendium*

8 December 2014

Tonight, Agnes is sleeping over at Kirsty's and Niall has invited me to meet his boyfriend. What would be a commonplace but delightful dinner date in New York feels an almost transgressive novelty in Fascaray. Perhaps I'm too immersed in McWatt's *Compendium* and his early accounts of fundamentalist Presbyterianism – what would the Reverend William Buchanan have made of the invitation?

The apartment over the schoolroom offers more New York echoes. It's light and uncluttered, with Danish furniture and a wall of books separating the bedroom from the dining area and kitchen. Jamie is in his early forties, sandy-haired, stocky and good-looking in a jockish sort of way – that's athletic jock, not the Scottish type, although he's also Scottish. In conversation, he is anything but a US-style jock. He talks softly, with modesty and authority, about his work at Auchwinnie, about carbon dating and geomorphology and, while Niall prepares supper, he quizzes me for details about the museum and archives.

'That's some deadline you've got there,' he says. 'I hear your administrator's on compassionate leave. That's tough. We'll be spending Christmas on the mainland but before then I'm sure I could take some time off – the idea of being a lowly intern in a museum start-up takes me back to student days. Really, anything we can do to help . . .'

I thank him.

'So what have you learned about Grigor McWatt?' he asks, pouring me a glass of wine. 'The man I mean. Not the poet.'

'Not enough, to be honest,' I say. 'I've got nothing concrete on his early life. He guarded his privacy fiercely and even his memoirs seem evasive.'

'Do you have any primary sources apart from the *Compendium* and his newspaper columns?'

'I've got some letters, a Festschrift pamphlet of contemporaneous reminiscences of McWatt by locals, and I did some audio interviews – with the old postmistress here, Effie MacLeod, and Donald MacInnes, his lodger, who helped him out with the animals, as well as Dolina MacPartland, the sister –'

'Ah yes, sister of the star-crossed lover, Lilias Hogg.'

'You know the story?' I say.

'Doesn't everyone?'

Over dinner – Donal MacEwan's hand-dived scallops – we talk of their trip to New York for a family wedding in City Hall. Like a true exile, I'm avid for news of the old country. Just hearing the names of neighbourhoods gives me pleasure; Bushwick, Battery Park, Bed-Stuy, Cobble Hill, Williamsburg, the West Village – my Blessed Litany.

Niall, clearing the plates and setting out coffee cups, steers the conversation back to Fascaray.

'Jamie's keen to hear more about the museum,' he says.

'I'm not sure *I* am,' I say. 'To be honest, right now I feel I've reached a dead end on this one.'

'Well, tell me about your primary sources. The interviews,' says Jamie.

'Effie MacLeod was entertaining, but more on island history than on McWatt himself. Donald MacInnes was borderline hostile – to me, not McWatt – and Dolina MacPartland . . .'

'I can't imagine she had much to say in McWatt's favour.'

'Who does?' I say.

'You'd be surprised,' says Niall, pouring my coffee.

'Okay.' I'm suddenly irritated by this teasing hint of prior knowledge. I've been working on this for months. 'Surprise me.'

He leans back in his chair, unfazed.

'You're still looking for primary sources?'

'That would be nice, but I've exhausted them all.'

'You give up too easily,' Niall says.

Now I'm really annoyed.

'Maybe,' I say, biting back my anger. I don't want this evening to finish on a bad note.

'Well, you're looking at another one,' he says.

'Another what?'

It's late, I'm tired and I really want to get to bed.

'Another primary source,' Niall says.

He laughs at my frown.

'Not me. Jamie.'

Jamie smiles, shakes his head at Niall, and says, 'Don't torment her.'

He turns to me with an apologetic shrug.

'I've been meaning to tell you all evening.'

'Tell me what?'

'I knew Grigor McWatt – pretty well, as it happens – and I'm happy to help you in whatever way you want.'

So now, just as the evening is ending, I take in Jamie's full name for the first time. Jamie MacDonald. James Frances MacDonald, son of Jamie MacDonald, hero of the *Morag May*, and of the late Marsaili MacDonald.

'Jamie the Hose!' I say.

'You know the story?' Niall asks. 'The Fascaradian David who felled the Big House Goliath?'

'Doesn't everyone?' I say.

And so Jamie's story unfolds, of McWatt's generosity to his widowed mother and his aunt Jessie after the *Morag May* disaster, of the poet's continued financial support of the families – 'food, clothing, rent, utilities, presents at birthdays and Christmas' – and of Marsaili's business – 'he kept the Bothy afloat really. It would have gone bust without him' – and how McWatt encouraged and enabled Jamie, his siblings and cousins to stay on at school, then gave them each an allowance when they went to university.

'He supported me through my postgrad studies, too, and did the same for two others. I'm not saying he was a saint. He hated change, modernity of any sort, could be bigoted, especially about the English, and he had some hare-brained schemes – that crazy menagerie! He was waspish and bad-tempered and he was fanatical about his privacy. If anyone spoke about him to the press he'd cut them dead. He was difficult, no question. Lilias Hogg suffered, I know, though she wasn't the pure martyr-to-love the press have made her out to be. But there's a counter-narrative to the tale of the misanthropic recluse. Here's the good word that no one has had to say about McWatt – he was a generous man. He transformed my life and the lives of my siblings and cousins.

We've most of us done well – one's a marine biologist in Edinburgh, two are working in the tech industry in America, one's a cardiologist in Canada – and there is no question that we owe it all to Grigor McWatt.'

It is not until he stops speaking that I notice the candles have gone out. We sit on in silence in the darkness before I realise it's time to go.

McWATT'S NEED TO RETREAT TO CALASAY AND RECOLLECT IN tranquillity had never been in greater jeopardy. A team of construction workers arrived and set up camp in a large tent on the Calasay cliffs. Under orders from Tupper International, they erected a 6ft-high wooden fence behind An Tobar, cutting McWatt's access to the cliffs and obscuring his view, and the poet was sent a £2,000 bill – 'for labour and fencing materials'. The workers also cut the pipeline to An Tobar's water supply, apparently accidentally. 'I tried to engage with them,' McWatt wrote in the *Pibroch*, 'but they are under strict instructions to avoid contact with locals.'

Tupper, a flamboyant figure 'with the petulance of a spoiled child,' had not reckoned on two factors – Fascaradian weather and the stoicism of a Scottish veteran commando. For McWatt, the loss of piped water at An Tobar was an inconvenience that, he wrote in the *Pibroch*, 'became an unexpected pleasure. For years I took my bucket to the burn to draw water direct from the source and it has felt good, these past months, to return to this simple early-morning and late-night ritual which confers a special intimacy with the natural world.'

For the construction workers, shivering under tarpaulin in the fierce north-easterlies, this intimacy with the natural world wasn't going so well. One morning at 3 a.m., when a force-nine gale ripped their tent from its moorings, they sheepishly knocked on McWatt's door seeking shelter. He made them tea laced with whisky and let them sleep in the byre. The next day, after reconnecting An Tobar's water supply, they walked off the job and took the ferry back to the mainland. The gale had also blown down Tupper's fence, providing McWatt with enough firewood to keep him warm for the next two months.

More than a million Facebook users registered with Piers Aubrey's 'Scupper Tupper' page and signed its online petition against the development. The world's press besieged Fascaray and McWatt's photograph, kilted and uncompromising at the door of An Tobar and lit by the ominous flare of a Calasay sunset, became a contemporary emblem of Scottish grit and of that universal story: the small man of integrity pitted against monstrous avarice.

Tupper, irritated by the protest campaign, applied to a now-quiescent Auchwinnie Council for a compulsory purchase order on McWatt's croft.

'It does not make business sense for my high-end guests at the Calasay Tupper Links Leisure Resort to look out on this slum,' he told the *Pibroch*.

In response, Piers Aubrey came up with a scheme whereby Scupper Tupper supporters could, for the sum of one pound, purchase a square foot of McWatt's two-acre back field. The scheme, launched with another Facebook page, was oversubscribed; it took less than a month to raise £87,120 and a further six weeks for all 87,120 donors to be registered as owners of the land and receive their official title deeds. Even Tupper's dedicated lawyers blanched at the prospect of the volume of paperwork required to press ahead with compulsory purchase orders.

Aubrey, for all his eccentricities and Englishness, was a man of probity, and ploughed the money back into the campaign. He rented a derelict one-roomed cottage in the grounds of Finnverinnity House from the Schneiders, renovated it to use as an office, and engaged the services of a public relations company in Glasgow to promote the campaign. He also commissioned a documentary on the issue which went on to win a Special Jury Prize at the Sundance Film Festival. A fifteen-minute trailer for the film was viewed 152,132 times on YouTube. Unusually, without demur and waiving royalties, McWatt consented to the use of 'Hame tae Fascaray', in the recording by the Corries, during the documentary's closing credits. As the issue of the island's future received worldwide attention, McWatt dug in deeper in Calasay, continuing to record in *The Fascaray Compendium* the imperilled natural world around him.

A Granite Ballad – The Reimagining of Grigor McWatt,
Mhairi McPhail (Thackeray College Press, 2016)

chitons (*Mollusca Polyplacophora*): known as cradills, coat-of-mail shells, sea-sclaters, lunschochs or jocky coats. Flattened molluscs with articulating plates which allow the creature to curl up defensively, like the domestic woodlouse or sclater (*Millepes asellus*). Found on rocky shorelines, particularly beneath the Calasay cliffs, clinging beneath loose boulders and stones. Unpleasant ammonia tang on the human palate. Their chief predators are crabs and fish.

limpets, whelks, winkles (*Mollusca Prosobranchia*): called bishop, fiorin, rooklo, spikilurie, spick, foofacks, wulks, catties, kitties, gulsoch or pirlie. Characterised by shells, of various sizes, made up of a single whorled unit with ornamental ridges, ribs and spires. Abundant on rocky shores, particularly under seaweed. Their culinary uses are well known. The spikilurie (limpet) also makes invaluable bait, known as furto, forebait (when crushed, or chewed, before scattering or spitting on the water), ligny, saithe or kupi. The creatures are prised from rocks using a knife known as a muttle or sprud and the bait is then kept in a box called a krobbek. When the bait is cast on the sea, it creates a smooth, oily surface on the water known as an oothy or smelt.

mussels, cockles, clams, scallops (*Mollusca Bivalvia*): known as missels, crocklins, horsos, maddies, clabbydhus, yams, echans, gaikies, cracken, gaubertie-shells, dobs. As their Latin name suggests, these creatures are encased in a shell of two halves, hinged by fibrous ligaments or byssus threads. Mostly sedentary, though the scallop can swim by flapping its two halves together, castanet-style. Found abundantly at sea or onshore. Culinary uses immeasurable.

jellyfish (*Cnidaria Hydrozoan* and *Cnidaria Scyphozoa*)

Portuguese man o'war (*Physalia phisalis*): known for its gas-bubble float, livid Medusa-like tentacles and deadly sting. Called locally a scowder, a Fascaray bramble, a bangi, a selch and seal-skitter. Traditionally thought to be the saliva of seals.

common or moon jellyfish (*Aurelia aurita*): distinguished by its four violet horseshoe-shaped gonads. Known as the barnet, the slub and the skulp. After warm spells they can be washed up on the shore and stranded in rock pools in their hundreds.

Grigor McWatt, 2010, The Fascaray Compendium.

It's now 2 a.m. and, with Agnes away on her sleepover, I'm sitting at my laptop with a mug of coffee, having spent the past hour dithering over drafts of an email to Marco – veering between conciliation and recrimination – before steering myself back to McWatt and to Fascaray's recent history. I don't know exactly how Jamie's new information will fit into the story but it certainly makes me feel better disposed towards my subject. I'm rereading another McWatt inventory when I'm startled by the sudden ping of a new email.

For a moment I think it might be Marco again. But no, it's Ailish. She's up too, also working apparently. She wants to know if she can call me on the landline.

'I think I've traced McWatt's Jean,' she says. There is, for the first time since I've worked with her, real excitement in her voice. 'She's still alive. Still in Woking. In Acacia Crescent, just round the corner from Abbotsford Drive. Her last name, her married name I imagine, is Turner.'

'Turner' – not exactly redolent of the misty Highland hills of home. Stolidly English, I would guess. A double treachery for McWatt. Had the mysterious Bonnie Jean, the unimpeachable Muse and victorious rival of poor Lilias, married an Englishman and moved south like a perfidious swallow?

'Are you sure?' I ask.

'The age fits. First name and address too. All on the electoral register. I've got her phone number too. I'll ring her later this morning.'

'No,' I say. 'You've done enough. *I'll* get in touch with her.'

If this is Bonnie Jean I need to see her quickly. She must be in her eighties. With her testimony – I hope she's still neurologically intact – and an interview with Jamie, I could at last start to build an authentic picture of the Bard of Fascaray. After this evening's talk of New York, I welcome an excuse to get away from the island again. Woking is a long way from Williamsburg. But it's away.

491

WHILE THE LEGAL BATTLE WITH TUPPER DRAGGED ON, THE ISLAND broke with centuries of sabbatarian tradition when Sunday ferry services were finally introduced in December 2010. Tempest, pestilence or flood did not afflict Fascaray as a result of the flouting of the Lord's Day, despite the predictions of the Reverend Angus Cumming, a hard-line Free Church minister in Auchwinnie, who lay down on the harbour slipway in protest at the ungodly innovation. McWatt observed, 'Archie Tupper's plan may be the nearest thing to a plague that has ever been visited on this island, but it pre-dated the Sunday ferry.'

Some islanders were now in the awkward position of betraying their own sabbatarian views by catching the Sunday ferry in order to worship in Auchwinnie. Other, less devout Fascaradians welcomed the convenience of an extra weekend's sailing to get supplies from the town's supermarket, which had been open for business on Sundays since 2009, despite protests from the Reverend Cumming, who lay on the pavement outside the supermarket's automatic doors on its first morning of Sabbath business until heavy rain forced him to abandon his one-man demonstration.

In his *Fascaray Compendium* entry for January 2011, McWatt recorded that Netta and Sandy Macfarlane had moved to Argyllshire and the lease on Finnverinnity Shop and Post Office had been bought by Akbar Shah, owner of the Raj, 'the popular curry house in Auchwinnie'. Akbar installed his son and daughter-in-law, Iqbal and Reza, to run it, retaining Margaret Mackenzie as postmistress.

McWatt's appetite for local gossip seems undiminished. That year, he notes: 'At Lusnaharra, Ben Guthrie has tired of insular life and, defeated by the task of turning the wrecked church into an arts centre and tea room, parted from Alison and moved to London to take up a job as a senior civil servant, while Alison has set up home with Piers Aubrey and their respective children in the manse. One wonders what the Reverend William Buchanan, late of this parish, would have made of this new "bidie-in" arrangement at his former home.' Meanwhile Jinny Aubrey had moved into the Lodge as a full-time Seeker and member of Evelyn Fletcher's personal staff.

The Balnasaig Seekers had undergone another expansion, taking over Tam Macpherson's farmhouse from his grandson Innes, who was moving to Wales. Evelyn Fletcher announced that Tam's old farm would be refurbished and opened as a residential College of Mindfulness and Past Life Studies.

The kirk had been sold to a Swiss restaurateur who planned to convert it into holiday flats, while two women from London, keen sailors and vegetarian cooks, had bought the former Temperance Hotel, purged the building of its baronial artefacts, repainted it in polychromatic stripes and renamed it Watergaw House Hotel. Within months of its opening, recorded McWatt in the *Compendium*, there were enthusiastic reviews in the travel pages and food columns of the national papers. He was ambivalent about the increase in tourism on the island. 'It does bring in money to the islanders, I suppose. As long as the day trippers stay well away from Calasay, I won't complain,' he wrote.

Nigel and Gill Parsons were also drawing new visitors to the island with their Whale Watching Cruises. 'Actual whales have yet to be spotted,' noted McWatt, 'but the sightseers seem happy enough pointing at the shoals of dolphins and porpoises seen off the north-west coast of the island.'

In January 2012, while Tupper's lawyers were still grappling with the stalled Calasay project, the tycoon announced further plans for the island. 'He is seeking permission from Auchwinnie Council to extend Fascaray Airport runway to accommodate planes large and luxurious enough to carry his golfing clientele over the Atlantic,' reported McWatt in 'Frae Mambeag Brae'. 'Tupper has now demanded that the council impose a compulsory purchase order on Fergus McKinnon's croft, which sits on what would be the southern edge of the expanded airport.'

Piers Aubrey and Alison Guthrie got to work immediately and within weeks had ensured that two acres of the McKinnon smallholding was now owned by 10,000 supporters worldwide. A new recording of 'Hame tae Fascaray' in 2012 by the singer KT Tunstall, with backing by classical violinist Nicola Benedetti, brought timely publicity to the island's cause. Barry MacLeod, 'of whom', McWatt wrote in the *Pibroch*, 'it can truly be said that he has followed in his father's footsteps', had returned from Glasgow after a scrappy divorce and was now the Fascaray postman, regularly delivering sacks of letters from all over the world, some simply addressed to 'The Poet McWatt, Scotland'.

Finally, news broke in February 2013 that, in a fit of pique, Tupper had withdrawn his plans for the island. The Scottish government had granted permission for an offshore wind farm within sight of the Calasay cliffs. 'Archie Tupper, the rampaging King Kong of kitsch, who has so far demonstrated little concern over the aesthetic and environmental impact of new development,' McWatt wrote, 'is incensed that the turbines would spoil his golfers' views.' Tupper announced that he would now focus on his political ambitions in America. 'Pity America,' wrote McWatt.

In Fascaray, 'the blustering billionaire' had been defeated. But at a price.

'Can it be that for once we are in accord with Archie Tupper?' wrote McWatt in the *Auchwinnie Pibroch* on 7 February 2013. 'We are, naturally, delighted to see the back of him and his vulgar holiday-camp proposals but this is a pyrrhic victory. The vast wind farm, three times the size of our island, will blight the seascape, destroy bird life and be as disfiguring, alien and unwelcome in our beautiful home as a gargantuan golf course and leisure complex.'

The Trondfjord Fascaray Array would comprise 160 turbines, each 600ft tall, rising from the seabed three miles north-west of the island, within full view of the cliffs of Calasay and Doonmara.

'As technology, it is pitifully inefficient and grotesquely expensive, but the greatest cost of the Array would not be financial,' McWatt wrote. 'It would industrialise our landscape, threaten its fragile ecology and diminish forever the timeless quality of a place in which we can look around and see in its topographical features, its hills, glens and burns, its machair grasslands and the wide unvanquishable sea, the lineaments of a beloved face; the same face that our Fascaradian ancestors gazed on eight thousand years ago. *Dùthchas*, the tender respect for the land born of a sense of birthright and belonging, has always, for the Fascaradian, also applied to the sea. Wha loues the sea, awns the sea, an the sea awns him. My hope is that the Scottish government in Holyrood comes to its senses and puts the long-term future of its island peoples and our precious marine resources first, before the quick hit of a fast buck.'

For some old and combat-weary Fascaradians, however, the new battle against the wind farm seemed a fight too far. Even McWatt, as he wrote in the *Pibroch* a week later, conceded that finally, at the age of ninety-one, he could no longer take a front-line position in the ongoing battle for Fascaray: 'We old-timers, *bodachs* and *caillachs* as we call ourselves here, have been struggling for nearly seventy years to preserve our island from the whims and depredations of feudal lairds and from ravening corporate greed. Is it cowardice, now our personal gloamins are upon us, to finally step aside, pass on the fiery baton, urge a younger generation into battle and wish them well in the fray?'

It was not a true son of the island, not a McWatt or a scion of the immortal Five – neither a MacDonald, nor a McPhail, nor a McPhee, not a MacEwan or a McNeil – who took up the banner against the wind farm but an Aubrey, the English incomer Piers, energised by the campaign against Tupper, who seized the latest chance to mobilise popular support in what McWatt called 'this new fight for the soul of Fascaray'.

In his column for the *Auchwinnie Pibroch* on 18 September 2013, a year to the day before the planned referendum on independence, McWatt extended a hand to those 500,000 English people now living north of the border and therefore deemed eligible to vote for or against Scotland's freedom. It is surely not fanciful to suggest that Piers Aubrey's pivotal role in the Scupper Tupper campaign and in the new No Fascaray Array movement prompted this sudden softening in McWatt's attitudes to the English. Certainly, the article suggested a surprising cessation of old hostilities and a more forgiving, inclusive politics. His veteran literary enemy Professor Alastair Galbraith, writing in the *Quill & Thistle*, took a different view, describing McWatt's opposition to the Array as 'the absurd performance of a Caledonian Quixote tilting at wind turbines', and suggested that the poet's new conciliatory tone was 'either an example of senile benevolence or, more credibly, the tactic of a wily old Nat desperate for independence at any cost – even civility to the English'.

A Granite Ballad – The Reimagining of Grigor McWatt,
Mhairi McPhail (Thackeray College Press, 2016)

This may come as a shock to some of my regular readers, but I ask them to bear with me as I make the case for the non-Scot. This is not, I hasten to add, an eleventh-hour epiphany. I have not finally, with life's last cairn in view on the final bend in the track, come round to the English. The hoar frost of age may be upon me but I am not completely gowkit. No, the non-Scots of whom I speak are those with roots outwith our land who fell in love with our glens, straths and hills, rubbed along quite well with our people, and strove to serve them and their land.

Their place in our history is assured, from the time of the Norse settlers who took our native Celtic women as their brides. Their children were called Gallgaels, foreign Gaels. Since then, many a Gallgael has worked to shape our nation. Robert the Bruce was, of course, of Norman extraction; William Wallace was, as his name suggests, Welsh; Mary Queen of Scots was to all intents and purposes French, and the Italian-born son of a Polish mother and English father became Scotland's Bonnie Prince Charlie.

More recently, our independence movement has included such distinguished figures as Sir Compton Mackenzie (English); James Graham, the (London-born, Eton-educated) Duke of Montrose; and Gwendoline Emily Meacham, the redoubtable Scottish patriot who adopted the name Wendy Wood when she left her native South Africa and gained fame and notoriety for tearing down the Union Jack at Stirling Castle. The Summer-Isle-dwelling pioneer of Scottish ecology, Frank Fraser Darling, was an Englishman whose Scots-sounding middle name was acquired thanks to a brief early marriage.

In the sphere of Scots music, folk singer Hamish Imlach was born in Calcutta; his near namesake, the folk-song collector Hamish Henderson, was actually baptised James and raised in England; Margaret Fay Shaw, another great folk-song collector, described as the 'saviour of Scotland's Gaelic tradition', was from Pennsylvania, and her husband, John Lorne Campbell, self-styled Laird of Canna, was himself half American, while

Ewan MacColl, the singer and songwriter who celebrated the Scottish street song in such a curious accent, was in fact an Englishman named Jimmy Miller.

In my own field, Charles Murray, author of much-anthologised Scots poems including 'The Whistle that the Wee Herd Made', though Scots-born, was another man of the veldt, and the inestimable Sydney Goodsir Smith, who did so much to advance the cause of Lallans with verse including 'Under the Eildon Tree' and 'The Grace of God and the Meth-Drinker', was a New Zealander, educated in an English public school and at Oxford which, when I last looked, was firmly located in England.

Even the great Hugh MacDiarmid, whose real name was the more anglophonic Christopher Grieve, was born just six miles from the border with The Enemy and it does not seem completely implausible, indeed geography and human nature suggest it, that somewhere, at sometime in his past, there was a little Sassenach penetration into Grieve's otherwise irreproachable genealogy. Perhaps this also explains his later-life desertion of the Scots language for the sort of fantoosh vocabulary that might be heard in the science departments of English universities.

Let us not forget that even the Scots-born can get it wrong, as demonstrated by our politicians' recent collaborations with Yankee billionaires, as well as their support for the bird-slaughtering, peace-destroying, landscape-blighting Fascaray Array. We should remind ourselves that many sons of Caledonia – lowlanders, granted, but Scots nonetheless – served under the Butcher Cumberland at Culloden and slaughtered their Highland kinsmen on behalf of their English masters.

Conversely, many Irishmen enlisted with Charlie's Jacobite army to fight for Scottish independence. We cannot deny the well-intentioned Gallgael's contribution to our nation's life. It is their tragedy that they are less Scottish than they, and we, would wish. They might never be truly one of us, these outliers and incomers – folk of whom we say in Fascaray they are 'frae away' – but, surely, some respect is due.

They must not be confused with those incomers who see themselves as old imperialist 'white settlers' living in hostile terrain and treating the natives accordingly, or the absentee landlords – English lairds and their descendants – who twice a year tramp across our nation's hills in quasi-military garb, with hip flasks of malt and polished guns, slaughtering our wildlife. Annual attendance at a ceilidh and a familiarity with the steps of the Dashing White Sergeant do not a Scot make.

These colonising incomers are like the rhododendrons that their status-conscious Victorian predecessors planted in their gardens here. They take to our soil, these rapacious foreign blooms, and then they take over, escaping their cultivated confines, rampaging through the wild, leeching the soil of nutrients, destroying the habitats of our native species and threatening the delicate balance of our entire ecosystem.

So what makes a Scot? Or, more to the point, what makes the worthiest faux Scot a Gallgael? It is in the end about a modest stoicism, a sense of social justice, a distrust of rank and the trappings of fame and an unbragging appreciation of the beauty and majesty around us. It's about accepting the challenges of climate and terrain and knuckling down and getting on with it. It's about loving the land, accepting our subservience to it, and giving to it, rather than taking from it. Wha loues the laun, awns the laun, an the laun awns him. Oor ain laun fur oor ain fowk!

Grigor McWatt, 18 September 2013, *Auchwinnie Pibroch*

We'll Gang Nae Mair Stravaigin

We'll gang nae mair stravaigin,
Sae late intae the nicht,
Though the hert be aye as louin,
An the muin be aye as bricht.

Fur the sgian-dubh rusts ower
An the saul ootwairs the breist,
An the hert maun paws tae pech
An loue itsel maun rest.

Tho the nicht was made for louin,
An the dawk back-comes tae suin,
Yet we'll gang nae mair stravaigin,
By the licht o the muin.

Grigor McWatt, efter Lord Byron, 2013[21]

21 *That's Me Awa*, Smeddum Beuks, 2013.

THE MANNER OF HIS DEATH SEEMED PROFOUNDLY OUT OF character; he slipped away, on 15 January 2014, without fulminations or protest, meekly acquiescing for the first time in his life. Barry the Post was the last person to see McWatt alive. The poet was fishing for grayling on the Lingel that final morning and Barry, pausing from his rounds 'for a wee cigarette break' by the river, had waved to McWatt who was wandering with his rod across the stones to the far bank. Barry stamped on his cigarette butt and was getting back in his van when he heard a cry – 'more a soft moan than a shout', he said later. He looked up to see McWatt keel over, hand on heart, head first into the water.

The poet's pulse had already given out by the time Barry reached him, turned him over and dragged him to the bank. McWatt lay there, mud-spattered, eyes closed. 'He'd a sleekit smile on him,' the postman reported later, 'as if he was about to deliver a punchline.' Barry desperately tried to pound the old man's heart back into life but McWatt lay cold and unresisting. There was nothing to be done but to drive for help and return, load the body onto a trailer and, in a grim parody of McWatt's regular commute, convey him to the Finnverinnity Inn.

Barry's brother Kenny phoned Auchwinnie and, while they waited for the undertakers to arrive on the *Bonxie*, the regulars stood solemnly round the corpse stretched across the window seat and raised a glass to the Bard of Fascaray. Chic McIntosh reflected that, while McWatt's presence continued to dominate the inn, this was one bar-room conversation he wouldn't interrupt.

His death was reported in all the national newspapers (on the front pages in Scotland, inside pages in England), was a lead item on Scottish television news, the last item on the BBC's *Newsnight* and trended on social media for two days, with the hashtag #BardofFascaray.

The Scottish government issued a statement about McWatt's 'incalculable contribution to our culture and to our understanding of who we are,' and there were suggestions that McWatt's funeral would be a national event, a rallying point for the independence movement, generating some useful publicity before the referendum in nine months' time. But in his will and testament, drawn up in Auchwinnie six months before his death, McWatt had stipulated 'a small local, secular funeral ceremony in Fascaray'. In the same will, apart from an endowment to his former assistant Donald MacInnes, he bequeathed his estate, including the regular stream of royalties for his famous song, for the 'benefit of the community of Fascaray'.

On the day of the funeral, Finnverinnity School was closed and the entire population of the island filled the village hall, where McWatt lay in a closed wicker coffin garlanded with yellow spikes of early-flowering gorse picked by local children in Calasay. There were readings of his poems by older islanders and, to the young reporter covering the ceremony for the *Auchwinnie Pibroch*, it seemed 'as if the touchingly halting recitations, the crying of babies and the whispering of bored children reinforced the sense of community and illustrated so vividly the fact that McWatt was a true poet of his people'.

At McWatt's request, there was no mention of the song that had made his name and his fortune. Instead, eleven-year-old Marsaili-May Mac-Donald, niece of fisherman piper Shonnie, great-great-granddaughter of soldier piper Shonnie and great-great-niece of Murdo MacDonald of the Fascaray Five, sang unaccompanied the lovely traditional Gaelic song 'Griogal Cridhe', Beloved Grigor, with its *puirt-à-beul* mouth-music chorus.

> 'S ioma h-oidhche fhliuch is thioram,
> Sìde nan seachd sian,
> Gheibheadh Griogal dhòmhsa creagan
> Ris an gabhainn dìon.
>
> Sèist:
> Obhan obhan obhan iri
> Obhan iri, o!
> Obhan obhan obhan iri
> 'S mòr mo mhulad, 's mòr.

Many a night of rain or wind,
Weather of the seven elements
Grigor would find for me a rocky shelter
Where I would take refuge.

Chorus:
Obhan obhan obhan iri
Obhan iri, o!
Obhan obhan obhan iri
Great is my sorrow, great.

After the ceremony, the coffin was reverently carried from the hall and lifted onto the back of Kenny MacLeod's Land Rover, watched by silent islanders blinking against a sudden shaft of winter sunlight. A disorderly cortège of quad bikes, tractors, trailers and pickup trucks followed the makeshift hearse through Finnverinnity Glen to Ruh and across the strand, for McWatt's burial behind An Tobar, on the edge of the Calasay cliffs under a simple driftwood cross.

He had, presciently, written his own epitaph weeks before his death. It was engraved on a granite slab and transported across the island the following month with some difficulty by Kenny MacLeod and Chic Macintosh, using a quad bike, trailer and ropes. In a quiet dedication ceremony, on a bright windless day of light snow, McWatt's memorial stone was erected, like the Clach na Saorsa monument to the Fascaray Five, on the slopes of his beloved Beinn Mammor.

GRIGOR McWATT
POET, FASCARADIAN, SCOT
1921–2014

Ablo the braid an starnie sky
Sheuch the graff an lat me lee,
Gled did Ah live an gledly dee
An Ah laid me doon wi a wull.
This be the varse ye cairve fur me;
Here he ligs whaur he langed tae be:

Hame is the fisher, hame frae the sea
An the hunter hame frae the brae.

Grigor McWatt, efter R. L. Stevenson, 2014

A Granite Ballad – The Reimagining of Grigor McWatt,
Mhairi McPhail (Thackeray College Press, 2016)

10 December 2014

The bungalow, set on a close-cropped lawn edged with rows of orange pansies bounded by a low privet hedge, is a miniature McMansion, its exterior as bland and tidy as a show home. I push open the picket gate and walk up the path to the front door before hesitating; I must have the wrong house. In the window is a poster declaring support for the UK Independence Party, UKIP, a wacko English Tea Party outfit. McWatt's Jean can't live here, surely. But the house number is correct, confirmed in my phone call yesterday to a terse Englishman who told me he was Jean Turner's husband. When the door is opened, I'm still puzzling over the lurid yellow-and-purple poster and my expectations are low. It would be unreasonable to expect to see, after all this time, any trace of the enchantress who ensnared McWatt, and I'm only mildly disconcerted to be greeted by a wide-hipped grandmother in pastel knitwear.

'You must be Mhairi McPhail. Do come in.'

What does shock me is that Bonnie Jean seems to have gone native, adopted the inflections of the English estuaries and eradicated every trace of her Scottish accent. For Grigor, this surely would have been the ultimate betrayal.

Transcription of interview with Jean Turner, Acacia Crescent, Woking, 10 December 2014. Conducted by Mhairi McPhail.

'How long is this going to take? My husband will be back from his golf in an hour and I have a hair appointment later . . .

'No, of course. I've been expecting a call ever since he died. You're in charge of his legacy? You live on the island? . . . You're plainly not Scottish yourself . . . New York? We've been to Florida twice. Loved it. I'm one for the sun. We head south whenever we can. Madeira. Majorca. Marbella. The Med. I can't see the appeal of the north – cold, dark, rainy. We get enough of that here. But each to his own, I suppose.

'No. I was never invited. He was very cloak-and-dagger about it all. Scotland in general never had much appeal to me anyway. Awful climate. Filthy food. Miserable people . . .

'To be honest, we hadn't been in touch for years. I did write now and again but he returned most of my letters unopened.

'No, it wasn't so much a row between us, more a kind of falling away, an estrangement. We had a shared past, you couldn't argue with that – though he tried – but in the end, when it came down to it, we never had much in common . . .

'Yes, I suppose I did know him longer than anyone. He was a romantic, if that's the word for it, right from the start. Always away in his room, dreaming, reading . . . to be honest he thought he was too good for the rest of us, especially after he got into the grammar school . . . Others can judge the writing. I was never one for poetry. Especially not foreign poetry. Never could make head nor tail of it.

'Didn't mind the song though. Catchy tune. For a while it was hard to avoid – every time you turned on the radio. Extraordinary, really. I liked the Three Tenors best. Some of the pop versions leave me cold. Must have made him a fortune, though . . .

'I'm not sure that success changed him, as such. It just made him more so . . . more of a fantasist, more convinced of his genius. It certainly dug him in deeper to that depressing little island he called home. We were out of touch for so long, I couldn't say whether the fame went to his head. He certainly didn't throw his money about, I can tell you that.

'So the Scottish Parliament has actually given a grant for a Grigor McWatt museum on the island? [LAUGHS] It's not for me to say, but surely they could find a better use for public money? Or do they just splash it about like cheap whisky up there?

'And since we're on the subject of money, can you give me an idea of the sums involved? . . . You did say you were in charge of his legacy? I know the Scottish legal system's different from ours but I thought you might have some news for us on his will . . . You know, his estate? . . .

'What? Are you serious? `. . . The money's going to the island? All of it? . . . You came all the way here to tell me that? . . .

'A misunderstanding? You're talking about another legacy? . . . I don't believe it! . . . Well, poetry and history won't be much use to Arthur and me.

'So he was stubborn and vindictive to the end. Your phone call raised my hopes that he'd finally decided to make amends. But things were never going to be straightforward with Geoffrey . . .

'No. Geoffrey. You – the world – knew him as Grigor. I knew him as Geoffrey . . . It wasn't a "pet name", no. We weren't on "pet name" terms.'

*

The transcription, which will not be displayed in any form in the Grigor McWatt Heritage Centre, ends here. There are another five minutes of tape – my stuttering questions, her dismissive replies – and then my notes tell the rest of the story, which was interrupted by the arrival of a coughing, bent-backed old man in khaki slacks.

'Arthur, she's not who we thought she was. She's not a lawyer,' said Jean Turner. 'She's setting up that ridiculous museum on the island.'

He lowered himself slowly into a leather armchair and I found myself wondering how this desiccated pensioner once beat McWatt in a duel for Jean's hand.

'So, no news on the will?' he asked.

I repeated that McWatt had left most of his estate to the people of Fascaray and that the purpose of my visit was to interview Jean about McWatt's life for the museum and archive.

He exchanged a look of astonishment with his wife.

'The old scoundrel,' he said. 'We should have known better than to have had expectations. He gave you nothing in life. Why should that have changed in death?'

I tried to use their disappointment to my advantage, steering us back on course with the narrative.

'I can imagine you're dismayed,' I said, 'considering the important role you, Jean, played in his life.'

'His early life,' she said. 'There's no denying it. Though I never got any thanks for it.'

'But you were an undeniable inspiration. An early muse.'

She laughed bitterly and shook her head.

'Really? If I was, it hasn't done me much good, has it?'

Their patience was waning. I had nothing to lose. I went for a direct question.

'Tell me, how did you meet? You and Grigor?'

She frowned, then looked over at her husband. Now they were both laughing, as if I was an idiot.

'I suppose that would be down to our parents . . .' she said finally.

Arthur's laugh had turned into a hacking cough.

I persevered: 'Family friends then?'

'Yes, family. But friends? I think it's plain we weren't friends.'

This was getting nowhere. I pressed her further.

'When did you start . . . courting?' I hoped the coy word, used by my parents, might be less offensive to her. She was not offended. Jean Turner was giggling like a teenager.

'Courting? Me and Geoffrey?'

Arthur's cough became a spluttering laugh.

'Another misunderstanding,' said Jean. 'A day of misunderstandings. Maybe a lifetime of misunderstandings.'

'But the elusive "Bonnie Jean"?' I asked. 'His lost love and muse? It's all part of the myth – the legend – of Grigor McWatt.'

She shook her head.

'I did see some magazine story about him once. He'd got himself a couple of fancy women, they said. That came as a surprise to me. In fact I didn't believe it, to be honest. They make that stuff up, don't they? I could never see him as a ladies' man. Was one of them called Jean? It didn't register. I mean it's not exactly an unusual name, is it? Not like yours. What is it again? Maori? Myree?'

She had composed herself, her mirth was replaced by cold anger, and she began to talk. For the second time in a week, my assumptions about Grigor McWatt were overturned.

'You call it a legend. I call it a lie,' she said. 'Grigor McWatt for a start. His name is the least of it. You ask me why I call him Geoffrey? Well, that's because Geoffrey, Geoffrey Watkins, was his name. Before my marriage to Arthur, I was Jean Watkins. I wasn't the poet's "lover" but his sister. Geoffrey Watkins was no more Scottish than me. Like me, he was Surrey born and bred. As English as cream teas and cricket.'

Pechs There the Loon

Pechs there the loon wi saul sae deid,
Wha niver tae hissel hae said,
This is ma ain, ma native laund!
Whase hert hae niver in him burn't
As hame his fitstaps he hae turn't
Stravaigin oan a furrin strand?
If such there pech, ye mind him well;
Fur him nae Makar's raptures swell;
He micht hae titles tae impress,
Ayebidin wealth an aw the rest;
Despite the gowd o aw high heid yins,
In him the basest metal rins,
Alive he's but a cowrin ootcast,
An deid twice ower he'll sink fast
Tae putrid smurach whence he came,
Ungreet't, gunkit an unthrain't.

Grigor McWatt, efter Walter Scott, 2013[22]

22   *That's Me Awa*, Smeddum Beuks, 2013.

11 December 2014

I caught the sleeper back to Scotland yesterday in a daze. I didn't leave England entirely empty-handed. I came away from Acacia Crescent with an envelope containing three photographs and two letters. They are Jean Turner's gift to the museum, and her curse on it. She handed me the small haul of memorabilia saying: 'Take it. Most of our old family stuff was lost in a fire at our previous house. That's all that's left. I've neither use nor space for it.'

As I stretched out on my narrow bunk in the train I felt a crushing despair. I've just diligently researched myself out of a job. The book's finished. We can't go ahead with the museum. McWatt – Watkins – was an impostor. The whole enterprise, the poetry, *The Fascaray Compendium*, and now the museum, has been built on the deception of a crazy fantasist. I have to resign and hightail it off the island with my daughter, back to New York and an uncertain future, in disgrace, a figure of ridicule. It will be hard for Marco not to gloat. If our positions were reversed, I'd do the same.

Jean Turner's photographs and letters bear out her story. The earliest picture, cracked and faded with age, shows two chubby toddlers with severe haircuts standing before a floral clock in a municipal park. They are wearing oversized coats and holding two small Union Jack flags. Another black-and-white snapshot is of a boy aged about nine standing by a bicycle whose wicker pannier, attached to the handlebars, is filled with books. In the background is a corrugated-iron building, single-storey with a narrow spire – a bizarre architectural hybrid, somewhere between a shed and a church. On the back of the photograph is a hand-written note identifying the boy and the building: 'Geoff outside Woking Library, in the old St Dunstan's Church, Percy Street, 1930'. You can see in the boy's high forehead and faintly suspicious gaze the face of the old man he would become. The same boy, taller, and two years older, stands at a picket gate in school uniform: an old-fashioned blazer, cap and short pants. It's easy to read pride and self-importance in that straight back and uplifted chin. 'Geoff's first day at grammar school,' reads the note on the back.

There is one letter from Jean to Grigor – I still find it hard to think of him as Geoffrey – and one from him to her.

At first, Jean Turner told me, once she had tracked him down to the island, she wrote to him using his real name. All her letters addressed to Geoffrey Watkins had been returned unopened.

'Ridiculous. He actually went to the length of changing his name by deed poll. An insult to our parents. To me,' she said.

'Eventually, when I urgently needed to get in touch with him after the death of our mother, I backed down and addressed the letters as he wished. But that wasn't enough. He wanted to wipe out his past. He didn't even stir himself to come down for our parents' funerals.'

The siblings, she told me, had been born eight years apart (he was the older) in Surrey to an assistant bank manager father and a full-time mother, intelligent but under-educated, who channelled her thwarted energies into raising her children, running her home and active involvement in the Women's Institute. The siblings were sent to the local Church of England primary school until they were eleven, attended church services every Sunday, and were brought up to be polite and neat.

'I can see, from Geoffrey's point of view, it wasn't exactly an exciting life,' Jean said. 'Not the best grounding for a poet, perhaps. We were well provided for. No complaints. And poets need something to complain about, don't they? But Geoffrey was always a bit odd. He never fitted in. Never had friends. Never settled to anything.'

Unlike Jean, he passed the entrance exam to the local grammar school. 'He never let me, or anyone else, forget it.' He was always a keen reader – 'Lost himself in books. Fantasies, adventure stories . . .' – and his passion for verse irked his sister. 'He memorised poems obsessively and would stand up and recite them at every opportunity. Our family holidays in Dad's Morris Minor were blighted by Geoffrey droning on in the back seat about ancient mariners and highwaymen and rolling English roads. You couldn't shut him up. It was just another form of showing off, really.'

He left school, and home, as early as he could and moved to the north London suburbs where he got a job working in a small branch library.

'At the outbreak of war he joined the services and ended up training in Scotland,' Jean continued. 'He came back to see us after the war, just the once. He was very secretive about what he was doing and made no effort to keep in touch after that. I tried, for our parents' sake. Tracked him down to that wretched island. He didn't want to know.'

At this point, Arthur intervened, addressing me.

'I really don't see the point of dredging up all this. You've made it plain – there's nothing in the will for us. Another slap in the face. Why do you need to know more? He's dead now. What difference will these details of his life make to anyone now?'

'It makes quite a difference to me,' I said. 'And to Fascaray. To our cultural identity . . . To twentieth-century Scottish history.' I was conscious that I was parroting Gordon Nesbitt and the Auchwinnie Board.

'The Scots can stuff their history,' said Arthur, his face reddening alarmingly. 'They want independence? They can have it. The sooner they break away, the better. What about independence for England? We've been carrying the burden of those lazy Jocks for years.'

I didn't want to be sidetracked. I turned to his wife.

'He's a figurehead, your brother. There's an entire industry built around him. Around the myth of him. It will have to be dismantled, if what you say is true.'

'Of course it's true!' Arthur shouted.

His wife, clearly used to these outbursts, told him to calm down.

'Remember your angina. What the doctor said . . .'

Then, as an afterthought, she asked me: 'Will there be much of a fuss, do you think? When the truth comes out? In the papers?'

'You could say that, yes.'

The press, particularly the English press, will love it. Famous Scots Poet Exposed as English Fraud. The myth will be publicly demolished and with it my job, my life . . .

'Oh no. I don't want to get involved with the press,' said Jean, suddenly panicky, her hands fanning at her face. 'I don't want reporters camping on my doorstep.'

'Look,' Arthur intervened, 'we just want a quiet life. That's all we've ever wanted. If there's no money in it for us, let's forget it. We don't want to be dragged into this, especially at our age. Let's just agree this conversation never took place. My wife's done without a brother for more than seventy years. There's no point in raking all this up now.'

And that's when Jean, not-so-bonnie Jean, stepped in, getting to her feet and shoving the brown envelope in my arms.

'My so-called brother was dead to me for years before they actually buried him. As far as I'm concerned, I never want to hear another word about him again.'

The first letter she gave me is from her, to her brother, dated 25 February 1967.

Dear G,

   The latest cheque arrived, and I must say we were a little disappointed. We had hoped for something more substantial this month. You might be prepared to live in an unheated hut but Arthur suffers with his chest while I, as you know, feel the cold bitterly. This last winter was harsh and central heating is a necessity not a luxury for us.

   I'm delighted to see Grigor's continued success – we watched the White Heather Club at the New Year, where they sang the song three times! – and I trust it brings Geoffrey substantial financial rewards. It would be nice to think that he remembered his family down south, the family that brought him up and then complied with his wishes to keep their distance and stay silent about the awkward fact of their existence.

   Tah-tah for now,
   Jean

The second letter is from Grigor to Jean, dated 14 August 1973.

Dear Jean,

   Will this do? You may not be aware but I do have other financial commitments, which I'd rather not go into.

513

Please see this cheque as full and final settlement of whatever arrangements there may have been between us. I am returning your letters, and will return all future letters I receive from you. I was happy to revoke my claim on our parents' financial estate in your favour. As your older brother, the likelihood is that I will predecease you. I have written my will and when I am dead you will find that its contents reflect the full extent of my historic obligations and loyalties.

Until then, I would appreciate it if the distance – and silence – between us is maintained.

G.

————————————

Alane

Frae bairnhuid's oor Ah havnae been
As ithers were; Ah havnae seen
As ithers saw, didnae draw oot
Ma passion frae a common spoot.
Frae likesome source Ah havnae taen
Ma dule; Ah couldnae wauken
Ma hert tae joy at their refrain
An aw Ah loued Ah loued alane.

Grigor McWatt, efter Edgar Allan Poe, 2013[23]

23 *That's Me Awa*, Smeddum Beuks, 2013.

12 December 2014

I must tell the development board, scrap the museum, spike my book, blow up the whole bogus enterprise, chuck in my job and move away. So many people to disabuse and let down, Agnes among them. And Fascaray? The only hope for retaining its status as a cultural centre would be to rebrand it as the scene of the biggest literary fraud since 1760, when James Macpherson passed off his cod epic poetry as the ancient Gaelic verse of Ossian. But I'm not sure you could build a business model round that. Defining the issue as one of identity politics – the fact that McWatt *identified* as Scots, just as transexuals identify with genders they weren't 'assigned at birth' – isn't going to help here; Canadians and New Zealanders won't make Fascaray a way station on their diasporic pilgrimage once McWatt the Scot is revealed as English Watkins, and the island will sink back into obscurity, becoming the butt of jokes for metropolitan types in the know.

There'll be another wave of economic emigration from the island, the population will dwindle further and the school will face closure, the Bothy and the Watergaw will shut down, the gift shop and tea shop will close, the Lusnaharra distillery will pack up before it has a chance to get going, and the holiday homes – number 19, the kirk – will stand idle, fall derelict and eventually subside into the earth like Hector's home in Killiebrae.

As for the Heritage Centre and Museum, some Internet entrepreneur from Edinburgh might be persuaded to buy the freehold sight unseen and commission a young architect to turn it into a streamlined weekend bolt-hole – an energy-efficient box of triple-glazed UV-filtered glass, exposed brickwork and recessed lighting whose clean lines, empty splendour and unimpeded sea views might feature in an issue of *Architectural Digest* before the owner, deterred by the weather, the inconvenience of the journey and competing attractions in warmer, drier and brighter zones, will put it up for sale. It will, of course, fail to find a buyer and within a year the building will regress to its former state, reverting to a derelict herring-packing shed, albeit one with triple-glazed UV-filtered glass and recessed lighting. And for the island as a whole, with no fishing industry and little tourism, the best the Fascaradians can hope for in an uncertain world is that the market in ditsy etherealism continues to expand and the Balnasaig Sanctuary is anointed as the Vatican of the New Age.

Winter is the fierce and unforgiving season in which daylight appears but briefly in an endless night, as the swift clang o a dungeon door. Colour has fled the land, heather flowers are sere and the surviving red beads of rowan have been picked by departing birds. We wake in darkness and by noon the brief gloaming of the day is already fading into darkness again. This is the time of demonic storms, when the wind pummels our frail homes, moans in the chimney, howls at the door and rattles the windows, encrusting them with sea-spray salt. Fences are flattened and fence posts whirl in the wind like matchsticks; slates are whisked from the roof and hurled through the air like autumn leaves.

This is the time of ceaseless rain, unrelenting floods and impassable bogs when the burn in spate rips away the roots of trees and funnels mercilessly through the land, wrecking bridges and sweeping boulders down to the sea as if they were pebbles. All this water – the rain, the sea, the angry burn and the loch battering its banks – creeps into the soul. One is always damp, wringing out clothes, vainly trying to dry sodden boots, constantly wiping the eyes as if overcome by grief. In these blackest of days, one looks for light and warmth in a glass of whisky and a fire, whose quivering flames tell a thousand diverting stories.

In this island, protected by the Gulf Stream, snow does not often fall. But when it does it means business. There are no pretty scatterings of flakes but blinding, annihilating blizzards. The burn freezes, the well freezes, organ-pipe icicles hang from the roof and one stirs from one's bed, breathing dragon clouds of steam, and looks out onto a bleached world of lilac shadows and silence.

Grigor McWatt, 2013, *The Fascaray Compendium*

Such good cheer and diligence. The scene in the museum puts me in mind of those old Soviet propaganda posters depicting the wholesome joy of collective labour. Eck Campbell and Kenny MacLeod are up on ladders finishing the paintwork, Lori from the Watergaw is on her knees sorting out the electrics, Chic McIntosh whistles as he washes windows, Reza and Iqbal are wiping down the cabinets, which Jamie carefully fills with letters, manuscripts and first editions of the poetry collections. I go through the pantomime of choosing and setting out *The Fascaray Compendium* notebooks in three separate display cabinets while Margaret Mackenzie, in floral apron and yellow rubber gloves, cleans the bathroom. Dot arrives from the Watergaw with a tray of mince pies and makes more tea. I can't bear it.

Before applying the wrecking ball to all this industry, I must tie up some loose ends. Diversionary tactics, I know. Closing the door on the museum, I go to sit at my desk and phone Jim Struan.

'I just wanted to prevail on your memories of Finnverinnity House one more time . . . No. Not about Grigor McWatt. I know you drew a blank there. Another name. Geoffrey. Geoffrey Watkins.'

All I hear is Jim's laboured breathing at the other end of the line and I feel such guilt for pressing him further. Jim must be in his nineties himself now. Can't I just leave him alone to get on with what remains of his life?

When he finally speaks, though, he sounds cheerful and alert, delighted by a new challenge and eager to help.

'Watkins . . . Geoffrey . . . Now that might stir something. The faintest echo. A funny wee fellow? Bit of an oddball? He wasn't one of us, strictly speaking. Could he have been a conchie? Look, I may be completely wrong here. Let me ask around and I'll get back to you.'

Outside, the rain has turned to snow. It is 3 p.m. and soon it will be dark as midnight.

cold *n*: caal, cald, caul, cauld, fuachd, fuarachd, jeel.

dark *n* and *adj*: daurk, derk, doilleir, dorch, douth, dubh, mirk.

drench *v*: bogaich, dook, drook, druidh, fliuch, sap.

drizzle *n* and *adj*: braon, dreeze, dribble, drowe, mug, rag, skiff, smirr.

dull *adj*: dorcha, dowie, dreich, dùmhail, loorie, oorie.

mist *n*: ceathach, citheach, drowe, gull, gum, haar, rouk, sgleò, smuchter.

rain *n*: blash, fearr-shìon, frasachd, saft, smirr, uisge, weet. *v* (*to rain heavily*): blatter, ding, ding doon, doirt, fras, pish, pish doon, plump, teem, trom-shileadh, tuil; *v* (*to rain softly*): sileadh, skiff, skirp, smirr, snith; *n* (*continuous rain or snow and the consequent foulness of roads and paths*): glashtrocht.

rainbow *n*: bogha-frois, watergaw.

snow *n*: snaw, sneachda, snyauve, stour.

storm *n*: ànradh, an-uair, blatter, doinionn, doireann, gaillionn, snifter.

wet *n*: drookit, fliuch, fiuchadh, sypit, uisge.

wind *n*: gaoth, oiteag, souch, tirl, ween, win, wun.

Grigor McWatt, 1 January 2013, *The Fascaray Compendium*

14 December 2014

Agnes has just finished Skyping her father – what do they find to say to each other for a full thirty minutes? – and I've sent her, too excited to sleep, up to bed to read. I pick up the final volume of the *Compendium*, dated Winter 2013, and riffle through it.

There is a brief inventory of 'flotsam and jetsam' washed up beneath Calasay cliffs after a storm – 'two left shoes, of the kind called by Scots "sand shoes"; one pink rubber hot-water bottle; two yellow plastic bottles that once contained bleach; a rusty boot-polish tin, empty; lengths of serviceable nylon rope; a tiny peaked cap, which looks as if it was made for a doll or a monkey (probably a sailor's shrunken hat), two old fish boxes, stamped "Peterhead", useful for kindling; a coconut; a bottle of cognac, empty; a 13-point deer antler, picked clean by crows and bleached by the sea; two clear plastic bottles that once contained mineral water.'

Here he is, banging on about grouse shooting again: 'The burning of heather on grouse moors to facilitate this inane so-called sport causes the disintegration of peat, damages our delicate ecosystem and releases carbon dioxide into the atmosphere, thus accelerating climate change.' Probably a draft column, one of his last, for the *Auchwinnie Pibroch*. There are more lists – 'predators of the earth: pine martens, badgers, wildcats, hill foxes; predators of the air: eagles, falcons, ravens, buzzards, hooded crows, hen harriers' – and further fulminations – 'To protect the alien pheasants, so they can live long enough in their prison pens to die at the hands of wealthy tweed-breeked killers from the south, gamekeepers hunt down and destroy our beautiful native predators. The hen harrier, with its elegant aerial displays and exultant song – its Scots name, *gled*, is somewhere between gladness and the bright fire of *gleed* – is now an endangered species. And so, once more, I conclude that the most ravening predator in Scotland, without ameliorating physical grace or nobility of spirit, is the Englishman.'

There are more 'reimaginings' – of Donne, Shakespeare and Tennyson – and I'm beginning to wonder whether he was no more a poet than he was a Scotsman. The translations – for that, in the end, is surely what they are – are fine as far as they go but the only original poems I've found are the acrostic verse to Lilias and the lyrics of 'Hame tae Fascaray', which he tried to disown anyway. He looked like a poet, though, wild-haired, kilted and frowning in the majestic wilderness, and he thought he was a poet, and other people thought – and continue to think – he was a poet. Maybe that's enough.

The landline rings and for an irrational moment, in which I'm both pleased and annoyed, I think it's Marco. To my relief, and disappointment, it's Jim Struan.

'Mhairi. I've something for you. I finally got through to Tex Bertaud in Arizona. He'd been in hospital. Prostate trouble. Doing fine now. A big character, an oil man by trade, with a prodigious memory. He's helped me out on several queries – missing bits of the jigsaw – in the past. He was one of the first American recruits in 1943 who came from Greentop Camp in New York to help with resistance work in France. Arrived in Gourock after a five-day voyage on board the converted *Queen Elizabeth* – couldn't believe their luck with their cabins, the ballroom – before slumming it for the rest of the journey to Fascaray.

'Remembered your Watkins instantly. Had several run-ins with him at Finnverinnity. "An ornery son of a bitch," he called him. Aye, Watkins was at Finnverinnity House. But I was right. He definitely wasn't one of us. He'd come up from London for one of the "warfare weekend schools" we used to run for the Home Guard, you know the miscellaneous bunch of amateurs who were going to defend our realm, in the event of invasion, with pitchforks and catapults, God help us.

'He was a hopeless soldier by all accounts. Chippy too. Bit of a joke even among the Home Guard. But he took a shine to the place, the life, and volunteered for the selection course. He loved to tramp about the hills, though manoeuvres and any kind of soldiery were beyond him. We had a bit of a problem with the dropouts and failures in fact. Those who didn't make the grade were considered a security risk, usually through no fault of their own.

'Policy was to keep them on for a few months before sending them back to their units, not internment, strictly speaking – they never knew they were doing anything but making a valuable contribution to the war effort. We just kept them isolated, busy and occupied doing those pointless tasks: brass cleaning, that sort of thing, daft routines that our boys have always been so good at devising. We set up a foundry there, using scrap metal to make climbing gear and crampons, boat hooks and training equipment – tin targets on the firing ranges, that sort of thing. Watkins also cleaned latrines and worked in the kitchens. We were short-handed and he made himself useful. Up to a point. He was partly responsible for the terrible food we had to put up with there.

'Tex used to joke that Geoffrey's cooking was part of the training – a toughening-up preparation for the catering arrangements in the POW camps. But he had staying power, Watkins, by all accounts. Saw out the war in the Big House, anyway. So what's your interest in him? And did you turn up any info on your poet? The Bard of Fascaray?'

Ma Hidlin Life

Yer richt, ma duds hae seen
Faur better days, an Ah'm fair skint
But ben ma hert Ah've faur mair wealth,
Than onie tycoon's fantoosh pelf.

Fur Ah've a hidlin life naebdy
Can aye howp tae see;
A preevat girtholl nane
Micht skair wi me.

Abeich Ah staund oot frae the fray
An ben ma hert's a sang,
An here on lownly Calasay
Ah tae masel belang.

Ginst lairds an tyrants Ah rebel,
An dinnae fear defeat,
Fur tae ma datchie citidaille
Ah'll aye retreat.

Och ye who hae a hidlin life
Forby this dowie day,
When greed an grief are runnin rife
Gang cannily away.

Haud yer refuge tae yer hert,
Untae yersel be true,
An aye protect frae dreich despair
The Rael You.

Grigor McWatt, efter Robert Service, 2012[24]

---

24   *That's Me Awa*, Smeddum Beuks, 2013.

15 December 2014

Eck Campbell and Chic McIntosh have patched up the *Silver Darling*'s hull and wheeled the boat to the beach outside the museum. It looks a long way from seaworthy but Eck is confident. Even under canvas drapes she's attracting a crowd of admiring children and reminiscing seniors.

The school breaks up for the holidays next week and Agnes is excited about Christmas – maybe unreasonably excited. I'm not sure I can deliver the fiesta of high-octane pleasure she seems to be anticipating. She's writing out her lists – one of presents she would like from 'Santa' (I notice she has started putting the name in quotes), the other of presents she wants to buy for friends and family.

She has already, in some secrecy, wrapped and posted, with Margaret's help, a small present to her father. She's now angling for a shopping trip to Auchwinnie.

'The village store is okay for basics,' she says, authoritatively making the case for urban life, 'but Auchwinnie's got more to choose from?'

She is even more excited about the Hogmanay ceilidh and the Ne'erday Ba'; Lori at Watergaw House plans to reintroduce the traditional island shinty match on New Year's Day.

'It's kind of like hockey? Only she's using, like, a foam ball? So no one will get hurt. It'll be so fun. I can't wait.'

I can. The ceilidh will mark the New Year and the official 'soft' opening of the museum, with Gordon Nesbitt, islanders, local press and the provost of Auchwinnie Council. I haven't been able to reach Nesbitt – he's on annual leave until 29 December. I have to see him then and tell him the truth, blow up the whole project three days before its launch. I can't believe I've let this happen, that the exhibits will all be in place, the museum will be up and running on schedule, and then I'll light the blue touchpaper and retreat.

They've been practising the ceilidh dances at school, Agnes tells me.

'It's like a barn dance? Only more fun.'

Finn O'Kane stood on her foot during the Strip the Willow, she says, and Kirsty spun out of control and collided with a chair during the Dashing White Sergeant.

'What do you think I should wear?' she asks. 'My plaid skirt? Or the red dress? Or maybe my jeans and sneakers would be better for dancing?'

This concern about her appearance is new, too.

She talks me through the the Gay Gordons and the Bluebell Polka: 'and then you take your partner – there are more girls than boys so I'm dancing the boys' part – and you do this little skip to the side . . .'

I listen vaguely, knowing I should be taking pleasure in her excitement but I am absorbed in my gloomy task as I go through my last box of Calasay papers – more displacement activity. I pack up the books from McWatt's collection; still I think of him as McWatt. Agnes kicks off her sneakers to demonstrate.

'So in the Eightsome Reel there's lots of steps to remember and you can spin real fast and you make, like, this little scream . . .'

My arms are full as I walk across the room.

'Only you're screaming cos it's fun . . .' she continues.

'Damn!' I shout, stumbling over her discarded shoes. I put my hand out to steady myself on a chair and drop my armful of books.

'Sorry,' she says, crushed, all gaiety gone. You'd think she'd endured a childhood of slights and smacks.

Jamieson's, M to W is the only casualty. The pages have fanned open and the spine seems to have cracked.

I quickly pick it up to avoid further damage and a manila A4 envelope falls to the floor. There are several letters inside, some documents and an old chequebook. A few weeks ago I would have been exhilarated by the find. Today I feel only despair. What does it matter now? The old professional instincts soon kick in, however – I must see this project through to its end, to the crack of doom – as Agnes apologetically tidies away her shoes and fills the kettle to make me a cup of tea.

Opening the envelope carefully, I feel a churn of self-loathing.

'Shit.'

'I said sorry,' says Agnes, her lower lip jutting.

'No. No. I'm not cross with you. I'm cross with me,' I say.

Here I am, even at this stage, still hoping at some level to find the proof that vindicates the Bard of Fascaray, that ensures the legend of Grigor McWatt can prevail.

Inside the envelope is a document: a small folded booklet, yellowing pages bound with rusty staples and a waxed board cover. A 'Soldier's Release Book'. The frontispiece is stamped with the words 'Home Guard. Any person finding this book is requested to hand it in to any Barracks, Post Office or Police Station for transmission to the Under Secretary of State, The War Office, London SW1.' The name on the booklet is 'Geoffrey Watkins'.

'Don't be cross with yourself, Mom,' says Agnes.

She has no idea.

The package also contains several bills, invoices and a letter, Grigor to Lilias, with a note, attached by paper clip, written by Lilias, which reads: 'Oh what a tangled web we weave . . .' She must have returned his letter to him in one of their periodic stand-offs.

The chequebook is from the Royal Bank of Scotland. It's empty, apart from the stubs, which he has scrupulously filled in with the names of payees, sums and dates – from November 1972 to August 1973. Most of his cheques were made out that year to Lilias Hogg. £200, £550, £150. In February, he paid £500 to Murdo McIntyre, the original fiddler of 'Hame tae Fascaray'. There are two cheques each for £2,000 dated 31 March. The payees were Marsaili and Jessie MacDonald, recently widowed by the *Morag May* disaster. The final stub in the chequebook, made out in August 1973, makes me start. It's for £10,000 – a fantastic sum in 1973 – and was paid to Jean Turner. Full and final payment. So the wily old blackmailer got her conservatory and central heating.

There are two receipts from a private nursing home in Perth, from 1973 and 1974, for 'payment for the care and treatment of Miss Lilias Hogg' and three from an Aberdeenshire convalescent home in 1980 and 1981, also in Lilias's name. A receipt, dated seven years later, is from an Edinburgh undertaker acknowledging payment for Lilias's funeral and headstone.

I turn back to his letter, dated September 1973. The handwriting is as familiar to me now as Marco's and the tone is concerned and solicitous, even loving. He writes, 'You must take better care of yourself dear Lilias. I worry for you.' But there are also signs of tentative disengagement –

'Though I might wish to, I cannot drop everything, leave this place and journey south to come to what you call your "rescue". The hard fact, dearest lass, is that the only person who can rescue you is yourself.'

Across the top in red ink, partially obscuring his address, she has written in an angry scrawl: 'A poet with no soul. Mean of spirit, tight of fist . . . Fause, Fause, Fause.'

Poor Grigor, I find myself thinking for the first time. Or Poor Geoffrey.

Vieveness

Fause life, a blaflum an nae mair, when
Will ye win awa?
Ye sleekit cheatrie o aw men,
Ye jink the suith, ye wampler.

Yer a muin-like darg, a blin
Self-murgeonin fash,
A mirkie sprattle o bowds an brinn,
A mere carnaptious stramash.

Grigor McWatt, efter Henry Vaughan, 2013[25]

25   *That's Me Awa*, Smeddum Beuks, 2013.

In Scotland, we've never had much time for Christmas. To good Presbyterians, there's something offensively papist about the celebration; with its combined focus on women and childbirth, gluttony and financial extravagance, it is seen as an incitement to incontinence of every sort. In Fascaray's harbour village of Finnverinnity, under the eye of the manse, the only concession to Yuletide is the sudden appearance in the village shop several days before the event of fresh fruit – apples, oranges, bananas and the occasional exotic Conference pear.

We go about our business as usual on the day itself. Until the last decade, local children were expected to attend school on 25 December. But over in Lusnaharra, where the left foot is dominant, Christmas Eve ushers in three days of excess, marked in the poorest of households with feasting, the exchange of gifts and long, operatic Masses in the Church of the Sacred Heart and Immaculate Mary. These revels, no matter how profligate, are but a pallid run-through for the wild bacchanal that is Hogmanay.

On this, Catholic and Presbyterian agree (unless the Presbyterian is teetotal, or the Catholic a drink-forswearing Pioneer, or unless Hogmanay falls on a Sunday, which rules out celebration for the Presbyterian community) and the lanes and paths are busy with the menfolk on their unsteady first-footing rounds with lumps of coal, a bannock and a half-bottle of whisky, while our isle is suddenly full of noises – bagpipes, fiddles, accordions. Every house (bar the manse and Mistress Geddes' Temperance Hotel) is transformed into a Ceilidh House and an outbreak of dancing is general throughout Fascaray.

The following morning, as daybreak lifts the hem of night, every islander – no matter how infirm after the Hogmanay excesses – makes his or her way to Lusnaharra Strand for the annual Ne'erday Ba' – a communal game of shinty. The ball made from hazel root, carved and boiled, and the curved caman sticks, whittled from willow, can inflict serious injury but, heroically disregarding the physical risks and the exertions of the previous evening, players and supporters hurl themselves into the game with a degree of boisterousness that is almost suicidal.

Injuries have been sustained – broken bones, sprained ankles, blackened eyes – but no fatalities have been recorded so far. Naturally such valour must be rewarded and the quantity of drink taken through the afternoon and into the evening has ensured that the day is known as the Wee Hogmanay. That is, of course, unless it is a Sabbath, in which case the good Presbyterian members of the community stay away, stoically nursing their hangovers in silence over the family Bible while the papists battle it out at strand and inn.

Grigor McWatt, 24 December 1955, *The Fascaray Compendium*

25 December 2014

I'm woken on Christmas morning by a howling wind and by Agnes, who stands by my bed, eyes bright with excitement. Outside, black clouds scud across a grey sky. The sea, battered by relentless rain, looks as bilious as I feel.

'Happy Christmas, Mom!"

'You too, sweetheart!'

This Christmas business must be got through.

Agnes is holding the stocking I left at the foot of her bed at midnight and settles next to me to open it. She's an instinctive conservative, like all kids. Tradition is everything. There's been a stocking, in some form or another, every Christmas of her life. This one's red felt, decorated with plastic holly leaves, bought on my behalf by Margaret in Auchwinnie, and filled by me late last night with an assortment of plastic trinkets, fruit and candies, also bought by Margaret.

Agnes squeals with pleasure over every small item – a tube of pink glitter, a miniature disco ball, a set of tiny clockwork chattering teeth, a red balloon, gummy bears, some bright popper beads (way too young for her new pre-teen tastes), a foil-wrapped chocolate Santa, a tiny diary, a magnifying glass – 'Perfect for examining my shells!' she exclaims – and a little red-and-white packet stamped with the words 'Fortune Teller – Miracle Fish' above a cartoon of a sassy salmon, or possibly a cod, thrashing about in high seas. Agnes maintains the fiction, for my benefit I'm sure, that this cheap novelty is entirely new to her, despite the fact that she has found one in her stocking every year for the past seven years.

She takes out the fish-shaped strip of cellophane and reads out the instructions.

'"Place fish in palm of hand and its movements will tell your fortune . . ." Look, its head and tail are moving. It means I'm in love! Ewww. Gross! I don't think so . . .'

She places it in my palm and it curls up and turns over. She frowns over the instructions on the packet.

'It says you're false! What does that mean?'

'Telling lies.'

'Crazy fish,' she says, slipping it back in its envelope. She is done with the fortune teller for another year.

Before we go downstairs she has a surprise for me: a small stocking, one of her own red-striped socks, heavy and carbuncular with gifts.

'From Santa,' she says, handing it to me.

In it are some of her treasures – a pink scallop shell and a nugget of fool's gold – as well as six wrapped Christmas cookies, shaped like snowmen and snowflakes, made with Margaret, a small bottle of the perfume she and Ailsa made from broom flowers under Johanna's supervision, and one of the neon friendship bracelets she also made with Ailsa and her mother. How did Johanna find the time and patience to make all this stuff with the girls? Against my thoughtless shop-bought offerings, this stocking and its contents seem a rebuke to a mother who makes nothing but trouble.

We go down for breakfast – those home-made cookies – then turn to the presents under the tree. More exclamations of delight from Agnes as she opens the asked-for flower press, two grown-up field guides to the flowers and birds of Scotland, a field guide to shells from Margaret, a box of coloured nail polish and stickers, and a pair of red roller skates, which she insists on putting on straight away. From Canada, my parents and Aidan have sent her glow-in-the-dark gloves and a selfie stick. She immediately clamps her cell phone on to it, loops her arm round my neck and tells me to say Happy Christmas to the camera. I oblige, my cagey smirk upstaged by her full-beam smile. She immediately sends it to her father, who instantly pings a reply, which I don't ask to see. What time is it there? What's he doing up at this hour? Where is he anyway? Agnes saves Marco's present to last. Carefully wrapped in purple paper and green ribbons it was delivered a month ago. It's an expensive kids' smartwatch, with games and a camera. Her evident pleasure seems muted for my benefit.

'He liked my movies and wants me to make more,' she says, fastening it to her wrist.

She wants to road-test her roller skates but first she has a special present for me. It's a tissue-wrapped lozenge of frosted turquoise sea glass, pierced and threaded with leather.

'I found the glass on the beach at Lusnaharra. It's just like a jewel made from frozen waves. Mr Kennedy drilled a hole in it for me and put in the lace.'

'It's beautiful,' I say, putting it on. She carefully adjusts it at my throat.

Outside, the rain has eased but we're buffeted by the wind. Agnes grips my hand and propels herself unsteadily in her skates along the deserted street. We walk past my office, and the museum, which rebukes me with its spruceness. It's ready for business. The *Silver Darling* is emerging from her canvas chrysalis, too. Eck has been busy. By the time we turn along the road to Finnverinnity House she's mastered the skates, lets go of my hand and races past me. This is how it's going to be, I reflect, standing alone and shivering in the cold, left with the receding echo of my daughter's laughter as she speeds towards the horizon. The rain rescues me, bringing her scooting back and we hurry home, holding hands again.

In the evening, she Skypes my parents and Aidan in Canada, waving her gloves at the screen, showing off the selfie stick and her other presents. My mother, who seems suddenly frail, asks me how my work is going. 'Fine,' I say, and ask her how she's feeling. 'Fine,' she says. I'm not so sure. My father tells me: 'You know your grandfather would be awful proud of you . . . and we're awful proud of you too.'

Agnes Skypes Marco next and I skirt the room, glimpsing his face on the screen. He's grown a beard, I notice. I also notice, to my irritation, that it suits him. He leans in to tell Agnes some inconsequential story about a neighbour's pet poodles. She shrieks appreciatively at the punchline, which involves some vigilante action over dog mess. I diplomatically retreat upstairs, out of range.

She seems sheepish when she comes to get me once they finish their call and is guarded when I ask her how her father is.

'He's good. He had Christmas with Nonna Lucia and cousin Enzo yesterday. You know, Christmas Eve is their Christmas. They ate fish.'

We eat nut roast with carrots and Brussels sprouts, though we both loathe Brussels sprouts.

'We've got to have them,' she'd insisted. 'It's traditional.'

So are the shiny Christmas crackers she bought from Finnverinnity

534

store, and the plastic toys and terrible jokes and paper hats inside them. We sit there wearing our flimsy coloured crowns and on this family day in our little cottage on this northern isle lashed by wind and rain, we make lonely, dispossessed monarchs far from home.

In the evening we watch television – a cartoon about insufferably cute snow creatures. I keep my reservations to myself. Later, she paints my nails turquoise with frowning concentration; an artist at work.

'It's the colour of the sea, in summer,' she says. 'To remind you.'

On her way to bed she has another regressive turn and asks me to read her a bedtime story.

She chooses *The Treasure Seekers* again.

'From the beginning. Please!'

This time there is no escape.

'"There are six of us besides Father,"' I read. '"Our Mother is dead, and if you think we don't care because I don't tell you much about her you only show that you do not understand people at all."'

Did Marco ever pause to read this stuff before he gave it to our daughter?

I read on and her eyelids grow heavy as she drifts towards sleep.

'Thanks, Mom,' she whispers. 'That was a brilliant Christmas.'

The Herkeners . . .

. . . anely a thrang o bogle herkeners
That bided in the lane hoose then
Stuid leetin in the saucht o the muinlicht
Tae thon vyce frae the warld o men:
Stuid croudin the shilpit muinbeams on the daurk stair,
That gangs doon tae the tuimt haw,
Leetin in an air steert an shoogelt
By the lanely Traiveler's caw.
Niver the least steer made the herkeners,
Though ivery wird he spake
Fell echoin through the sheedaeness o the lown hoose
Frae the wan man left awake:
Aye, they heard his foot onwart the stirrup,
An the soond o airn on stane,
An hou the seelence plyped saftly backlins
When the breengin hooves were gane.

Grigor McWatt, efter Walter de la Mare, 2013[26]

---

26 *That's Me Awa*, Smeddum Beuks, 2013.

26 December 2014

'So today is St Stephen's Day – that's what some people call Boxing Day. Tomorrow is St Fabiola's Day and then there is the feast day of the Massacre of the Holy Innocents,' Agnes informs me.

Is this new fad for the lives of saints the influence of Catholic Oonagh? I wonder. I caught them giggling and cooing over photographs of Oonagh's first communion dress last week.

'The 28th of December is the day', Agnes continues, 'when Herod heard about the Baby Jesus and sent his army out to murder all the baby boys.'

I don't know whether to be worried about religious indoctrination or pleased at her retentive memory.

'This isn't necessarily historical fact . . .' I caution.

Agnes rolls her eyes.

'Mom! It's folklore! It has value too!'

I postpone a definitive view. I have my own Massacre of Innocence to address.

It's a calm, cold day of silvery-blue skies and high thin cloud when we set out on the quad bike. It's taken me this long to master driving the thing, just as we're about to leave, and there won't be many opportunities for all-terrain biking once we're back in Brooklyn, or whichever blighted North American industrial town I wind up working in; running automative industry heritage tours in Detroit, perhaps, or managing the gift shop in the Baltimore Babe Ruth Interactive Museum.

We're heading for Calasay to check that An Tobar and the library have survived the storm. I want to bid a private farewell to the house, to McWatt and the whole venture, as well as to my professional credibility, and ensure that I am leaving it in good shape before breaking the news to Gordon Nesbitt and giving in my notice on Monday. I can't postpone it any longer. The opening celebration on Wednesday will have to be cancelled. The Fascaradians can still have their Hogmanay ceilidh but the museum is finished. And so am I. The ceilidh will soften the blow

537

for Agnes, who is going to find it hard to leave the island. Though she doesn't know it, this is her farewell to Calasay too.

'This is so fun,' she squeals, as we ride up Finnverinnity Glen towards the Calasay Strand. The tide is out when we get to Ruh and it's a dry run across the sand with the wind behind us and the sea, under the winter sun, a distant harebell meadow. We leave the bike on the machair and while Agnes admires the worm casts in the sand I set out a picnic – bread, cheese, apples, a flask of hot broth and Christmas cake, made by Margaret.

'We're so lucky,' says Agnes, watching two red-beaked oystercatchers patrolling the shore.

'Why's that?'

'We live in the most beautiful place in the world.'

After lunch we walk up to An Tobar – 'The Source', as I now know, of the myth of Grigor McWatt. Against the brilliant blue backdrop of sky and sea it looks absurdly picturesque. Whatever else can be said against the old fraud, he chose well. Suburban Surrey or this place? I know what I'd choose. For him, as well as exceptional natural beauty, the island must have offered escape and peace, the chance to shake off his past for whatever reason, to reinvent himself and be a better, cleverer, stronger man. It took grit to withstand those many, many bleak days when the wind and rain and battering sea conspired to enact a clearance of their own and drive the faint-hearted from the land. Whoever he was, there was no denying Grigor McWatt loved the place, respected it and gave something back to it and its people.

While I linger, taking in each room for the last time, Agnes dashes round the cottage taking pictures.

'It was creepy when we first came,' she says. 'But it's kind of grown on me. Papa would really love this place.'

I go to the desk, waiting for her to finish, and idly lift the lid. There, where McWatt left them before he died, are the fountain pen, ink, pencils, eraser, sharpener and felt-tip pens; the tools he used to dig his way out of his drab past and, over seventy years, build a bold and brilliant story for himself. Who wouldn't, given the same options and opportunity?

I realise I'm no longer angry with him. In fact I'm beginning to feel a sneaking admiration. Whoever he was, there's no denying his achievement – the translations, 'reimaginings', whatever he called them, whatever tradition they were drawn from, still speak up for Scots as a vital and distinctive language, or dialect, or whatever you want to call it. Does anyone care that English wasn't Nabokov's first language? Or that Beckett chose to write in French? McWatt, or Watkins, mastered the Scots language, no question. And no one can deny that, as a comprehensive account of island culture and natural history across the twentieth century, *The Fascaray Compendium* has no rival. He was the ultimate self-made man. And he paid heavily for his deceit; the price of a lifetime secret is loneliness.

We lock up the house and I walk across the yard to check on the byre. Agnes goes off to look for wild flowers to press for her new collection.

'Maybe there'll be some of those tufty sea pinks by the cliff?' she says.

In December? I doubt it, but I don't want to spoil her fun. I'll be doing plenty of that in the coming weeks.

I can hardly bear to look at the library, this impressive collection amassed and preserved so lovingly over a lifetime to bolster a lie he may even have come to believe himself.

The musty smell breaks the bad news. There's been a leak. A small pool of water on the floor by the north wall confirms it. I look up to the rafters and see a ten-inch dark patch on the ceiling which has spread across the shelves all the way down to the floor. 821: English poetry. This is still my responsibility. I reach up and start to take out some of the casualties; their spines are wet to the touch. *The Oxford Book of English Verse* is saturated, as is *Palgrave's Golden Treasury*. I spread them out on a dry area of the floor and try to mop them with my scarf. The *Palgrave's* slips free from its boards and the thick wedge of pages lies there sodden as a bathroom sponge. I might as well chuck it. It wasn't worth much before; it's worthless now. I glance at the pale bookplate pasted to the endpaper. Printed below an elaborate coat of arms are the words: 'Royal Grammar School, Surrey. June, 1935. School Prize for English.' The name of the recipient is written in copperplate: 'Geoffrey Watkins'.

I can do no more here. I turn and leave, locking the door behind me for a final time.

It's then that I hear a scream. The air vibrates with it. Agnes's scream. I run towards it, scanning the cliff edge for sight of her. She's not there.

Stumbling wildly I follow the fading echo and make a bargain with a god I don't believe in.

'Let her be all right. Please. Let her be okay.'

Nothing in the world, no one, matters to me but my beautiful daughter, to whom I have been such a careless mother.

'Please let her be okay.'

I look out over the cliff to the waves crashing on the empty beach far below. Then I see her just beneath me, lying on a wide grassy ledge five feet down, her eyes closed, legs crooked. There's no sign of blood. I scramble towards her and reach her in time to see her stir. Her eyes open and – here's the miracle, the answered prayer – she is laughing. She is okay. Agnes is okay.

She sits up, rubbing her knee as I reach her.

'I'm fine. Mom, really I am. I was trying to pull up this pretty blue flower and I just tripped and fell. I saved myself by grabbing that stone sticking out of the side of the cliff.'

She points to a rectangular object, still partly wedged in the rock and soil.

'Can we bring it back with us?' She is on her feet, unscathed, reaching for the stone. 'As a souvenir? I can show Papa when I tell him the story?'

'No,' I say firmly. 'Let me.'

I help her back up to the cliff path then lower myself down again to examine the stone more carefully. It is, in fact, not a stone but a hinged box of wood and metal. I prise it carefully out of the cliff face. It's about the size of a shoebox, shaped like a small roofed house and covered with what looks like hammered gold and silver plate, decorated with carved animals entwined in the Celtic fashion. There are three red enamelled studs on the lid. I put my ear to the box and shake it gently. There's a muffled rattle; something's in there but I know better than to force open the lid myself. I'll leave that to the experts. The tide is coming in and we don't want to spend the night in An Tobar. I wrap the box carefully in my spare fleece, put it in my backpack, rejoin my daughter on the cliff path and we hold hands as we hurry back to the quad bike. It's time to say goodbye to Calasay.

A Fareweel

Wi aw ma wull, bit sair agin ma hert,
We twa noo pert.
Ma Cushie Doo,
Oor solace is, the dowie road rins true.
It needs nae ert,
Wi fent, avertet fit
An greetin ee,
Alang oor contrair paths tae pechin flee.
Awa you Sooth, an Ah'll gang Nor.
We wullna say
There's onie howp the day.
Bit aw, ma braw,
When greetin's ower,
An bubblin disnae blur oor ees,
Tae see the heather bloom neath gloamin skies,
Mebbe we micht
Gar fu circle o oor unco exile,
Mak bricht day oot o derkest nicht,
An meet agin upby oor blisset isle.

Grigor McWatt, efter Coventry Patmore, 2012[27]

---

27 *That's Me Awa*, Smeddum Beuks, 2013.

27 December 2014

I texted Jamie a picture of the box last night and he and Niall arrive this morning from the mainland.

'It's too soon to say what it is, exactly,' Jamie says, turning the box carefully in his hands. 'But I think this could be really big.'

We go with them up to Calasay on the quad bikes and he pokes around the cliff edge with a small hand tool.

'I don't want to disturb the site any more,' he says. 'We need to get a proper team here.'

He and Niall secure the area with a fence and we head back to number 19. Agnes is exultant.

'Is it treasure, maybe? Kind of like *Treasure Island*?'

'Maybe,' says Niall. 'Without the pirates and the parrot.'

She shows Niall her blue flower, retrieved and pressed after her fall – *Galium McWatti*, McWatt's mattress, he tells her.

'Wow!' she says. 'The poet's flower? That's so cool.'

As we drink our tea, Jamie admires her collection of shells and rocks by the window, poking through them with his index finger. He pauses and lingers over the grubby fish-shaped piece of burnt wood she picked up in the cave three months ago.

'Where did you find this?' he asks, holding it up to the light.

'At Slochd. In Uamh a' Chlàrsair Chaillte,' she says, pronouncing the Gaelic with impressive fluency. 'The Cave of the Disappearing Harpist . . .'

'You've got a good eye, Agnes,' he says. 'This is really interesting. Could I borrow it and get it checked out?'

THE CALASAY RELIQUARY CASKET, AS IT HAS COME TO BE KNOWN, proved to be a prime example of Insular art, its decoration – stylised animals, griffons and dog-like beasts biting their own tails, are interlaced with spirals, circles and other geometric patterns – characterised by a fusion of Pictish and Irish Celtic design with Anglo-Saxon metalwork techniques. The Latin inscription – *Hic est Rufus* – was a clue to its contents: a small hessian-tied bundle of eight brittle ivory shards which the monks of Calasay had believed to be the miraculous bones of St Maolrubha.

The casket turned out to be only part of the Fascaray Hoard, a priceless collection of early-medieval ecclesiastical metalware excavated carefully over the following two months from the site just west of Grigor McWatt's grave by a team of archaeologists led by Jamie MacDonald.

The prize piece was a large, richly decorated two-handled chalice of gold, silver, lead pewter and enamel on a copper-alloy stem. Around its silver bowl, the names of the apostles are engraved in a frieze below a ring of wirework panels incised with animals and birds. Next to it, MacDonald unearthed a silver plate – the 'paten' on which the Eucharist would have been placed – with twelve amber studs, one for each apostle, set in brass medallions around the rim. In addition there was a large basin of hammered bronze, in which the chalice and paten must have been placed by monks before they hastily buried their sacred hoard and tried to flee the Vikings.

The story of the Fascaray Hoard, first broken in the *Auchwinnie Pibroch* in March 2015, was picked up by the world's press; reports quoted the Scottish government's Culture Secretary, who described it as 'one of the most valuable and historically significant archaeological finds of the last two hundred years, contributing priceless new insights to our understanding of life and culture in early-medieval Scotland and shedding new light on the deepest roots of our nation'.

Some press reports the following month also carried news of the identification of another significant, and even more ancient, historical artefact. Carbon dating revealed that a small piece of charred wood, discovered in 2014 in a Fascaray cave by a nine-year-old girl sheltering from the rain, was, according to a curator at National Museums Scotland, part of the carved bridge of a lyre dating back more than 2,300 years, making it the oldest stringed instrument found in Western Europe. Its discovery proves that music, ritual and verse, which such instruments would have accompanied, played an important part in the lives of Iron Age Fascaradians. It has also led to a new understanding of the Pictish people and has rewritten the history of complex Western music, pushing back its origins by a thousand years, and demonstrating the remarkable continuity of the Celtic love of music, song and poetry.

A Granite Ballad – The Reimagining of Grigor McWatt,
Mhairi McPhail (Thackeray College Press, 2016)

The Flane an the Sang

Ah shot a flane intae the aire,
An where it fell Ah didnae ken;
It flew sae fest that human sicht,
Couldnae follae in its flicht.
Ah peched a sang, intae the aire,
An where it fell Ah didnae ken,
Fur who has sicht sae shairp an lang
That it can keek the flicht o sang?
Years oan Ah foon the flane intact,
In an aik tree, an that's a fact.
An ma sang Ah foon again,
In the herts o richteous men.

Grigor McWatt, efter Henry Wadsworth Longfellow, 2000[28]

---

28 *Thoog a Poog*, Smeddum Beuks, 2012.

But first there is the ceilidh. In the end, Agnes settles on a plaid shirt, jeans and the pink cowboy boots her father bought her in Tucson.

'Good choice,' I whisper as we walk, swaddled against the chill in our down jackets under a starlit sky past the museum, which is in darkness, past the *Silver Darling*, transformed, a thing of beauty, freshly painted and fully seaworthy, her red sails tightly furled, ready for her first voyage next week.

The hall is crowded and noisy with elated chatter. The children are dressed, like Agnes, for a hoedown while most of the adults, me included, are in variations of hiking gear. My concession to style is Agnes's glass pendant. The only kilts I can see are worn by a party of Seekers and by Reinhardt Schneider, who is also wearing a tartan bonnet trimmed with pheasant feathers.

Niall has had the pages of Agnes's 'My Hero' project enlarged to poster size and it's displayed on boards around the hall. She barely notices – there's too much going on – and she slips my hand with an excited cry; she's seen Johanna and Ailsa, who returned from Aberdeen this evening, and she runs to join them. I wave. I'll catch up with them later.

Niall is here with Jamie, and we move towards each other and embrace in the crush.

Across the stage, a banner made by pupils from Auchwinnie School, reads 'Wha loues the laun, awns the laun', and under it the musicians are setting up. Jessie McIntosh, studying for her Highers at Auchwinnie Academy, is playing her great-uncle Iain's old fiddle; Shonnie MacDonald is shouldering his great-grandfather's treasured bagpipes and Donal MacEwan is strapping on an accordion. Between them Iqbal Shah the Shop sits cross-legged on a cushion flexing his fingers over two tabla drums. For the purposes of the evening, the musicians, who play a gentle jig to warm up, have named their ad hoc band Dùthchas.

There is a tug at my sleeve. Agnes is back.

'Ailsa's papa's getting better,' she says, shouting to be heard over the din.

'Something else to celebrate,' says Niall.

'Her mom says he's turned a corner. Is that a metaphor?' she asks.

I nod and stroke her hair, which she's braided with more patience and competence than I could ever manage.

Gordon Nesbitt stands by the bar. In the rush of events I haven't found time to tell him the truth about the Bard of Fascaray. He waves and I walk towards him, queasy with dread. I pass Ailish, who's whispering to the Provost of Auchwinnie, a small man wearing an outsize gold chain that would be envied by an old-school rapper. Piers Aubrey is talking to Nigel Parsons. They're jubilant; Nigel's recent sighting of a group of basking sharks off the island's north-west coast has been confirmed and the sharks' protected status means the wind farm is likely to be scrapped.

Two journalists from the *Pibroch* have joined Gordon and, as I force my way through the crowd to reach them, Kenny MacLeod turns to me, bows and mimes applause, then other heads turn and there is an outbreak of clapping and cheering. I can't shake the sense that I'm being mocked. Then I realise they are cheering not me or the museum but Agnes. News of her discovery at the Calasay cliffs has got around fast. It will be months before excavations are completed and we find out what exactly is there and what story it tells. But for now rumours of 'buried treasure' add to the party euphoria.

By the time I reach the bar, Gordon has moved towards the stage. I order a couple of sodas – Margaret serves me but refuses to take any money – and Agnes is already off with Ailsa, Oonagh, Henry and Finn, practising dance steps.

The musicians stop their warm-up, put down their instruments and make room for Gordon on the stage. The hall falls silent as he coughs into the microphone, testing the sound. But before he can begin his speech there is a sudden loud bang – the door has blown open in a gust of wind. A latecomer has arrived, bringing with him a flurry of snow. Agnes runs to him.

'Papa!' she shouts, burying her head in Marco's big coat.

He sees me and waves hesitantly. I wave back but I've no time to gauge my feelings because Nesbitt is speaking now, celebrating the opening of the new museum, congratulating all those involved, praising me for my 'diligence and resilience' and citing Grigor McWatt, 'whose art, generosity and love for the island have made this whole project possible'. The audience nods and there are scattered whoops.

'The recent exciting archaeological find', continues Nesbitt, 'may eventually mean a shift in focus for the museum but I am confident that McWatt himself would have given his approval. Meanwhile, tonight, we celebrate this remarkable island and its people, and in particular we thank Mhairi McPhail, descendant of one of the Fascaray Five, for uprooting her life and crossing an ocean to honour the birthplace of her grandfather.'

Now they're all cheering. Anyone looking at me closely might mistake my flushed cheeks for modesty, or even early menopause. No one will guess that it's a blush of guilt.

The applause dies away and Gordon leaves the stage. As the band starts to play I steel myself and make my way towards him through the throng.

But I'm intercepted. It's Agnes, holding her father's hand.

'You can do this one too, Mom. Please?'

Marco's taken off his coat and I notice he's wearing a pendant round his neck. Pale blue sea glass on a leather lace.

'I have no idea,' I say.

'Just follow us,' he says.

'Don't worry, Mom. Papa and me worked it out. He's got a book and he looked at YouTube and we went through it on Skype. He knows all the steps.'

Of course he does.

The crowd disperses and reconfigures into circles of four pairs and I am swept along in the dance with everyone else. Niall takes my hand while Agnes partners Marco. Jamie and Lorna McKinnon join us with Margaret and Kenny. We bow to each other, laughing. The tune is jaunty but sedate enough for me to follow the steps, which involve skipping, weaving and partner swapping – a long way from the free-form dry humping that passed for dancing in my bachelorette years. I find myself holding hands with Marco – when was the last time we did that? – and then it is over, we move on and I am bowing once more to a gallant Niall.

The tempo of the next dance is wilder and I move to sit it out, find Gordon Nesbitt and have my difficult conversation with him. But Agnes calls me back.

'It's Strip the Willow! You got to, Mom! It's so fun!'

The crowd divides into two long lines and we all clap as the first couple, Eck and Isa, dance towards the end of the hall linking arms and spinning everyone in turn before moving on. Then Margaret and Chic take their place. It's chaotic but good-natured and everybody has a go; Dot is linking arms with Barry MacLeod, Gordon Nesbitt is jigging hectically with Ailish, Balnasaig Seekers are dancing with fishermen, game seniors with scampering children, Campbells with MacDonalds, MacEwans with McIntoshes and McKinnons with MacLeods. This is how I come to have the odd experience of grasping my ex-lover's hands and revolving with him at such reckless high speed that, when I'm not panting, I'm laughing so hard that tears brim in my eyes.

Agnes looks concerned.

'You okay, Mom?' she mouths over the music.

I nod.

By the time the dance is over even the children are out of breath. The band signals a change of pace and Jessie steps forward to perform a fiddle solo as a guest singer is helped onto the stage. It is Hamish McIntosh, Jessie's grandfather, now eighty-four, frail and stooped, here to perform the song he first sang in the Finnverinnity Inn as a young boy seven decades ago. He adjusts the microphone with trembling hands and as he starts to sing his voice is light and wavers on the higher notes.

> *Blaw winds,*
> *An dae your warst!*
> *Stormy seas rise up!*

But the purity of pitch is still there and as we watch him a curious thing happens; his voice gathers strength, he stands more erect and he seems to grow younger, summoning the old passion and pride of a group of men and women brought together by a sense of injustice.

> *Spite lashin rain*
> *An England's shame,*
> *We're comin hame.*

And now the chorus. Agnes looks up at her father, then at me.

'You know the words, right?' she says, reaching for our hands. 'Hame? It's kind of a metaphor?'

We take a breath and then, with every Fascaradian in the hall – old-timers, incomers, Scots, Gallgaels, settlers and visitors – we lift our voices to join in.

> *Hee-ra-haw, boys,*
> *We're awa, boys,*
> *Gangin hame*
> *Tae Fascaray.*

ACKNOWLEDGEMENTS

Thanks to Alma McTavish, my scrupulous editor at Thackeray College Press, Pennsylvania, and to my colleagues at the Morgan Library and Museum, New York, who generously granted me leave of absence to finish this book, which would not have existed without the backing of the Fascaray Trust and Auchwinnie Regional Development and Enterprise Board.

Thanks are also due to Sandy Balfour and Isabella Kerr of National Museums Scotland, Morag Maclennan of the National Library of Scotland and Ailish Mooney, current director of the Fascaray Hoard Museum and Grigor McWatt Study Centre. The late Jim Struan, former commando, Finnverinnity House veteran and historian of the SOE, was unfailingly generous in his response to my enquiries about Grigor McWatt's war years.

My biggest debts of gratitude are to the people of Fascaray – in particular Effie MacLeod, James MacDonald and Niall Kennedy – to my husband Marco Bartoli, and to our daughter Agnes, whose sweet nature and boundless curiosity illuminated a dark northern winter and helped to unearth the hidden history of that beautiful island.

Mhairi McPhail, New York, 22 June 2016.
(A Granite Ballad – The Reimagining of Grigor McWatt, Thackeray College Press, 2016)

GLOSSARY

A

aa – all
abeich – aloof, apart
ablo – under, below
abreed – wide apart, open
abuin – above, overhead
acause – because
aefauld – honest, faithful
agane – again
agin – against
agley – awry, astray
Ah – I, first-person singular
ahint – behind, late
aiblins – perhaps
aik – oak
ain – own
airn – iron
airt – direction, *to airt out* – to discover
ane – one, an, a
anely – only
aneath – beneath
antrin – occasional, rare, odd
asclentit – aslant, aside, astray, 'to the one side like Gourock'
asure – blue
athin – within
atweesh – between
aw – all
awfie – awful
awra – all the
aye – yes, always
ayebidin – everlasting
ayont – beyond

B

bahookie – backside
bairns – babies, children
bampot – idiot, person of low intelligence or away with the fairies (see *sidhe*)
bangster – ruffian
barelins – barely, hardly
bauchle – untidy, clumsy or old person
bauld-daur – audacious
bawbee – coin, penny
bawheid – idiot
bayin – to lift up the voice loudly
beekin – shining
ben – in, inside, indoors, as in 'ben the hoose'
beuchs – boughs
bevvy – alcoholic beverage
bickety – trifling
bide – stay, couples who reside together conjugally without marriage are known as 'bidie-ins'
big – build
bing – a heap
binna – except, unless
birl – to rotate rapidly, revolve, whirl
birlinn – long-oared boat, galley
birses – bruises
birsie – hot-tempered
blae – blue
blaflum – hoax, illusion, nonsense
blash – a splash of liquid
blashy – gusty
blether – prattle, idle talk
bletherskite – fool, babbler

552

bliss – bless

blooter – a jelly-like mass, blast of wind

blootert or *bluitert* – drunk

boak – retch, vomit

boch – rapture, ecstasy

bodach – old man

bogey – flawed, invalid, as in 'the gemme's a bogey'

bogle – spirit, ghost

bonailie – a farewell drink

bonnie – beautiful

booral – small bedroom

bosie – bosom

bothy – hut, primitive shelter

bouk – body, carcass

bowd – billowing waves

bowsie – fat, puffed up

brae – hill

braibit – depressed

braid – broad

brall – to soar, to fly

brammle – berry

braw – fine, splendid

breenge – plunge, rush recklessly

brinn – piercing, dry wind

broch – a prehistoric tower

broukit – broken

browstary – embroidery

bruim-buss – broom bush, genista, whin

bucht – bend

buchtit – abundant, weighty bowers

bunnet firs – Scots pines

burn – river, stream

bygae – go by

byous – wonderful, extraordinary

C

cadgy – happy, cheerful

cailleach – old woman

callant – stripling, youthful

caller-killt – freshly killed

camsheuch – crooked, deformed, perverse

camsteirie – wild, excitable, riotous

cannie – wise, shrewd, cautious

cantie – lively, cheerful

cark – anxiety, care

carnaptious – quarrelsome, crabbed

cauld – cold

caunle – candle

caur – left

caw – call

chap – (1) knock (2) lay a claim

chaumer – room

chib – blade, knife

chirker – cricket

chitterin – shivering

chuckie – a small stone, pebble (for throwing, skimming)

clachan – hamlet, small village

claggie – sticky

clashmaclavers – gossip, idle talk

clatty – dirty

claucht – caught, seized

cleed – clothe

cleeked – hooked

cleuch – gorge, pit, ravine

clonger – wild rose

clourt – beaten, dented

cludgie – restroom, toilet

clype – to inform on someone, tell tales

cogie – bowl

colf – fill

collit – shaped

con – squirrel

coof – rogue, blade

coolks – reeds

corrieneuchin – intimate conversation

coupon – face

couthie – pleasant, sympathetic, good company

cowp – upset, fall, lay low
crack – conversation, gossip
crammasie – crimson
cranreuch – frost
creesh – fat
cried – called, as in name
crochan – mud
crood – cooed, sang
crottle – crumble
crooch – crouch
cruin – croon, mournful song
cuckoo-brogue – violet
cuddie – donkey, horse
cuild – cooled
cuitle – please, gratify
cuman – milking pail
curnawin – hunger
cushie doo – darling dove, term of
    endearment
cutty – short
cutty-stool – low three-legged stool

D

dachlin – dawdling, going slowly,
    hesitating
daedle – linger
dag – day
darg – work
dashelt – worn out
datchie – secret
daud – lump, piece
daunder – saunter, stroll
dautie – darling, pet
dawk – dawn
deid – dead
deil – devil
dern – hidden, secret, to hide
diacle – compass
dicht – washed, cleaned, wiped
diddies – breasts
dings – beats
dinkly – dainty

dirl – whirl, gust
dirr – numb
dishantit – abandoned, deserted
disjaskit – downcast, dejected,
    depressed
dit – close
doistert – frenzied
doitert – confused
donsie – luckless, unfortunate
doo – dove
doon – down
douce – sweet, pleasant, sober (usage
    in religious households only)
dover – sleep, doze
dowe – fade, wither
dowf – weary, stupefied, dull,
    melancholy
dowie – melancholy, sad
dowp – to sit, buttocks
dowre – to sleep
draik – drench
dree – suffer, endure, see *thole*
dreich – wet, dull
drouthie – thirsty
dùchthas – ancient Gaelic spirit of
    connection with and kindness to
    the land
duds – clothes
dufftie – soft, spongy
dule – sorrow
dunt – batter, beat
dwaum – dream, reverie, trance
dwm – dumb
dwyne – wither, fade, waste away

E

eariwig – eavesdrop, overhear
eelist – envy
eik – grow
een – eye, eyes
e'en – (1) evening (2) even
ensenzie – motto, slogan

erch – coy, timid
ettle – desire
eydent – intent, busy

F
factor – bailiff, estate manager
fae – (1) from (2) foe
fank – (1) confusion (2) sheep pen
fankelt – mixed up, confused, tangled
fash – trouble, annoy, irritate
fauld – sheepfold
fause – false
faw – fall
feart – afraid
fecht – fight
fedders – feathers
fegs – faith
feuch – rage
fire-flaucht – lightning
fit – foot
fiver – fever
flane – arrow
flaucht – weave
fleech – flatter, wheedle, beseech
flicht – flight
flirry – blossom
flit – move, as in moving house
flochter – flutter
flum – flattery
fog – moss
forby – besides, as well, in addition to
forfauchelt – exhausted, worn out
forhou – forsake
fou – drunk, full
fouth – abundant
fowed – forked
fower – four
fowk – people
frae – from
freuch – hard, dry
fung – kick, toss, fling

furrin – foreign
fykie – intricate
fyle – foul

G
gab – mouth, beginning
gairdie – hand, fist
gallus – reckless, bold
gallehooing – noisy, foolish blustering
gamawow – a fool
gamf – mimic
gang – go
gangrel – vagrant
gar – make, coerce, cause
geck – scorn
gealit – frozen
geggie – mouth
gemmster – gambler
gey – very
gillum – jewel, jewelled
gin – if
girn – grimace
girtholl – sanctuary
gizz – face
gizzern – throat
glagger, glaggin – to yearn, long for
glaikit – foolish
glaise – to warm, as at a fire
glaister – glitter
glaur – mud, ooze, slime
gleed – glowing coal, burning peat or
 ember, fire
gleek – peep, glance
glen – valley
glisk – glimmer, glance
gloamin – twilight, fusk
glormach – gaudy
gluives – gloves
goad – god
gowan – daisy
gowd – gold
gowen – gown

gowk – fool, cuckoo

gowp – stare gormlessly

graff – grave

graig – gurgling noise

gree – prize

greet – cry, weep

grotho – sorrow, vexation

gru – atom, particle

grue – horror

gruggie – cloudy

guddle – mess, confusion

guga – young gannet, hunted by Fascaradians for centuries

gullion – a marsh, a swamp

gunkit – bitterly disappointed

gurley – wild, stormy

gyrie – circuit

H

haar – mist

haffet – cheek, temple, face

hain – protect

hairiken – hurricane

hairst – autumn, harvest

haiveless – meaningless, senseless

hame – home

hamelt – belonging to home, internal, native, domestic

hameseek – homesick, selfish

hamesucken – the offence under Scots law of premeditated assault on a person in his own dwelling place

handsel – a present to bring good luck to a new enterprise, be it a new home, a baby or the New Year at Hogmanay

hap – cover

hauch – low ground, meadow

haulflin – adolescent

haw-buss – hawthorn

heeld – to lean, slant

hecht – vow

heeze – to rise

heich – high

heid – head

heiv'n – heaven

hen – affectionate term for a woman

hend – end, last

hert – heart

heuch – to shout joyously, as at a ceilidh

hewit – colour, hue

hicht – height, exalted position

hidlins – secret, hidden

high heid yins – self-anointed rulers

hingins – curtains

hinmaist – last

hinnie – honey

hishie – murmur, whisper

hissel – hazel

hochmagandy – sexual congress

hod – hold

hollae – hollow

hoob – land exposed at ebb-tide

hoor – whore

hooshit – silent, hushed

howdie – midwife

howdiein – birth

howe – deep, hollow, hoe

howff – a public house or inn, meeting place

howked – dug

huff – blow

huily – slowly

hummel – humble

hyne – far away

hynie – distance

I

ilka – each, every

ill-kyndit – ill-willed, *th'ill kyndit yin* – the devil

ill-mynded – forgetful

ilsket – malicious

imalded – overwhelmed, buried
impignorate – to pawn

J

jamphi – mocking, jeering
jessamine – wood anemone
jink – to move nimbly, dodge, dart
jouk – play truant
jube – deep place, bog or morass

K

kail – kale, leafy-green vegetable
  originally part of Scots diet, now
  universal
kailyard – sentimental school of
  Scots writing dealing with rural
  domestic life
keech – excrement
keek – glance, peep
keelie – rowdy fellow (see *ned*)
ken – to know, knowledge
kenspeckelt – familiar
killie–shangie – uproarious argument
kinchie – merry
kinrick – kingdom
kirn – mix
kittle – to stimulate, please, perplex
knock – time, the hour
knowe – small hill
knype – to knock, strike
kowk – to retch, vomit
kye – cows
kythe – appearance

L

laich – low
laid – load
laith – hatred
laldie – a thrashing, perform
  vigorously
lang – long
lave – remainder, rest

laverock – skylark
laylocks – lilacs
lea – field
leal – loyal
lee – lie
leep – period of warm weather
leid – language
leif – life
lettern – desk
lig – recline, lie, rest
limmer – harlot, rascal
lin – rest
linn – waterfall
lintie – linnet
list – wish, desire
loon – young man
loorach – tattered, trailing
lootch – stooped
loue – love
lounder – severe thrashing
lown – quiet, silent, peaceful
lowp – leap
lowsin – loose
lugs – ears
luim – loom
lum – chimney
lumber – a date, as in 'lookin fer a
  lumber'
lum-scutcher – chimney sweep

M

machair – low-lying land covered
  with wild grasses next to seashore
mair – more
mairchlessness – infinity
makar – a poet
mak-on – impostor
malafoustert – destroyed
mane – moan, grieve
marrae – equal
mauchtless – powerless
maumie – ripe, mellow

maun – must

mense – honour, dignity

merk – mark

messages – shopping

midden – dunghill, rubbish dump, compost heap

mind – remember

mindin – memory

mirk – dark, black, gloomy

mishanter – misfortune, disaster

mixter-maxter – motley, jumble

mizzle – vanish

moch – moth

molligrants – grumbles, small complaints

moue – mouth

mozin – decay

muckle – much, large, great

murgeon – mock

murl – mould, decay

myndin – remembering

mynt – aim

N

ned – lout

neshie – tender, soft, fragile

neuk – corner

nieve – fistful

nipscart – a crabbed, bad-tempered person

nocht – nothing

numpty – idiot, eejit (see *bampot*)

nyaff – a puny, worthless person

O

oan – on

ochenin – dawning

onie – any

onwith – onwards

oor – (1) our (2) hour

oorit – cold, tired

ootby – outwards, a little way off

ootwith – outside, beyond

orra – other

orra man – odd-job man

ort – waste

ower – over

owersettin – translation

oxter – armpit

P

pap – touch

pattle – spade

pawkies – gloves, mittens

pech – breath, pant, gasp

pechan – stomach

peelie-wallie – sickly, pallid

peerie – little

pelf – possessions, plunder, wealth

perjink – neat, trim, fussy

perlustrin – surveying

pewlie – seagull

piece – sandwich, snack

pilked – shelled

pirlin – twisted, crooked, twirling

plack – cash, money

pleuch – plough

pliskie – trick, practical joke

pluff – puff, plump up

plype – soft, sudden sound

poost – strength

pouk – pluck

powl – pole

pree – kiss, taste

prink – wink

puckle – small quantity, a little

puddock – frog, toad

puddock-stuils – toadstools

pudgetie – dumpy

pug – to hide, play truant

purvey – church tea

pushion – poison

pynes – pains

Q

quaich – shallow drinking cup with two handles
qued – vile
queir – choir
quine – young woman

R

rack – stretch
racket – rotten branch, firewood
radge – rage, fury, wrath
rael – true, honest, genuine
rairie – roaring, as in drunk
raivelment – muddle, disorder, tangle
rammie – fight, scuffle
rammish – impetuous, wanton
ramsh – to munch, chew noisily
rath – early, premature
rauchle – Loose, untidy, disorder
raucle – bold, rash in speech or action
redd up – to tidy, clear away
reeshelt – rustled
reiver – robber, thief
rissle – twig
rive – tear, rip
roch – rough
roo – quiet, peace, rest
routhie – profuse, abundant
ruchelt – strong, rough
ruise – praise, flatter
rumballiach – tempestuous

S

saorsa – freedom
saucht – peace, tranquillity
saul – soul
saut – salt
scabbit – bare
scart – trace, track
scaum – burn, scorch
scheme – housing project
sclim – climb
scob – willow or hazel cane
scodge – drudgery, menial labour
scoosh – gush, splash
scowe – flat-bottomed boat
scran – food, scraps
scriddan – torrent
scrieve – write
scrimpit – meagre, scanty
scud – naked, nude, as in 'in the scud/scuddie'
scug – shade
sculdered – ruined, smashed
scunner – sicken
scurrivaig – vagabond
seabhag – falcon
seannachie – storyteller, bard
seelent – silent
seendil – seldom
seggie flooers – yellow-flag irises
seil – happiness, good fortune
ser – serve
shaikle – icicle
shaw – wood
sheilin – remote summer hut near grazing cattle or sheep
sheuch – trench, to dig, to sink, to plant
shilpit – puny, thin, ill-looking
shoon – shoes
shot – turn, as in a game
shoogle – shake
sic – such
siccan – such
siccar – certain, safe, cautious
sidhe – fairies
siller – silver, money, wealth
simmen – rope made of straw
simmer – summer
simmet – vest
skair – share
skaithe – hurt, injure

skellum – rogue, scoundrel

skep – basket

skilderin – soft glaze

skiftin – wainscot, skirting board

skiggan – bright

skink – to pour

skirl – shriek, scream, sound of bagpies

skoosh – spray, squirt

skyce – slip away unnoticed

skyre – glitter, brightness

slaister – splashy mess, smear, daub

sleekit – sly

slig – lie, deception

slinge – to lounge or loaf

sloch – to drink, quench thirst

sloonge – to idle

smattert – shattered

smeddum – spirit, drive, resourcefulness, energy

smeeg – kiss

smoch – smoke

smoorach – kiss, cuddle

smouch – secret smile

smue – smile, smirk

smuir – (1) to extinguish a fire (2) a covering of smoke

smurach – fine dust, dross

sneist – gibe, taunt

sneith – polished, smooth

snellit – sharp

sneuter – weep, blubber

snig – pilfer, cut

snod – trim, spruce

snoke – hunt

sonse – good fortune, prosperity

sonsie – fine, buxom (f) handsome (m), cheerful

sook – sycophant, to suck

sottlin – cooking

souch – sigh, breeze, wind

sowans – oatmeal soaked in water

sowe – shroud

sowf – doze, slumber, snore, whistle softly

spaes – prophecies, predictions

spaewife – woman fortune-teller

spairge – spray, dash, sprinkle

spang – pace, stride

speal – a spell of time

speeach – stick, log

speir – to ask, enquire

spiel – a game

spirlie – slender, spindly

splairge – splash, spatter

spoot – spring, spout

sprattle – contest

sprauchelt – climbed, clambered

starn – star

stech – to stuff, cram

steek – stitch, sew

steg – prowl, stalk

stell – place, position

stentless – boundless

stieve – firm, fixed, stable

stocious – drunk

strae – straw

straigly – straggly

straik – streak

stramash – row, uproar, commotion

stravaig – wander, roam, stroll

streeks – stretches

sturken – restore

stushie – argument, uproar, brawl

stychelt – stifled, suffocated

suith – truth, veracity

swallae – (1) drink, esp. alcohol (2) fork-tailed songbird

swee – swing

swith – fleeting, brief

syne – since

syple – an impertinent, large-bellied person

syte – grief, sorrow

sythment – recompense, compensation

syver – a gutter

T

tack – lease

tap – top

tapsalteerie – topsy-turvy, chaotic

tapster – innkeeper

tapteed – passionate, eager

tashit – tarnished

taury – sailor

telt – told

teuk – chicken

thirlt – bound

thole – suffer, bear, put up with

thon – that

thonder – yonder

thoog a poog – a lie, a hoax, a leg-pull

thortout – utterly

thrain – lament

thrapple – throat

thrawartlie – contrary

thrawn – stubborn, contrary

threep – to argue assertively

thrie – three

throstle – thrush

tinkie – gypsy, member of the travelling community (respectful rather than derogatory)

tirl – spin

tirran – brawling

toosht – loose bundle

trailach – trailing

trinnlin – rolling

tuim – empty, vacant, a tomb

tulzie – skirmish, fight

twa – two

tyne – lose

U

unco – strange, unfamiliar, unusual

undeemous – enormous

ungrutten – unmourned

ungubbed – sober

untashit – untarnished

unvinkishable – invincible

upby – up the way, up there, heaven

V

vauntie – jaunty, proud, showy

vieve – (1) life (2) bright, quick

virr – energy, vigour, force

voar – spring (the season)

vowtit – vaulted

W

wabbit – weak, feeble, exhausted

wae – woe

wally dug – porcelain dog

wampler – a rake, reprobate

ware – spend, pass

waucht – drink, quaff

waws – waves

wean – child

wechtie – heavy

ween – to guess, surmise, think

whase – whose

whaul – whale

wheech – whisk

wheen – a small amount

wheer – odd, quiet

wheesht – quiet, often used in the imperative

whids – lies, as in Black Donald of the Whids (the devil, or deil)

whigmaleerie – a fancy, whim

whilk – which

whilli-wha – highwayman

whin – broom, gorse

whumgee – frivolous

whummel – to empty

whumleeries – hopes, desires

whurl – wheel

wicht – valiant, bold

wid – (1) wood (2) would

willie-waught – a hearty swig, copious draught

windlestrae – thin stalks of meadow grass

winze – curse, swear

wiss – wish, desire

wraith – wrath, anger

wynd – narrow winding lane

wyteless – blameless

Y

yairn – (1) wool (2) story

yask – dust, ash

yauks – aches

yetts – gates

yin – one

yink – dedication

yird – earth

yowes – ewes

yowt – roar

yowtherin – plodding

SELECT BIBLIOGRAPHY

GRIGOR MCWATT

Knox-Cardew, Charles, *A Vulgar Eloquence* (Glenton University Press, 1987)

McPhail, Mhairi, *A Granite Ballad – The Reimagining of Grigor McWatt* (Thackeray College Press, 2016)

McWatt, Grigor, *The Fascaray Compendium*, ed. Mhairi McPhail (to be published in seven volumes by Cumlin Press, 2017)

Collected journalism

Frae Mambeag Brae: Selected Columns and Essays of Grigor McWatt (Stravaigin Press, 1980)

Wittins: Mair Selected Columns and Essays of Grigor McWatt (Stravaigin Press, 2011)

Memoir

Forby (Virr Press, 1962)

Ootwith (Smeddum Beuks, 1994)

Poetry

Kenspeckelt (Virr Press, 1959)

Kowk in the Kaleyard (Virr Press, 1975)

Wappenshaw (Virr Press, 1986)

Warld in a Gless: The Collected Varse of Grigor McWatt (Smeddum Beuks, 1992)

Teuchter's Chapbook (Smeddum Beuks, 1998)

Thoog a Poog (Smeddum Beuks, 2010)

That's Me Awa (Smeddum Beuks, 2013)

The Whigmaleerie's Ower – The Complete Collected Verse of Grigor McWatt, ed. Ailish Mooney (Smeddum Beuks, 2015)

CULTURE

Bold, Alan, *MacDiarmid* (John Murray, 1988)

Carmichael, Alexander, *Ortha Nan Gaidheal: Carmina Gadelica* (Floris Books, six-volume facsimile, 2006)

Fergusson, Maggie, *George Mackay Brown, The Life* (John Murray, 2007)

Green, Stanley Roger, *A Clamjamfray of Poets* (Saltire Society, 2008)

MacDiarmid, Hugh, *Lucky Poet* (Jonathan Cape, 1972)

Nic a' Phi, A., *The Fascaray Songbook* (Gartcosh Press, 2015)

Shaw, Margaret Fay, *From the Alleghenies to the Hebrides* (Birlinn, 2008)

ETHNOGRAPHY

Grant, Isabel, *Highland Folk Ways* (Routledge, 1961) and *The Making of Am Fasgadh* (NMSE, 2007)

McPhail, Mhairi, *The But'n'Ben Baroness* (Aikenhead Press, 2010)

Webster, Joseph, *The Anthropology of Protestantism: Faith and Crisis among Scottish Fishermen* (Palgrave Macmillan, 2014)

HISTORY

Allan, Stuart, *Commando Country* (National Museums Scotland, 2007)

Devine, T. M., *The Scottish Nation: A Modern History* (Penguin, 2012)

Goring, Rosemary, *Scotland the Autobiography* (Viking, 2007)

Hunter, James, *On the Other Side of Sorrow: Nature and People in the Scottish Highlands* (Birlinn, 2014)

Lynch, Michael, *The Oxford Companion to Scottish History* (OUP, 2001)

Rixson, Denis, *Knoydart, A History* (Birlinn, 1999)

Struan, Jim, *Silent Killing for Cubs and Scouts* (Buirlie Books, 1973)

ISLAND LIFE

Brown, George Mackay, *Portrait of Orkney* (John Murray, 1988)

Campbell, John Lorne, *The Book of Barra* (Routledge, 1936)

Dressler, Camille, *Eigg: The Story of an Island* (Birlinn, 2014)

Gordon, Seton, *Hebridean Memories* (In Pinn, 2013)

Haswell-Smith, Hamish, *An Island Odyssey* (Canongate, 2015)

Maclennan, Donald John, *Dalmore – Tales of a Lewis Village* (Create Space, 2013)

McPhee, John, *The Crofter and the Laird* (House of Lochar, 1998)

Rea, F. G., *A School in South Uist* (Birlinn, 1997)

LANGUAGE

Jamieson, John, *Etymological Dictionary of the Scottish Language* (Alexander Gardner, 1879 edition, 5 volumes)

Macafee, Caroline, and Macleod, Iseabail, eds, *The Nuttis Schell: Essays on the Scots Language* (Aberdeen University Press, 1987)

MacLennan, Malcolm, *Gaelic Dictionary* (Acair and Mercat Press, 2001)

Macleod, Iseabail, and Cairns, Pauline, eds, *Essential Scots Dictionary* (Edinburgh University Press, 1996) and *The Scots Thesaurus* (Aberdeen University Press, 1990)

NATURAL HISTORY

Botting, Douglas, *Gavin Maxwell: A Life* (HarperCollins, 1994)

Cunningham, Peter, *A Hebridean Naturalist* (Acair, 1979)

Fish, J. D. and Fish, S., *A Student's Guide to the Seashore* (Cambridge University Press, 2011)

Maxwell, Gavin, *Ring of Bright Water Trilogy* (Penguin, 2001)

Shepherd, Nan, *The Living Mountain: A Celebration of the Cairngorms* (Canongate, 2011)

POLITICS

Ascherson, Neal, *Stone Voices* (Granta, 2003)

Brand, Jack, *The National Movement in Scotland* (Routledge, 1978)

Harvie, Christopher, *No Gods and Precious Few Heroes: Scotland 1914–1980* (Edward Arnold, 1981)

McIntosh, Alastair, *Soil and Soul* (Aurum, 2001)

Marr, Andrew, *The Battle for Scotland* (Penguin, 2013)

Wightman, Andy, *Who Owns Scotland?* (Canongate, 1996) and *The Poor Had No Lawyers* (Birlinn, 2013)

ONLINE RESOURCES

Dictionair o the Scots Leid: *http://www.dsl.ac.uk*

Historical Thesaurus of Scots: *http://scotsthesaurus.org*

The Online Scots Dictionary: *http://www.scots-online.org/dictionary/index.asp*

ScotlandsPeople: *http://www.scotslandspeople.gov.uk*

Scots Language Centre: *http://www.scotslanguage.com*

Scots Leid Associe: *http://www.lallans.co.uk*

Scots Radio: *http://www.scotsradio.com*

APPENDIX I

Receipts, or Recipes, from *The Fascaray Compendium*

Broth

INGREDIENTS

One nieve of barley
One nieve of split peas
One nieve of lentils
Four leeks or onions
Butter or lard
Two nieves of chopped carrots
One and a half nieves of neeps
Three pints of mutton or chicken stock
Nieve of parsley if available

METHOD

Soak barley, peas and lentils overnight. Boil for an hour in salted water then drain. Fry leeks or onions in butter or lard until soft. Add remaining vegetables. Fry for five minutes then add stock. Bring to boil then add drained barley, peas and lentils. Simmer for half an hour, add more stock as needed, then serve with parsley. Keeps for a week if kept outside in the cold in a skillet weighted with bricks to keep out rats, mice, pine martens, etc.

Cranachan Ice Cream

Can only be made in spells of exceptionally cold weather.

INGREDIENTS

One nieve of oatmeal
Daud of unsalted butter
Spoonful of honey
Spoonful of raspberries
Two cups of cream

METHOD

Fry oats in butter until light brown and crispy. Add honey, cream and raspberries. Spoon into empty, cleaned tin can, tie securely in a bag and leave in the lower reaches of the burn over night, supporting it upright with stones.

Fish Piece

INGREDIENTS

Leftover cooked herring or kippers, or tinned sardines
Packet of potato crisps
Two slices of bread and butter

METHOD

Layer fish in sandwich with butter and scatter with potato crisps. Serve.

Guga

INGREDIENTS

One dried bird per person
Water to cover

METHOD

Boil guga in pan of water, skim off grease and reserve. Add more water, boil again and skim off grease once more. Repeat as necessary, up to a dozen times. Serve the bird with boiled new potatoes and kale. The grease can be used as furniture polish, floor wax, wheel lubricant or face cream for the ladies (though it can be ill-smelling).

Mealie Creeshie

INGREDIENTS

One nieve of oatmeal
Daud of bacon fat

METHOD

Fry oatmeal in bacon fat until light brown and crisp. Can be served with fried onions if available.

Nettle Soup

INGREDIENTS

One onion
Butter
Three nieves of nettle leaves (preferably young tops, harvested using gloves)
One potato
Stock made from boiled bones (mutton, beef or chicken)
Salt
Pepper
Swirl of cream if available

METHOD

Fry onion in butter. Dice potato, skin on, and fry for five minutes with onion. Add stock. Once potato is soft add two nieves of chopped nettles. Boil for twenty minutes. Add remaining nieve. Boil for five minutes. Serve with pepper, salt and swirl of cream.

Pancakes

INGREDIENTS

One and a half nieves of self-raising flour
Two tablespoons of caster sugar
One teaspoon of baking powder
One egg
One cup of sour milk or buttermilk

METHOD

Mix dry ingredients. Add egg, mix well, then milk. Mix again. Put one spoonful of mixture onto hot greased griddle and cook until bubbles begin to form. Turn over and cook other side briefly. They should be shiny and golden brown. Serve hot with butter.

Pea Brae

INGREDIENTS

One nieve of dried marrowfat peas
One teaspoon of salt
Three cups of water
Two cups of malt vinegar

METHOD

Soak peas with salt in water overnight. Boil till soft then add vinegar. Mash, drink the liquid hot and eat the pea mush with a spoon.

Soda Bread

INGREDIENTS

Four nieves of flour
One teaspoon of salt
One and a half teaspoons of bicarbonate of soda
One and a half cups of buttermilk

METHOD

Sift dry ingredients. Add buttermilk. Mix to soft dough. Knead. Shape into flat round. Bake for 30 minutes on moderately high heat.

Soorocks Salad

INGREDIENTS

Handful of soorocks (wood sorrel)
Tomato
Small onion

METHOD

Wash soorocks. Scatter over sliced tomato. Garnish with chopped onion.

Tablet

INGREDIENTS

Half a pound of butter
One pint of water
Four pounds of caster sugar
One tin of sweetened condensed milk
Optional: nieve of walnuts; drop of vanilla essence

METHOD

Melt butter in water in pan over low heat then add sugar and bring to the boil, stirring constantly. Add condensed milk and simmer for 30 minutes, stirring frequently to prevent sticking. Remove from heat and add optional ingredients if desired then beat well for five minutes. Pour into a greased tin and score into squares when partially set.

Tattie Scones

INGREDIENTS

Half a pound of floury potatoes, boiled and mashed
One ounce of butter
Half a nieve of flour
Salt
Pepper

METHOD

Mix in the flour with potatoes, butter and seasoning. Roll out the dough on a floured board. Prick with a fork and cut into rounds. Mark the rounds into quarter wedges with a knife. Cook on a hot greased griddle for about four minutes each side, or until golden. Serve with butter.

Whisky Toddy, or Hot Toddy

An island cure-all.

INGREDIENTS

Whisky
One lemon
One spoon of honey
Water (if required)

METHOD

Boil water. Squeeze lemon into large mug. Add similar amount of boiled water if required. Mix with honey. Fill to the brim with whisky. Serve. Repeat as necessary. Good before a voyage and by the fireside, as a morning stiffener and an evening soother, in the mirk of winter and the skyre of summer, to lubricate companionship and celebrate solitude, to aid story-telling and ease silence. Recommended treatment for *Morbus Fascariensis*.

Grigor McWatt, 2010, *The Fascaray Compendium*

HAME TAE FASCARAY

Words & Music by
McWATT / McAFEE

Melancholy or martial
♩ = 100

[Verse]

Blaw winds, An dae your warst! Stor - my seas rise up!___ Spite la - shin rain An En - gland's shame, We're ___ co - min hame.___ Hee -

[Chorus]

ra - haw, boys, We're___ a - wa, boys, Gang - in hame Tae Fas - ca - ray.___

AUTHOR'S NOTE

Scotland has, in my view, the finest landscape in the world and one of the richest and best-documented histories and cultures of any small nation in western Europe. Only a few of the sources drawn on for this novel could be cited in the select bibliography.

I would like to thank early readers of the book in typescript – Carmen Callil, Richard Eyre, Jane Maud, Gail Rebuck, Mary Kaye Schilling and Peter Straus – for their encouragement and astute comments. Ellie Steel and Elizabeth Foley have been shrewd and sensitive editors.

Special thanks are due to my family – like my sources, too numerous to mention in these pages – but I single out my cousin Bobby Winslow, teacher and musician, my nephew Calum McAfee, scholar of Scots and Irish literature, and historian Cornelius McAfee, my Irish twin and fellow-Fascaradian, all of whom lent their expertise to this novel.

For the Scots language my debt is, once more, primarily to my family, in particular to my late parents and to my aunts, maternal and paternal. Alison Lang gave invaluable assistance with Gaelic (any mistakes are mine); Sabhal Mòr Ostaig college on the Isle of Skye gave me grounding in the basics of this remarkable endangered language, spoken by fewer than two percent of Scots, which survives in some of the most beautiful regions of the country and is memorialised in its place names and in a wonderful tradition of song and verse.

Thanks are also due to Glasgow musician and singer Callum Rae, who with his band The Corellas – David McLachlan, Alex Smith and Jim Lang – recorded a stirring version of 'Hame tae Fascaray', with backing vocals by my brother Conn McAfee and cousins Alex and Nick Muir.

Finally I am indebted, as always, to my husband, Ian McEwan, for his wise suggestions, gently offered, and for his patience and support.

Annalena McAfee,
November 2016

CREDITS

All poems cited are translated from the original English into Scots, with the exception of Hugh MacDiarmid's lines from 'A Drunk Man Looks at the Thistle', which are reprinted in the original Scots.